THE MISSING PIECE

She had never been kissed. But it didn't take her long to figure out how it should be done. His lips guided hers. His arm in the small of her back flattened her body against his as he took her measure. Her arms wrapped under his and around his back where her hands skimmed over his scars. His hand moved down lower and pressed her against his rising manhood.

Shannon. He wanted her. She filled holes that were missing in his mind and in his heart. He didn't need the past when he had her. His life started here, now, with Shannon. He would leave the past behind him and not give it another thought.

She let out a whimper as his tongue with its whiskey taste found its way between her lips, caressing her, teasing it, teaching her the game. Her hands moving on his back were driving him wild. The scars didn't exist when she touched them.

The scars. Where did the scars come from? What was he doing? She didn't deserve this. What if he was married? What would it do to her if he made love to her and then left her?

Other *Leisure* books by Cindy Holby:

CROSSWINDS
WIND OF THE WOLF
CHASE THE WIND

CINDY HOLBY

Windfall

LEISURE BOOKS NEW YORK CITY

Thanks, Mom and Dad.
And thanks to Matt and Helaina Burton

A LEISURE BOOK®

December 2004

Published by

Dorchester Publishing Co., Inc.
200 Madison Avenue
New York, NY 10016

ISBN 0-8439-5306-3

The name "Leisure Books" and the stylized "L" are trademarks of Dorchester Publishing Co., Inc.

Printed in the United States of America.

Visit us on the web at www.dorchesterpub.com.

Windfall

Chapter One

Something was different. His mind swirled through the darkness that was forever pressing down upon him. It struck once again for the surface where the light was waiting. He sensed the presence of the light but found it out of reach. He strained for something familiar, for something to trigger the consciousness that his body fought for.

He knew what day it was. It was announced to his still form every morning by a booming voice. He knew by the feel of the cool breeze that washed over his body. He knew that he was kept clean and shaved. Gentle hands soothed his body and worked the muscles that threatened to atrophy after months of disuse. He knew everything that went on around him. Everything except who he was and what he was doing there. He knew everything except his name.

The voice was missing. The sweet soprano that sang

to him while gentle hands routinely exercised his weakened limbs and massaged his lean fingers and toes. His ears strained for the sound of her footsteps on the wood floor as his skin ached for the cool touch of her fingertips.

Where was she? His mind turned circles as it sought release from its prison. For as long as he could remember she had been at his side. If only he could move. Maybe then she would come. If only she knew how much he needed her, how he longed for her. She was the only anchor he had in the deep ocean of darkness that covered him. Desperate, he tried to make his body respond, but in vain.

An observer would have seen full lips part slightly in a pale face that had gone too long without the warmth of the sun. A slight flush of pink creep across high cheekbones that were separated by the strong nose characteristic of his Nordic forebears. There was a slight movement of neatly trimmed hair the color of corn silk as his head turned slightly to search for the voice . . . but no one was there to see. His part of the ward remained empty and silent. The one who had been his constant did not come. He fell back into the fog that held him prisoner. The emptiness swallowed him once again.

Shannon Mahoney's bare feet did not make a sound as they flew over the firmly packed dirt of the trail that led into town. The air was crisp after the frost of the night and her feet were chilled, but shoes were hard to come by so she saved the wear and tear on hers whenever she could. Her shoes bumped against the swirl of her well-worn brown skirt as they swung to and fro on a rope looped over her shoulder. Her flaming red hair slid over the left side of her face from the hastily jerked knot she had twisted as she escaped the confines of the small cabin on the mountainside. The heavy curtain covered the bruising and swelling that had appeared around her vivid green eye. She brushed back the straight-as-a-stick mass and blew at the stray tendrils that lingered over her face.

I wonder if he's awake. She had missed a day. She hadn't meant to. She had been coming faithfully to work at the hospital every day since the beginning of the war and she felt a personal attachment to the silent and sleeping patient in the ward. After all, she had been the one who found him lying in the stream covered by the bloated body of a dead horse. She had stilled her father's hand when he had raised a rock to finish the job that the Union forces had started. It was one thing to plunder the bodies of the dead for the small treasures they possessed. The fallen men didn't need them anymore and if her father didn't take advantage of the situation, somebody else would. But murder, that was something else entirely.

"Thou shalt not kill," Shannon had said as she quoted the commandments that Gran had taught her from memory. She had surprised both of them with her impudence, but Da had been feeling generous that day and allowed her to drag the man out of the stream and load him onto the back of their tired horse. It had not occurred to him to help her in her struggles, nor had she thought that her attempt to move the injured man might further damage his broken body. She was tall and she was strong from years of hard work, and she had delivered the man to the hospital where he still lay, three months later, in what Doctor Blankenship called a coma.

Faithfully she came each day and tended the men in the ward. She bathed them and shaved them and bandaged draining stumps and gaping wounds. Most of those men had gone on now. The passage of the injured through these parts had slowed to a mere trickle. She always saved the quiet one with the scars on his back for last. His wounds were on the inside, Doctor Blankenship had said. Broken bones and a swelling in his brain that kept him from waking. The bones had healed and the swelling had dissipated but the quiet one slept on, oblivious to the happenings of the world around him.

She hadn't meant to miss a day, but Da had been gone with the drink as he so often was now. She wondered what he had sold in order to buy the whiskey. "Probably another of the man's possessions," Shannon mused out loud. After he'd had a few he would turn mean. He hadn't been that way before, when Gran had been around and Will. . . .

Shannon usually made herself scarce before it happened, but a sudden cold downpour had left her trapped in the cabin and his rage had erupted suddenly and without warning. His fist had found her face and she had struck her head on the table as she fell to the hard dirt floor of the cabin. He had left her there unconscious until the whiskey he drank had overcome him and he had passed out on the narrow cot that was his bed. Shannon had finally stirred into wakefulness and hid in the loft. He would be even meaner when he woke with the hangover that always followed. He would be angry because she wasn't there to fix his meals and clean up his mess but the small pittance she made working at the hospital would help to calm his anger and improve his mood until the cycle started again.

"If only Will had not died things would be different for sure," Shannon sighed to the squirrels that were busy gathering their food for the winter. But Will, along with so many others, had fallen at Gettysburg in the fruitless efforts of generals who threw men at cannons as if they were nothing and the generals God himself. They had neither known nor cared that Will was the center of the world for a poor heartbroken father with a busted leg and a lonely younger sister who lived deep in the mountains of what was now the independent Yankee state of West Virginia. Will, who was tall and strong with a crop of flaming red hair so much like her own. Will, who could calm the world with one of his ready smiles. Will, who played the guitar that now lay silent and still in the loft where it would be safe from the drunken rampages that now consumed her father. It was safe in the loft where she slept because Da couldn't climb the ladder with his twisted leg. He would sell it without thinking if he got his hands on it. He scavenged and stole if the need arose to pay for the drink that helped erase the memory of all he had lost.

If only she had died instead of Will. She deserved to die. Hadn't it been giving birth to her that had killed her mother? Gran had told her it wasn't her fault, but she had heard folks' whispers as she had grown to be as tall and strong as a man.

"God's will," Gran had said. Why had it been God's will for Will to die in the war? Why couldn't it have been she who died? She was big enough that she could have gone to war and fought in Will's place and he could have stayed at home to work the small plot of land and play the guitar and continue to be the light of Shamus Mahoney's life. Instead Da was stuck with a twisted leg that pained him, a daughter with no prospects and a bleak future on the side of a mountain in the wild woods. If only Will were still alive. . . . But he wasn't, and the light and hope and happiness that had once been part of their lives had died with him.

Shannon had reached the outskirts of town. She paused a moment under a tall pine to clean the fragments of leaves and pine needles from her feet before she put on her shoes. Across the river she could see the grand white inn that had become a hospital during the war, and once again she wondered if the quiet man was awake yet.

On the wings of a dove
flies my true love
'neath the moon
through the mist
o'er the mountain.

The words danced though his head, carried by a sweet soprano voice. He felt the cool hands on his body massaging the legs that would not move on their own. Strong fingers found the arch of his foot and rubbed down through his toes. His ears picked up the sound of water being wrung into a bowl and he knew that the cloth would follow on his skin and the night terrors would be washed away. The nameless faces that haunted his dreams would dissipate and he would be left again in the fog, searching for the identity that escaped him. If only he could open his eyes, then maybe the answer would be revealed. Who was he? Where was he? Why was he here?

Shannon gasped as she caught the flash of pale blue beneath her patient's surprisingly dark lashes. She dropped the damp cloth into the bowl and leaned forward to look closely at his still face. Was that an eyelid that twitched? Shannon leaned in closer, not daring to blink, holding her breath as she searched the face that had become so familiar to her.

She saw a twitch, then a flutter, followed by a glimpse of pale blue that resembled the ice on the creek in the wintertime.

"So you've decided to join us," she said as the eyes blinked and searched and finally focused on her face.

The sound of her voice was as musical as the song he had heard, and he looked up into eyes that were as green as the forest that had once surrounded him. Why did he remember the forest? Bright red hair tumbled untidily around an elfin face with an upturned nose that was dusted with freckles. A bruise discolored one side of her face, swelling the lid over the deep-set green eyes. It angered him to see it and he didn't understand why. Questions tumbled through his mind but the words would not form. There was so much he needed to ask, so much his mind craved to know. Where should he start? How should he begin?

"Who?" he thought he said, but his voice, so long unused, failed him. The deep green eyes looked down on him in confusion and she shook her head. She didn't understand. He wet his lips and tried again. "Who?"

A quick smile greeted him. "I'm Shannon."

His neck ached with the effort to shake his head and

he realized that any movement on his part was almost impossible. "No. . . ." A croak came forth from his throat. "Who . . . am . . . I?"

Shannon stood upright, stunned by the question. How could he not know who he was?

"You're Jacob Anderson." Shannon opened the drawer of the bedside table and pulled out a much-creased letter. "That's what the name on this letter says. You had it in your pocket."

"Read . . . it . . . to . . . me. . . ."

Shannon looked down at the face and saw that the eyes held no recognition of the name. She looked at the neat flowing letters that filled the paper and knew how he felt. Just as he did not recognize his name, she had no recognition of the words written there. Her face flushed with embarrassment and she was shocked to find that she didn't want him to know that she couldn't read. It wasn't as if the entire town didn't know that already.

"I'll go get the doctor." It was he who had told her the contents of the letter.

Before he could protest, she was gone, taking with her the light and his anchor. He felt the fog coming around again, felt the darkness consuming him, felt his mind sinking back into the quagmire that had been his existence. But this time there was a life line. It was his name. Jacob Anderson. His name was Jacob Anderson. It meant nothing to him, but it was something to hold on to. He gripped it tightly with his mind as he spiraled off into unconsciousness.

Chapter Two

The waking was different this time. His mind had become used to the struggle against the darkness as he reached mentally for the surface and the light. His name was Jacob Anderson and he was in a hospital of sorts. That was all he knew and he grabbed hold of the information and held it close. He took the time to take careful inventory of his body parts and was relieved to find that everything was still attached. He was conscious of his limbs and knew that he had feeling in them, but moving them about was beyond his capability at the present time. He knew without looking that there were scars on his back, but the wounds were old and not responsible for his presence here. Whatever injury it was that had brought him here and how he'd come to be injured were complete mysteries, but mysteries that he hoped could be solved by the people who were caring for him.

Shannon. Who was she? Did she know him from before? He decided immediately that she didn't from the conversation they'd had. How long had he been here? Once again he was overwhelmed by frustration. He needed answers. He needed to know more than what his name was. He needed to know who Jacob Anderson was. He turned his head to the bedside table where Shannon had found the letter. Were there answers in it? Why hadn't she read it to him?

"Welcome back to the land of the living, Mr. Anderson." An elderly man peered over his glasses from the end of his bed. "We thought you were going to sleep forever."

"Are . . . you . . . the doctor?" His voice was still weak from disuse but it was working.

"Yes, I'm Doctor Blankenship. I've been caring for you since Shannon carried you in some three months ago."

"I've been here three months?"

"Yes, and unconscious for all of them."

"What happened?"

Doctor Blankenship sat down on the edge of the bed. "Shannon found you half submerged in a stream on the other side of the mountain. Apparently your patrol had fallen to a Federal attack. . . ."

"Patrol? Federals . . . I don't understand. . . ."

The doctor cocked his head to one side as he considered his patient. "You don't understand what?"

The young man seemed to search for words. "Was I a soldier of some sort?"

"Yes, in the Confederate Army from the looks of your uniform."

"Confederate?"

"The War Between the States."

The pale blue eyes clenched shut in apparent confusion.

"Son." The doctor's voice was gentle as he laid a hand on his patient's arm. "Why don't you tell me what you know and maybe we can figure it out from there."

The thin face against the pillow was pale as desperation showed in those clear blue eyes. "I don't remember anything."

The doctor rose from the bedside and considered his patient for a moment. He took off his glasses and cleaned them with a finely pressed linen handkerchief as he carefully sought the words that would keep the man lying before him from going into a panic.

"As far as we know, your name is Jacob Anderson. We found a letter in your pocket addressed to that name, so we assumed it was yours. Considering the type of injuries you had, it does not surprise me that you have some memory loss, although I have never heard of this degree of amnesia."

"What were my injuries?"

"Both legs were broken, along with your pelvis, several of your ribs, and your collar bone. Along with that you had a dislocated shoulder and a bump on your head the size of my fist. All that combined with a case of pneumonia left you in a coma for the past three months. To be quite frank, it's a miracle that you're even alive, and you can thank Shannon for that."

"What happened to me? I thought you said my patrol was attacked?"

"There was an attack. Shannon's father was pilfering the bodies of the dead soldiers when they found you. She said it looked as if your horse had gone over the trail and rolled over you down the hill. She found you underneath the horse's body in the stream. The horse had a broken neck. It's only by God's grace that you didn't have one yourself."

"Then there were no survivors?"

"You're the only one we know of. A storm came through and washed away most of the signs and then the Union forces came and buried the bodies. They took some prisoners with them. That's all I know."

"The letter?"

"I assume you can read?" the doctor asked.

He thought about it for a moment. "Yes, I can read, though I'm not sure how I know that."

"There's some who can't, you know."

Doctor Blankenship handed him the letter from the drawer and then pulled a basket out from beneath the bed. "These are the clothes you were wearing. The money we found in your boot and your weapons are in my office for safekeeping."

"Weapons?"

"A rather nice set of ivory-handled pistols."

A blank stare was his only response.

"I'll leave you to your letter." The doctor considered the patient for a moment. "I'll see about getting you something to eat."

"Food?"

Doctor Blankenship laughed. "Yes, food, although it will be something easy on your stomach. Shannon's been dribbling soup down your gullet for the past three months. That young lady was determined to keep you alive. I guess she felt responsible for you since she saved your life."

"She saved my life?"

"She found you in the stream, remember?"

"She found me in the stream and brought me here." He repeated the statement as if that would help him remember it. He clutched the letter in his hands as the doctor walked away.

The letter was addressed to Jacob Anderson. The rest of the words in the address were lost, although he could make out "Cavalry" and "Carolina," but whether it was North or South was indecipherable. The doctor had said that Shannon found him lying in a stream. He hoped that the water had not made the letter illegible.

Dear Jake—whoever had written this letter called him Jake.

Dear Jake,

I hope this letter finds you well and in good spirits. Things are much the same here . . . Where was here? . . . *Lucy Ann continues in her constant disapproval of my actions while Parker has many opinions on how the war should be fought and won. Penelope and I have taken to spending our days together and I have come to love the dear woman as if she were my own mother.* Who were these people? *Daddy writes that things are still the same back home and we are all still missed. He said that Zane is quite lost without the companionship of you and Caleb, although he does find some relief by picking on Dan and Randy. He also said that the boys are growing like weeds and have taken to feeding themselves, although they finish with more food on the outside than the inside. He was proud to say that Fox has the same appetite as his father. Even though he is a few months younger than Chance, he is much the same size. I'm sure caring for the two of them is quite taxing on Jenny and Chase, but the joy they must feel at having them, especially Fox, must outweigh the burden.* Were these people family? Were they friends? Where did they live so he could find them and ask? There had been no clue as to where the letter came from, where "back home" was, or where and when the letter was written. *I look forward myself to the day when we shall be blessed with a baby.* We? His eyes scanned the page as a new paragraph started.

I miss you and pray every day for your safe return. Please tell Caleb the same if his letter does not find him. And tell Ty . . . The ink faded and ran together and the message to Ty, whoever he might be, was lost. His eyes dropped to the bottom of the page. *With great love and affection . . . Cat.*

He squeezed his eyes shut as the names circled in his head. Lucy Ann, Parker, Penelope, who was somebody's mother. A father from somewhere else, Zane, Dan and Randy. Babies named Fox and Chance who belonged to someone named Jenny and Chase. Caleb and Ty, whom he had apparently served with. And then a woman named Cat who was anxiously awaiting the day that *we shall be blessed with a baby.* Was she waiting for him to come back and make her a mother? Was she his wife, lover, or sweetheart? He opened his eyes to glance at his left hand. There was no band on his ring finger and no indication that one had ever been there. But then again, hadn't the doctor said that Shannon's father had been robbing the bodies of the dead? Could he have slipped a ring off his finger before Shannon had the decency to bring him in here instead of allowing him to die in the stream? The names meant nothing to him; they just added more to the muddled confusion that swirled in his brain. The only name that had a face to go with it was Shannon's, and he looked up to see her coming toward him carrying a tray.

He had not noticed before how tall she was, or how bright her hair was. The afternoon sun pouring through the long row of tall windows lit up the untidy mass. He also hadn't noticed her smile, which revealed a row of perfect white teeth. Doctor Blankenship had said that she had carried him in here. Looking at her, there was no doubt in his mind that she could do it.

He suddenly became aware that he was wearing nothing but a night shirt. He also had a vague impression of strong hands massaging his limbs and a cool cloth cleaning his body. He felt heat rush to his face as she arrived at his bedside and he felt like cursing at his weak attempt to pull the blanket over his chest. The letter flew off the blanket and fluttered to the floor, landing right at her feet.

Shannon placed the tray on the bedside table and stooped to pick up the letter. Her untidy bun slid over her face as she bent and she came up with the letter in one hand and holding her bright red hair back with the other. She dropped the letter on top of the blanket and hastily refastened her hair with the few remaining pins that she had. She was always losing them, it seemed.

"Did reading your letter help you with your memory?" she asked as she finished tidying her uncooperative hair.

"No." Dang, why did he feel so nervous in front of her? She had already seen his most private parts. She probably knew more about his body at this time than he did, but he still couldn't resist the urge to pull the blanket up closer. He felt so weak and vulnerable, and he didn't like the feeling at all. He didn't like the fact that the side of her face was bruised and she had a black eye, either.

"I brought you some eggs and fresh-baked bread. I didn't know how you liked them so I just scrambled them." The lilt of her voice seemed familiar and his mind recalled the singing he had heard while trapped in his dreams.

"Scrambled is fine." He felt his stomach flip-flop as the aroma from the bread filled his nostrils. "I really don't recall how I like them."

Shannon placed her hands on her hips and studied the face that had grown so familiar to her over the past few months. It was strange looking at him with his eyes open and flashing pale, icy blue in the sunlight. "I guess if you can't recall your name, then how you like your eggs would be one of the last things you'd be worried about."

A smile flitted across the man's lean features, revealing a flash of white teeth and deepening the creases around his eyes. He must have spent a lot of time in the bright sun to have creases like that while still so young. If he was a confederate soldier, then he must be from the South, Shannon reasoned. But his voice didn't betray the accent that a lot of the Southerners had and there was something about him that spoke of wide open spaces. Maybe he was from Texas. She had heard tales of the state, and its rugged wildness seemed to fit him. And he had been wearing that brace of fine pistols that her father still asked about as if waiting for the poor man to die so he could claim them as his own. Wherever her patient was from, he must have been in trouble at some time. She had seen the scars on his back and knew that they came from a whip.

"Does the letter say where you're from?" she asked.

"It's just a series of names without places. Just news about people I don't remember." He picked it up and looked at the name on the front. "Here, read it yourself, maybe you can recognize some of the names."

Shannon had no choice but to take the letter from his outstretched hand, which trembled slightly with the effort. She glanced at the name on the front. Jacob Anderson. She knew that much of what it said. "I couldn't. It's not proper to read other people's mail." As if she ever got any herself. She folded the well-creased missive and placed it safely in the drawer. "I don't know many people around these parts anyway, unless they're from the old country. Anderson isn't an Irish name by any means."

"But you might have heard of them."

"Doctor Blankenship read it and he didn't recognize any of the names or else he would have had those fine people down here to look at you." She reached for the blanket to pull it back.

"What are you doing?"

"You can't eat lying flat on your back."

The thought of sitting up seemed an impossible task and he quickly realized that he would need her help to do so. He nodded wearily. The day's events had already overwhelmed him. Strong hands reached under his arms and pulled him up. Shannon braced him against her shoulder as she reached behind to rearrange his pillow. His nostrils caught the scent of the deep woods and strong lye soap along with the sweet smell of the bread. She leaned his body back against the head-board and gave him a broad smile as she placed the tray on his lap.

"Would you need some help with the eating of it?"

His mouth watered as he looked at the food. But he knew he didn't have the strength to lift the fork to his mouth.

"Yes." It was hard for him to ask her for help.

Shannon saw his reluctance and resisted the urge to shake her head at men and their pride as she sat on the side of the bed. Her own brother had been proud, but not so proud that he would turn away a hand when she offered it. After all, she was almost as strong as he had been, God rest his soul. She scooped up a bite of eggs and offered it. "The doctor said you should take it easy. We don't want you losing what you eat."

His mouth watered as he chewed the eggs. Did all food taste this good? "I'd hate to make another mess for you to clean up," he finally said when he had managed to swallow.

Shannon paused as she brought the fork up with another bite. This one was prideful. She had seen her share of them here in the ward and the humble ones too.

"It's all part of my job to clean up the messes and take care of the wounded."

He glanced down at the row of beds, most of them empty. "I guess I should thank you, for saving my life and taking care of me since."

"You're welcome." Her smile flashed brilliantly and she cocked her head as she waited expectantly for him to take the eggs off the waiting fork.

"Shannon . . ." He had to stop to chew the eggs.

"At least we know your mother raised you with some manners."

Had she? He didn't know, nor could he remember.

"Shannon, was I wearing a wedding ring when you found me?"

The deep green eyes flashed sparks. "Oh, and are you accusing me of stealing such a ring from your finger as I pulled your broken body out of the stream?" She jumped from her seat indignantly as her hair tumbled from the last remaining pins.

"No." Why did he suddenly feel so nervous? "I was just wondering if there was a possibility that I could be married to the woman who wrote the letter."

"Well, if you are, you weren't wearing a ring when I found you." Her lilt became more pronounced with her anger. "And you aren't wearing one now. What you wore before is none of my concern, nor is what you did with the ring, if there was one." She stalked away from the bed with her head held high and her bright red hair streaming down her back. He watched her walk away, wishing he could call her back.

Jake looked at the tray on his lap and at the fork that had landed on the floor. He had one friend in this world and he had managed to offend her. What kind of person was he? He picked up the bread with trembling hands and managed to break off a small portion of it. He was suddenly very tired.

Shannon counted her pennies as she stalked across the bridge into town. Her last pin was gone and she would have to stop at the mercantile to buy some more. She prayed that Da had not been in and bought anything on credit. She had asked the storekeeper not to extend him credit, but Shamus had the gift of gab and could talk the hide off a bear when the mood hit him. The mood hadn't hit him since Will had died. It seemed now as if all the joy had been taken out of him. He had no one to share his joys and sorrows with.

"And now the sins of the father are resting on the daughter," Shannon said to the water gurgling over the rocks as she crossed the bridge. Her patient had accused her of stealing from him. And after she had saved his life! Of course Doctor Blankenship had probably told him about Da pilfering the bodies. Everyone in the county knew that Shamus was always out scavenging things, but her father couldn't work with his crippled leg. It had been different when Will was alive. Everyone had loved Will. . . .

Quit crying over spilt milk, Shannon, she told herself as her long stride quickly covered the steps to the mercantile. *There's nothing to be done but getting on with your life, such as it is.*

"Good afternoon, Shannon," the storekeeper greeted her as the tinkling bell announced her arrival.

"Good afternoon, Mr. Farley. I need some pins for my hair."

"You just missed your father," Mr. Farley informed her as he counted out five pins.

"And what was he after?"

"Nothing from here. He sold me a fine rifle that he had found on the battlefield." Mr. Farley pointed to a rifle lying on the counter behind him, and Shannon recognized it as the one that had been in the stock of the quiet man's dead horse.

"He has a name," she mumbled to herself as she wondered what Da was up to now.

"I beg your pardon?" Mr. Farley asked.

"Nothing, sir, just a bad habit I have of talking to myself. Did you happen to notice where Da went when he left here?"

"He took off toward the west."

The tavern was west. Their home was east. No doubt whatever money he'd received had been traded for a bottle of fine Irish whiskey. She gave the storekeeper a penny and started for the door.

"Yoo-hoo, Shannon!"

She had hoped to escape without falling into the clutches of Mrs. Farley, who felt it was her duty to matchmake for every eligible maiden in the county. Unfortunately for Shannon, all Mrs. Farley ever had in mind for her was crippled widowers who needed a strong woman to care for them in their waning years. Shannon could stay home and do that and not have the burden of the marriage bed in the bargain. Another old man's wife must have died, giving Mrs. Farley another name on her list for Shannon's potential mate.

"Good afternoon, Missus Farley."

"I was hoping you would come in, dear. We just got in this ribbon and it's a color that matches your eyes."

Shannon blinked those green eyes as she looked at Mrs. Farley in disbelief. The portly woman was rummaging through a box under the counter. "I put it away so no one else would buy it." The round face appeared with a triumphant smile. "See, the color is perfect for you."

Imagine that, a piece of ribbon for my hair, Shannon

thought as she went to the counter. She had never had a ribbon for her hair before. Gran had always braided it and tied the ends with string when she was little. Of course, the braids had always come loose and she had invariably ended the day looking like a scarecrow, but Gran would always brush it out and then braid it again the next day. Shannon rubbed the soft strip of satin between her fingers.

"We could cut you a length to tie in your hair and then another two lengths for your bonnet."

"I don't have a bonnet, Missus Farley."

"Well, you should. Anybody with skin as fair as yours should protect it from the sun at all costs."

"The trees hereabouts are too thick for much sun to land on my face." Shannon had always been practical.

Mrs. Farley let out a discouraging *tsk* and rewound the ribbon. Shannon watched her with some regret and suddenly had an image of a shy smile on a lean face with pale blue eyes.

"Wait," Shannon said as she opened her coin purse. "How much for a length for my hair?"

The precious ribbon was coiled and placed in her pocket. No telling what Da would say when he saw that bit of extravagance. So now she could go face the devil himself or go home. She'd rather go home. It looked like the clouds were gathering for rain. Shannon took the time to glance back across the river where the quiet man, Jacob, was probably still struggling with his dinner. "Serves him right, accusing me of stealing. As if I would do such a thing."

Was he married? He had said that he might be married to the woman who'd written his letter. How could he not know? Either he was or he wasn't, her practical side told her. But apparently the letter had raised questions in his mind. "That's all he's got in there right now—questions." Shannon snorted as she turned toward the west and the tavern. Who had written the letter? Obviously it was a woman, one who might or might not be his wife. It must not have been too personal, or else why would he suggest that she read it?

"We've missed you in choir lately, Shannon."

Distracted by her musings, she had practically walked right into the thin chest of Reverend Mullens.

"Sorry, sir." Shannon dropped a quick curtsy. "But I feel as if the wounded men across the river have more need of me than the choir right now."

"Ah yes, the poor souls." The pastor looked at the former inn, which now served the wounded of both sides. "God has laid his hand on your heart to lead you into such service." He looked up at Shannon. "But still we miss your beautiful voice. What are the chances of your coming back in time to sing for our Christmas pageant?"

"If time allows, I'll be there, sir."

The pastor bid her good day and she scurried on toward the tavern. Lead her into service, indeed. He talked of her as if she was one of the Sisters of Mercy instead of a poor lass trying to make a living for herself and a worthless father. Of course, Da had never approved of Reverend Mullens. His church wasn't Catholic, for one thing. Better not to go at all than set foot inside another denomination, Da always said. And better for her to be a nun, in her father's opinion, than to be an old maid. Certainly no one would want her for a wife.

Was there a wife looking for the quiet man right now? Was there a Mrs. Jacob Anderson mourning the loss of a good husband? Did she know every inch of the man's body as Shannon did?

There were many who disapproved of an unmarried woman caring for the patients as she did, but there was no one else around who was willing or able to do it, and she needed the money. Shannon didn't see what all the fuss was about. As far as she was concerned, men had all the same equipment as bulls and stallions and the dogs that hung around the porch and licked themselves just because they could. There was nothing new there, nothing that shocked her maidenly sensibilities. She had seen her brother in the altogether every day of her life until her own body had started to blossom and curve.

But still, if she were the man's wife, she wouldn't want another woman to know his body as intimately as Shannon now knew Jacob's.

As if an old maid like you will ever be anyone's wife, she chided herself.

Boisterous laughter poured out of the tavern doors and faded into the singing of a limerick. Shannon recognized the voice. Da was entertaining the patrons, undoubtedly fortified with strong drink. She hoped the horse was here so she could get him home. If not, he'd have to sleep it off in the shed behind the tavern, and there was no telling how many fights he would get into when the good feelings wore off and the bad ones took over. Not that he'd win any of them. But that wouldn't keep him from taking a swing at somebody if the mood suited him. He was just like the mangy rooster that tended to their hens. A lot of crow with nothing to back it up.

He had been something in his day, Gran had said. He could hold his own with the best of them before the gang wars in the city of New York had left him with a busted-up leg and two hungry children to feed. That was when the four of them had come south to West Virginia, where Shamus had hoped to find a plot of land that would support his family better than the dried-up piece he had left in Ireland. The only good thing it held in its earth were the bodies of his father and his dear sweet wife, dead in childbirth.

But that had all transpired before Shannon could remember. Her life had always been here in the wild mountains, where the four of them had made a home together. Their lives had been decent ones until the war had taken Will and a particularly harsh winter had taken Gran. Shannon saw their one tired horse tied to the rail and patted the gelding's neck as she went by.

There he was, standing in front of the fireplace with a glass of whiskey in his hand reciting the verses that told the life story of Padriac O'Shaunessey and his one-eyed bull. The audience roared with laughter as Shannon eased her way into the room, wincing as the limerick described what the one-eyed bull did with the cow. Ingrid the bar maid bumped her with a tray full of empty tankards as she went by.

"Have you come to take him home?" the woman asked as she recognized Shannon.

"I reckon it's about time."

"Indeed," Ingrid agreed.

"Och and look, gentlemen, it's me lovely daughter

come to escort me home," Shamus announced to the room as he finished the verse. "What other man here wants to be so lucky?"

"Let's go, Da," Shannon said steadily, hiding her fear of where the conversation was leading.

"Come on now, gents, look at her. What man wouldn't be lucky to have such a helpmate as me own daughter?" Shamus waved his hand in Shannon's direction while she wished for the floor to open up and swallow her. "She's strong enough that you could hitch her up to yer plow and save yer horse for ridin'."

Shannon felt her cheeks flush at the implication. Better to ride a horse than take a chance on riding her in the marriage bed. That was fine as far as she was concerned. What woman in her right mind would want the likes of these men?

"I'm taking the horse, Da. If you don't want to walk, I suggest you come on."

Shamus waggled his eyebrows at her mild threat, which drew another wave of laugher from the assembly. "Best leave the beast for me, daughter."

"I think not, Da. He's old and the weather is chill. He needs to be home in his shed instead of spending the night out in the weather."

"Go on, Shamus, take your horse home," someone in the crowd encouraged.

"Yes, take both of them," added another, which bought more laughter from the patrons.

Shamus smiled broadly at the joke. "So I'll go, gentlemen. I'll ride the gelding, and the chestnut mare can follow." He took off his hat and bowed to the still laughing crowd as he took his leave. Shannon squared her shoulders and followed as he whistled a lively tune on his way out the door.

"Shame on you, Shamus Mahoney," Ingrid said as he passed. "If I wouldn't have to clean up the mess, I'd let you have it with this tray."

"Me daughter is me own business, missy, and I'll thank ye to mind yours," he retorted.

" 'Tis nothing, Ingrid," Shannon said, flushing as she walked by. "Thank you anyway." The sound of Ingrid's tirade about men and their lack of sense followed her out the door. Shamus strode on ahead, proud of himself for some reason. Shannon squared her shoulders. She knew a battle was coming; she was the one who was going to bring it.

"Da, how could you?"

"How could I what?" He untied the gelding from the post and started to mount the poor beast.

"Sell the man's rifle."

"He has no need of it lying flat on his back in that bed day after day."

"He's awake, Da, and you promised me you would keep his things safe in the shed."

"Awake after all this time, did ye say? Hmmm." He swung up in the saddle with his brow furrowed in mock concern for her patient. "Well, there's nothing to be done about it now. The rifle is sold and the money spent."

"You mean wasted on whiskey and song." Shannon easily matched the slow gait of the gelding as they followed the street out of town.

"That's none of your concern either."

"It's mine when you're stealing, Da."

"What do ye mean, stealin'?"

"The rifle didn't belong to you. It's stealing."

Shamus blustered about for a retort but failed to find one.

"Was there a ring in his things?"

"A ring?"

"Yes, Da, a ring. A wedding ring. Did you see one among his things?"

"Can't say that I did. Why do ye ask?"

"Because he may be missing one."

"Well, either he is or he isn't. Which is it?"

It was too much for Shannon to explain, and she knew that her father would use the man's memory loss as an excuse to sell off the rest of his possessions. "Was there a ring?"

"Why such concern over a ring?"

Shannon could see the wheels turning in her father's mind. If there was a ring, he hadn't found it yet and he was trying to buy time to look for it. She'd best get the man's saddlebags from the shed and take them to him.

"Because he thinks I took it from him."

Shamus laughed.

"I'm not a thief, Da, nor am I a horse, and I don't appreciate being called either." They were on the trail to the cabin now and the wind had picked up, bringing with it a touch of the north and the promise of a cold rain. Shannon gathered her shawl close against the darkness that seemed to be approaching more rapidly than usual.

"I don't appreciate your tone, daughter."

"Well, I don't appreciate being the butt of your jokes. You should treat me with more respect, Da."

"What's to respect?" Shamus snorted.

"Don't I take good care of you?"

"You do what's expected, like the Bible says. 'Honor thy father and mother.'"

"I do honor you, Da."

"By calling me a thief?"

"What would you call it? The Bible also says 'Thou shalt not steal.' The things are not yours. They belong to somebody else."

"Dead people who can't use them."

"But this man isn't dead."

The trail was steadily rising now, winding its way around the mountainside to the small clearing where their cabin stood. "Da," Shannon said in exasperation. "What has happened to you? You weren't like this before."

"Before what?"

"Before Will died."

"Don't mention his name to me, daughter."

"But he would not approve of what you're doing!" Shannon's voice rose with the wind that swirled around her skirt. "And he would not approve of the way you treat me!"

Shamus jerked the reins of the gelding and staggered from the back of the horse. Shannon stood her ground as he came toward her. He raised his hand and struck her across her right cheek, turning her face with the impact.

"Do not mention his name in my presence again." They stood eye to eye in the gathering darkness of the storm as Shamus trembled with indignation. "It should have been you who died instead of him. It should have been you who died instead of your dear, sweet mother. If you had died, she would have given me more sons to comfort me in my old age."

"I wish it had been me who died, Da. Better to be dead than living this life the Lord has seen fit to bless me with." The flaming tendrils of her hair swirled about her face. "I'm twenty-two years old and have nothing to look forward to but more of the same." She smoothed her hair away from her face and held it back as she stepped closer to her father. "But know this, Da. You can beat me until I'm dead and it will not bring her back, nor will it bring back Will. Do not tell me not to mention his name. I remember him with love and honor his memory. You bring shame to it with every breath you take." Shannon stepped around the still trembling form of her father and attacked the trail with her long stride.

"Yer forgettin' yer place, daughter," Shamus yelled after her departing form.

"I'm leavin' ye, Da," Shannon yelled back. "I'll not be a part of your misery. I've got my own to deal with."

"How far do ye think ye'll get out there on your own?"

Shannon ignored him as her strides took her around a bend in the trail.

"Nobody wants you!"

The words stung harder than the slap. Shannon blinked against the raindrops that pelted their way through the thick canopy of branches. At least the water cooled the flaming sting of her cheek. There was no balm that could help the hurt she'd been dealt by her father's words. She held her head up high. "It's fine with me if nobody wants me. Seems like life is safer that way," she said to the rain and the wind.

She went directly to the shed and found the saddle-bags. There was no time to look through them to see if there was a ring. She'd let the man do it himself. A trip to the loft took but a moment as she stuffed her one nice dress, her nightgown and the few personal items she owned in a pillowcase. A gleam in the corner caught her eye and she tenderly picked up Will's guitar. Shannon heard her father blustering as he settled the gelding in the shed. She snatched up the quilt that covered her narrow cot and wrapped it around the guitar.

"Surely ye weren't serious about leavin' me now, daughter." Shamus tried to charm her with a smile as he entered the cabin.

"I was and I am." Shannon flung the saddlebags over her shoulder and clutched the other things to her chest.

"But it's pourin' rain and I've yet to have me supper."

"Fix it yourself." She gathered the shawl over her chest. Shamus stood in the doorway, blocking her way. Shannon's determined green eyes met the bloodshot ones of her father.

"Ye have yer mother's eyes, ye know," he said as he moved to the side.

"Thank God for that." Shannon didn't bother to close the door behind her as she stepped out into the rain.

Chapter Three

Doctor Blankenship had given him newspapers to read but beyond bringing him up to date on the happenings of the war, they were useless. From what he had read, things looked bad for the Confederacy, which meant he had been on the losing side. Why was he not surprised by that bit of information? Jake looked in frustration at the papers piled up on the floor. If he had the strength, he would pick them up, but he didn't and that knowledge just added to his misery. He wanted to get up, he wanted to get out, but mostly he wanted to remember something, anything of his past.

The rain beat a steady tattoo against the panes of the tall windows that ran the length of the ward. The lamp mounted on the wall by the door cast a soft, warm glow over the row of mostly empty beds. The patients slept on, lulled into their dreams by the drumming of the rain. Jake didn't want to sleep. He had been asleep for three months straight. He needed to move; he needed to do something. He needed to apologize to Shannon for accusing her of stealing a ring that probably didn't exist. Her anger with him only added to his misery, but that was something he could fix if she ever came back.

He flexed his hands and looked at his long lean fingers. Doctor Blankenship had mentioned his weapons, a set of ivory-handled pistols. Why did he ache to hold them and feel the cool touch of the handles in his palms? Was it the weight of them that he missed on his hips? Maybe he just needed to put on a pair of pants. Jake glanced at the floor, at the basket that contained his clothes. Chances were that even if he managed to get them on, they would puddle around his ankles. He was nothing but skin and bones.

How did he know that he was skinnier now than before? Maybe he had always been this thin. Jake flung his arm over his forehead in frustration. He just knew. He just knew that he had been bigger, just as he knew how to read and how to talk and how to eat. He knew there were scars on his back and he knew how to shoot a gun and that he was good at it. So why didn't he know anything else? Why was his name a mystery? Why couldn't he recall the identities of the faces that continually flashed across his mind?

He heard the creak of the door and the sound of a long stride coming toward him. Shannon. He turned his head and saw that she was dripping wet. In her arms she tenderly held something beneath a sopping, brightly colored quilt.

An image flashed through his mind. He saw a beautiful woman with a bruised face and golden blond hair that flowed down her back. She was wrapped in a quilt of soft blues and pinks and was carried in the arms of a man with long dark hair and snapping eyes. The scene surrounding them was one of death and destruction but the man's tenderness for the woman was evident in the way he held her and the way he looked at her. Who were they? The faces were familiar and the names were there on the tip of his tongue, just waiting to be spoken. Then the memory passed and the image faded from his mind as Shannon approached his bed.

"I brought you your things." She dropped his saddlebags on the end of the bed.

"You could have waited until it stopped raining." But he was glad she hadn't.

"I found I was going to be out anyway." Her hair streamed down the side of her face and dripped over her shoulders.

"Making deliveries in the late evening, are we?" *Now where did that come from?* he wondered as he watched her face light up at his remark.

A smile curled her lips. "I see that you recall your sense of humor."

"That's assuming I had one before," Jake commented as he noticed how sweetly her mouth curved into a smile. "I don't know if I did or not."

"That's not something you gain or lose. You either have one or you don't." Her tone was teasing and he found that he enjoyed the banter.

"You're very wet for someone who seems to be so practical."

"I didn't consider the weather when I decided to move."

"Move?"

"Out, from my father's house." Shannon shivered with cold.

"Oh." Jake toyed with the edge of his blanket. "Don't you think you should get out of those wet clothes before you catch your death and wind up a patient yourself?" He was suddenly embarrassed. He hoped she didn't think he was suggesting anything. Especially after he had practically called her a thief.

"I'm waiting for Doctor Blankenship to find me a key."

"A key?" Apparently she had missed the double meaning of his comment.

"To one of the cottages out back. This house was an inn before the war. Rich people came to take the waters for healing. There are several cottages on the grounds where the staff used to live. Most of them are empty now."

"So I guess that means I'll be seeing more of you?"

"I suppose." Shannon noticed a warmth gathering inside of her even though her skin was freezing. Was he pleased that she would be living on the grounds? She tried to study his face but it was lost in the dim light of the room. His hair, usually the color of corn silk, seemed to be white against the angles and shadows of his face, and his pale blue eyes glittered like ice as they caught the glow from the lamp. She found no answers there; his meaning was as vague as his memory, but still his words warmed her.

"Shannon." He had to look up as she stood over the end of the bed. He found the words hard to speak but was determined to get them out anyway. "I'm sorry for what I said about the ring."

"You didn't mean anything. You just have a lot of questions in your head."

"Like where did you get that fiery temper of yours?"

Her laugh was as musical as her voice. "Now I'm sure that's the last thing on your mind."

"Well, I have to admit there are other things I'd rather know first. But it seems to me like it might have something to do with your red hair." A voice from the past entered his mind. *She should have been the one with the red hair.*

"You're remembering something?" Shannon saw the confusion as it flashed across his features.

As suddenly as it came, the memory was gone. He wanted to scream his frustration, to break something or throw something; instead he just squeezed the ends of the blankets between his fingers. "They never stay long enough for me to remember them," he whispered more to himself than to Shannon.

"It will come."

"What if it doesn't?"

"Then you'll start from here, the beginning of your remembering."

She stood at the end of his bed, dripping wet and holding what appeared to be all of her worldly possessions. He briefly wondered what it was that she held so carefully beneath the quilt. "Do you think you could tell me about what happened when you found me? Not now, but tomorrow when you're dry and not being so practical."

"You will find that I am always practical, but I'll be happy to oblige." Doctor Blankenship waved to her from the door. "And since I now have a place to get dry, I think I will be practical and do so." She walked away, still holding her bundle.

Jake slid down on the mattress and rolled on his side, pulling the blanket up over his shoulder. Why had he thought apologizing to her would be so hard? He had dreaded it but at the same time had wanted to do it. Was it something he hadn't done in the past? He felt the weight of the saddlebags with his feet and kicked them off the mattress. He was too tired to look through them now. He'd rather wait until morning when Shannon was there to go through them with him. Maybe they held some answers. But then again, maybe they didn't. The rain beat steadily against the windows and he hoped that Shannon didn't have too far to go to get to the cottages. He smiled at the sight of her standing tall and proud and dripping at the end of his bed. Dang but she was pretty, even when she was sopping wet. He fell asleep, lulled by the sound of the rain.

Jake awoke before dawn, feeling hungry and restless. He longed to get out of bed and stand on his own two feet but he knew he was weak from the months he had spent flat on his back. He doubted seriously if his legs would support him. At least he knew his insides were working correctly as the urge to relieve himself overcame all other feelings. The previous morning a man named Mose had come in at dawn to wake the patients. Jake had recognized the booming voice from his time spent in the coma but he was surprised to see that it came from a withered former slave who had the good luck to live in a part of Virginia where the slaves had now been emancipated. Jake wondered how long it would be before Mose made his appearance.

The pressure became worse and he sat up in bed. That hadn't been as difficult as he'd thought it would be. He moved the blanket off and managed to swing his legs over the side of the bed. Doubts assailed him as he surveyed the long thin limbs that dangled over the side of the bed. There was only one way to know if his legs would support him and that was to try them out. He prayed that he wouldn't wet himself if they didn't.

His legs trembled as he slid off the bed and precariously balanced himself on the two sticks that served as his foundation. He swayed and then reached for the bed beside his own, bracing his hands on the mattress. Jake gritted his teeth. "Come on, you can do this." A screen stood in the corner, just across from the bed he was leaning against. He knew there was a chamber pot behind it. He slid his feet and inched his hands down the mattress until he stood at the end of the bed's narrow length. Four steps would get him there. *It might as well be four miles,* he thought as the coming dawn revealed the chasm that lay between him and relief.

"Move," he commanded his legs through gritted teeth. He held his hands out to his sides as dizziness overcame him and he teetered at the edge of the bed. "Move!" Jake felt himself falling and his hands grabbed the air as he crashed face-first into the aisle beyond the bed. His forehead broke out in a sweat as he dragged himself toward his goal. His legs felt useless and his shoulders shook with the effort. After what seemed like an eternity, he reached the screen and was relieved to see a sturdy chair alongside the chamber pot. Sheer determination was the only ally he had as he dragged himself up, using the chair as a support. He had made it and relief was gained along with a sweet feeling of victory.

The feeling faded quickly, however, as his strength gave out and he slumped onto the chair. If only he had thought to bring his pants with him. The draft from the huge windows chilled his bare legs, which the nightshirt covered only to his knees. His bed looked inviting but it might as well be a hundred miles away. He knew he would never make it alone. But he had to.

Jake gained his feet using the chair as a support. It was a sturdy chair and made of oak, which made it heavy. It slid easily across the wood floor and Jake managed to shove it along and drag himself after it.

"Whatever are you doing?" Shannon called as she entered the ward.

Jake groaned in frustration. Mose was usually the first one in.

"Are you out of your mind?" she added as she came rushing toward him.

Jake didn't answer; it took every bit of his strength to maneuver across the aisle. He heard the sound of her hurried feet and it became a race for him. He had to reach the bed without her help. He had to.

"Don't touch me!" he managed to get out through gritted teeth as Shannon came up on him. Sweat poured down his forehead.

The concern showed on her face but Shannon obeyed as she held her arms out at her sides to show they were not anywhere near him. Jake grasped the footboard of the bed with one hand and the back of the chair with the other. His chest heaved with the effort he had put forth. Shannon stepped to the end of the bed and he straightened to his full height, letting go of his supports as he did so.

The top of her head was only a few inches lower than his. Deep green eyes met pale blue as they exchanged a smile, silently agreeing that he was indeed taller than she, but not by much. The bruise around her left eye had faded some, but now there was a slight redness on the right, as if someone had slapped her.

"What are you doing out of bed?" she asked with the smile still curling the corners of her lips.

"It was time to get up."

"Stubborn fool."

"Who did this to you?" He gently touched a finger to her cheek and then his legs gave out. In his descent he grabbed the first thing available, which happened to be her shoulders. Shannon wrapped her arms around his waist and lowered Jake to the bed.

"You should have waited for help."

"I didn't want any help," he protested. "You didn't answer my question."

"Lucky for me the rest of the men in this ward aren't so foolish or I would be spending my day picking the lot of you up from the floor."

"I wasn't on the floor."

"You would have been," she assured him. She flipped the blanket back as he lowered himself to the bed.

"Wait." He grabbed her arm before she could cover his legs. "I want my pants."

Shannon threw up her hands in disgust. "Why? Are you planning another trip?" She pulled the basket from under the bed and produced the blue pants with the gold stripe that were part of the cavalry uniform. "Lucky for you they have suspenders. Most likely they'll just fall off."

Jake leveled an icy stare at her as she waited expectantly by the side of his bed to offer help. "Ooh, you are a stubborn fool," she finally exclaimed as she turned on her heel and stalked away. She stopped a few beds down to talk to another patient, but her eyes were on Jake. He continued to stare at her as he lay in the bed with the pants clutched in his hands, and she realized that he wouldn't make a move until she had left the ward. The sound of her voice making disparaging remarks about his stubbornness carried the length of the room and the slamming of the door gave added punctuation to the expression of her opinion.

Jake felt much better once he had his pants on. He then realized that she had never answered his question about her face.

Shannon returned later with a breakfast tray. Jake's stomach growled as she literally dropped the tray on his lap, causing the glass of milk to splash over the pancakes and sausage. "Since you're so determined to be on your own, you can start by feeding yourself," she announced as she walked away. "I told the doctor about your adventure this morning. He'll be in to see you in a bit."

"Shannon?"

She turned on her heel and glowered down at him. Obviously she was afraid he was going to ask about her face again.

"Can we talk later, about the day you found me?"

The green eyes softened and her glorious smile curled the corners of her lips. "We can talk," she agreed. "I'll be by later to get your tray."

Doctor Blankenship came to talk to him while he was eating, and after telling him to take things slow and easy, he bid him a good day. Jake remembered his saddlebags and the doctor handed them to him before he took his leave.

Inside he found a shell jacket in a light gray with gold trim. His rank was corporal; he recognized the insignia.

There was a white linen shirt with the initials *JA* embroidered inside the neck. At the bottom of the seam on the inside button placket he found the initials *JD*. The stitching was fine and neat and he could see that the shirt had been sewn with extreme care. He assumed that the *JA* stood for *Jacob Anderson,* but who *JD* was remained a mystery. He also found a pair of leather gloves with a soft fur lining and a hand-knit muffler in a light gray yarn. At least he would be warm when winter came. The rest of his possessions were the typical utensils of a man who lived in the open: a razor, a sliver of soap, a towel and some eating utensils. A small white sack revealed a few stray beans. There was nothing there to identify him, no photographs, no journal and no evidence of anyone who knew him or might be looking for him.

Jake held up the razor as if looking at it for the first time. He suddenly realized that he didn't know what he looked like. He scanned the walls of the ward. There was no mirror present. The urge to know what he looked like overwhelmed him. If he saw his face, would the memories come back? His hand found his face, felt the skin, which was relatively smooth and youthful except for the shadow of a beard, felt the fine wrinkles at the corners of his eyes. How old was he? He ran his hands through his short cropped hair. What color was it? It was too short to see and for some reason he felt as if it should be longer. His breath came in short gulps. He had to know; he had to see. Where should he go?

His impatience at his predicament overcame his self-restraint. The breakfast tray, which was sitting on the bedside table, went flying into the aisle beyond his bed with a crash as his frustration took control. *Who, where, why?* The questions never stopped. The questions haunted his every waking moment. Where were the answers? Would he forever be condemned to the hell of not knowing who he was, where he had come from? Had he left loved ones behind? Were they looking for him? Did anyone even care that he was still alive and needed some answers? He felt totally adrift and totally alone. He kicked the blankets away and covered his face with his hands, scrubbing them up through his hair and down again.

He heard Shannon's flying feet coming toward him and prepared himself for the tongue lashing he was sure to get. Let her scream her lungs out at him; it would be a distraction from the never-ending circle of questions that spun in his mind.

Without a word she knelt and picked up the shattered fragments of plate and glass and placed them on the tray. She set the tray on the table and folded her arms as she looked at his sullen face. "I thought you might like to go for a ride." She tilted her head toward the door where a wheelchair was parked. "Maybe get some fresh air?"

Jake looked at the chair doubtfully but knew it was his only escape. He sighed and nodded.

"Put on your coat then. You'll catch your death." As she walked away he noticed that her hair was pulled back and tied at her neck with a length of green ribbon. It made a nice contrast with the bright red of her hair. *Why would anyone want to hurt her?* he asked himself as he shrugged into the short jacket. He discovered it to be loose around his waist, as his pants were, but it fit well across the width of his shoulders and chest.

Shannon lined the wheelchair up beside the bed and

stepped back. Apparently she was willing to let him move himself. He managed to get into the chair pretty easily and felt proud of that accomplishment until Shannon wheeled him down the aisle of the ward. He hated feeling so helpless. She pushed him out the main door onto a wide porch that faced the north.

Patches of frost that had so far escaped the early morning sun gave the wide expanse of lawn in front of the hospital the appearance of a quilt. The huge oak trees that graced the curving drive still hung on to dried brown leaves that rattled among the thick branches with the stirring of each breeze. A long line of hemlocks bordered the road to the west and a bridge to the east led over a shallow river and into a small town. Beyond were mountains that sprang up from the ground without warning and overshadowed the small valley.

"Where are we?" Jake asked as he looked around in wonder at the landscape. After his months of confinement and darkness the view before him was too big, too broad, too bright. He blinked his eyes as if seeing it all for the first time.

"The new and independent state of West Virginia. We're close to the Virginia line. It's maybe ten miles or so away."

"Where did you find me?"

"A few miles east of here on a trail that cut through the deep woods toward the river."

"Which river?"

"The New. This is the Greenbriar River. It runs into the New River south of here."

Jake nodded as if he understood, but the names and places meant nothing.

"Was there anyone else around?"

"There were bodies, if that's what you mean. Some were Confederate, some were Union." Her voice trailed off. "A few were blown to bits." Her stomach turned with the memory of the body of a young man with his face missing. Shannon maneuvered the wheelchair down the few steps to the crushed stone pathway that led up to the porch. The ground was frozen solid and she managed the wheelchair easily over the lawn. Shannon parked the chair next to a bench and settled herself beside him. "It wasn't a pretty sight." She shivered with the remembering.

"Doctor Blankenship said you found me in a stream?"

"The stream ran below the trail. I saw the body of a horse trapped between some boulders so I went down to see what I could find. You were below it with your head lying on a sand bar. That's why you didn't drown. From the signs it looked as if your horse had gone over the trail and rolled both of you down the hill before he landed on top of you. The water was deep enough where you landed to float the horse's body and I just pulled you out. That's when I noticed you were still breathing."

"That's all?"

It wasn't all but Shannon didn't want to tell him the rest of it. What good would it do to tell him that her father had wanted to kill him by crushing his head with a rock?

"That's all. We put you on the back of our horse and carried you here. When Da went back the Union soldiers were there with some prisoners, burying the bodies."

"Prisoners? So some survived the attack?"

"Yes." Shannon laid a hand on his arm. "But that was

months ago. They'd be up north now in one of the prison camps."

"Months ago. What month was it?"

"Near the end of July."

"And now it's the first of November."

"Yes, it is."

Jake looked up at the swaying treetops to where a pair of squirrels were busy chasing each other around and over the branches. Their furious activity knocked loose a clump of leaves that fell a few feet, only to become entangled in the lower branches.

"They'd best get busy," Shannon observed as she followed his gaze to the squirrels. "There'll be snow soon and food will be hard to find."

"Maybe they're looking for someone warm to pass the winter with." Jake's pale blue eyes settled on Shannon's face, which was still upturned toward the treetops. The long line of her throat was creamy white against the drab colors of her blouse and shawl. Her skin was flawless, he noticed, except for the spattering of freckles across her upturned nose and the bruises around her left eye.

"You never answered my question, you know."

"Which question is that?" She turned her attention from the squirrels to Jake. Her cheeks flushed pink when she saw the intensity of his icy gaze.

"Who did this to you?"

Her hand covered the bruise self-consciously. "It was an accident, that's all."

"Somebody's fist accidentally hit your face?"

"It's none of your concern." Shannon jumped to her feet and grabbed the handles of the chair, turning him back toward the hospital.

"Wait, there's something else I need to know."

"Which is?"

"What do I look like?" Why did he suddenly feel shy asking her the question, especially when his questions about her bruises had been so personal?

She stopped pushing him toward the door and stepped around to the front of the chair. "I guess it makes sense that since you don't remember your name, you wouldn't remember your face." She pushed him back to the porch. Jake held up his hand when they got to the steps.

"I can manage these," he declared as he stood. He grasped the banister and pulled himself up the three short steps to the porch. He turned to look at Shannon with a pleased look on his face. She shook her head and brought the chair up easily, positioning it behind him.

"Sit down," she instructed. "I'll be right back." She left, only to come back a few minutes later with a mirror inside a wide gold frame. Obviously she had removed it from a wall somewhere inside.

The face looking back at him was that of a stranger. The nose was strong, along with the chin. The lines in his jaw were all angles because of the weight he had lost. The eyes were pale blue with dark lashes that contrasted sharply with the blond of his brows and hair.

"You didn't look as you do now when I found you," Shannon said as she saw the despair come into his pale blue eyes. "Your hair was long—" she showed him the length with her hands about her shoulders. "And you had a goatee." Her hand brought an imaginary beard to a point on her own chin.

"What happened to it?"

"It was easier to keep you clean without it." She didn't

dare admit that she had wanted to see his face without the covering of the beard.

"Anything else?"

"You were tanned, all over except for . . ." Her face flushed scarlet as she realized that she had just entered very personal territory.

He let her slip pass by. It was humiliating enough to know that someone had had to clean up after him without discussing it. "How old do you think I am?"

"Twenty-five or more by your face. You look about the same age as my brother. He was twenty-six." She didn't mention that Jake's eyes looked so much older than Will's.

"Was?"

"He died at Gettysburg."

"I'm sorry." He didn't remember Gettysburg. Had he been there? Had he fought alongside her brother? A thought suddenly occurred to him. "Which side?"

"He fought for the north."

He could have been the one to kill him if he had been there. "What was his name?"

"Will, Will Mahoney." The name rang in his mind. A vision filled his eyes. A battlefield covered with smoke and blood and bodies lying on the ground. He was on the ground with another man and he was shaking a body, calling out a name, trying to get him to respond.

"Willie?" Jake gasped as the images swam and danced and then dissolved like the smoke that at one time had surrounded him.

"No, it was always Will."

His head hurt. He placed his right hand over his forehead and rubbed his temples with his finger and thumb. Shannon had lost a brother named Will in the war. He had known someone named Willie. It was a common enough name. Why was that trivial piece of knowledge still lodged in his brain while the important things like who he was and where he was from were missing? He felt the anger boiling up from within once again.

"Shannon?" It hurt to speak. It wrenched his gut and made bile rise in his throat. Why couldn't he remember? "Do you think there's someone who misses me? Who might be looking for me?"

Would anyone look for her if she was gone? She'd like to think so. Certainly her Da would spare a thought as to who was going to fix his dinner, but that wasn't even an issue now since she had moved out. Mrs. Farley might notice she was gone the next time a widower became available. Reverend Mullens missed her voice in the choir, but not enough to come knocking on her door and invite her back. The men in the ward might miss her when they realized there was no one around to clean up their mess.

"There's the woman who wrote the letter. She cared enough to write to you."

Jake nodded in agreement but he was not satisfied. "Do you think she could be looking for me?"

The pale blue eyes were lost and searching and Shannon felt her heart tumble in her chest as his weakness was exposed to her.

"I would, if it were me." What was she saying? Shannon turned away and looked out over the porch railing to the lawn, where the squirrels were now furiously at work burying their winter's stores. What must he think of her? Was she a wanton for saying she'd search him out if he were lost to her? What had possessed her to say such a thing? Why would she even presume that she would care for him, that he would care for her. . . . ? "I have to go. You're not the only patient I take care of, you know." She took the mirror from his hands and disappeared into the building.

Jake, lost in thought, watched the squirrels tumble about the lawn. Shannon was right, there would be snow soon.

Chapter Four

It's not too soon to be thinking about Christmas, Jenny Duncan said to herself as she carried the bundle of laundry over to Grace's cabin. *It will be here in less than a month. . . .*

Her mind made a list of the things that needed to be done before the holidays were upon them. She needed to talk to Jason's housekeeper, Agnes, about the decorating of the big house. The three women needed to decide about the baking of the usual Christmas treats. She would put Chase, Caleb and Zane in charge of the search for a perfect tree and that would leave all the shopping for gifts to her. And then, of course, there was the figuring out of where she was going to put all the unnecessary gifts that Jason would shower upon the boys.

The list was nothing more than a minor distraction from the bittersweet sadness that filled her mind. The memories of her twin brother, Jamie, were always stronger when the holidays came upon them. It had been Christmas night when they enjoyed their last time alone as brother and sister. It had been New Year's Day when he was gunned down without mercy on the street right after his wedding to Sarah.

Chase swore Jamie was still with them. He claimed that her brother's spirit had been responsible for Ty finding him half dead in the snow two years ago. Her husband also believed that Jamie was watching her. But if that were true, why didn't his spirit visit her?

Maybe he does and you're just too foolish to see it. His spirit was obvious in the countenance of his son, Fox, whom she was now raising as her own since his mother had died in childbirth. He was the image of his father, with his wide grin and russet hair, and at three years old, he was already showing signs of having the same kind of personality. Fox studied the world around him down to the smallest detail and showed great concern for his extended family on the ranch just as his father had. Jenny's own son, Chance, was more restless and quickly lost interest in everyday things. His deep blue eyes, looking shockingly bright beneath his dark lashes, were always looking away from the ranch, toward the mountains and the wilds of the untamed land. He was quiet, keeping his emotions locked inside, while Fox's flashed across his face, as readable as a book. Chance reminded Jenny of herself when she was a child, except her frustration had come from being a girl in a man's world. Chase assured her that he had been a quiet child also, finding his companionship in nature, but still Jenny worried about her son as only a mother would.

The boys were like every other child in one respect.

They were wild with excitement about Christmas coming. Their great-grandfather Jason had been adding fuel to that fire for weeks now with veiled hints of fantastic presents that would be making an appearance if both boys promised to be good until the day arrived. Jason had both of them up at the main house now, already instructing them on their letters so they would be prepared to start school when and if they ever got the building done and a teacher hired. With all the local unrest, it would be a miracle if the school was ready by the time the boys were old enough to attend.

The sky above was heavy with clouds as Jenny stomped the snow from her boots and shook her long blond braid free from her heavy coat. She frowned as she entered the cabin that was the center of her small universe; Grace had already started the laundry. The older woman really should be taking better care of herself in her delicate condition.

"Grace," Jenny said as she came through the door. "I thought I told you to leave that until I got here." As she entered the cabin, a large black dog thumped his tail against the colorful rag rug.

"Zeb got the water for me," Grace said by way of explanation as she looked up from the washboard. Her softly protruding stomach made her movements slightly awkward. Grace put a hand to the small of her back and arched against it.

"Grace, you need to rest."

"I know, I know, a woman my age has no business having a baby." Grace continued scrubbing the shirt across the washboard. "But yet here I am, thirty-seven years old and with child for the first time in my life. But that doesn't mean that the world is going to stop turning and the chores are magically going to get done."

Jenny dropped her bundle on the floor and pulled Grace's hands away from the washboard. "Have you told Cole yet?" The father of Grace's baby had stayed in New York with his niece Amanda after he and his friends from the ranch had rescued her from a house of prostitution. Amanda had been kept complaint with opium and she was addicted to the drug. Now she was in a clinic where Cole hoped she could be weaned from the influence of the drug.

"No, I haven't mentioned it in my letters. The funny thing is I was pregnant before he left and never knew it. I've never been regular in my life and figured that was why I never got with child."

"You need to tell him," Jenny gently urged. Grace had been like a mother to her since she had arrived at the ranch five years before.

"Amanda needs him more than I do." Grace resumed her washing. "He's all she's got."

"He'd want to know."

"He'll find out soon enough. In about four months, as near as I can tell." Grace wiped her forehead and left a soapy trail.

"Grace, let me do the laundry." Jenny pulled Grace's hands away once again. "You start lunch. Chase said they were taking Caleb out on the range today to get him used to riding again. You know they'll all be starved when they get back."

Grace agreed, knowing that the meal needed to be done as much as the laundry, and Jenny took over at the washtub. She watched Grace with a worried eye as the older woman went about the business of preparing lunch for the group of men who worked the ranch. Grace's beautiful cheekbones were more prominent now and her sparkling brown eyes were tired with worry. There were even a few gray hairs mixed in with the rich chestnut brown that was twisted into a knot on top of her head.

If only Cole were here, Jenny knew, everything would be fine. He would marry Grace and they could look forward to the arrival of the tiny blessing that had come so late in life to both of them. He should have married Grace before he'd left, but his first obligation had been to his niece, and Grace had understood that. But that had all been before there was a baby. Having a baby made all the difference in the world.

Jenny self-consciously laid a hand over the flat plane of her stomach, secretly wondering if she were once again in that condition. Only time would tell. It was poor planning on her part if she was. Chance had been born in the high summer and that experience was not something she was looking forward to repeating. She had been miserable with the heat. Her husband Chase had been wonderful and understanding, however. The memory of an afternoon spent together on the lake while she was heavy with child brought a blush to her cheeks and a warm rush to her stomach. She would know for sure in a few more weeks.

Now if only Cat could get pregnant, too. Jenny felt a pang of regret for her dear friend. Cat wanted desperately to have a baby and Jenny was sure she was taking advantage of the fact that she was trapped in North Carolina with her husband Ty to work on it. The two of them had returned to the south after Ty had escaped from prison camp. Ty had sworn himself to the South-

ern cause and would fulfill his obligation, no matter
how fruitless he thought the effort.

A stomping on the porch announced the arrival of a
huge black man.

"Looks like we's gonna get some mo' snow," the deep
voice boomed, filling the cabin.

"A lot more than you're used to, Zeb," Jenny
observed.

"Yes, ma'am, we didn't get this much back in North
Carolina. We might get some but it would all melt away
befo' we'd get mo'."

"A few winters ago we had it drifted up as high as the
rooftops," Grace added from the stove. Jenny shivered
as she recalled that winter. That had been the winter
that Chase left the ranch to go after Logan, Jamie's killer.

"Don't know if I'd care to see it get that bad, Miz
Grace." Zeb sat down at the table and Grace set a plate
before him. She knew that the great size of the man
required more fuel than most and she had quickly
taken to feeding him a snack between the regularly
scheduled meals, just as she had with Jamie when he
was alive.

"Are you going to work with Jason today on your letters?" Jenny asked as Zeb took a bite from the sandwich.

"Yes, ma'am. Mister Lynch said to come on up to the
big house as soon as I gets done with the chores. Won't
my momma be proud when I writes her a letter all by
myself?"

"She'll be writing to you, too, before you know it."

"Yes'm, I'm sure that Miz Catherine will have her
readin' and writin' in no time."

"Just don't let those two little outlaws distract you

from your lessons," Jenny said with a grin, knowing how much the former slave had come to cherish the two boys. She made a note to herself to find Zeb a special Christmas gift.

Zeb left for the big house with Cole's dog Justice on his heels. The poor creature really missed his master and latched on to anyone coming or going, hoping they would take him to Cole.

Zeb had been a godsend as far as Jenny was concerned. He had a way with the horses that reminded her of her father and relieved her of a lot of the physical chores involved with caring for them. She was able to spend more time on individual training for the foals. Her stock was quickly gaining a reputation for speed and stamina along with intelligence, and Jenny was highly selective about who could purchase the animals. For top dollar, of course. Jason was sure that as soon as the war ended, their reputation as a breeder of fine horses would extend from coast to coast.

Jenny wasn't so sure. The foals they had sold so far had been sired by Storm, the stud who had belonged to her father. He was gone now, the final link with her father. All she had left now were the wonderful memories of her father, mother and brother and the things that had belonged to her mother. She was grateful to have the quilt and the Bible. Those things had led her to the discovery that she was not alone, even though her father, mother and brother were dead. The discovery that Jason was her grandfather had helped soothe the lonely corners of her heart. And then there were her boys, Chance and Fox, and the ever-growing family of friends and coworkers on the ranch. And, of course, there was Chase.

What would she do if something ever happened to Chase? The regally handsome face of her half-Kiowa husband filled her mind. She had almost lost him the winter after Jamie had been killed. His broken body had come back to her that spring, but it had taken his spirit longer to return. Then they had almost lost each other again when Wade Bishop kidnapped her. But Chase had taken care of him, dropping the evil man to his death from a window in New York City. Chase had asked her if she had any more enemies before he passed out from blood loss after the fight. She had assured him there were none, and the dreams that had always been a portent of evil in their lives had stopped. She hoped they were gone forever.

And why wouldn't they be? Jenny wrung out a tiny shirt that she had carefully stitched and hung it on the rack in front of the fireplace. She hated being melancholy, especially when she had so much to be grateful for, and so much to look forward to. She made up her mind to think only happy thoughts during the holidays. There were so many blessings in her life that it would be ungrateful to do otherwise.

"Here they come," Grace announced as she looked out the window over the sink. The sounds of horses in the yard and footsteps on the wooden planks of the porch confirmed the arrival of the men who worked the Lynch ranch.

"Dang, but I'm hungry," Zane announced as they came clomping through the door.

"Don't know why, you didn't do a thing out there," Randy commented as he and Dan both tried to shoulder through the passage at the same time.

"You boys had it all under control, near as I could

tell," Zane retorted as he went to the pitcher and bowl to wash his hands.

"Had what under control?" Jenny asked.

"Tearing down a dam on the stream that comes out of Elk Canyon." Part of Zane's answer was lost in the brisk rubbing of a towel across his face. "And don't worry; we didn't let Chase lift anything." Chase's shoulder had been seriously injured during his fight to the death with Bishop. Thanks to the surgical talents of Jenny's old friend Marcus, he hadn't lost his arm, but it was still weak.

"Beavers?" Jenny asked.

"Not unless they've started using stones." Jenny arched a delicate eyebrow at Zane's reply and then looked toward the door, where Caleb's uneven gait could be heard.

"Why would anyone want to dam up a stream?" Grace picked up a platter to carry it to the table, but before she could take a step, Zane took it away, flashing a dimpled grin as he did so. Grace sighed in exasperation and turned to slice a fresh loaf of bread.

"So our stock couldn't get water," Caleb said as came through the door.

Jenny saw the regal face of her husband over his shoulder and bestowed a gentle smile on him. He always made sure that Caleb did not feel inadequate with his wooden leg, even if it was only seeing that Caleb wasn't the last one through the door. The smile he gave her in return assured her that Caleb's first big outing since his return to the ranch had gone well, although his dark eyes showed some worry over the damming of the stream.

"But there are plenty of watering holes around."

Grace pulled the plate of bread slices away from Zane's willing hands and put it on the table herself.

Zane slapped two slices of bread on his plate as a foundation for a sandwich. "It's a nuisance, nothing more. We're going to check all of the holes tomorrow." He jumped up as Grace reached for a crock on the shelf over the window. Quickly moving her hands away, he placed the crock on the counter with authority. He raised an eyebrow at Grace, daring her to do the slightest thing that might be considered strenuous. Grace crossed her arms over her protruding stomach and gave him a look that would have made him shiver if he hadn't known her so well. Dan and Randy filled their plates, oblivious to what was going on. Caleb limped from the washstand to the table and eased himself into a chair with his left leg held out stiffly before him. He lifted his thigh and the leg fell into place with the proper bend in the knee.

Jenny smiled at Zane and Grace's private battle and then her deep blue eyes met the dark ones of her husband as he dried his face. *How was Caleb's ride? I'm worried about Grace.* Little comments on everyday life passed between them with a glance.

Who is responsible for this sabotage? Why would someone dam up a stream that everyone in these parts needs? Those bigger questions had been haunting all of them in the past few weeks. Chase's dark eyes held no answers but she caught the glint of steely resolve in them. Their lives were being threatened again. He would not rest until the threat was over.

Chapter Five

Cole Larrimore gently held his niece's upper arm as they stood on the platform waiting for the train to arrive. She was so thin that he was sure a stiff breeze would blow her slight body off the platform and onto the track, where it would be cut to pieces by the approaching train. The traveling ensemble he had bought her for their journey to Wyoming hung on her weakened frame and served only to accent her thinness instead of wrapping her in comfort and security as he had hoped when he purchased the coat and dress for her. He had picked out a warm gray to match her eyes but the color of the soft wool had turned her eyes into a haunting violet shade that stood in sharp contrast to her pale face. Her mother had always insisted that she had his eyes. He hated to think that his ever looked like that. He gripped her arm tighter as she shivered in the damp cold of the late-November day.

The past month had been hell for her. Jenny's friend, Doctor Marcus Brown had wanted to wean her off the opium slowly and gently, but she had refused to take the doses he prescribed, turning her head away and giving herself over to the violent trembling and nausea that shook her body.

Cole knew in his heart that she was seeking her death in this abrupt withdrawal from the opium that Wade Bishop had been feeding her through the years. He could only imagine the hell she must have experienced at the bastard's hands to drive her to wish for such an end. She had spent four years as his prisoner after being kidnapped on her way home from work at a small Texas newspaper. Cole had told her that her mother, his only sister, had died from the grief of losing her. She hadn't even reacted to that news, just maintained her stoic silence. There was no sign of the spirited and creative young woman who had written stories and had aspirations of becoming a newspaper editor, a daring dream in itself for a young woman from Texas.

Marcus Brown waited with them for the train. Cole could tell that the doctor was anxious to head west himself. His tall, lean body paced the platform restlessly, and his compassionate brown eyes gazed down the track. He needed to finish his schooling, Cole knew, but after watching the miracle he had worked on Chase's shoulder, Cole thought the young man was competent enough to show his instructors a thing or two about medicine.

A whistle shrieked in the distance, announcing the coming of the train. "Home by Christmas," Cole said gratefully as the mighty steam engine churned into view. He missed Grace, he missed Justice, he even missed the two little boys who were always getting underfoot. How much had he missed by not being a father himself? His relationship with Amanda was the closest he had come to parenthood, being a temporary father after she had lost her own at such a young age. Her father had been his best friend growing up, and they had become Texas Rangers together. It was only right that Tom Myers had married Cole's sister Chloe. The only wrong thing was that Tom had died soon after Amanda had been born, the victim of an outlaw's bullet.

Cole wished again that it had been he who died that day. Tom had had everything to live for; Cole had only made mistakes. He had married Constance, the spoiled daughter of a Spanish aristocrat, only to lose her a few months later because she was bored. She had run away with an actor from a troupe that was passing through town, and when he finally caught up with them in San Francisco, he had been informed of her death by the same handsome young man. "She died of regret," he had stated dramatically and even showed him her grave while shedding some tears. Cole was sure the tears were nothing more than practice for a role he was working on, but headstones didn't lie and the one he was looking at declared Constance Larrimore was lying beneath it.

From there he had gone back to Texas and built his reputation as a lawman, but it could not replace his family. He had failed Amanda by not protecting her from Bishop and he had failed Chloe by not protecting Tom and Amanda. He was a hero, all right, but only in the dime novels that had faded from sight since he had left the Texas Rangers.

Grace had saved him. He had never thought to find love in his lifetime, not the kind he felt for Grace. If only he had met her when they were both young. If only he had taken her from the gambling halls that her father had raised her in and kept her from the knife of Wade Bishop. If only they had spent their youth together and created a home and had a family.

There was no sense in regretting the past. But they could have a future. The only thing that had been holding him back was his obligation to Amanda. He had found his niece and she was safe now. It was time to move on with his life. He couldn't wait to see Grace.

"All aboard!" Amanda blinked as if waking from a dream as the porter made his announcement.

"I guess this is it." Marcus extended his hand to Cole. "Take care of yourself."

"Come see us when you come back west."

"Oh, don't worry, I will. I want to see what Jenny's boys look like."

Amanda said nothing, silently letting Cole guide her to the train. He settled her into a seat next to the window and was gratified to see that her empty eyes looked toward the figure on the platform and she raised her hand, for just a moment. It was doubtful that the man waving good-bye on the platform saw it but at least she had responded to something. It gave him hope.

"You'll like Wyoming, Amanda." Was he trying to convince himself or her? "Jenny will be there. You remember Jenny, don't you?"

There was no response, as usual. She did what she was told. That was all. The motion of the train was relaxing and Cole put his arm around her and gently tilted her head down against his shoulder. "Try to get some rest; we have a long trip ahead of us." The city faded from sight in much the same way as Marcus had. Cole closed his eyes, his mind like the train, heading west.

Chapter Six

Jake leaned on the pitchfork and watched from the loft as Shannon lifted her shawl over her bright red hair and rushed through the rain toward the back door of the hospital. He shook his head as she ran by; she always seemed to be in a hurry to do something. She had barely spared him a glance since that day a month ago when they had talked about her finding him. Since then he had worked on getting his strength back and had moved into the tack room in the barn and taken over the care of the three horses and the red milk cow that resided there. He might as well earn his keep. He had also begun to help Mose with some of his more strenuous duties about the hospital. Jake hadn't bothered to explain to Doctor Blankenship that he had no place to go, no memory of anywhere or anyone who would want him.

He extended his arm and flexed his bicep as he stretched his hand out with fingers splayed wide. He felt strong and could put in a full day's work now without tiring easily as he had a few weeks earlier. He had pushed himself hard in the past month. He hated feeling weak and was determined to put that vulnerability behind him.

The questions in his mind were still unanswered. Every morning he woke up and looked into the tiny square of mirror tacked to the wall in his room. Every morning a stranger looked back at him. Like the scars on his back, his entire existence was a mystery.

Aside from the memory loss, he really had nothing to complain about. He was healthy and strong again. He had a warm, dry place to sleep and he had three square meals a day. Every day he discovered knowledge that was ingrained in him, such as taking care of the animals, hitching up the wagon and saddling a horse. He knew he could ride as well as he walked; it was as natural to him as breathing. He had picked up a rope one day and lassoed a tree stump with surprising ease. There was no mystery in the things he knew about himself, no mystery at all except who he was.

Jake continued to watch as Shannon picked her way through the puddles while holding her shawl above her head to keep the rain off. Her attention was on her feet so she missed the sight of the door swinging open and the withered form of Mose as he backed out, his arms full of something as he exchanged words with someone inside. Shannon's foot reached for the step just as his was coming down. Mose stepped on Shannon's foot instead of the wooden plank he was searching for and

lost his balance. Shannon teetered, but when Mose
landed against her knees, she toppled backward, landing squarely in a puddle on her behind.

Jake howled. The pitchfork was a weak support when
laughter was doubling him over. Shannon couldn't help
hearing him and she blinked up at the loft as the water
ran into her deep green eyes. Jake could see her anger
from where he stood, still laughing. Her shawl was covered with mud, and she flung it away in anger. It landed
in another puddle, spraying more water upon her. Mose
tried to help her as he gathered together the things he
had been carrying in his arms but Shannon pushed
him away.

Jake wiped his eyes and suddenly saw two women
sitting in a puddle instead of one. Neither was Shannon.
One was as tall as the redhead but instead of flaming
hair, she wore a golden braid and had sapphire blue
eyes that danced mischievously as she wiped mud from
her face. The other was smaller, with golden brown
curls and snapping green-gold eyes that had the look of
a cat's.

"Cat?" Jake reached out a hand as if he could touch
the two women who had mysteriously appeared before
him. Just as quickly they were gone, washed away by
the downpour that beat steadily on the roof of the barn.
Jake blinked, hoping to bring them back, but all he saw
was Shannon, standing beneath the small shelter of the
roof over the back door. Her shawl had been pitched
over the railing and she placed a long leg beside it to
peel off a stocking that was soaking wet. Jake watched
as the well-defined muscles in her legs flexed and she
wiped the moisture from the flawless white skin of her
calf, but his mind was on another woman.

The woman who had written him the letter—Cat.

Had he just seen her face in his mind? Had she played an important role in his life? The image he had seen had been an amusing one. Who wouldn't find two beautiful women covered with mud amusing, except possibly the women themselves? But they hadn't looked mad. What role had he played in their mud bath? His hand went without thought to the back of his head and smoothed down the hair that now touched the collar of his shirt. His hair had been long when they'd found him. Was that why he didn't recognize his face when he looked in the mirror? Shannon said he had worn his hair long and had a goatee. It was foolish to think that a little bit of hair would make a difference to his memory.

Shannon spared one last angry look toward the loft before she stormed into the hospital. No doubt she would have a few choice words for him because he'd laughed at her misery. If she even spared him the time for a bit of conversation. The only thing he had heard from her lately was the soft sound of her voice accompanied by a guitar as she sat on the porch of her cottage and played and sang each night. The guitar must have been what she'd had wrapped up in the quilt the night she came in to see him all dripping wet. Jake smiled again at the memory. She must love the rain to spend so much time tromping through it.

"Mister Jake?"

"Up here, Mose." Jake propped the pitchfork against a beam and quickly climbed down the ladder to the barn floor. "You look a little wet, Mose." Jake smiled at the smaller man who seemed to be all gleaming white teeth.

"Yassur, me and Miz Shannon done had a meetin' and a baptism all together on the back step. Miz Shannon done got the worst of it but I reckon you knows that already."

"I was watching."

"Dat girl sure do get het up when someone gets the best of her, that's fer sure."

"I think it has something to do with the red hair." *The wrong one got the red hair in that family.* . . . . Jake shook his head to clear the cobwebs. "What you got there, Mose?"

"Doc Blankenship done tole me to fetch yer guns out to you." Mose handed Jake a sack that was a bit mud-splattered but otherwise none the worse for the collision it had been in. "And he said this here's the money that wuz in yer boot. He didn't take none out fer yer care. He says he's a gonna write up a paper on yer condition and get famous." Mose swelled his narrow chest at the prospect as if he had written the paper himself.

"I don't know much about my condition, or how it could make him famous. I don't reckon I'm even cured yet." Jake felt the weight of the small pouch that Mose handed him and was pleased.

"Far as I can see yer a lot better off than most of them fellers that comes through here. You got both yer legs and both yer arms. Yer breathin' and walkin' and appear to be fit as a fiddle."

Jake opened the bag and handed Mose a coin. "Sounds like you got a better handle on my condition that I do, Mose. I appreciate your taking care of me all those months."

Mose smiled his toothy smile as the coin gleamed in

his hand. "Miz Shannon done most of it, Mister Jake. But I do 'preciate it all the same."

"Tell me about Miss Shannon," Jake asked, leaning against a stall. One of the barn cats jumped up on the ledge next to his shoulder and Jake absentmindedly stroked the orange fur between its ears. "What's her story?"

Mose loved to talk and saw that Jake was an interested audience. He also knew that there were several floors that needed mopping inside. The longer he could put the task off, the more likely it was that Shannon would tackle the job herself. Mose propped himself on a hay bale and considered the facts for a moment before he began.

"Miz Shannon is a good girl and a hard worker. Her daddy ain't no account at all, though. Ever since her brother got hisself kilt in the war, he ain't done nothin' but drink and steal. He started hittin' on her too."

"Her father is the one who beats her?" Jake's hands clenched in anger.

"Yassur, sho' nuff. It weren't like that befo'. When Mister Will was alive things wuz different. That boy was the friendliest and the funnest boy I ever did see. He was always smilin' and jokin' and singin' and tellin' stories and such. It 'bout broke everybody's heart when that boy got hisself killed in the war. Miz Shannon in particular. Those two were closer than peas in a pod. And they sounded like the angels when they wuz singin' together."

"I've heard her sing. She has a beautiful voice."

"Yassur, sho' nuff she does. Shame she don't have no looks to go with it."

"What do you mean, no looks? She's beautiful."

"Maybe if she wuzn't so big . . ."

"There's not a thing wrong with the way she looks!" Jake stood up straight and squared his shoulders. The orange cat meowed in distress as the rubbing stopped and then became preoccupied with the frayed end of a whip that hung from a nail on a post.

"All I knows is what I hears, Mister Jake. Missus Farley over to the sto' done said that Miz Shannon is too big to be purty and she ain't gwanna get no husband unless it's one of them ole fellers who needs a strong back to take care of 'em."

"And I suppose this Missus Farley is the law on all the business that goes on in this town?" Jake asked in exasperation.

"Sho' nuff," Mose said with white teeth flashing into a smile.

Poor Shannon, condemned to spinsterhood by a know-it-all busybody. . . . Jake wanted to throttle the woman. "So why did she decide to start living here?"

"I hear tell she and her daddy got into it over to the tavern when he was drunk one night. He called her a horse and said no one would want to ride her. The men thought it was funny but Miz Ingrid was madder'n a wet hen about it."

"Miz Ingrid?"

"She works at the tavern. She gives me food and such when I hep with some of her chores."

Jake nodded at the explanation as the cat, bored with the whip now, made circles around his boots. He gently nudged the cat away. "Get on now, you've had your milk this morning." The cat, grievously offended, took a moment to wash a snow-white paw before making its exit into a stall for its midmorning nap.

"Mose!"

"She's got some lungs on her, sho' nuff." Mose snickered as Shannon's voice was heard through the pouring rain.

"Best you go see what she wants before she comes looking for you." Jake grinned as the withered old man sauntered from the barn.

He had forgotten about the guns.

A matching pair of ivory-handled pistols with a hand-tooled leather belt and holsters. Not standard issue for the Confederate States of America's cavalry. He pulled a pistol from its sheath and examined it. The memory of the feel and weight of it returned to his hand and he sent the gun through an intricate series of twirls and spins without thinking about what he was doing. Jake looked at the gun in his hand and wondered why he carried such a weapon. Weapons.

He replaced the gun in its holster and wrapped the belt around his waist. It fit low on his hips and the wear of the leather where it was buckled indicated that was how it normally fit, not just because he was still thin from his weeks of illness. Leather thongs dangled from the ends of the holsters and he tied both of them securely around his thighs.

Jake took a deep breath to clear his mind. He squared his shoulders and let his arms dangle freely at his sides. His fingertips caressed the handle of one gun as it protruded from its holster. He teased the well-crafted curve that fit his hand as if made for it. He eased his finger over the smooth polish of the ivory.

The gun cleared the holster in the blink of an eye.

"Dang. That was fast," Jake said to the milk cow, who really hadn't noticed. The orange cat jumped up onto a ledge and curled its tail around snow-white paws. It meowed as if in question as Jake spun the gun back into the holster.

He took another deep breath and tried again with his left hand. The results were the same. The cat blinked green eyes at him as Jake jerked the belt off and tossed it onto a crate. "Why? Why do I carry weapons like these?" He looked at the guns as if they were poisonous. "Only gunfighters carry guns like that." The cat jumped down and walked toward him with its tail straight up in the air. "Am I a gunfighter?" The cat trailed around his boots, purring its response.

What if he was? Would there be someone looking for him if he was? Did he have enemies out there in the world or did he have friends? Did anyone care if he was alive or dead? What if enemies found him first?

He picked up the holster. "I guess I'd better go see if I remember how to clean these things." The cat trailed behind him as he went to his room.

Chapter Seven

He had laughed! Shannon shoved the mop into the bucket with a splash and wrung it out, imagining her hands were wrapped around a certain man's neck and wringing the life out of him. He had laughed! The image of him standing in the loft bent over double with laughter galled her.

And Mose! Just when she had finally got him in to do the mopping, he had run off to town on some errand for the cook. He'd best not run his mouth about her mishap in the puddle. He'd have the whole town laughing at her as if they didn't already, thanks to Da. Shannon attacked the dirt on the floor as if it were an enemy. Now thanks to Mose she'd be late for choir and have to go soaking wet in the bargain. She had only one good dress to wear other than the clothes she had on, and she didn't want to ruin it in this weather.

The weather. One week it was freezing cold with

snow piled on the ground; the next it was warm and pouring rain. It was a wonder that the entire town wasn't sick with the extremes they'd had lately. The mop hit the pail again and she swished it up and down like a butter churn.

"I wonder how Da's doing," she mumbled to herself as she attacked the floor again. She hadn't seen him since the day she'd left but knew he was out and about from the reports Mose had given her. He'd been seen frequenting the tavern with regularity. "I wonder what he's stolen to pay his way with. Now that he doesn't have me around to act as his conscience, he's as free as a bird. . . ." Shannon talked to the mop as if it were a companion. Thank goodness Da hadn't seen her mishap on the step. That would give him new fodder for his tales. "How his homely old-maid daughter wound up sitting on her arse in a puddle . . ." Shannon mimicked the strong Irish brogue of her father.

He had laughed! Shannon looked out the window toward the puddle, which now reflected the weak efforts of the afternoon sun to peep through the clouds. She had to admit it probably was funny. She imagined her long frame teetering on the step and her arms windmilling toward the sky for support that was not to be found. A smile tickled the corners of her lips and she shook her head at the memory.

She liked his laugh. She had not heard it before, not like today. It came from deep within his belly. Will had had a laugh like that. Of course, Will had always been laughing and smiling and joking and singing. It was good to hear a laugh like that again. Will had always said you could judge a man's heart by where his laughter came from.

That was what she missed about her brother the most. The talking. The observations he made about life. When they were little, they had talked many a night away. They talked about nonsense, they talked about everyday life. They talked about their dreams. Now she had no one to talk to. Doctor Blankenship was wrapped up in his patients and papers. The grouchy cook barely grunted. She could sour water quicker than a lemon. Mose was good for gossip but not much else. She hadn't had a good talk with anyone since . . .

He had laughed! It would be nice to sit down and laugh with him. Shannon enjoyed a joke as much as anyone. Years ago she had been the one who dropped the ink in Mrs. Farley's tea when the busybody had been railing at Gran for not putting her in a proper school so she could learn to read and write. It wasn't Gran's fault that her father wouldn't allow it. Gran had done the best she could by teaching her what she remembered from the Bible. Da hadn't seen any use in education and Mrs. Farley had blamed Gran. The old busybody was talking with blue teeth for weeks after the ink incident, and Will had taken the blame and the whipping for it.

Why did Jake have scars on his back? Shannon leaned on the mop handle and looked toward the barn. Had he been imprisoned at one time? What had he done to deserve such a punishment? The wounds were old but the scars were deep. Had there been someone there to comfort him after it was done? Had he a mother or a sister or a lover who could ease the pain for him?

Shannon watched as Jake came out of the barn with a sure step. He was wearing his short jacket and his light gray muffler was wrapped around his neck against the biting cold of the strong wind that had blown up. His pale blond hair had grown some and stood straight up as the wind went through it. Shannon's fingers ached to smooth the tousled mass back into place. She watched his progress from the barn to the corner of the big house and wondered where he was going all bundled up against the weather. If he had been coming to the house, he would have stepped out in his shirtsleeves as he did every day.

Someone, somewhere, loved him. The finely knitted muffler was proof of that. Had the woman in the letter made it? Had she given it to him as a going-away present to remember her by? Had she wept at the thought of his leaving and did she weep now because he had not returned? An image filled her mind. Jake was standing next to a horse, handsome and strong in his fine uniform. The sun glistened off his hair and his pale blue eyes were looking into the eyes of a woman who was wrapping a light gray muffler around his neck. He bent his head and their lips touched. The woman leaned into his body and Jake wrapped his arms around her waist, pulling her close so that the entire lengths of their frames were touching.

Shannon felt the heat rising within her. Had she turned into a wanton since he had entered her life? Her cheeks turned as red as her hair as she imagined what it would be like to be that woman who clung to him. What would it be like to have his hands touch her and his lips kiss her own? What would it feel like to sleep next to him at night, to reach out and touch his body with her own? And once she had him, how could she ever let him go? Jake walked by the window with his hands buried in his pockets, his head down against the wind. "He's trying to remember," Shannon said to the mop. She leaned her forehead against the coolness of the windowpane to relieve the heat that had risen to her face. If only she could cool the rest of her body as easily. Keeping her distance from the man had not made it easier.

"Thou shalt not steal, thou shalt not commit adultery. Thou shalt not covet . . ."

"Did you say something, Miz Shannon?"

Mose grinned his toothy grin as he always did when he caught her talking to herself.

"Just reciting the commandments, Mose."

"Do you want me to finish up in here?"

In the next instant the mop spun into his hand as Shannon fled the room.

He was going to town. Shannon watched from the front door as Jake turned when he met the road. Whatever could he be going to town for? Panic overcame her. Was he leaving? Surely he wouldn't leave without a word. Had he said something to Doctor Blankenship? Or to Mose? Surely he would say good-bye to her. Wouldn't he? Shannon ran back through the house.

"Mose, I'm going to town!" she called as she flew by the room he was mopping.

"Sho' nuff, Miz Shannon." Mose slung the mop around, missing most of the dirt. "Everyone's all het up to go to town today. I'm goin' to town; Mister Jake's goin' to town and now Miz Shannon goin' to town." Mose laughed out loud as he realized the implications. "Best put on your Sunday dress, Miz Shannon. . . ."

It wasn't much of a town, Jake thought to himself as he crossed the bridge. At least the groupings of the buildings blocked most of the wind. He could see a church steeple before him, a general store to the right, along with a bank and a few other shops. Houses were to the left and a small schoolhouse was visible on the edge of the forest. Jake headed for the store.

Jake could tell as soon as he entered that the community wasn't accustomed to strangers. The storekeeper approached the counter with some trepidation while a portly woman looked on with ears perked to catch the conversation.

"I need some ammunition for a Colt forty-four," Jake said as the man came to the counter.

"Are you sure?" the man asked. "I notice you're not wearing a weapon."

"Am I sure of what kind of ammo I need or am I sure that I need it?" Jake knew the man was fishing for information. And the woman who was approaching the counter had to be the same Mrs. Farley who had condemned Shannon to spinsterhood because she didn't fit into her idea of beauty. He had a sudden urge to show the woman a mirror.

"What is it you're looking for, young man?"

"A box of bullets for a Colt forty-four." Jake turned away from the couple to discourage their questions. The table before him was covered with clothing. There were neat stacks of pants and shirts in all colors and sizes. But it was the thing that was out of place that had caught his attention. A cream-colored shawl had been carelessly thrown on top. Jake walked to the table and touched a corner of the shawl where the fringe began. He lifted the fabric and held it before him. The edge of it was embroidered with a vine and clusters of purple flowers.

"How much for this?" he asked.

Mrs. Farley shot an elbow into her husband's stomach. "That's a one-of-a-kind piece. It's special made; only one with that pattern of embroidery."

Jake knew she was feeding him a line but what she said fit his purpose. "That's fine with me, ma'am. It's for a one-of-a-kind, special-made lady." He looked over his shoulder at her. "How much?"

Mrs. Farley searched for a number that was high enough to make a profit but low enough to keep the sale. He didn't bat an eye when she announced it.

"Would you like it wrapped?" she asked eagerly.

Jake had a vision of Shannon's face as he handed her the gift. "Yes." A display of ribbon behind the counter caught his eye. "And could you tie it with a piece of that green ribbon?" He pointed to a length of ribbon that matched Shannon's eyes. Mrs. Farley started tallying numbers in her head as she went through a mental list of eligible maids in the community.

Jake wandered around the store while Mrs. Farley wrapped the shawl. He let his hands drift over the different items, hoping that something he saw would stir up some memories. A rack hanging on the wall held several dime novels. He picked one up and leafed through the pages. Something tickled the back of his mind . . .

"I know who you are," Mrs. Farley announced. "You're that man Shannon found in the creek." She turned to her husband. "Mose said he was fine now and working for the doctor. He's the one who doesn't know his name."

"I know my name, Missus Farley," Jake announced and was pleased with the shocked look she gave him when he pronounced hers. "It's Jacob Anderson." He moved to a glass display cabinet that held several guns. A Henry rifle lay along the back of the case. The walnut stock had been polished and it glowed with warmth amid the cold steel of the other guns on display. Jake's hands itched to hold it.

"I'd like to see that rifle also."

"It's not for sale," Mr. Farley said. Mrs. Farley hissed at her husband.

"May I just look at it?"

"No, I'm sorry, it's not for sale." Mrs. Farley gave her husband another swift jab to the gut. The storekeeper slapped the box of cartridges on the counter. "Anything else for you today?"

Jake regretfully tore himself away from the gun case. "That's all. How much do I owe you?"

Mrs. Farley gave him the total and Jake counted out the money.

"I thought you were a Confederate soldier," she commented as he gave her the bills.

"I was," Jake looked down at his uniform. "Why?"

"These are Yankee dollars."

"So they are." Jake looked at the bills. "Would you rather have Confederate?"

"No, we don't take it."

"Well, I guess it's a good thing I'm carrying Yankee money." Jake gathered his packages and left the store.

It was a good question. Why was a Confederate soldier carrying Yankee dollars in his boot? He dismissed it as easily as it came. It was just another question that he didn't have the answer to.

He wished he could have gotten his hands on that rifle. He just wanted to know what it felt like to hold it. It looked like a fine piece. Why was it lying in that case if it wasn't for sale? Jake looked around the town. There were a few people on the street, going about their business.

He called out to a man passing by. "Can you tell me if there's a saloon around here?"

The man scratched the back of his head as he considered the question. "Saloon? There's a tavern up that-a-way."

Jake thanked him and headed in the direction he'd indicated. Saloon? Tavern? Was there a difference? It just must depend on where you were from. Jake stopped in his tracks. Of course. People from these parts used the word "tavern." He'd said "saloon" without even thinking about it. Did people from the South call such a place a saloon? He didn't think so. He was also pretty certain he wasn't from the South. He definitely didn't talk the way most of the folks around here did. Where was he from? He had once again gone around the endless circle that held no escape and no answers.

It wasn't much of a tavern. The two-story wood-frame house had a common room on the first floor and some rooms for rent upstairs. He had the place to himself for the moment. Jake wondered if there was a woman who worked the rooms. He didn't even know how long it had been since he had been with a woman. If there was a soiled dove working the rooms, what would he do? An image of Shannon rose up before him. Her face was full of indignant rage, and sparks were flying from her deep green eyes. Jake had to smile as the image presented itself.

What difference should it make to her if he did go upstairs? Why should he care what she thought? Or that she might be hurt. Jake walked up to the bar with that thought reeling in his head. Did he care about Shannon enough to worry about hurting her?

A woman working the bar came up to him. "What would you like?"

"A beer." He dropped his packages onto the stool beside him.

Shannon had saved his life. On top of that, she had cared for him all those weeks when he couldn't care for himself. Of course he didn't want to hurt her. She was a sweet girl. She was sweet and she was pretty. She had a beautiful voice and an interesting personality. No, he certainly didn't want to hurt her. Why would anyone want to hurt her?

"You just get into town?" the woman asked.

Jake took a sip of the beer. "No, I've been here a while."

"Been keeping yourself busy?"

Jake looked directly at the woman with icy blue eyes that encouraged her to mind her own business. She walked back to the other end of the bar. He immediately regretted his unfriendliness. He took another sip of the beer.

"Are you Ingrid?" he asked.

"Yes." She looked at him expectantly.

"Mose mentioned you."

"Mose." The woman smiled. "You must be Mister Jake."

"I guess I am."

"He told me about you. Said you had taken up residence in the tack room and were working for Doc Blankenship."

"Mose loves to talk."

Ingrid smiled as she wiped the bar down. "Yes, he does." She moved down to his position as she worked. "So tell me, Jake, what do you think of Shannon?"

Jake leaned back in surprise. "Shannon?"

"She was the talk of the town there for a while. There are lots of people who did not approve of an unmarried woman becoming so intimate with the patients over there."

"When you say lots of people, are you referring to Missus Farley?"

Ingrid laughed. "Mose does like to talk, doesn't he?" She topped off his glass from the huge keg behind her. "So what do you think of Shannon?"

"I'd be dead if it weren't for her."

"Yes, you would. And you could probably thank her father for it also. If she hadn't been along that day, he probably would have bashed your head in with a rock."

Jake looked at the woman in surprise. "Does Shannon make a habit of robbing dead bodies with her father?"

"Pish! Shannon tries her best to keep her father out of trouble. The smartest thing that girl ever did was leave him. There was no sense at all in the way Shamus treated her. He acts as if it was her fault that her mother died when she was born and her brother died in the war."

"How could he blame her for those things?"

"He blames her for her mother's death because they say she was too big for her mother. He blames her for her brother's death because he's just plain mean."

"Mose said he beat her."

"I wouldn't call it beatings, really, but he did hit her a lot. Especially when he was drunk."

"Someone should show him what it feels like." Jake took the glass between his hands and clenched it tightly. Ingrid gasped as it shattered and the beer foamed out onto the bar.

"Oh my goodness!" she exclaimed. "Are you cut?" She grabbed a towel and dabbed at the blood that oozed from the palm of his left hand. A piece of glass was sticking out of the cut and she extracted it as Jake looked on in amazement. "You should have Doc look at that. I think he'll probably need to sew it up."

Jake looked at the blood oozing from his hand. "You think?"

Ingrid folded a clean towel around his hand and then wrapped his fingers into his palm. "Yes. I do."

Jake picked up his packages and stuffed them under his left arm as he dug into his pocket for some money. "Thanks, Ingrid." He made his way to the door while she looked after his retreating form with shock.

He met a man coming through the door just as he was going out. The man was older than he, with faded red hair and a limp, dragging one leg behind him as if he couldn't bend the knee. The two of them turned in their tracks as they passed, each one sizing up the other. Jake raked his pale blue eyes over the older man's form. The man, in return, wiped a grimy sleeve under his nose and hitched up his pants.

"My dearest Ingrid, can ye spare a drop fer me tiday?" the man asked as he approached the bar. Jake followed his progress with icy blue eyes and then left.

"Who was that?" Shamus hitched a thumb over his shoulder as Jake left.

"He's the man your daughter saved."

"He's still hanging around?" Shamus sniffed the cheap brew that was all his coin would buy him. "I wonder what he's after."

Chapter Eight

His hand was starting to throb. Jake turned to go toward the bridge but stopped when he saw the flick of skirts around a strong, sure stride. Shannon had come to town. And she was wearing a pretty green dress, along with a green ribbon in her hair, which had been pinned up into a surprisingly neat knot. He noticed that she had her arms wrapped around herself to ward off the cold and remembered the sight of her shawl dripping on the porch rail.

Instead of turning to go over the bridge, Jake cautiously walked after Shannon in the dimming light of early evening. Her stride had to be as long as his, because he wasn't catching up with her. Of course, he wasn't sure if he wanted to. Jake was several yards behind her and stopped to watch as she entered the doors of the small white church at the end of the street. A few other people went in also, including Mrs. Farley, who seemed to be in a hurry as she gathered her wide skirts and huffed her way across the street. Jake went to the end of the boardwalk and waited until he was sure no one else was going to show up. Organ music drifted out of the entrance, and he used it to cover the sound he made as he slipped through the door and into the corner where the end of a pew was hidden in darkness.

There were seven women and five men gathered in seats on the platform at the front of the church. One man was so thin that it looked as if a stiff breeze would blow him away. Jake recognized him as the pastor from several visits he had paid to the hospital. The reverend clapped his hands and the group directed its attention to him. He nodded to the organist, who began playing a sudden burst of music with both her hands and her feet. The pastor waved his hands in time to the music and then with another nod of his head, the assembled voices rang out.

Jake easily recognized the four parts of the music. It was a Christmas piece and he realized that he knew the words. One voice seemed to be out of time with the rest and occasionally hit a discordant note, especially when the tune went into the higher octaves. Jake looked to see if he could identify who was off key. It couldn't be Shannon. He had heard her sing many times and knew her voice as it soared above the rest. Her face was glowing and he thought her hair must be freshly washed as it shone brightly in the soft light of the lanterns. An especially bad note was heard and Jake laughed to himself as Shannon took a half step away from the broad form of Mrs. Farley. The pastor kept on waving his hands and the organ continued. After meeting the woman, Jake figured there was no changing her. She probably thought she had the most beautiful voice in town.

It was then he noticed that everyone was holding

music except for Shannon. She must know the music well, along with the words. But as they went through several songs, Jake wondered how she could remember them all. It was amazing how she just sang without any effort and without missing a word. She must have an incredible memory.

"Thank you, everyone," the pastor finally said. Mrs. Farley fanned herself with her music as if she had just run a race. "Everyone can go unless you wish to listen to Shannon practice her solo."

Everyone found a seat except for Mrs. Farley, who rushed down the aisle in a flurry of huffs and puffs. She blew right by Jake without seeing him, a fact that made him feel immensely grateful to the Father whose house he was sitting in. He leaned forward in anticipation and then became confused when the organist stepped out from her box and joined the small group that had gathered in the front pews.

Shannon stepped to the front of the platform. She folded her hands in front of her and Jake couldn't help noticing the bit of white lace that stood up around the collar of her dress, accentuating the length of her neck and the pale perfection of her skin.

Hark the herald angels sing,
Glory to the newborn king.
Peace on earth and mercy mild,
God and sinners reconciled.
Joyful all ye nations rise,
Join the triumph of the skies,
With the angelic host proclaim,
Christ is born in Bethlehem.

Hark the herald angels sing,
Glory to the newborn king!

Jake had a thought as her voice filled the church. Bring in the leaders of the North and South. Bring in the generals and the admirals and the presidents of both nations. Let them listen to this song. Let them hear these words. Surely the goodness and beauty that was pouring forth from Shannon would end the war if they would only listen.

Jake shook his head. It was beautiful. But it made him sad. He wanted to weep.

He hated himself for his weakness, yet he couldn't tear himself away.

She sang the second verse and then the third and her voice was strong and gave witness to the words. Her soul shone through her eyes and her spirit showed in the glow of her face.

Leave, now, before it's too late.

He couldn't move.

He didn't have a clue as to what he had done in his past. But he knew without a doubt that she was much too good for him.

She finished the song. She had seen him. He was trapped.

A smattering of applause filled the front of the church. The pastor had been especially moved and jumped to his feet to show his appreciation. Shannon blushed at the accolades and accepted the compliments as she made her way to the back of the church, where Jake stood with the package clutched under his arm and his hand throbbing in the towel.

"What are you doing here?" she asked him.

"I . . . I don't know . . . I heard the music . . . ," he said helplessly. A row of curious faces appeared behind her. "Can I walk you back?" He needed to get out of there as quickly as possible.

Her smile was glorious. "Thank you. What happened to your hand?" Jake placed the injured hand on her back to guide her out the door.

"I cut it."

"On what?" Shannon reached for the wounded hand.

"Ow! Wait!" They paused on the step outside the church. Jake could still feel the eyes of the pastor and choir on them. It wouldn't have surprised him if they had their faces plastered to the windows. "Hold this." He handed her his packages and then he slipped off his short battle jacket. "Put this on."

She looked at him in amazement as he swung it over her shoulders and then placed the packages back under his right arm. He then looped her hand under his left arm.

"So you've done some shopping?" Shannon looked at the packages curiously.

"I have." They stepped out into the darkened street.

"And cut your hand in the meantime?"

"You can look at it when we get back."

"You've had quite an adventure for your first trip to town." He could see the smile curling the edges of her mouth as they passed beneath a lamp.

"From what I can see, I think I've done it all."

"Been to the tavern, have you?"

"And what if I had?"

"You smell like a brewery."

Jake sniffed his sleeve and was suddenly embarrassed at the realization that he had gone into a church smelling of strong beer. "That's how I cut my hand. A glass of beer broke in it."

"Must have been some strong beer."

Jake stopped in the middle of the street. "Are you laughing at me?"

"Well, you were laughing at me." Her smile was dancing across her face.

"It was funny."

"Wish I could have seen it," Shannon retorted dryly. She grabbed the jacket with her hand and gripped it around the front to keep it from sliding off her shoulders. She should have just put it on. It would fit her as well as him but she liked the way it felt when he placed it on her shoulders. It was almost as if he cared . . . for her.

They walked on in silence, except for an occasional chuckle, first one, then the other. Their shoes made a hollow sound on the bridge.

"The river will probably be frozen up again by morning," she said.

"We'll probably have snow again in a few days," he returned.

"Indeed."

"Shannon?"

"Hmm?"

"Your singing . . . it's beautiful."

"It was much better when Will was around."

"I can't imagine it being any better than it was . . . tonight."

She stopped and looked out over the river that was

flowing peacefully beneath the bridge. "I don't feel like myself when I'm singing."

"Whom do you feel like?" Jake stopped beside her.

"Like someone else." Her eyes glittered in the moonlight like the ice that formed alongside the banks. "I feel like someone who's beautiful."

He turned to look at her. "You are beautiful."

She lowered her head and he touched her chin to raise it with the injured hand. "You are," he insisted. A small sigh escaped her lips and turned into fog in the crisp night air. He turned her face toward his and leaned forward. Her mouth was just a few inches below his. Her lips were slightly parted, trembling, waiting . . .

"You're bleeding!" she exclaimed and grabbed his arm. She held it so his palm was up and over the water. Blood had run down his arm and soaked the sleeve of his shirt. She quickly unwrapped the blood-soaked towel and looked at his wound. "I can't see. It's too dark." She wrapped the towel back around his hand and raised his arm in the air. "Hold it like this," Shannon commanded and then proceeded to tow him across the bridge while holding on to his arm.

She guided him into a small office in the hospital and showed him a chair before she lit a lamp and placed it on the table. She dropped his jacket on a chair and then did a quick examination of his hand. "Dolt. You should have had this looked at right away." She was talking more to herself than to him and was surprised when he answered her.

"I got distracted." He felt like a child who had been caught with his hand in the cookie jar.

Shannon rummaged around in a drawer and returned

with some supplies. "It's going to need some stitches. Should I go get Doctor Blankenship?"

"No. You can do it." His eyes were silver in the lamplight as he looked up at her. Her smile danced at the corners of her lips as she realized that he trusted her to take care of him.

"I can." Shannon pulled another chair up to the table and sat down across from him. She placed his hand out flat beside the lamp and gave a small *tsk* of disgust as she looked at the wound. "This is going to hurt," she warned him. She grabbed hold of his wrist with one hand and poured liquid from a crock with the other.

"Ahhh!" Jake yelled as she held his hand down. He slapped the table with the other. "What was that?"

"Whiskey. It cleans the wound of poison."

"Why is it in a crock?"

"So Mose won't find it and drink it."

Jake, find me some whiskey to pour in this wound. It will keep it from getting infected. He shook his head to clear the fog as she stuck a needle in his palm.

"What now? Are you trying to kill me?"

"Hold still. If I wanted to kill you, I'd use something bigger than this needle."

"Ow!"

"It's a good thing you were in a coma when you came here. I would have bashed you on the head myself if I had to listen to your whining like this for three months."

Zane, quit your whining!

Shannon bent her head over and blew on his hand as she took the next stitch. He leaned closer to look.

"Watch it; you're in my light."

"Do you ever stop?"

"Stop what?"

"Fussing."

"Fussing?" She took another stitch and blew on his hand again.

"That tickles."

"So who's fussing now?"

"I don't fuss. Women fuss, men just gripe."

"So before you weren't whining, you were griping?"

"Yes, I mean no. Are you about done?"

Shannon pulled the thread up and snipped it at his palm. "Yes, except for the bandaging." She took her instruments and put them away, leaving the bottle on the table. Jake picked it up and took a quick swig while she had her back to him as she searched for a bandage. She soon had his hand wrapped to her satisfaction and then looked skeptically at his shirtsleeve as she stood to clean up the mess.

"It's going to have to be soaked to get that blood out."

Jake couldn't control himself. She had been so superior while taking care of his hand that he had to turn the tables. He stood and whipped the shirt over his head in a quick motion and handed it to her. "Thanks. I appreciate the offer."

The pale skin of his chest glowed in the lamplight. The air in the room was cool and his skin quickly reacted to it. How many times had she touched his chest? How many times had she wiped a cool cloth over it to chase away the dreams that troubled his sleep while he lay in the bed caught in the darkness? How many times had she looked at him in his troubled state and wished that she could help him?

"It looks like I got some blood on your dress too." He touched a finger to a few dark spots in the pleats of her skirt. "I could return the favor, if you want."

Her breath caught in her throat. Her body burned beneath the layers of her clothes as his finger brushed the droplets of blood that had dripped from his hand. The same hand that now drifted gently up her arm, barely touching the sleeve of her dress with his finger-tips curled to protect the wound in the palm. The other hand gripped her forearm and pulled her a step closer to him and to the bare chest that glowed in the soft light. *Quit looking at his chest, Shannon. You're a wanton.* She tore her eyes away and raised them to his face. He pulled her in another step. Her breasts brushed against his chest and they tingled and swelled at the soft impact. The tip of her nose was even with his mouth. Another step and his arm slid behind her. The fingertips of his bandaged hand brushed against her temple, down her cheek, lifting her face and her trembling lips.

She had never been kissed. But it didn't take her long to figure out how it should be done. His lips guided hers. His arm in the small of her back flat-tened her body against his as he took her measure. Her arms wrapped under his and around his back where her hands skimmed over the scars. His hand moved down lower and pressed her against his rising manhood.

Shannon. He wanted her. He needed her. She filled the holes that were missing in his mind and in his heart. He didn't need the past when he had her. His life started here, now, with Shannon. He would leave the past behind him and not give it another thought.

She let out a whimper as his tongue with its whiskey taste found its way between her lips, caressing her, teas-ing, teaching her the game. Her hands moving on his back were driving him wild. The scars didn't exist when she touched them.

The scars. Where did the scars come from? What was he doing? She didn't deserve this. What if he was married? What would it do to her if he made love to her and then left her?

"Shannon." His lips protested as he pushed her away. They wanted more but his mind screamed that it was wrong. That he would hurt her.

She stood before him gasping for breath. Her hair had lost some pins and the knot had slid to the side; the ribbon was barely hanging on.

"I'm sorry." Jake reached a hand out to touch her arm and then just as quickly dropped it.

She threw a hand up to her mouth and looked at him through green eyes brimming with tears.

"I can't."

She ran from the room with a sob caught in her throat.

"Shannon. Wait." She didn't hear him. She was gone.

The flickering of the lamp was nothing compared to the flames that raged within him. Jake fought for control over his body as he heard her footsteps pounding through the hall and then the slamming of the door as she found her escape. With a sigh he ran his fingers through his hair, causing the blond tips to stand on end. He was cold and his shirt lay in a puddle of white and red on the floor. He picked it up. She was right. It would have to be soaked to get the blood out. Cold water worked best for such things. *How do I know that?* He could use a soak in some cold water himself. His nether parts were still rebelling.

Jake found his jacket where she had left it on the back of a chair. He put it on over his bare chest and gathered up his shirt and packages. He took a moment to look at the shawl, which was wrapped in brown paper and tied with green ribbon. He had meant it for Shannon as a Christmas present but after tonight she would probably throw it in his face. And he would justly deserve that action.

The light was on in her cabin when he emerged from the back of the building. Maybe he should go and apologize. And maybe she would clobber him with whatever weapon she had handy. Jake sighed and made his way to his room in the barn.

The cold air on his naked body did nothing to help his arousal as he slid between the blankets. Just how long had it been since he had a woman? He groaned as he rolled over on his side. It looked like it was going to be a long, sleepless night.

The gentle sounds of a guitar drifted through the clear stillness of the night air. The strings vibrated with a haunting melody that seemed to be from a different world after the joyous music of the season he had heard in the little white church. Shannon's voice soon joined in, but instead of the clear soprano she had used before, she now sang in a throaty contralto that filled his body with the memory of the kiss they had shared.

My true love has gone away,
Now I try to fill my days
With memories and bits of song
That fill my soul and make me long
For my time on earth to end
And my broken heart will mend.

The orange cat jumped onto the end of his cot and carefully crept up over the bend of his legs and into the crook between his thighs and arms. It sat and stared at Jake for a moment, with a deep purr rumbling in its throat.

Jake flopped over on his back and the cat jumped off, taking a moment to lick away the insult to its dignity after it landed on the floor.

"That's a good idea, cat." Jake looked at where the cat sat in a sliver of moonlight shining through the window. "Maybe I should just go too." He threw an arm over his forehead as the song continued. "But where will I go?"

Chapter Nine

Jason was worried. He held in his hand a letter from another rancher who lived east of them. Someone was buying up land and didn't care what he had to do to get it.

"So what is your friend going to do?" Chase asked as Jason folded the letter and placed it on his desk.

"He's leaving. Packing up after putting forty-some years into his place. He was here before I was. He told me I was foolish for buying up all the property from the government. He said I should save my money and take advantage of the free range. Now his range is gone and his son was killed in the bargain. He's going back East to live with his daughter."

"Any clue as to who's doing the buying?"

"He sold out to a man named Petty. He's pretty sure that the thugs who were doing all the sabotage worked for him too. He said life had gotten downright impossible in the past few years and everyone was selling out. He just didn't have the heart to fight it anymore."

"So you think this Petty might be moving west?"

"It would explain a lot of things, wouldn't it?" Jason unrolled a map and placed it on the desktop. His finger found St. Louis and trailed across the territories until it reached Wyoming. "Civilization is moving west, Chase, and the railroad is going to bring it. Congress has already passed a resolution to buy up land. Maybe this Petty is trying to make a buck off the U.S. government."

"You mean steal the land from the locals and then sell it to the government?" Chase walked away from the desk. "Some of these homesteaders are barely making it. They wouldn't have a chance against hired guns."

"Exactly." Jason went back to his perusal of the map. "From what I recall when the surveyors were out here a few years back, they were looking at a route that went south of here."

"So it would miss us?"

"For the most part. Look at this." Chase came back to the desk and stood next to Jason. "You say that the creek coming out of Elk Canyon was dammed?" Jason's finger trailed the creek as it wandered over the map. "That creek feeds the south pasture." His other finger moved across the map to the east, where his friend's ranch had been located.

"Which is in the path of the railroad."

"Maybe you and I should pay a visit to some of our neighbors down in that direction and see if they've noticed anything."

Chase nodded in agreement just as two little boys came bursting through the door.

"Daddy, Agnes gave us cookies!" Fox announced as

they bounced into the room. "We saved some for you if you want."

"Thanks." Chase grinned as his hands ruffled the hair of the boys who clung to each of his legs.

"What's that?" Chance asked and went around the desk to his grandfather.

"It's a map." Jason pulled Chance into his lap and the two heads bent together as the elderly man pointed out various landmarks to his great-grandson. Fox, not wanting to be left out, claimed the other knee and the three were soon engrossed in a question-and-answer period.

"Bring them down when you're tired of them," Chase said as he left.

"Chase—" Jason looked up from the map. "Best tell the others what's going on."

"I will." Chase left the house with Justice following along and went down the hill to Grace's, his mind turning over the discussion he'd had with Jason. There was a threat coming to the ranch, he was sure of it. It was the first time, however, that Jenny hadn't dreamed of a threat. As far as he knew, she had been sleeping peacefully through the night since they returned from their near disaster in New York. Of course, with everything she did during the day, it wasn't a surprise that she slept so soundly. She took care of the boys, she worked with the horses and she did her best to relieve Grace of her more strenuous duties because of her friend's advancing pregnancy.

But all in all, Jenny seemed unworried. He knew she was relieved by the recent letter saying that Ty and Cat were still safe at Ty's plantation; Caleb seemed to be getting along well, and as soon as Cole returned with Amanda, things would be set right at the ranch.

They all missed Jake, of course. He had been the quiet one of the bunch but that didn't mean he hadn't added his own brand of spice to their conversations. He had a way of coming up with dry observations that usually set everyone to laughing. Life had been fun then. . . . They had all been carefree in those days before the war. The summer before the drive had been one of the best of Chase's life. Jenny loved him, Jamie had been alive, Jake had been alive, Caleb had been whole . . . Would he trade what he had now for what they had lost?

The answer to that was easy. No, he couldn't and wouldn't make that choice. But there were days when he looked at Fox and missed Jamie so much it hurt. It hurt to know that the precious little boy would never know how wonderful his father was. And now Jake was gone. The two boys had never even seen him. All he would ever be to them was a name.

Laughter poured forth from Grace's cabin. Zane telling a tale again. Must be a good one. He heard Caleb's low chuckle along with Grace's and Jenny's.

She hadn't had any dreams lately, he reminded himself. Maybe things would be all right. He walked into the cabin.

"Hey Chase, do you remember Spotted Tail?" Zane asked as soon as he came through the door.

"The Brule chief?" Chase nodded. "From the Dakota?"

"Yes." Zane jumped into his story. "You remember how his daughter was always watching the soldiers on the parade grounds? Well, apparently she just up and died and Spotted Tail brought her back to be buried at the fort. Colonel Maynadier went all out and gave her a

Christian burial. The chaplain was out there praying over her for nearly an hour."

"Did any of it rub off on you?" Grace asked and Zane sent her his most charming smile with dimples flashing.

"So that's what took you so long in town today," Jenny added.

"Had to see what was going on now, didn't I?" He lifted a lid on a pot that was boiling on the stove. "All those Indians were hanging around all dressed out in their good duds. For all I know, they could have been getting ready to go to war."

"Shut up, Zane," Chase snapped.

Zane looked at Chase. "You sounded just like Jake when you said that." Zane pulled open the oven door. "What's got you all bent out of shape?"

Grace smacked his backside with a towel. "Go make yourself useful and tell the others that dinner will be ready in a minute."

"Yes, ma'am." Zane went to the door just as Justice started barking. "Sounds like we might have company. . . ." He opened the door and jerked his head toward Caleb. Caleb slowly rose from his chair and joined Zane on the porch. A tall, rangy man stood outside with a foolish grin on his face.

Cole walked up the steps to the cabin with Justice bounding around his legs. "You boys gonna say hi or just stand there and look at me?" A woman sat on the buggy seat behind him.

Zane let go with a left to Cole's jaw that sent him flying off the step. Then Zane jumped off and quickly went to Cole's side to help rescue him from Justice's cold nose and wet tongue.

"What the hell did you do that for?" Cole asked as Zane pulled him to his feet. He tested his jaw and dusted off his backside while Justice wagged his tail at the new game.

"Just so dang glad to see you, Cole." Zane hung on to his arm.

"Let go of me, you fool." Cole jerked his arm away. "It will take more than a punch from you to keep me from getting up these steps."

Caleb planted his feet, both the real and the wooden one, firmly on the porch. He swung at Cole and struck him squarely in the jaw. Cole stumbled back down the steps where Zane was waiting to catch him. Justice starting barking again, not really sure what was happening. Caleb lost his balance and grabbed on to the post to set himself right. Chase came out the door to see what all the commotion was about.

"Have you two lost your minds?" Cole hollered and wrested himself away from Zane.

"You want a shot at him, Chase?" Zane asked.

"Why not?" Chase grinned and jumped off the porch. Zane grabbed Cole's arms so Chase would have a free shot. Chase dropped him in the dirt again and Cole stayed there, propped on one hand while he rubbed his jaw with the other.

"When I get up from here, I just might kill all three of you," Cole growled.

Chase extended a hand. "We just really missed you, Cole." Jenny walked out and leaned against the door with arms folded.

"I don't think so. I don't think you missed me a bit." He looked dubiously at Chase and let him pull him to his feet. "If Zeb comes out and takes a swing at me, I'm leaving the territory."

"Oh, we wouldn't let him do that." Zane made a production of dusting off the dirt and handed Cole his hat. "But now if Grace decides to have a go at you, we will all hold you down."

"Why would Grace want to hit me?"

"Why don't you ask her?" Jenny said from the door.

Cole looked at all of them as if they had lost their minds and tentatively walked up the steps. Caleb held his hands up and away as Cole walked by.

Cole looked down to see him standing on two legs. "I couldn't tell the difference," he assured him as he went by.

Jenny looked up into his gray eyes as she stood in front of the door, barring his way. "I always thought you to be a decent man, Cole Larrimore. I hope you don't disappoint me."

Cole was sure they'd all lost their minds as he reached past Jenny for the latch. She stepped out of his way and he walked into the cabin.

Jenny saw Amanda sitting on the buggy seat and went to her. "Hi, remember me?" she asked the frightened young woman.

Amanda nodded with gray eyes wide.

"Don't mind these maniacs. They just have a strange way of doing things."

"Glad to see you finally made it," Chase said as he came up behind Jenny.

"Howdy!" Zane added.

"Where's Uncle Cole?" Her voice was barely above a whisper.

"He's got some catching up to do with Grace," Jenny explained. "Why don't you come sit on the porch until they're done?"

Chase offered a hand but she refused it, climbing down by herself.

"Amanda, this is Zane, and that's Caleb."

"Ma'am," they both said together.

Amanda walked to the porch and set a foot on the step. On the second one she slipped and stumbled forward. Caleb, still next to the post, quickly grabbed her arm and kept her from falling. Her arm trembled beneath his grasp and her eyes were wild as she looked up at him.

"Are you all right?" he asked, his warm brown eyes looking into the depths of her wide gray ones.

She nodded and he released her arm. Amanda went to a chair and sat down, her back stiff, her eyes looking off into the distance.

"I'll go tell the boys that dinner might be late," Caleb offered as Jenny came up on the porch.

"That might be a good idea," Jenny said. She was at her wits' end as to what to do with Amanda.

"Pretty girl," Zane said when Caleb stepped in beside him.

"She's lost."

Zane looked over his shoulder at where Amanda was sitting, staring off into the distance. "What do you mean, she's lost?"

"Look into her eyes, Zane. I don't know what that bastard did to her when he had her, but I can tell you this much. She's lost." They had almost reached the bunkhouse.

"Well, maybe she needs some help to find her way."

Caleb whirled and grabbed Zane's shirt collar. He pushed him against the wall of the bunkhouse. "Don't do it, Zane. Don't mess with her." Caleb ground the words out between clenched teeth.

Zane threw his hands out to the side in supplication. "Fine, I won't, you can have her."

"Zane . . ."

"I'll leave her alone, Caleb. I swear."

Caleb released him and haltingly stepped away.

"I'm sorry, Zane; I don't know what came over me."

Zane grinned at his friend. "I know what came over you. A pretty girl came over you."

"It's not that. . . . I mean, yes, she is pretty, but that's not it."

Zane laid a hand on Caleb's shoulder. "I understand, Caleb. Don't worry about it."

Caleb nodded, not sure if he understood what had just happened himself.

"For a guy with one leg, you sure did bust a good one on Cole," Zane laughed. "I'm pretty sure you hit him as hard as I did."

"You think?"

Zane threw his arm over Caleb's shoulder. "Come on; let's go tell the boys about it. By the way, did you see what you just did? That was amazing. Are you sure you aren't just faking that missing leg?"

"Shut up, Zane."

Grace had her back to him when Cole entered the room. He was sure she must know of his arrival after all the noise they had made outside. He waggled his jaw against the pain. Both sides hurt. Zane's left and Caleb's right had wrung him out good. He tried to remember what Chase had hit him with and couldn't. For a guy who had come seriously close to losing an arm, he had done pretty well with it.

Grace continued with whatever it was she was doing. Cooking dinner probably. It sure did smell good.

"Grace?"

"Hello, Cole." She didn't turn around.

"I get the sneaking suspicion that I've done something wrong." He walked toward her. "Would you mind telling me what it is?"

"I wouldn't exactly call it wrong." Grace laid down the knife she had been using. "Just poor timing on your part."

"Aren't you even glad to see me?" He stopped before he reached her, more confused than he had ever been in his life.

"That depends on how glad you are to see me." Grace took a breath and then turned. Her stomach bulged beneath her apron in a neat round mound.

"Grace?" Cole looked at her belly with his mouth hanging open.

"Congratulations, Cole. In a few months you're going to be a father."

"I am?"

"There hasn't been anyone else knocking on my door lately." Her tone was challenging but her warm brown eyes were worried.

"Grace . . . I . . . dang . . ." He came to her and laid a hand on her belly. "I can't believe it's real."

"Oh, it's real enough, believe me, and in about four months the reality will really set in." She was close to crying and fought her tears.

Cole grabbed her hand and knelt before her. "Grace, will you marry me?"

"Get up, you fool."

A grin covered his face. "Not until you give me an answer. And just in case you think I'm just saying this because of your condition, I'm about to prove you wrong." Cole reached into his jacket pocket and pulled out a tiny satin bag. He opened her palm and shook out a delicate gold ring set with an opal. "I bought it in New York. Amanda is safe now and I have nothing holding me back. Will you marry me?"

"Oh, Cole."

"I take it that means yes?" He came to his feet and took her in his arms. "And I hope you don't believe in long engagements."

Grace melted against him. "I didn't think you were ever coming back."

"You should have told me."

"I didn't even know until after you'd left. I thought I was going through the change."

"Wouldn't it have been a bit early for that?"

"You never know."

"So why didn't you write and tell me?"

"You had to take care of Amanda." Grace wiped a tear. "Where is she?"

"Outside. I hope Jenny is taking care of her." They turned to go out. "So that's why I got the reception I got. Did you see what those guys did to me?"

"I was watching."

"I bet you enjoyed it too," Cole laughed.

"It was kind of fun."

He pulled her into his arms again and kissed her. "I love you, Grace. It's so good to be home."

Chapter Ten

Jake wondered if he would ever get used to the smell coming from the hot spring that bubbled up behind the huge house. After all this time he should have become accustomed to it, but it still assailed his nostrils with the scent of rotten eggs. But more importantly, it haunted his mind with ghosts of the past. Ghosts without faces and without names.

Jake walked through the fresh snow that covered the lawn to Shannon's cottage and wondered if she would pitch him back down the steps once he climbed them. They had not exchanged more that two words since the night he had kissed her. Doctor Blankenship had even suggested that he ask her to take the stitches out of his palm, but he had decided he'd rather do it himself than face the hurt he anticipated in her deep green eyes.

He had decided to leave. There was no reason for him to stay. Except for one. And she probably wanted him as far away as possible. If only he knew where to go. He hoped the expedition that he was about to set out on would provide him with some answers. Jake climbed the steps to her porch and knocked on the door.

Shannon didn't say anything when she answered. She just stood there looking at him with her mouth set in a grim line and her arms wrapped securely around her waist.

"Hello, Shannon," Jake said nervously. "I was wondering if you could help me with something."

"As if I haven't helped you enough already?" She moved to slam the door.

Jake braced his hand against the portal before it could shut in his face. "We need to talk."

"I heard you well enough the other night." She stepped out onto the porch and looked out over the rail, putting her back to him. It was safer than having him come into her home.

"Shannon, you have to understand. I didn't want to take something from you unless I could make things right between us."

She glanced over her shoulder at him with a confused look on her face.

"You're not the type of woman who wants a one-night stand. And that's not what I want from you."

"What do you want from me, Jake?" She looked back over the rail again and made sure she kept a firm hold on it. For some reason her hands wanted to smooth down the pale blond locks that were sorely in need of a trim. The tips of his hair hung down and mingled with the darker color of his brows and eyelashes.

Her words seemed encouraging, so he stepped up

behind her. He reached a hand toward her shoulder but then thought better of touching it. Her posture seemed as tense as that of a deer caught in a hunter's sights, and he wasn't sure if she would run.

"I want to be with you, Shannon, but I don't want to make love to you unless I can stay with you. You wouldn't be easy to walk away from."

Her head turned again and her deep green eyes were brimming when they lighted on his face. "Do you mean that?" Her lower lip trembled.

He wanted to kiss her. He forced himself to regain control over his body.

"You're not just saying that?" she continued.

"No, I mean it. But until I know who I am and where I come from, I can't."

Dang, Jake, you done got yourself whipped just like the rest of them.... A familiar voice laughed in his head.

"Because you think you might be married to the woman who wrote you that letter." *But he might not be ...*

"That's one of the reasons, but not the only one." *Tell her the real reason....*

"Your scars," she said as she turned completely to face him. "You don't know why you have them."

"There has to be a reason for them. I must have done something to deserve them." He was sure he had.

"Maybe you didn't. Maybe you were trapped by someone else's madness and meanness." She was talking about herself and her father. She had not deserved the bruises he gave her but that had not mattered to him at the time he was hitting her.

Jake stepped up to the rail beside her. "Maybe you're right." He looked at her then and smiled. "I'd like to think you are." He cursed himself for a fool as her smile danced at the corners of her mouth. "I've missed you," he said.

"Is that why you've been hanging around outside the church during choir practice?"

"You saw me?" *I am a fool.*

"Only once."

Jake felt himself turn scarlet and looked away in embarrassment. He had been listening to her music, waiting until he saw her leave in the evenings and then showing up outside the church when he was sure she was already inside. It was the only time he really felt at peace with himself. When she was singing he could forget about the things that twisted his insides. He could forget that he had forgotten. When she was singing, all that mattered was the moment. "I love listening to you sing."

"Thank you," she whispered, embarrassed at the compliment.

They stood awkwardly in silence for a while until Shannon gave in and dug an elbow into his side. Jake pretended to be mortally injured and they both laughed at his antics.

"So what is it you need me to do for you?" Shannon asked. "Now," she couldn't help adding. Probably all he wanted was a haircut.

"I want to go to the place where you found me."

"Do you think it might help?" Her heart jumped in her chest at the thought of going off with him, even on a short excursion.

"It couldn't hurt."

"It will be covered with snow."

"I know."

"It's a long walk."

"I saddled the horse."

"Only one?" She hoped the heat she felt inside didn't show on her face.

"Doc Blankenship took the wagon."

"I'd best get my shawl."

"Don't you have a coat?"

"No."

She started the ride sitting ramrod straight behind him and trying her best to keep from touching him. She clung to the back of the saddle and gave directions, but the trail had some ups and downs and after feeling her slip several times, Jake grabbed her arm and wrapped it around his waist.

"What'd you do that for?" she asked with some hostility in her voice. She didn't want him to think that she was used to that type of thing. She wasn't.

"I'm tired of your squirming around," he barked back. "Unless you want to fall on your backside again." He looked over his shoulder at her angry countenance. "After all, it's been several days since I've had a good laugh."

Shannon's answer was to wrap her other arm around his waist. And then she squeezed him tight.

"Hey!" The horse danced as he yelled. "Not so tight." Dang but she was strong.

She released her hold, satisfied that she had made her point, but Jake noticed that she now had her body pressed firmly against his back and her chin rested on his shoulder.

The day was bright with a few scattered clouds in a pale blue sky. The sunlight danced off the icy surface of the snow and dazzled their eyes. They rode by a stone house set in a meadow below the wide curve of a mountain and then went over a covered bridge. Shannon pointed north and they followed the trail upstream awhile. Another trail branched into it and soon they were in a deep wood on a bank that rose some ten feet above the stream on the left and rose over their heads on the right. The way turned into frozen earth and the horse's hooves made a hollow sound compared to the earlier scrunching in the snow. The branches were so thick over their heads that the snow had not penetrated and the shiny deep green of the mountain laurel was a welcome respite from the blinding whiteness that had surrounded them earlier. A huge pine leaned out from the side of the trail and hung over the ravine. Past it was the remains of a fallen tree.

"There were bodies here," Shannon said as they moved on. "Two older men, Confederates. Also horses and mules." They kept going. "Here," she said finally.

Jake stopped the horse and she slid off as he dismounted. She walked over to where the trail fell away to the creek below.

"There was a body here." She pointed to the ground. "I think he was young." Her voice dropped to a whisper. "His face was gone."

Jake knelt at her side and ran a gloved hand over the snow. "Why?"

"Da said you were carrying powder. There were pack mules and kegs. Some of the bodies were in pieces."

Jake looked up and down the trail, trying to remember something of the day. There was nothing, just the silence of a cold winter's day.

"I found you down there." Shannon pointed to the creek bank below. The skeletal remains of a horse lay there, the ribs sticking up through the snow.

Jake slid down the embankment and walked over to where the water bubbled merrily along, undeterred by the ice that encrusted its sides. He kicked at the snow, hoping to find some answers hidden among the drifts and shallows but there was nothing except for the tracks of some animal that had come to the carcass, hoping for one last meal.

Chase would know from the tracks what kind of animal it was. Jake quickly looked up and around, hoping against hope that more information would funnel into his brain. There was nothing. Shannon stood on the bank above, her mouth set in a grim line. She had said the bodies were in pieces. *It must be hard on her to come back and remember the gruesome sight.*

He crawled back up the bank with the help of her extended hand and they walked on up the trail, leading the horse behind them. They soon came to a meadow that was blanketed with snow. Beyond it was the river and more deep woods that covered the side of a mountain.

"Which direction do you think we came from?"

"It's hard to say." She looked around. "If you were carrying powder, you must have been coming from the caves."

"Caves?"

She pointed to the north. "They were making powder in the caves. I've heard they've stopped. There's no way to get it out."

"The Confederates were making powder?"

"Yes. Or so they say."

"And my squad was carrying it." Jake looked back down the trail. "Wait here." He swung onto the horse and headed back into the woods.

Jake gave the horse his head and closed his eyes, willing the memories to come back. He plodded along in silence. Shannon had said there were several bodies. How many had been with the squad? How many had died? Had they ridden in single file, two abreast? There had been pack mules. Had they driven them? Were they leading them? They must have made a horrendous noise as they traveled. He tried to imagine it.

A face entered his mind. It was all planes and angles but the mouth was soft and the eyes gentle. It was the face of a boy who was quickly growing into manhood. He was eager and he rode leading a string of mules behind his horse. Jake pulled his horse up and opened his eyes and found himself looking at the spot where Shannon had said a boy's body had lain, his face gone.

A sob tore at his throat and he ground the heels of his hands into his eyes to remove the image that filled his mind. Had he seen it or was it because Shannon had told him? He had known the boy, he was sure of it. He cast his head from side to side, searching for something, anything that would give him an anchor.

Willie?

"Jake!"

Shannon was coming down the trail at a run.

"What's wrong?"

"Some men are coming." She looked behind her. "Soldiers."

"Union?"

"Yes." Her eyes were wide with fear. Jake was wearing a Confederate uniform.

He swung up on the horse and then Shannon used his arm to swing up behind him. "We can't let them see us," he tossed over his shoulder as he kicked the horse into a gallop. "But we can't outrun them."

"There's a cave down below. We can hide there until they pass."

She pointed to where the bank softened and they could cut down to the stream. Jake handed her the reins and she led the horse down to the stream while he took a broken tree branch and smoothed out the snow where they had disturbed it. He could hear them coming now. Jake tossed the branch aside and ran in the direction Shannon had taken.

"Jake," she whispered. She was standing in the entrance of a cave. A dead tree had fallen in front of it and neatly hid the opening from view.

The voices were clear now. Jake ducked under the tree and counted five riders with one horse doubled up coming toward them. And he had foolishly left his guns in the sack under his cot. Shannon silently urged him to safety and he ducked into the cave.

The horse tossed his head so Jake held the bridle down and talked soothingly to the animal, praying that he wouldn't call out to the other horses as the sounds of their hooves hitting the trail echoed above. The noise of their heavy breathing from the dash filled the hollow darkness of the cave.

"What do you think they're doing this far west?" Shannon whispered when the noise had faded.

"I don't know." Jake ducked his head out and cautiously looked around. "Deserters maybe? The last newspaper I read said the conditions are really bad for both armies this winter."

"Where are they supposed to be?" she asked. If only

she could read, then all this information would be available to her.

"Surrounding Richmond in this part of the country." He stepped out of the cave, confident they were gone. "From what I've read, I couldn't get back to the Confederate Army even if I wanted to. The entire Union Army is standing in my way."

"I hate to think that they were deserters."

"We'd better take it slow going home." Jake led the horse out as Shannon disappeared into the back of the cave. "What are you doing?"

"Wait a minute, I've found something."

"What is it?"

"I don't know. It's too dark to see." Shannon came out carrying a piece of paper. "Someone had a fire back there at one time. I found this behind it." She stepped into the light and looked at the piece of paper. Suddenly her face turned white and she looked at Jake with wide eyes.

"What's wrong?"

Shannon handed him the paper. It was a drawing, exquisite in its detail, done in charcoal. It showed a man leaning against a wide tree trunk in what seemed to be a restful pose but the set of his shoulders and the look in his eyes showed that the man was alert and ready for anything that might come along. He was wearing a Confederate uniform and a set of pistols with white handles. His wide-brimmed hat was slouched forward, shading pale eyes that seemed to be frozen over with ice. Long light hair flowed from beneath the hat and the face wore a goatee. The man in the drawing was dangerous and deadly and there was no need of a caption to identify those qualities. The artist had done a remarkable job of conveying them with his talent.

"Don't you recognize it?" Shannon asked as Jake looked in amazement at the paper. His pale blue eyes had the look of a lost child's and her heart wept for him. "It's you, Jake."

Chapter Eleven

They rode on in silence. Jake had stuffed the drawing under his shirt. When he buttoned the first button on his jacket, he looked at Shannon, who was holding her shawl up around her neck to ward off the cold. Her cheeks were as red as her hair and the tip of her nose was dripping. He took off his jacket and handed it to her.

"I can't take this," she protested. "All you're wearing is a shirt. You'll freeze."

"Put it on. Cover it up with your shawl." His teeth were already chattering but he wasn't sure it was from the cold. The sight of the drawing had done something to him. Something he didn't quite understand yet. "In case we run into them." He tilted his chin down the trail.

Shannon tried to cover as much of his torso as she could with the shawl when she wrapped her arms securely around his waist. He had the gray knitted scarf and he was wearing gloves, but she knew he must be cold and it would be dark soon. The day, which had started out so bright, had turned gloomy and now it looked as though there would be more snow.

Shannon wondered about the picture. Jake had not said a word about it since he had stuck the paper in his shirt. She had seen the signature in the bottom corner but the name had been just as much as mystery as everything else. If Jake recognized it, he hadn't said so. The portrait was a perfect likeness of his features. She wondered what it was that had made him look so violent. Maybe it had been done right before a battle or right after one. Surely that would explain the deadly air the drawing imparted.

Jake laid a hand over hers as he pulled the horse to a stop. They had passed over the bridge and gone by the stone house, taking their time to allow the group of soldiers to move on. They were in the woods again and coming up on a ridge. She smelled smoke.

"Didn't you say that place was deserted when we came by it earlier?" He pointed at a cabin that sat down in the gully below. Smoke poured from the chimney and a group of horses stood in the open shed.

"Yes."

"It's not now. Is there another way down?"

"We'd have to walk. It's too steep to ride."

They dismounted and she led the way back in the direction they had come from. A game trail led down the side of the mountain and she took it. Jake and the horse followed her down the winding path through the mountain laurel that covered the mountain side. The way was slick and dusk had settled over them. Luckily there was a half moon out and it reflected off the snow in the areas where it had made its way down through the heavy boughs of the pines. Heavy clouds were gathering and occasionally they blocked the light. Jake hoped the weather would stay clear long enough for them to find their way. The horse was having trouble; he kept sliding onto his haunches and pulling against the reins. He finally lost his footing altogether and Jake shoved Shannon into the mountain laurel as the horse careened by.

"Well, that does it." Shannon said as the branches broke beneath them and they landed in a whoosh on the ground with Jake's body prostrate over her own.

"Does what?"

"I'm soaked to the bone. I'll probably catch pneumonia or at the least a cold."

"So? We can keep each other company while we're sick."

"You dolt!" She smacked the side of his head. "I won't be able to sing for the Christmas program. It's only a few weeks away!"

They heard more crashing and then the whinny of the horse.

"Do you think he's all right?"

"I hope so." Jake raised his head and listened. "Sounds like he's up on all fours."

"I reckon that's a good thing."

"Should be."

"So are you going to lie on top of me all night, or are we going to check on him?"

Jake tilted his head to look at her and his eyes caught the reflection of the moon off the snow. "I don't know. I'm pretty comfortable and you are keeping me dry."

"I've got a branch poking me in the backside!"

Jake laughed. "Quit squirming or you'll have a branch poking you in the front side also."

Shannon suddenly lay very still. Her breath had caught in her throat at his words and her lips parted slightly. Her skin seemed to be as pale as the snow in the moonlight and her eyes were fathomless as he lowered his head and kissed her.

Why did she have to answer him so? Why did she return what he gave her and leave him wanting more? They were both shaking with the cold but he didn't want to stop. Her lips clung to his and he took possession of them and cursed himself for not having the willpower to stop before they both caught their death from the weather. He had to stop but stopping would mean he would see the hurt in her eyes again. He pulled away, just enough so he could look at her.

"I don't want to remember," he said in a voice as soft as falling snow.

"Maybe you never will." Shannon's heart pounded in her chest. Surely he could feel it. He lay so close it was almost as if they were one. What would it be like to be one with him? She wanted desperately to find out.

"You said I could start my life from here." He almost believed it. Saying the words out loud made it seem like it could happen.

"From the beginning of your remembering." His face hovered above hers and she wondered what she could do to start the kissing again. The kissing would lead to more. She wanted all of him. She wanted him now when he was thinking of her instead of what was right for her. He was always thinking of what was right, and what she wanted was very wrong . . . or was it?

"That would be you." He kissed the tip of her nose. "You're the beginning of my remembering."

Her breath caught in her throat.

"Shannon. Would you go with me?"

"Go where?" Yes! Yes! Let's go now before you draw away from me like you did the last time. Be calm, Shannon. This is the rest of your life he's talking about. Yes!

"Anywhere. Away. To start my life." He kissed her again, making her breathless as she clung to him. "To start our life."

"Do you mean it?" *He wants me. . . .*

"I wouldn't say it if I didn't."

"What about . . . ?" *I don't care.*

"The remembering started with you. There's nothing behind it."

"I'll go." She was foolish and she was a wanton. She'd follow him to hell. He would break her heart and leave her when his memory came back. Where would she be then?

He stood and pulled her to her feet. "You know, I fell in love with you the first time I saw you."

Her mind continued to chastise her impetuous heart as it exploded into a thousand pieces. How could she stand there and remain so calm when he had just said he loved her? "It was earlier for me," she said as she moved into his arms. "You see, I fell in love with you the first time *I* saw *you.*" Her eyes were level with the bridge of his nose. They were a perfect fit as far as she was concerned. And she would stay with him for as long as he would have her and worry about the consequences later. At least she would have these few tender moments to get her through the lonely days when he left her.

"So I guess you had a bit of a head start." His shy smile was quick and crinkled the lines around his eyes.

"I was hoping you'd catch up." She berated herself for acting like a common whore as she leaned against the long lean length of his body. She could get used to acting this way very easily. She wanted more.

He kissed her again and as he wrapped his arms around her, he noticed how wet she was. "You are soaking."

"To the bone," she agreed. Then she sneezed. *Now that was romantic, Shannon.*

They found the horse standing at the bottom of the ridge with nothing more than a small cut on his foreleg. Jake lifted Shannon on to his back and he led the animal to the trail with her directions. The promised snow soon started and by the time they arrived back at the cottage, they were both shivering violently.

"You'd better get out of those wet clothes," Jake said as he helped her down from the horse.

Shannon nodded. She was too cold to speak.

"I'll be back as soon as I get the horse settled."

He quickly took care of the animal and stopped in his room for a moment before he headed back to her cottage. The orange cat was sleeping in the middle of his cot and mewed when he came into the room. Jake turned the lamp up and sat down on the cot to look at the drawing that was stuffed in his shirt.

At least he knew why he carried the guns now. He was a killer. There was no doubt in his mind after looking at the drawing. He wondered if there were WANTED posters out with the same likeness on it. And like the fool that he obviously was, he had just asked Shannon to leave with him. What kind of life had he just condemned her to? Would they forever be running away from something? Would they be constantly looking for his past? It was easy to say he didn't care about it, but what if he did remember something? What if he was married, had children and a home waiting for him? What if he was a criminal who had used enlistment to hide from his crimes? What would happen to Shannon if he took her from everything familiar and then had to leave her in the middle of nowhere?

He would never do that. But he might break her heart if his past did catch up with him.

The name in the corner of the drawing said Caleb Conners. Was he friend or foe? Jake's brain made the logical progression. This Caleb Conners must have been in the same squad as he in order to draw the picture. And he must have survived the attack. Why else would he have been in the cave with a fire? He had used some of his drawings to start a fire. He had probably been hurt and holed up in the cave until he was well enough to move on.

He needed to find Caleb Conners. Maybe this unknown artist would have the answers he was looking for. But hadn't he just told Shannon that he didn't want those answers?

His head hurt. Jake placed a hand over his face and rubbed his temples with his thumb and middle finger. The orange cat decided that he liked the looks of that activity and bumped his arm.

"What do you want?" Jake asked the cat, who touched his hand with a snow-white paw. He rubbed the cat's head and the animal closed its eyes in contentment, letting forth a great rumble from its throat.

"What do I want?" Jake asked the cat. A green eye

barely opened and the cat mewed. "You're right. I want Shannon." He stuffed the drawing in the sack with his guns and placed it back under his bed. The orange cat yawned and curled up in the center of the cot.

Chapter Twelve

Cole and Grace stepped off the boardwalk to cross the street to the finest restaurant in Denver. Cole kept his hand protectively against the small of Grace's back as she lifted her skirts to pick her way through the puddles. After all, she was his wife now, and not only that, but she was with child. His child. His heart swelled at the thought that in a few short months he would be a father. He had never imagined that his life would turn out this way. That he would find such happiness and contentment at such a late age. He was forty-three years old and past the time for such nonsense. A brand-new father at the age when most men were grandfathers. He hoped he was up to the task.

The bonnet Grace wore helped to hide the scars on her face from the prying eyes of strangers, but it also limited her vision and kept her from seeing the closed carriage that was heading straight for them. Cole wrapped an arm around her waist and swung his new wife out of the path of the matched blacks that were coming straight toward them at a quick trot.

"I guess it's been too long since I was in a big city!" Grace exclaimed as he lifted her to the walk before the restaurant.

"The driver wasn't looking where he was going either." Cole snorted as he watched the passage of the carriage. "Some rich folks think they own the road." A woman wearing a hat with a veil leaned out of the carriage window, apparently to see if any pedestrians had been injured by their passage. Cole resisted the urge to shake his fist at the carriage. After all, it was his wedding day, and he was taking his wife to dinner.

"Are you sure that you don't mind leaving Amanda alone so soon?" Grace asked when they were seated at a corner table. Cole sat with his back in the corner and Grace faced him to keep strangers from looking at her scars. The people in Laramie had become used to them but they still drew attention when she met strangers. All Cole saw was how beautiful she was in her cinnamon-colored suit with the lovely cameo brooch on the collar. When she smiled, one hardly noticed the scars as they fell into the lines of her face. How any man could do such a thing to a woman was beyond his comprehension. And yet Wade Bishop had done it without a second thought. At least Amanda had been spared the devil's blade, but she still had scars. Deep scars.

"She'll be fine," Cole assured her as he grasped her hand.

"She seemed to be very nervous at the wedding," Grace continued. As a judge, Jason had conducted a simple ceremony in the parlor the night before. Amanda had stood in a corner the entire time and then escaped to her room as soon as she was able.

"It's the men," Cole explained. "She's terrified of all the men."

"But surely she knows that none of the men on the ranch are going to hurt her." So much had happened in the few weeks since Cole had been back that Grace had not had time to get to know Amanda well, although she had tried to include her in as many of the wedding preparations as possible.

"She knows, I told her, but it's still hard for her to comprehend it."

"I guess we'll never really know what happened to her in those years that Bishop had her."

"No, we won't. Marcus also said that because of the opium, it would be hard for her to remember what was real and what was a dream."

"I guess the best thing would be for her not to remember at all."

"If only it were that simple."

"We'll just have to give her time. Get her involved in something."

"Maybe the baby will help. After all, it will be her cousin."

Cole took Grace's work-worn hands into his callused ones. "I still find it hard to believe. We're going to have a baby!"

"If I didn't know you better, Cole Larrimore, I'd say you were downright giddy with excitement."

"I am." Cole laughed. "Hard to believe it, but I am. I can't wait."

Grace placed a hand over her stomach. "I can't wait either. Just so I can get this baby out. He kicks like a horse."

"She's spirited."

Grace laughed. "I guess time will tell which one of us is right."

"It's good to hear you laugh like that."

"Well, I'm happy."

"I am too, Grace. I never thought I would be this happy. . . ." The words trailed off as he noticed a tall, slim woman approaching their table. She was wearing a stylish wine-colored hat with a black veil pulled over her face. A matching suit and gloves completed the ensemble. Something about her was familiar. Cole recognized her as the same woman who had stared at them from the speeding carriage, but there was something more. . . .

"Why, Cole Larrimore," the woman purred as she pulled the veil back from her exquisite face. "I thought you would never leave the borders of Texas."

Cole felt the floor sink beneath his feet as the elegant woman with the glowing dark eyes and carefully styled black hair bestowed a dazzling smile on the two of them. What was she doing here? For the past fifteen years he had thought her dead and buried. He had even seen her grave in San Francisco. Yet here she was, looking more beautiful than the last time he had seen her, if that was possible. Grace looked at him in confusion.

"And I thought you were dead, Constance."

"Why, Cole, darling, whatever gave you that idea?" Her smile was dazzling.

"I saw your grave."

"You mean you came looking for me?" Constance looked at Grace, who was still in a state of confusion. "Isn't that sweet?"

"That was a long time ago, Constance." Cole fought back the urge to choke her. "Where have you been in the meantime?"

"Oh, Cole, I have been around the world. You know how I always wanted to travel. Of course, there wasn't much chance of that happening when we were together." She tilted her head toward Grace as if she were sharing a confidence. "He was so wrapped up in his job, you know. I married him because I thought he could give me adventures."

"You married him?" Grace looked from one to the other.

"Why, yes, I did. Foolish me. I was just a child then, anxious to get away from the confines of my father's house and old-fashioned ways. We are descended from Spanish nobility and my father thought I should stay in a convent until he found me a proper husband. I thought marrying a Texas Ranger would be more romantic. I was wrong about that, so I left Cole for an actor. As I said earlier, I'm foolish. But I guess I am still married to Cole, since I never bothered to get a divorce." She laughed as if it were all a big joke. "How about you, Cole? Did you get a divorce without notifying me?"

"Like I said, Constance, I was under the impression that you were dead."

She laughed. "Oh, that. Stephan was so clingy. And overly dramatic. Of course, he was an actor but not a very good one. He just couldn't provide me with the things I wanted. And he wouldn't take no for an answer. It was easier for me to die than to leave him."

"So you pretended to be dead in order to dump him?"

"Something like that. It was Francois's idea."

"Francois?"

"Yes, I met him in San Francisco. He was quite a fan of the theater. He's the one who took me around the world." Constance looked up at the ceiling. "I wonder where he is now. He was sweet."

"Cole, I'm afraid I'm not feeling very well." Grace's face was pale.

"Oh, I'm sorry, did I interrupt your dinner? And we haven't even been properly introduced." She extended a gloved hand toward Grace. "I'm Constance Arguelles Larrimore. Mrs. Cole Larrimore. And you are?"

Grace fought back the urge to slap the woman.

Cole stood and took Grace's arm to help her up from the chair. "This is my wife Grace."

"Oh my, I guess my being alive may change all that. Have you been a bigamist for long, Cole?" The smirk Constance wore gave evidence of her sarcasm. "Oh, and you're expecting too. When is the little bastard due?"

The sound of Grace's palm hitting Constance's face brought all conversation in the fine restaurant to a stop. Two sets of dark eyes narrowed as the women took each other's measure.

"Where are you staying, Constance?" Cole ground out as he placed Grace safely behind him. "Obviously we need to talk."

"Sorry, Cole, I'm on my way to Laramie, Wyoming. My companion has some interests in that area." Constance placed her hand on the lapel of Cole's jacket with wifely familiarity. "I'll probably be bored out of my mind in that dinky little town," she said with a pout.

"Well, how fortunate for us that we live up that way." Cole's face was pleasant but Grace felt the rage coursing through his body as he removed Constance's hand and turned to help her with her coat. "I'll look you up next week." When Grace started toward the door, he turned and leaned close to Constance. "And if you ever say anything like that to my wife again, you'll find that you need that grave out in San Francisco," he promised in a low growl.

"I guess this means that you haven't really missed me at all." Constance's mouth formed a flirty pout, but her eyes glittered evilly. "And I was thinking of telling you how handsome you still look. The years have been kind to you, Cole. Don't you think they've been kind to me? It's not as if I have scars. . . ."

Cole gripped her upper arm and squeezed. "You don't need me to tell you how beautiful you are. You've had plenty of practice telling yourself."

Constance hissed as she jerked her arm away from his grip.

"I'll see you in Laramie." Cole walked away, taking Grace's arm as he reached the spot where she was patiently waiting.

"And I'll see you in hell," Constance snarled at his retreating form. "Both of you."

Chapter Thirteen

"Grandpa, tell us a story." Jason looked up from the hearth where he had just laid a log on the fire to maintain the warmth in the parlor. Fox and Chance were lying on the rug playing with a set of hand-painted lead soldiers that had belonged to Jason in his boyhood. In the corner Amanda sat quietly, as usual, reading a book. In the days since she had arrived, she had made herself as inconspicuous as possible after moving into one of the upstairs rooms in the house. It was obvious that being around the men made her nervous. After what she had been through, her feelings were understandable. She barely spoke to anyone, although she did feel comfortable enough around Jason that she would sit in the parlor with him in the evening.

Cole and Grace had gone off to Denver to enjoy a short honeymoon. Jenny, Chase, Zane, Dan and Randy had gone to the annual Christmas dance that was given by the officers of the fort. Caleb had declined to go and was keeping company with Zeb down in the bunkhouse. Which left Jason to his favorite pastime, taking care of his great-grandsons.

"Tell you a story?" he asked. He settled down in his favorite chair and the boys came over to lean on his knees.

"Have I told you the story of 'The Sutler's Daughter'?" They both said no. "Well, many years ago when Fort Laramie had just been built, a man came to run the store and he brought his daughter with him. She was young, about fifteen years old, and loved to ride her horse. Every day you could see her out riding around and around the fort. And every day her father would tell her not to go too far, to stay where she could see the fort because something might happen to her. But she never listened to her father and went farther and farther out every day. Well, one day she got a beautiful new riding habit. It was dark green and had a hat with a big feather in it and she couldn't wait to show it off. So she put it on and went out for her ride and never came home."

"Never?" the boys asked in wide-eyed wonder.

"No. The soldiers all mounted their horses and went looking for her. They searched for weeks and never found a sign of where she had been."

"Dad would have found a sign," Chance said.

"Well, that is true. Your dad is a very good tracker. But they didn't have a good tracker like your dad at the fort then and so they never found her."

"So what did her dad do?" Fox asked.

"Well, he was so sad because his daughter was lost that he packed up all his possessions and went to California. But there have been people who say she's still out there riding. They say they've seen her wearing her green habit and running her horse while using the crop on him. She just keeps on riding."

"I can't believe you guys haven't heard that story," Zane said as they came up on the outskirts of town.

"There are no ghosts at Fort Laramie," Dan said. "You're crazy."

"Ask Private Johnson. He saw her. Saw her plain as day. Said she went flying by just beating the tarnation out of her horse. Had the green riding habit on and everything."

"Hey, Zane, is she pretty?" Randy asked.

Jenny burst out laughing from her place in the buggy. They were on their way to the dance and their spirits were high even though they had felt bad about leaving Caleb. He wasn't ready for dancing yet, he had said. Zane had told Dan and Randy the ghost story to distract everyone as they rode into town.

"What do you think, Chase?" Dan asked. "Is there a ghost girl riding around Fort Laramie?"

"I don't know why there wouldn't be. There have been lots of reports of sightings through the years."

Dan wiggled his shoulders. "I don't like to think that there are ghosts riding about, pretty or not."

"Just because she's a ghost doesn't mean she's a bad ghost," Zane said. "There can be good ghosts as well as bad ones."

Jenny slipped her hand around her husband's arm. Hadn't he said many times that Jamie's ghost had come back to help him the day that he was dying in the snow?

"That's right, Dan. If you believe in God, then you have to believe in the devil. If you believe in angels, then you have to believe that demons exist also," Chase added.

"Isn't this all a bit morbid for Christmastime?" Randy protested. "Shouldn't we be talking about candy and presents and singing carols?"

"You go right ahead and sing," Zane laughed. "I'll join you in the chorus."

Randy called his bluff and started singing "Joy to the World." Jenny joined in and soon they were all singing at the top of their lungs as they rode through the middle of town.

There was joy in the world. Jenny went over her list of blessings as the horse and buggy rolled on. Grace and Cole were fine; Amanda was safe, although she had a long road to recovery ahead of her. As did Caleb. He still had not picked up his sketchbook, but everyone hoped that would come back in time. Cat and Ty were in North Carolina at his brother's plantation. With luck, the war would be over soon and he wouldn't have to go back to the front. Zeb's escape from the plantation to the ranch had been a blessing. He had taken over so much of the heavy work with the horses, leaving her more time for the training. The boys were healthy and growing every day and Jason adored them. If only Jake had survived, her happiness would be complete. Perhaps if the baby she was carrying beneath her heart was another boy, they could name it after him. She would suggest the idea to Chase when she told him. And she planned on telling him tonight, after the dance.

Jason looked over the heads of the two boys to where Amanda sat in the corner. He had noticed during the storytelling that she had been listening. He wondered if he had made a mistake, telling that story. Jenny would

have a fit if the boys woke up screaming from night-
mares about the sutler's daughter. They had gone back
to playing on the rug but now one of the painted lead
cavalry riders had taken on the role of the ghost and
was mowing down a line of toy soldiers.

The logs cracked and popped in the fireplace and the
tall case clock ticked away the minutes as the parlor was
filled with peace and warmth. Jason picked up his
newspaper. He turned to news of the war. The only general who seemed to be on the move was Sherman, and
he was burning a wide swath through the south. Though
Jason did not approve of his tactics, he could understand the reasoning behind them. Hood and his men
had suffered some blows on the western front. It looked
as if it was almost over for the South. Cat's last letter had
said pretty much the same thing. He hoped the men in
charge would come to the same realization before any
more had to die.

There were some articles about the problems ranchers were having to the east. Water holes had been
fouled; cattle had been stolen and then their carcasses
showed up in prominent places. People were selling
out and moving on. Sometimes the land just wasn't
worth a man's life. Sometimes it was. Jason hoped the
coming of winter would put a stop to the worst of it.

A shot was heard ringing through the cold night air,
followed by a second. Amanda looked up, her gray eyes
wide with fear. Justice's wild barking could be heard
across the valley.

"You boys stay here with Amanda," Jason instructed
as he rose to go to the door. As soon as he left the room,
they ran to the window.

Caleb was coming up the hill as quickly as possible

with his awkward gait. He was carrying his pistol.

"What is it?" Jason asked as Caleb stomped breathlessly onto the porch.

"Horse thieves," Caleb spat out. "Took one of the yearlings out of the corral."

"What?"

"We heard Justice barking and then Storm Cloud started kicking up a fuss. When Zeb went to check on him, he saw someone taking off with one of the yearlings. They only took one. They even closed the gate. Zeb hollered and I got off a few shots, but they were gone. There were three of them near as I can tell. Zeb's saddling the horses right now."

"I'll get my stuff," Jason said. "Go ask Amanda to take care of the boys. If she doesn't feel up to it, tell her to wake Agnes." Jason took off through the house to get his coat and weapons. Caleb limped into the study.

"Caleb! What happened?" The boys had a hundred questions.

"Someone took one of the horses. We're going to go after the thieves." Caleb looked at Amanda, who stood in front of the window. "Can you take care of the boys?"

"Ye-yes." She seemed to be scared to death. "I will."

"You can wake Agnes if you have to."

"She's not here. She went to town to stay with her daughter." Amanda covered her mouth. That was the longest sentence she'd uttered since her arrival.

Jason returned with his coat and rifle. "Think you can handle these little outlaws?" he asked Amanda. "I forgot about Agnes going to town."

"We'll be good," Fox assured him.

"We'll be fine," Amanda assured him somewhat nervously. She was rewarded with a smile from Caleb.

"Zeb's bringing the horses around front," Caleb said.

"Let's go." They took off toward the front of the house, where Zeb was waiting. He had placed Caleb's horse next to the porch, which made it much easier for him to mount. "You got a weapon, Zeb?" Jason asked.

"No, sir. Don't know how to shoot no gun. But I gots a knife."

"How are you rigged, Caleb?"

"I got a rifle and my pistol," Caleb answered. "I sure wish I still had that Henry you got all of us a few years back."

"Since it came down to choosing your own life over the rifle, I think you made the right decision."

"You can thank Ty and Cat for that." They took off toward the east, which was the direction the horse thieves had taken.

"Miss Jenny shore is gonna have a fit when she finds out that colt's gone," Zeb said as they took off into the night.

"Let's get him back before she finds out," Jason replied.

The dance had been perfect as far as Jenny was concerned. Zane wasn't so sure. There hadn't been any fights, and it was the same group of girls that had been around last year. He was ready for some fresh blood. Still, they had all enjoyed themselves and were in high spirits as they rode home.

Chase let the buggy fall behind as Zane, Dan and Randy rode on, comparing stories of their conquests of the night. The moon was close to being full and the reflection of it off the snow gave the night a fairytale glow. Jenny placed her hand over her stomach to settle it back into place after all the spinning and twirling she had done at the dance. She felt a bit nauseous and had already lost her breakfast a few times with this pregnancy. She hadn't been sick a day with Chance, but at that time she'd had other things on her mind.

"Are you all right?" Chase leaned over to ask.

"Yes, why?"

"You were looking a bit green a few times tonight," he replied.

"I was?" She snuggled up closer to him on the seat.

"Maybe it's the baby?"

"How did you know?" she demanded.

"Your eyes. They're looking inward, like the mares'."

"That's the same thing Jamie said to me when I was pregnant with Chance. He knew almost as soon as I did."

"I shouldn't have left you then." His arm came around her shoulders and he kissed her temple where the blond hair had been pulled back to cascade in curls down her back.

"You did what you had to do to protect us." Her gloved hand danced down the long muscles of his thigh and he felt the slow burn that always came over him when Jenny touched him.

"So when will this one be here?" His eyes glowed in the moonlight as he looked at her.

"Same as last. High summer."

Chase made a face. "I seem to recall that it wasn't much fun."

"I was pretty miserable." Jenny leaned into the hollow of his side. "Except for the day we went to the lake."

"Hmm, that was nice." He looped the reins over the

buggy rail, confident that the horse would get them home. "We should go up there more often." He brought his other arm around her and bent his head to give her a long, lingering kiss. "I hope this one is a girl," he whispered as he caressed her lips. "I hope she looks just like you."

"Woohoo, watch out, Dan!" Zane hollered from the road in front of them. "Sutler's daughter is coming to get you!" The sounds of pounding hooves were heard breaking across the countryside. The horse drawing the buggy tossed his head and Chase regretfully let go of Jenny to take up the reins.

"That sounds like more than one horse," Chase said.

"It looks like there's a fire up there," Jenny said as she peered forward to where the silhouettes of their friends could be seen on horseback.

"We're almost at the crossroads."

"Why would someone have a fire there?" Jenny asked. The flames grew brighter the closer they got and they realized that torches had been set in the ground at all four corners of the intersection. Six riders were gathered at the junction; they knew three of them were Zane, Dan and Randy.

"That looks like Zeb!" Jenny exclaimed as they got closer.

"It is. Caleb and Jason too."

Jenny's stomach jumped into her throat as her thoughts flew to her children. Zane heard their approach and rode back to meet the buggy.

"Jenny, you don't want to see."

"What is it, Zane?"

Zane grabbed the bridle of the horse to stop it. "It's one of your yearlings."

"What?" Jenny jumped down and took off toward the light, with Chase falling in beside her.

"Maybe you shouldn't look," he said. He reached for her arm but she pushed him away.

"I need to know." She came into the light between Caleb and Jason, who were still mounted.

Zeb was kneeling over the body of a horse. It was one of the two-year-olds that she had been working with. He had been a flashy bay with deep white stockings and a thick blaze covering his face. Now he lay in the center of the crossroads in a pool of blood. His throat had been cut and he had been gutted.

Chase grabbed Jenny's waist before she could reach the body of the once-beautiful animal.

"I don't understand, what happened?" she cried as she turned and buried her face in Chase's shoulder.

"Someone stole him. We were on the trail and found this," Caleb explained.

"But why?" Jenny sobbed. "Why would somebody do this?"

"They wanted you to find it," Jason said. He slapped his gloves against his thigh and a curse exploded from his lips.

"Bastards," Zane added.

"Wait a minute," Chase said. "They wanted us to see this. Which means whoever it was knew our plans for tonight."

"They figured everyone would be at the dance and it would be easy to steal the horse?" Zane asked.

"Amanda," Caleb said.

"What?" Zane asked.

"Amanda is alone at the ranch." He looked at the circle of friends. "With the boys."

"Chase, take my horse. I'll bring Jenny in the buggy," Jason commanded.

"Hurry!" Jenny gasped as they rode out. "Please."

Amanda hadn't been sure she would be able to handle the two little boys. They had started out asking a hundred or more questions upon the departure of the men, then finally settled into a game of chasing horse thieves with the tiny mounted soldiers.

"Take that!" Chance plowed over a horse and rider with one of his own. Fox picked up an infantry officer that held an extended sword and attacked the downed rider.

"I'm cutting off his leg!" he exclaimed.

"So what, he can just get a wooden one like Caleb," Chance said. "Besides, Zane says they hang horse thieves."

"Really?"

Amanda thought the topic of conversation should change and jumped on the first thing that popped into her mind.

"Caleb has a wooden leg?" she asked as she knelt on the carpet beside them.

"Uh-huh," Fox responded. "Aunt Cat whacked his real leg off with a sword." He went down the line with his toy soldier, whacking at legs.

Amanda barely remembered the petite young woman she had met in New York and could not imagine why she would whack off Caleb's leg.

"Fox, are you sure that's how he lost it?"

"He got it hurt in a 'plosion," Chance explained. "Aunt Cat had to help him 'cause he was going to die, so she hid him in a cave from the bad soldiers and cut it off.

Then the doctor did the rest but he wasn't there when it happened, so Aunt Cat had to do it."

"Oh," Amanda said. She had barely known there had been a war going on. She remembered soldiers, lots of them coming to her room, but they were all part of the painful haze that had been her life for the past four years. She knew that Jason's daughter, Cat, and her husband, Ty, were back East because of the war. She had picked that up from listening to the polite dinner conversation that flowed around her. And Cole had told her about everyone who lived at the ranch on their trip out, but she had, for the most part, paid no attention. It didn't matter. She was dead inside so nothing really mattered to her.

Get out of the house now.

Amanda's head flew up and she looked around the room. "Did you hear that?"

The boys looked up and then looked at each other. "I didn't hear anything," they said in unison and went back to their play.

Amanda walked over to the door of the parlor and looked into the wide hall that ran from the front of the house to the back. The clock ticked behind her and the fire continued to crack and pop. The wide staircase loomed off to the side, leading to the dark floor above. She caught a reflection of light through one of the transom windows on either side of the front door. Out of nowhere a man suddenly appeared as if coming through the door. She could tell he was tall, but his features were indecipherable in the darkness.

Get the boys out of the house. Hide! He was talking to her, but the words were inside her head. Was the opium still in her system? Had she finally gone mad as she was sure she would? This couldn't really be happening, could it? Was she imagining a ghost because of the story Jason had told the boys earlier?

"Chance, Fox, come here," Amanda said in a trembling voice.

The boys came to the doorway and peered out into the hallway. "Is someone here?" Fox asked.

Amanda closed her eyes and looked back toward the front door where the apparition had appeared. It was gone. She trembled and realized that the air around her had suddenly turned very cold.

HIDE.

She had to be losing her mind. But why now, when she was responsible for two young lives? The voice still rang in her head, giving her a sense of urgency. It almost felt as if someone were pushing her down the hall toward the door that went out the back. "Let's go down to Grace's," she said and grabbed the boys' hands.

"But no one is there," Chance said.

"I know, but we have to make sure Justice is okay." *Hurry.* "I bet Caleb and Zeb forgot all about him." She pulled them to the back door.

"What about our coats?" Fox asked.

"We don't have time."

They're coming.

"Let's be quiet so we don't scare the horses any more."

They hurried out the back door and went speeding down the hill. The boys sensed her fear and were quiet, their eyes wide as they wondered what was happening in their world. The sounds of horses could be heard coming up the drive at the front of the house. Justice went racing by, the hackles on the back of his neck standing straight up, his teeth bared. There was the sound of breaking glass behind them as Justice flew around the house, barking and growling.

Amanda studied the cluster of buildings as they ran down into the small valley. There was still a lamp glowing in the bunkhouse. Grace's cabin was dark, but they would search both buildings when they were done with the big house. She saw the shower stall out behind the bunkhouse. "Come on." She pulled the boys after her and ran to the stall.

"What are we doing?" Chance asked.

"Hiding."

"I'm cold." Fox shivered.

"I know, I am too." There was a table and chair sitting outside the stall and she grabbed the chair as they went in.

"We have to hold our feet up," she explained to the boys. Amanda sat down in the chair and pulled her feet up on the seat. "Climb in my lap and stay quiet. We'll try to keep each other warm."

The sounds coming from above were horrendous. Windows shattering, the crashing of furniture, gunshots ripping through the air. The worst part was that they could no longer hear Justice. The horses were restless and the angry whinnies of Storm Cloud could be heard coming from the barn.

"Please God, spare the horses," Amanda prayed as she held the two shivering bodies close. They both had their heads turned toward the sounds and their eyes were wide. The sounds of hoofbeats could be heard coming down into the small valley.

"I want my dad," Chance said.

"Shhhh." Amanda did her best to comfort the boys. She knew how they felt. How desperately she had wished for her mother and her uncle when she had been taken. Even for her own father, whom she had hardly even known.

"Listen," she whispered. "If they come close, I'm going to go outside. No matter what you hear, I want you to hide and stay quiet until your mom or dad comes looking for you. Do you understand?"

They both nodded and Fox's arms crept around her neck.

She had nothing to lose. These men could take nothing that she hadn't already lost. If they killed her, it would be a blessing. At least she would have the satisfaction of knowing that she had protected the boys from harm. The sounds of windows shattering came from the bunkhouse and then they smelled the fire.

At least he had worn his gun tonight. He had almost gone without it but the past had taught him a hard lesson. Chase never went anywhere without his gun and his knife.

They were all checking their loads. They had pulled the horses up in the drive when they heard the destruction coming from the big house. The buggy could be heard careening up behind them.

"Zeb, you go around to the barn and get the horses. Drive them out and we'll find them in the morning. Dan, you and Randy go 'round back and take care of any of them that come running out that way. Zane and I will take the front." Chase moved over next to Caleb. "You're the only one who can keep Jenny out of harm's way. You know she's going to be a madwoman when she gets here." He pulled Jason's rifle from the scabbard. "Give this to Jason and you two be ready for any of them that come this way." Chase extended a hand to Caleb. "Take care of her for me."

Caleb grasped it in return. "I will."

The horses were tossing their heads and fighting the bits. It reminded Caleb of the tension they had felt before he'd ridden into battle with Ty and Jake beside him.

The men took off and Caleb wheeled his horse to meet the buggy, which had just careened into sight around a curve.

Jason pulled the buggy up and Jenny looked up at Caleb with eyes full of fear. "What's happened?"

"They're at the house." Caleb handed Jason the rifle.

"Oh, God." Jenny jumped from the buggy and Caleb moved his horse to block her.

"Jenny, Chase wants you to stay here."

The look she turned on him was murderous and they all turned as shots were heard. She jerked off her coat and threw it in the buggy.

"If you think I'm going to stand here while my boys are up there, you are insane."

Jason came around and took her arm. "Jenny, Chase has a plan. Don't make it harder on him."

"He wants us to cut off any that come back this way."

"What about the horses?" Jenny asked. "We could go get the horses out."

"Zeb's doing that."

Jenny pulled Jason's rifle from the scabbard. "I'm going to get my boys. The only way you can stop me is to shoot me."

Caleb shook his head and they fell in behind her,

Jason walking and Caleb on his horse. The horse pulling the buggy looked up in surprise and trailed along after them, as if he were wondering why his passengers had suddenly decided to walk.

The thieves never saw opposition coming. Were they so secure in their plans that it never occurred to them that someone would fight back? Chase took one down with a single shot as the man sat on his horse with a torch in his hand, ready to throw it through a broken window. Another came riding out of the front door on his horse and was dropped as the animal jumped off the porch.

Dan and Randy split up and took off around the house on either side. Gunshots echoed from the valley below as those who had gone down to continue the destruction came back to join the battle. Zane picked off one that appeared suddenly out of the darkness.

"How many do you think there are?" he yelled as more riders came.

"Three less than there were before," Chase yelled back. "Let's go 'round back. It sounds like the boys have their hands full."

The men who had come to wreak destruction quickly lost their desire when met with the blazing guns of those whose livelihood they were endangering. Another two went down and the remaining three took off around the front of the house toward the drive.

Caleb heard them coming and shoved Jenny into the grass beside the drive with a gentle nudge from his good leg as he urged his horse forward. He charged toward the three with his gun blazing and dropped one, wounded another. Jason knelt behind him and fired his pistol, but his shot went wide. A return shot hit the elderly man in the shoulder and he dropped in the road. The buggy horse nervously stomped his foreleg and Jason had the presence of mind to roll under the buggy as the horse moved toward him.

Jenny spit out the mouthful of dirt she had eaten when she landed face-first on the ground. She grabbed her rifle as the two remaining men came toward her. She looked at the buggy and then saw that Caleb had wheeled his horse and was chasing after them. Jenny pitched the rifle into the buggy seat and gathered her skirts up. In one move she jumped into the buggy. Picking up the rifle, she swung it at the first rider's head, knocking him backward. The second rider's horse jumped and shied and Jenny launched herself from the buggy. The two of them rolled into the dirt.

Caleb came up on a scene of skirts and petticoats flying as Jenny wrestled with the man, clawing at his eyes and using her knees to good advantage. The man came up on top with his gun drawn. Caleb took his shot and the stranger fell over on top of Jenny just as Zane came up behind him.

"Dang, Caleb," he said. "What exactly did you learn in that war?" Zane jumped down and pulled the body off of Jenny, who was still spitting and clawing.

"The boys?"

"Chase is looking for them."

"Jason's hurt."

"Zane, take care of Jason." Caleb extended an arm to Jenny and she swung up behind him. The horse was moving down the drive before her bottom landed behind him.

Zane helped Jason into the buggy. "Do you think the

boys are all right?" he asked as Zane settled him into the seat and looked at his shoulder. It was bloody but didn't look dangerous.

"We can't find them. Chase is tearing the house apart, which shouldn't take too long since the bad guys already did most of the work." Zane checked the two bodies lying in the road. "Dang. This guy got his neck broke."

"He ran into Jenny."

"Remind me not to make her mad." He tied his horse to the buggy and climbed in. "Again."

"Is it bad?"

"The bunkhouse is on fire. Dan and Randy went down to see what they can save. I guess Zeb is down there too."

"Dang," Jason said.

Zane laughed. "It just don't sound right coming from you."

Jason cursed.

"That's better."

Jenny slid off the horse as Caleb pulled the animal to a stop. She flew through the front door of the house.

"Chase! Chance! Fox!"

"Jenny!" Chase ran down the stairs.

"Where are they?"

"I don't know . . . I can't find them."

Jenny felt the room spinning around her. "Did they take them? They wouldn't have . . . Oh, God."

Chase grabbed her as her face went pale.

"Momma!"

Zeb came through the back with a boy in each arm, Amanda wide-eyed behind him. As soon as their feet hit the floor, the boys ran to their parents, who had both dropped to their knees in relief.

Jenny and Chase crushed the boys between them as they immediately began telling of their adventure. Finally the two adults understood what they were saying and realized that Amanda had gotten them from the house before the trouble started.

"How did you know?" Jenny asked as she took her hand.

"A ghost told me." Amanda shook her head. They would think she was insane.

Chase looked at Jenny. "What did he look like?"

"Who?" Amanda felt as if she were suffocating. They would surely think her mad and send her away.

"The ghost, what did he look like?" Chase grabbed her shoulders and then dropped his hands when fear showed in her eyes.

"I didn't see his face," she whispered. "He was tall, that's all I know."

Jenny laid a hand on Chase's arm and nodded her head to the boys, who were now running around, looking at the damage. "Don't, not in front of them."

Chase nodded in agreement. "Is the fire out?" he asked Zeb.

"Mostly. Can't save the bunkhouse but we got out lots of the clothes and such."

"The horses?" Jenny asked.

"Right as rain, Miss Jenny, but Storm Cloud's madder than a wet hen."

"We'll just have to run it out of him."

"Yes'um, he's gwanna give you a ride fer sure."

"Oh, my God, Jason was shot," Jenny said fearfully as her system returned to normal after the panic of the evening.

"I'm fine," Jason announced, coming through the

door supported by Zane. Amanda slipped out the back while the rest of them went to look after Jason.

Dan and Randy had begun the process of laying out the bodies, which were lined up in a gruesome row on the porch. Amanda blanched at the sight and went toward the front. She ran right into Caleb, who was trying with great difficulty to stand with the burden of Justice in his arms.

"Is he dead?" Amanda ran to his side and helped Caleb to right himself.

"No, but he will be soon. He's been shot."

They made it to the back porch, where Zeb saw their struggles and carried the dog into the house.

"Where should I put him, Miss Jenny?"

Jenny took one look at the dog and ran to the dining room, where she swept the broken pieces of china covering the table onto the floor. "Put him here," she commanded.

"How's Jason?" Caleb asked.

"He's fine. The bullet just grazed his shoulder. He was lucky."

"We're going down the drive to get the rest of the bodies," Zane announced.

"Somebody had better go for the sheriff too," Jason said from the doorway. His shoulder had been bandaged and he was wearing his arm in a sling.

"Is Justice dead?" Chance asked.

"No honey, but he's hurt real bad," Jenny said. Chase came in and he and Zeb turned the dog to find the wound.

They found one in his chest and followed it around to where it had come out behind his foreleg. "The bullet passed through," Chase announced.

"Thank goodness," Jenny sighed.

"He's just lost a lot of blood." The light from one of the few unbroken lamps showed the dog's hide covered in blood. Jenny picked up a table cloth that was hanging half out of its drawer and ripped it. They soon had the dog bandaged and settled on a blanket in front of the fire in the parlor.

"You boys are in charge of taking care of Justice." She needed to keep Chance and Fox occupied because the rest of the house was a disaster. "Make sure he's comfortable and if he wakes up, get him some water." She looked at the tall case clock that Zeb had righted after finding it lying on the floor. It had survived the night, miraculously unscathed, and showed the time to be close to midnight. Chase came in with an armload of quilts.

"I thought we probably should just sleep here tonight," he explained.

"How are the beds?"

"Tossed." Chase took time to rub Justice's head. "One of the mattresses will have to be burned."

"Did somebody wet in it?" Fox asked.

"Yes, they did." Chase swirled his hand through the russet hair.

Jenny made a pallet for the boys next to Justice.

"We're going to sleep here tonight," she explained. "And Momma and Daddy will sleep next to you."

Suddenly their eyes became heavy as they fell into her arms for kisses and hugs.

"Momma?" Chance asked. "Did we have a 'venture?"

"Yes, we did."

" 'Ventures are scary," Fox declared.

"Yes, they are."

"But you were brave." Chase dropped to the floor beside Jenny, and Chance crawled into his lap.

"Amanda was scared," Fox informed them.

"I was too," Chase confided.

"You were?" Chance asked in amazement.

"We all were," Jenny explained. "Everyone was scared. But the difference between cowardice and bravery is what you do when you're scared."

"We hid," Fox said. "In the shower."

"That was brave because it was the smart thing for you do to," Chase said.

"Why were you scared of the bad men?" Chance leaned back to look at his father's face.

"I was scared because I was afraid they had hurt you, Fox and Amanda. It scared me because I didn't know you were safe. But it turned out you were, because you were brave and did the right thing."

"But you weren't scared of the bad men," Chance said.

"No, he wasn't," Jenny said. "He was very brave." Her eyes glowed as she looked over Fox's head into the dark ones of her husband.

"So was your mother."

"Momma fought the bad men?" Chance asked.

"Yes, she did." Jenny made a face at Chase.

"Did she kill any of them?"

"One of them."

"But only because I was afraid they were going to hurt Grandpa," Jenny added hastily. "Now it's time to go to sleep."

"But we have to take care of Justice."

"You can. He's right here where you can touch him. You can watch him from your bed." They settled the boys on their pallet and then Chase led Jenny to the window.

"You shouldn't have told them that," she said quietly when they were out of earshot of the boys.

"They need to know they can count on you as well as me. I won't always be here to protect them."

"You planning on going somewhere without me?"

"Jenny, you saw how fast this happened. If there's danger I have to protect you."

"But they're all dead."

"Somebody hired them. They didn't do this just for the fun of it."

"But why?"

"They want the land. They're trying to run us off it."

"So it isn't over." Her face was covered with dirt and blood, as was the front of her dress. "I guess we'll just have to be ready, maybe hire some more men?"

"Ty needs to come home."

"So does Cat." Jenny leaned into his embrace. "Isn't it funny that I haven't had any dreams about any of this?"

"Maybe it's because of the baby." His hand slid over the flat plane of her stomach.

"Maybe it is." She placed her own hand on her stomach and then looked at her dress in disgust. "Why is it we always have these disasters when I'm wearing my best dress?" She looked up into Chase's dark eyes. "Do you think it was Jamie?"

"Who else could it be?" He kissed her forehead.

Caleb knocked on the door frame. "How are the boys?"

"Sleeping."

"We fixed Jason's bed and he's upstairs. Amanda is going to sleep on her mattress on the floor. Zeb's staying with the horses. Everyone else is on the floor."

"What about you, Caleb?" Jenny knew it was hard for him to get up and down off the floor.

"I'm going to sit up in the study and watch. In case someone else decides to pay us a visit. Jason said to wait until morning to get the sheriff. Dan and Randy said they would go then."

"Wake me up in a couple of hours and I'll relieve you," Chase said.

Caleb nodded.

"Caleb," Jenny called. "Thanks for saving my life."

He smiled at her, but it was a weary one. "My part in the plan was supposed to be keeping you out of trouble. I guess I didn't really succeed, but hey, at least it all came out okay in the end."

"I didn't actually think anyone could stop her, Caleb," Chase said. "I was just hoping you'd slow her down."

"Well, then I guess I did do it right." Caleb shifted wearily on his leg. "Good night."

"Caleb told me what happened out on the road," Chase said when Jenny had settled into his arms. They had stripped down to their undergarments and sought their pallet after making sure everyone else was settled for the night. The boys were both deeply asleep and Justice had opened one eye long enough to assure them he was alive when they checked on him. "Do you think that was wise, considering your condition?"

"Probably not." Jenny's hand traced down his neck and over his chest before it settled into its familiar place against his heart. "All I could think about was the boys. I didn't know if they were safe or not. I wanted to kill those bastards."

"I believe you did." He squeezed her shoulder.

"It's not over, Chase."

"I know." Chase rolled on his side and pulled Jenny against the length of his body, enfolding her in his arms.

"Just know that how you felt tonight is the same way I feel. And when it happens again, it will be a lot easier for me to fight them if I know you and the boys are safe. Promise me, Jenny, that you won't go jumping off any more buggies or have wrestling matches with killers in the road."

"It does sound kind of ridiculous when you put it that way."

"Don't change the subject." Chase placed a finger under her chin and tilted it up so he could look into the deep blue of her eyes.

"I'm not going to stand around while you're out fighting all the battles. I'll do what I have to do to make sure we're safe. All of us. Don't ask me to sit at home and wait. I've done that. Whatever happens, we're going to face it together." Jenny buried her face in his shoulder as his hands came up her back and ran through her hair.

"I still don't understand why you didn't get the red hair in the family."

"Maybe you're lucky I didn't. Maybe I have the mild form of stubborn."

"I love you, Jenny."

"I love you," she sighed as she melted against him. "But I'm not looking forward to tomorrow."

"We'll face it together."

"That's enough for me."

Chapter Fourteen

Shannon whacked the stick on the side of the tiny pot-bellied stove to break it. Normally she would just snap it with her hands, but she felt as weak as a kitten. Her adventures with Jake in the snow had given her a cold and knowing that she looked as bad as she felt didn't make it any easier. Fat chance that the declaration of love he had given her in the moonlight the previous evening would stand up to the light of day. He had come to her cabin after putting the horse away and she had greeted him with a sneezing fit. Her nose had suddenly turned as red as her hair and was running as fast as the river. He had laughed, tugged on a lock of her hair that had tumbled loose and then bid her good-night, leaving Shannon to fall shivering into her bed. He even had the gall to whistle a gay tune as he went back to the barn, knowing that she had just about caught her death because of him.

Or maybe not. After all, he had saved her from being run over by the horse, but still . . . She woke up with a fever and an ill mood to accompany it. "It's easy to say I love you in the moonlight when you've got a soft woman keeping you warm and dry." The crack of the kindling added emphasis to her words. "But when it comes time to pay the price for a roll in the snow, they all disappear like the wind." Not that she had any experience in such matters, but it helped to think this was a general rule, and that Jake's absence was not due to some lack on her part. She kicked the stove door shut and pulled her shawl up around her neck.

"The least he could do would be to bring me a bit of soup," she said to the table. Shannon shoved back her tangled hair. "It's not as if I'm fit enough to be trouncing about the countryside now." She wiped her nose with her sleeve and dropped into the rocking chair that sat before the window. She gathered her brightly colored quilt around her body. "Oh and there goes the man himself off to have his own hot meal." She watched as Jake made his way through the snow from the barn to the big house.

She had just settled down to a good pout when he reappeared, carrying a tray. "Good Lord!" she exclaimed. "He's coming here!" Shannon scrambled from the chair and ran to the mirror that hung over the washstand. She was a fright!

She hastily scrubbed her face with the cloth and then jerked the pins from her hair. She dragged the brush through it and frowned at the knots that had formed from falling asleep with wet hair. She poked her finger at a particularly large one that stuck out over her ear. There was no hope for it at all. She pulled the heavy mass back as tightly as she could, hastily formed a braid and then tied it off with the green ribbon.

Her nightgown was tattered and the tail of it hung to just below her knees. Her socks were falling down around her ankles and, of course, there was nothing she could do about her bright red nose.

She heard the sound of his boots stomping on the steps. If only that bump in her hair would disappear. She pushed at it with her finger but it seemed determined to stick out like a goiter hanging over her ear.

He knocked at her door. Shannon grabbed the quilt from the chair and rewrapped it around herself. At least it covered her raggedy gown.

"Come in," she called out.

Jake pushed the door open and entered the cozy cabin bearing a tray laden with dishes. And a book. Shannon swallowed hard when she saw it. *Good Lord, he doesn't know that I can't read.*

"Hungry?" he asked. The smells coming from the tray made her stomach growl in response and Shannon blushed to the roots of her hair. "I guess that means yes." Jake set the tray down on the table. "Cook fixed a pot of soup last night and there are biscuits too." He arranged the food on the table with some care as if he had prepared the meal himself. "I found this book too. I thought you might need something to help pass the day."

Shannon clutched the quilt to her chest. "I can pass the day just fine without your help, thank you very much."

Jake looked at her in disbelief as he held out the book. "It's Jane Austen. I thought it was the kind of thing you might like."

"Well, it's not."

"I guess our taste in books is not something we've had time to discuss."

"Not everyone has time to sit around and read fancy stories." Shannon's stomach rumbled again.

"The food doesn't come with the book." Jake wondered what he had done to offend her. She was obviously hungry. She was practically drooling.

"What?"

"Come and eat." Jake sat down at the table.

Shannon's stomach won out over her pride and she joined him. Jake watched as she attacked the meal. "I'm glad to see that your cold hasn't affected your appetite," he said jokingly.

The look she gave him shot daggers so he retreated to the safety of the book, opening it to a random page and glancing at the words. "I guess I haven't read this one."

"So what made you think I would want to?"

"I don't know." Her hostility was confusing, to say the least. "What difference does it make?"

Shannon took a sip from the spoon. "It makes no difference at all."

"If you don't want to read the book, you don't have to."

"I don't want to read the book."

"Fine."

"Fine." Jake slammed the volume shut and leaned back in the chair.

Shannon continued to sip her soup but the icy feel of his pale blue eyes unnerved her. She refused to look at him as she laid the spoon down and picked up a biscuit, hoping that the anxiety that rocked her insides wasn't showing. Would he still want her if he knew how ignorant she was? Why did he want her at all?

"So are you going to let me in on what has got your tail all twisted?" His arms were crossed casually over his chest, but his pale blue eyes remained intense beneath his dark lashes.

"My tail twisted?" Shannon asked, not sure if she had been insulted.

"Yes, your tail twisted." Jake leaned across the table. "Ever since I walked through the door, you've acted as if I were your worst enemy. So I just want to know what happened between last night and this morning that's got you so out of sorts."

"I really don't know what you're talking about." Her hostility betrayed her lie.

"Shannon!" He barked her name as he stood up and his tone made her jump in the chair. She looked up at him with deep green eyes wide with fear.

"Are you going to hit me now?" Her lip trembled as she whispered the question, remembering the drawing. It had shown a man capable of great violence. She had seen it as clearly as he had.

Jake was so taken aback by her question that he found he couldn't answer. But what frightened him more was that he didn't know the answer. Had he ever struck a woman? Would he if made angry enough? Shannon had been beaten by her father; he had seen firsthand the evidence of that and it had turned his stomach. The thought of any man striking her sickened him. He would kill anyone who so much as threatened her. But who would protect her from him?

The chair scraped across the hard wood floor as he pushed himself out from the table. He walked away from her as if he were held in a trance. His heart was sealed against the warmth and joy that it had felt when he had first come to know her. The cost was too much, the price too high. It was better not to take the risk. It was better not to feel. Jake left the cozy comfort of the cabin, shutting the door firmly behind him.

Shannon looked around at the empty room. "Well, you've done a good job of running off the first man who ever took a second look at you," she chided herself as she burst into tears.

The smell of rotten eggs once again assaulted his senses as he made his way across the lawn toward the barn. He didn't want to smell the smell. It nagged at the corners of his mind where memories lay hidden. He was tired of not knowing the answers. He was tired of wanting things he could not have. But mostly he was tired of hurting Shannon. Best to leave now before he couldn't stop himself. Best to leave before the burning passion he felt every time he looked at her consumed his common sense. Best to leave before the violence that lay hidden deep within him came bubbling to the surface and erupted with a rotten smell like the hot springs throughout the area. It was time to go. There was no reason to stay, no reason except for a strong Irish lass with flaming red hair and a fiery temper who deserved better than what he could give her. He had nothing to offer her, not even a name, since he truly couldn't say one way or the other if he was Jacob Anderson.

He needed a horse. He needed supplies. He had money. Where would he go? North, South, East or West, did it matter? *Just go. Away. Now. Get as far away as possible from the deep green eyes that are your salvation. Leave her now before you destroy her.* Jake turned from the barn and rounded the hospital. He might as well get started. He would start with supplies for the trail. And without a doubt Mrs. Farley would know who would have a decent horse for sale. If she didn't, then surely someone at the tavern would. Besides, he could use a drink. Maybe a drink would put out the fire that had been burning inside him since he had first kissed Shannon. Jake laughed out loud at himself and then fell into silence when the sound tore at the frigid air. No doubt he was a mean drunk too. He wondered if the town could handle it.

The store was full of shoppers; probably all of them were buying last-minute gifts. Jake stalked into the store and brushed by a woman with her arms full of packages. If he heard one more "Merry Christmas" he would toss the offender out into the street. Both Mr. and Mrs. Farley were busy with customers. Jake went straight to the gun case.

The Henry rifle he had admired on his last trip to the store still lay in its place in the case. Mr. Farley had declared it was not for sale when he had asked to look at it, but if he had been asking the price on the tag attached to it, no wonder the rifle was still there. Jake's hands itched to hold it. There was something about the weapon that tickled his brain, something about it that seemed familiar.

Jake looked impatiently at Mr. Farley, who was unrolling a bolt of fabric for a woman holding a baby. Mrs. Farley was bent over a catalog beside an older woman wearing a hat with a huge feather that threatened to pierce the tight bun on top of the storekeeper's head as the two women perused the catalog from opposite sides of the counter. A set of twin boys eyed jars of candy that lined another counter and then surreptitiously stole looks at Mr. Farley.

A set of keys hung on a hook behind the case. Jake took them down and unlocked the case without a second thought.

"Hey!" Mr. Farley called out as the Henry rifle was lifted from the case.

Jake ran his hand down the polished sheen of the walnut stock. His fingertips brushed over the ornate carving on the blue steel receiver. It was a fine piece. He turned the gun over and saw a set of initials in the oval center of the carving that had been added by the gun maker. *J.A.* they said in an ornate flourish. *J.A.* for *Jacob Anderson.*

There had been other initials on other guns. Faces flashed through his mind, the smiling faces of friends, filled with joy over the unexpected gift from a generous benefactor. He heard the sounds of laughter, of camaraderie, of heartfelt fellowship. It echoed in his mind and bounced against the hollow corners of his solitude. They came and they went, spinning away before he could place names on their familiar faces. His heart ached to see them. How could he miss someone he didn't even remember? Behind the faces candles glowed on a Christmas tree and giant snowflakes filled a wide expanse of window that held high mountains shrouded in the violets and blues of distance. Jake clenched his eyes tightly shut, willing the faces to stay, begging them to fill the loneliness that wrenched at his gut. It was a weakness, a weakness he couldn't afford to have. It would lead him to make mistakes and the cost would be too high. It was better not to feel, not to want, not to care.

The bolt of fabric hit the floor as Mr. Farley pounded toward the case. "What are you doing?"

"I've come for what's mine." Jake's hold on the rifle was firm as he turned his icy blue eyes on the storekeeper.

"What do you mean?" Mr. Farley asked, his face betraying his panic.

Jake arched his eyebrows and raised his voice so all in the premises would hear. "What I mean, Mister Farley, is that you are selling something that doesn't belong to you." Jake turned the gun so the storekeeper could see the initials. "This rifle is mine and I don't recall giving you leave to sell it."

Mr. Farley's bluster died as his lips clamped shut over his words. The woman with the feather in her hat looked indignant and Mrs. Farley turned a dark shade of red.

"We bought that gun off Shamus Mahoney," she intoned. "If you've got a problem, you need to take it up with him."

Shamus Mahoney. The man had helped himself to his possessions while he lay in a dreamlike state for months. Did Shamus have anything else that belonged to him? Shannon had given him back his saddlebags but what had been taken from them before that time? How much of his past was now in the possession of her father? Was there something the man held that could lead him to his home? Or had he sold another man's past for the price of a drink. "How much did you give him for it?" Jake asked, preparing himself for the lie.

Mr. Farley quoted a price, somewhere between what he had paid and what he was asking. Jake dropped some money on the counter. It wasn't as much as what the storekeeper had asked, but it was more than he had given. Mr. Farley rubbed his chin and looked at his wife.

"I'll be leaving soon," Jake said dryly. "I'll be needing some supplies." Mrs. Farley nodded in agreement and Mr. Farley picked up the money. Jake picked up a box of shells and dared the man to comment.

"Tell me how to get to the Mahoney place," he asked when Mr. Farley had backed out of his way.

"It's east of here. Follow the trail out of town and then take the cut toward the ridge. The cabin sits on a ledge over a spring-fed creek."

"Where can I buy a horse?"

"Check with the livery. The pickings are slim with the war, but if you got the money, there's one to be had."

"I got the money," Jake said firmly.

"Would you like me to get some supplies together for you?" Mrs. Farley asked, stopping Jake in his tracks as he stalked toward the door.

Bless her heart. She knew how to make a dollar. Jake smiled his cold smile as he turned to look at the woman. "Yes. And throw in a warm coat while you're at it."

"I'll have it all ready for you to pick up on your way back through town," she assured him. And no doubt he would pay top dollar for it too. He didn't care. What else did he have to spend his money on?

The horse he purchased was not pretty by any stretch of the imagination, but he was strong and sound and his eyes possessed a wisdom unusual at such a young age. The gelding also bore the scars of battle around his chest and flanks and that meant he possessed courage. Jake handed over his coin without any regret. He had got the better end of the bargain and a full rig besides. The dun's sure footing on the snow-covered trail sealed the bargain for Jake as they followed the trail east out of town toward Shamus Mahoney's cabin.

He didn't even know why he was going to see Shamus, unless it was to make sure he left no stone unturned in finding out about his past before he left. What he hoped to find out was beyond him at the moment; he just knew that he had to try. He needed a direction. He needed a reason for leaving. He needed to know that Shannon would be taken care of. . . .

Jake cursed out loud as the image of her elfin face and deep green eyes came into his mind. He hadn't even left her yet and already she was haunting him. "She can take care of herself!" he exclaimed to the deep woods around him. Heavy snow weighed down the branches of the hemlocks along the trail and a brown wren hopped beneath one for shelter from the angry words that disturbed the peace of the winter's day. The dun's ears turned toward the sound, learning the voice of the new man who now rode him.

He found the cut and marveled at the wandering of the trail. Shannon had walked this route twice a day in all kinds of weather just to take care of him. She hadn't known what kind of man he was. She hadn't cared. She had tended him each day. She was faithful.

Was he? Had he betrayed a woman who was anxiously waiting for him to return? Was it Cat, who longed for a child? Was she still waiting for him to come home, wherever that was, and make her a mother? Even though he had not lain with Shannon, he desired her. He had declared his love for her and asked her to go away with him. Wouldn't he someday betray her as easily as he was betraying the one, if there was one, who was waiting for him?

What if he was wanted for a terrible crime? What if the deeds of his past caught up with him? Jake was sure there was something there, something bad behind him. The scars on his back were proof enough of that. What did a man do to deserve a beating such as that? What crime befitted the punishment of being whipped until one's back was bloody and all that remained was a mass of scars crisscrossing one another? He must have deserved it. He must be evil. There was no other explanation for it.

He heard the bubbling sound of water tumbling over rocks. Farley had said the cabin lay on a ridge over a spring-fed creek. Jake started looking for signs of a homestead. Surely the man would have a fire on such a cold day. He sniffed the air and it was clear of the scent of wood smoke. The trail went over a rise and then he saw the clearing along the ridge where Shamus had made an attempt at raising a few crops.

The cabin was tucked below with its back against the mountain. A small shed was beyond and a scraggly brown rooster scratched in the yard. This was where Shannon had grown up. No wonder her clothes were so ragged. Her family must have barely gotten by. But maybe it hadn't been that bad. She had been close to her brother and with all the wild wood that surrounded them, they could have played for hours. And she had mentioned a grandmother who had taken care of her. Had she been happy?

The door of the cabin yawned open to the cold winter's day and a pie pan leaned precariously against the doorjamb as if it had rolled along haphazardly and never been picked up. Maybe Shamus was drunk.

"Mahoney?" Jake called out. The rooster jumped in

the air in shock and took off with a squawk and a flurry of feathers toward the shed. Jake could hear the hens inside clucking to their champion as he sought shelter within.

"Shamus?" Jake dismounted and looped the reins over the porch rail. The dun's ears perked toward the open doorway. Jake pulled out the Henry and cocked it. The air around the cabin was eerily quiet except for the blustering of the hens. He stepped onto the porch and noticed a dark stain on the scuffed wood next to his boot. Jake knelt and touched it with a gloved finger and then raised it to his nose. Blood. Frozen and congealed but still blood without a doubt. Jake leveled the rifle before him and walked into the dim light of the cabin.

Surely the man wasn't living in this mess. The one room was a disaster. The table and chairs were flipped over and broken pottery was strewn around on the floor. Had Shamus taken his anger out on his home since Shannon was no longer around to bear the brunt of his attacks? No wonder she had left if this was the result of his temper.

"Shamus?" Jake called out again.

A moan was his answer.

A ladder hung precariously from a loft. Behind it was a bed with the mattress hanging off one side. Jake kicked the mattress aside and saw the barrel of a shotgun. Another kick and a leg became visible.

"Shamus?" Jake set the Henry aside and pulled the mattress out of the way. Shannon's father was lying facedown on the floor. The back of his head was matted with blood. Jake turned him over and the man moaned.

"Shamus? Can you hear me?" Jake shook the man. "What happened?"

Bloodshot eyes fluttered about, never settling on his face. "Deserters . . . Bastards.

Robbed . . . me . . . blind . . ."

"When?"

"Early . . . morning . . . shot one . . ." Shamus weakly licked his lips. "Got any whiskey?" he asked.

"The deserters, were they Union?"

The man nodded as his eyes rolled back and he passed out. Jake checked to make sure he was still breathing. He must not be hurt too bad if he had the presence of mind to ask for a drink, but then again the back of his head looked as if it had taken a nasty blow.

Shamus had said that Union deserters had attacked him and one of them was shot. It must have been the same group that he and Shannon had run into on the previous day. This cabin was out of the way, but it wasn't that far from where the group had spent the night. Apparently they were looking for food and supplies to get them through the winter as they worked their way west. But now one of them was hurt.

Jake pulled Shamus up and threw him over his shoulder. He picked up his rifle and carried the man outside where he laid him over his saddle. A quick check of the shed revealed no horse inside. One of the deserters had been riding double, although if Jake remembered Shamus's horse correctly, taking it would not be much of an improvement. So not only were they deserters, they were horse thieves. Jake was glad for the Henry. Maybe he'd better start wearing his guns too. Of course he would wear them. He'd put them on and leave. As soon as he got Shamus taken care of. He owed it to

Shannon to help her father. After all she had done for
him, it was the least he could do.

He was on his way out when a hat hanging on a post
in the corner caught his eye. It appeared to be well broken in, with the sides turned up to drain off the rain and
the front bent over the eyes to keep out the sun. It
would take a long time to break in a hat like that. So
why would someone go off and leave it, especially after
taking care to hang it on a post out of the way? Why
would a deserter in the middle of stealing a horse take
time to hang up his hat? Something about it seemed
familiar. Jake settled the hat on his head and was not
surprised to find that it fit perfectly. He took it off and
looked at it.

It was his. It was the same hat he had been wearing
in the drawing. He flipped it over and looked inside.
Just as he'd known they would be, the initials were
there. *JA.* He must have been careful with his things.
Lucky for him that he was. It sure made it easy to prove
what was his.

Jake pushed his hair back from his forehead and settled the hat into place. *Jamie always did that.* . . . He
grabbed the post as the thought swirled in his head. A
wide grin, sapphire blue eyes that snapped with life
beneath copper hair that had a bad habit of falling into
his eyes. He saw it all as clearly as he saw the hens
pecking at his feet. And a name to go with the face.
Jamie . . .

Jamie always did that. Other names came rushing
back. Chase would know what kind of animal had
made the tracks. Caleb Connors had drawn the picture.
Willie had died. Some of the names had been in the let-

ter, he remembered. Chase was the father of the two little boys. And Caleb was his friend.

Was he actually remembering things? Would the flashes that came and went all fall into place? Had something as simple as putting on a hat triggered his memories? This was not the time or place to ponder it. Shamus was hurt and here he stood like an idiot getting excited because he'd found a hat. It would take him the rest of the day to get the man to the doctor. Jake hoped that the deserters didn't have the same idea of taking their injured comrade to the hospital. Doc Blankenship helped all who were hurt, no matter which side of the Mason Dixon line they fought on, but these men were dangerous; they had already proven that. Jake hoped that they had just moved on, but an uneasy feeling in his gut told him different. He gathered the reins of the dun and began the long walk back to town with Shamus.

He had a friend named Caleb.

Chapter Fifteen

Now all he had to do was find him. Jake's mind whirled
with possibilities as he led the dun back down the trail
with Shamus hanging over the saddle. Caleb had survived the attack. Had he gone back to war? Or possibly
he had mustered home. Were they from the same town?
Had they enlisted together as boyhood friends off to
seek adventure? Somewhere there had to be records of
the men who served. All he had to do was find out
where, and his name would be on a list along with
Caleb's. As soon as he found Caleb, the answers would
come. Excitement surged through his body. He would
make his way to Richmond and seek out Caleb's whereabouts. And then when he had the answers, he would
come back for Shannon.

Shamus moaned as the trail became steeper. Jake
checked the back of the man's head and was disap-
pointed to see that blood was still seeping out. He

picked up a handful of snow and packed it against the man's head, hoping that it would stop the flow. There had been no need for the deserters to injure him so badly. Shamus was not much of a threat although he had gotten off a shot. He was probably lucky that they hadn't come back and killed him when they saw the sorry shape the gelding was in. They wouldn't get far with a wounded man and a failing horse.

A chill ran up Jake's spine at the thought that the deserters might still be around. The pickings had to have been slim at Shamus's cabin and they were likely to strike again. Jake decided to stop at the Farleys' store on his way back and put out a warning.

An outburst of birds from the branches on the trail below gave warning of someone approaching on the trail. Jake whirled the Henry around and cocked it as he dropped the reins to the dun. Once again he congratulated himself on his choice. The animal stood still as a stone with ears perked toward the trail.

Shannon's bright red head appeared coming around the trail. She looked up in horror at the sight of her father hanging over the saddle.

"Did you have to go off and kill him?" Horror flashed over her features.

"He's not dead, but he might be soon if we don't get him to Doc Blankenship." Shannon ran to her father and examined the back of his head. "What did you do to him?"

"I didn't do anything to him, Shannon. He was in this condition when I found him." Jake's voice was hollow and without emotion although his heart ached at her accusations.

"Missus Farley came and told me you were going to

kill him for stealing your rifle." Shannon looked at him
hopefully. She hadn't wanted to believe Mrs. Farley
even though her accusation was plausible.

"Missus Farley is an idiot and needs to keep her
mouth shut."

A smile teased the corners of her mouth.

"He was conscious when I found him. He said that
some deserters from the Union attacked him. They stole
your horse, too, from what I could see."

"The men we saw yesterday?" Shannon hadn't realized she had been holding her breath until she let it out.

"They needed another horse."

Shannon lifted her father's head to examine his eyes.

"He shot one of them."

"Good for you, Da," she said tenderly. She turned to
Jake. "I'm sorry I said those things." Her cheeks were
flushed with fever and her nose was running. Jake ran
his hand down the side of her face; her skin was damp
with perspiration.

"You shouldn't be out here. You're sick."

"That's what Missus Farley said."

"Then why did she go to all the trouble of telling you
I was going to kill your father?"

"Some people like to stir the pot." She was dizzy from
her race up the trail and swayed unevenly on her feet.
Jake grabbed her arm. "I don't have enough horse to
carry both of you down the trail."

"Don't worry about me. We just need to get him down
as quickly as possible."

"I can't help worrying about you. Even when you're
biting my head off, I worry about you." *Don't do it, Jake.
Step away.* He picked up the reins. "Let's get a move on
before we all freeze to death."

"I see you got your rifle back." Shannon fell into step beside him as they moved down the trail.

"Yes, I did."

"And your hat. I must have forgotten about it when I left."

"Apparently so." His pale blue eyes were dark and dangerous beneath the brim.

His manner was cold and she looked at him curiously. "You said Da shot one of the deserters?"

"Just repeating what he said. And I found some blood on the porch."

"So he was talking to you?"

"Yes. He said he shot one of the deserters and then he asked me if I had any whiskey on me."

Shannon laughed out loud. "Sound's like he's not hurt too bad. He's probably playing possum."

"I don't know, the back of his head looks bad."

"He's got a hard skull." Shannon tapped her finger against her own red head. "Stubborn too."

"Must run in the family," Jake groused.

She couldn't disagree and wrapped her shawl tighter around her arms.

"Why don't you own a coat?" The sight of her trembling with cold angered him beyond measure.

"Can't afford one. We had to buy Will a good one before he left."

Jake blinked his eyes at the image of a boy wearing a coat that was a couple of sizes too small. Willie had quickly outgrown all of his clothes and they were constantly plundering the army hospitals to find him things that fit.

"Ty?" Jake gasped.

"What?"

He shook his head as the memories disappeared.

"Did you remember something?"

"Yes . . . no . . . I don't know." A scowl covered his face. He didn't want to talk about his lost memory. "Surely you make enough at the hospital to buy a coat."

"I don't. None of the patients pay. Doc Blankenship does what he can and uses his own money to buy food and medical supplies. I barely make enough to put food on the table."

Jake felt embarrassed. He held a sack full of Yankee money in his pocket and the doctor hadn't asked for a cent. "Tomorrow we're going to buy you a coat." His words rang with anger at himself and the situation.

"I don't want your charity!" she sniffed.

"Think of it as payment for taking care of me." Why did she have to be so stubborn?

"I didn't do it for the money," she raged back. She jerked the reins from his hands and pulled the horse after her. "I'll take care of my own. Why don't you go on and leave since that's what you're planning on anyway according to Missus Farley."

The dun tossed his head at the rough treatment. "Hey, take it easy!" Jake called after her. *Dang that Mrs. Farley, poking her nose in everyone's business.*

Shannon cast him a look that would freeze a lesser man.

"How do you expect me to leave without my horse?" he shouted after her in exasperation.

"Dolt!" she yelled to the treetops.

The rest of the trip was made in silence except for an occasional sniff or sneeze from Shannon. Jake rescued the dun from her righteous anger and took the lead on the trail. She followed along behind, occasionally checking on her father to see if he was still breathing. They soon reached the hospital, where Dr. Blankenship and Mose were waiting to take care of the patient. After hearing about Mrs. Farley's meddling, Jake was surprised to find that the undertaker and local magistrate weren't there waiting for him.

They finally had Shamus bandaged and bathed and resting in one of the beds. Jake disappeared during the proceedings, leaving Shannon miffed. She wanted him to remain close so she could ignore him. Or harangue him. Either one would do. Dr. Blankenship gave her orders to take a warm bath and go to bed and sent Mose to fetch the tub to her cabin. She agreed to go, but only under the condition that they send for her as soon as Shamus awakened.

She had just settled into the tub when the door to her cabin burst open. Shannon squealed and grabbed a towel, holding it over her breasts.

"What?" she gasped in shock.

Jake stood in the doorway and the frigid air swirled around him, whipping the window curtains up and stirring up the fire that roared in the stove. She noticed he was now wearing a heavy coat and held another one in his arms.

"Making deliveries." His pale blue eyes narrowed dangerously as he surveyed the pearly expanse of her skin. Her knees trembled above the water level and the towel molded to her breasts as they heaved in shock. Jake kicked the door shut and stepped into the cabin.

"Leave," Shannon commanded. She knew her face must be flushed as red as her hair.

Jake dropped the coat in the rocking chair.

"That's my plan." He took off one glove as he walked

toward the tub, gazing appreciatively at the sight before him. Shannon drew her legs up under the towel as he dipped a finger in the steaming water and swirled it around.

"What are you doing?" she whispered. "You said you were leaving."

"I bought you a coat." Steam rose from the water but whether her flush came from the hot water or embarrassment, he could not tell.

"I don't want it."

"Too bad."

"I'll take it back," Shannon ground out stubbornly.

"I explained to Missus Farley that she would be very sorry if she allowed that."

Shannon looked up in shock. "You said that to Missus Farley? I'll be the laughingstock of the town."

"So?" Jake flicked at the water with his fingers.

"Why are you doing this?"

"Doing what?" *Leave, you fool.* "Giving you a gift?" *Walk away.* "Because you saved my life."

"I don't want charity."

"It's not charity, you stubborn fool." Jake crossed his arms and looked down at her. "It's gratitude."

"Dolt."

"Idiot." He smiled shyly. "Beautiful idiot."

"Don't make fun of me." Shannon looked at her knees.

"I'm not." Jake knelt beside the tub. "I think you are the most beautiful woman I have ever seen. And the most argumentative too."

"Considering the only other woman around here that you've seen is Missus Farley, that's not saying much."

"Shannon." Jake's finger lifted her chin, making her look into his eyes.

"I've seen a lot of women. And you are beautiful." Her eyes were moist and soft as she gazed at him.

"Truly?" Her lower lip quivered with the question.

"Truly." He leaned across the tub and kissed her gently, only his lips touching hers. "Which makes it really hard for me to say good-bye." Jake leaned back and looked at her face glistening with moisture. A tendril of hair brushed across her bare shoulder and he twisted it back into the mass piled on top of her head. "But I'll always treasure the way you look at this moment."

"You're really leaving?" she asked. How could her heart feel so happy and sad at the exact same moment?

"Yes." His shy smile danced quickly across his face. "You see, I've figured out where to go and who to talk to. The man who drew the picture. Caleb Conners. He was mentioned in the letter, so I know he's a friend. All I have to do is find him and he can answer all my questions. He must have survived the attack since he hid out in the cave. I'm hoping he went back to the army and they'll know where I can find him."

"He'll help you to remember." Shannon looked down at the water. "And then what happens?"

"I'll come back." His voice was sad. He wanted it to be true.

"But what if you can't? What if you're married to the woman in the letter?"

"Then it's better this way."

"Not for me." She looked up at his face. The face she had come to know so well, along with every inch of his body. She could see it with her eyes closed and despaired that she would never see it again. "I want the memories."

"What do you mean?"

"I want you to stay with me tonight. I want the memory of you to keep with me. I don't have that many good ones to think about." She said it quietly, her voice drifting up with the steam off the water.

"Shannon, do you know what you're saying?" His gut twisted at the thought of it. Could he? Should he?

"I do. Do you want me, Jake?" Her eyes were full of her innocence, but the parting of her mouth, the moisture trailing down beneath the towel, the fullness of her breasts bespoke a woman made for loving.

Should he take the memory with him? Once he made love to her, would he be able to let her go? *Walk away, Jake.*

In one quick movement, he wrenched her from the tub. Shannon gasped as her shins caught against the side and the towel fell away, landing half in, half out of the water.

"Shannon." Jake swallowed hard, his pale blue eyes searching the green depths of hers. The cold air of the room hit her skin, causing her to shiver as they looked into each other's eyes, both finding what they had never hoped to find, what they never even knew they were searching for.

"Are you sure?"

"I'm sure. I love you. If this is all I can have of you, then so be it."

With a groan he planted a kiss on her waiting mouth, driving his tongue deep within the pliant warmth. Shannon fell against him and his hands caressed her back. Frustrated, he wrenched off his other glove. The buttons of his coat dug into the tender skin of her breasts and stomach. He couldn't wait. She was naked and shivering and he was dressed for high winter. They both fought with his clothes, fingers trembling against each other, buttons resisting them. Jake jerked the coat off as Shannon pulled his shirt tail from his pants. It caught on the suspenders and fell tangled around his waist. Her hair came loose from the pins and he ravaged it as he kissed her again, tangling his hands in the bright mass as he attacked her neck with his mouth. Shannon pulled at the buttons of his pants, wanting what she had seen so many times when he lay unconscious beneath her gentle care.

How many times had she imagined this moment? How many nights had she lain in her narrow cot in the cabin after caring for him during the day and wondered what it would be like to be loved by him? His mouth caught her breast, glancing over the nipple and she leaned back to give him better access. Her body tingled. Her legs trembled. Her insides boiled. This was what it was supposed to be like. The wanting was good. How could it not be? Why would God make a man and woman to fit together and not give them pleasure from the joining? Her hands delved inside his pants, freeing him. Why hadn't anyone told her it was supposed to be like this?

Jake growled deep in his throat. She was driving him mad with her searching. His head flew up and his hands grabbed at hers as they reached for him again.

"What did I do?" she asked tearfully.

He shook his head to clear it. He throbbed with wanting, he could feel his sex reaching for her, begging for her.

"I want it to be good for you," he gasped. "I don't want to hurt you."

"You're hurting me now!" she cried.

Jake scooped her up and carried her to the bed. They both fell onto the brightly colored quilt in a tangle of legs and arms and flashing red hair. Jake laid his hand against her neck and trailed it down between her breasts and over her stomach. She trembled at his touch. "It will hurt, Shannon, the first time, especially if you get me so wild that I can't think about what I'm doing. . . ."

"I'm making you wild?" Her smile danced at the corners of her mouth.

"Just be quiet for once. Let me do the talking." He bent and kissed her again, this time slowly and gently, his lips pulling at her mouth while his hand traced over her body. Shannon moaned as she melted against the quilt. "See?" His mouth nibbled at her ear and moved down her neck.

"Jake . . ."

"Shhh . . ."

"Jake . . ." Her hands caught in his hair, bringing the silky blond tips up on end.

"Shhh . . ." His hands dipped into her private parts and she gasped in surprise.

"Jake . . . I can't . . . oh, what are you doing?"

"Can you keep your mouth shut for one second?"

"Jake, please, oh . . . Jake . . ."

He moved over her, poised and ready as he watched pleasure run over her elfin features. She gasped and bucked against his hand and he caught her joy in his mouth with another kiss as he entered her innocence. He felt her gasp of pain, then the melting against him as her long pale legs wound around him and she caught the motion. Jake felt himself being swept away as she met him with her strength. The bright patches of the quilt, along with the red of her hair and the deep green of her eyes became a kaleidoscope of colors whirling around his head. He closed his eyes. It was too much. He was going to die. His passion overwhelmed him and he became lost in the colors. Shannon filled his mind, replacing all that had been lost.

He was weak, and he was a fool. He should have left her before it was too late. He knew why he had the scars on his back. He was evil. He also knew that for the first time in his life, he was in love. That had to be true. How could he ever forget feeling like this? He wrapped his arms around her and buried his head in her shoulder.

"Shannon, I love you."

"Dolt. I love you too." Her hands skimmed across his back, soothing the scars that marred his skin.

Jake laughed as he rolled the quilt around their bodies.

"Jake?"

"Hmm?"

"Can we do it again?"

Chapter Sixteen

He had thought he'd be gone by now. He should have left when he had the chance but he had lingered and now the prospect of leaving was more than he wanted to think about. As if he could have a logical thought while Shannon was curled up against him as she was at the moment.

The stove needed feeding. The fire had gone out in the night and the air in the cabin was frigid. But beneath the brightly colored quilt it was warm, especially where the skin of his body came into contact with the smooth surface of hers. It was like curling up with an open flame, she burned as bright as her hair. Of course she was a bit feverish at the moment, but he was certain she would be just as incandescent without it.

Shannon.

Maybe he should take her with him. She had said she would go. They could go into Richmond together, find someone who knew about Caleb and could send him in the right direction. And once he found Caleb, he would find the answers to his past.

But what if the answers were wrong for Shannon? In that case, wouldn't it be better to just leave her here and never come back than to take her from everything she knew and then abandon her?

He wouldn't do that. He couldn't do that. Jake wrapped his arms tighter around her body. His muscles trembled with the effort not to hold her too tightly; not to crush her against him.

Shannon. The remembering started with her. She filled his mind, closing the doors that hung half-open, giving him glimpses of things that might or might not have happened. Her face replaced the nameless ones that flashed through his brain.

He should go.

But not now. Christmas was just a few days away. Her father was hurt. It would be cruel to leave now.

Wait until after Christmas. But then you'll have the excuse of the weather. And the longer you stay, the harder it will be to go, for both of you.

Shannon rubbed her nose against his shoulder and her body stretched and quivered as she awoke into the peaceful stillness of the morning. Jake looked down to find bright green eyes gazing up at him without the fog of fever.

"Good morning," he said, smiling at her.

"And to you." She smiled back. "A cold one too."

"We let the fire go out."

Shannon peered over his arm at the stove. "Only one of them from what I recall."

Jake laughed heartily. "Only one," he agreed.

"So who's going to stoke the fire?" she asked as she snuggled deeper under the quilt, pulling it up over her nose.

Jake leaned on his elbow to look down at her. "Don't think you can boss me around." He pulled the quilt down from her nose.

"You seemed agreeable to that last night," she said as she pulled it back up.

Jake grinned evilly as he flipped the quilt back from his body to leave the comfort of the bed. Shannon felt she had won the battle so she settled into the mattress. As soon as she released her hold on the quilt, Jake yanked it away and wrapped it around his shoulders.

She shrieked at the cold and threw a pillow at his back as he bent over the stove, stuffing in kindling and hard knots of wood. He soon had the embers glowing and the little potbelly of the stove began its work of emitting warmth into the cabin.

Jake took great relish in casually warming himself before the fire, placing himself between the heat and Shannon, who shivered beneath the plain white sheet that remained on the bed. His toes curled against the floor where the frigid air came up beneath the crawl space and founds its way into the cabin by way of cracks in the boards. A rag rug lay at the foot of the bed and he hooked it with his toe, bringing it before the fireplace to stand on.

Shannon watched his torture from her pillows, knowing that he was enjoying the process of getting warm while she shivered with cold. He definitely needed a comeuppance. The sheet was doing nothing to save her from the chilblains, so she casually folded it away from her body.

Her bright hair tumbled down around her breasts, creating a curtain that partially hid them from his sight. Shannon caught the narrowing of his pale blue eyes as they roamed over her form and felt the new sensation that he had introduced her to the night before gathering within her. She was a wanton where Jake was concerned. The idea didn't bother her anymore.

She liked being a wanton for Jake.

Shannon made a great show of stretching and yawning. She gathered her hair up in her hand and ran her fingers through it, exposing her nakedness to his icy gaze. She glanced at him coyly from the side as she bought a long, muscular leg from beneath the sheet and arched her foot toward the end of the bed. She let out a casual sigh, as if she were bored and then looked him full in the face with a bright red eyebrow arching delicately in his direction.

He couldn't stand it. Jake recalled an old adage about being caught between a rock and a hard place. That's where he stood for sure. At this point he was damned if he did and damned if he didn't. He went to her as if he were a fish on a line and she were reeling him in.

As he sank into the mattress, welcomed by her open arms, the thought crossed his mind again that he should go.

He decided to think about it after Christmas.

"I'd better go check on Da," Shannon said much later when they were too spent to do anything more than lazily snuggle under the quilt.

"Doc said he'd send for you if there was a problem," Jake mumbled against the smooth skin of her stomach.

"But it's late in the morning. Surely he's woken up by now. If he hasn't, then that is a problem."

"Do you think that maybe they're just giving us some time?"

Shannon bolted upright in the bed. "You mean they know about this?"

"Mose saw me come up here last night."

"And he was probably watching for you to leave," she cried as she scrambled from the sheets and began the search for her clothes. "Dear Lord in heaven, the whole town will know about it by now." Her ranting continued as she pulled on her clothes. Jake watched her with an amused expression as she flew about the room, talking to herself and cursing the overactive tongues of Mose and Mrs. Farley, who would no doubt have her own issues with Shannon's misconduct. "I'll be barred from the Christmas service for sure," she cried as she crawled under the bed to retrieve a recalcitrant shoe.

Jake leaned over the bed to look at her flushed face. "Shannon, no one is going to care, especially not Mose. He's probably tickled pink that this happened."

"Oh Jake, you don't know. You don't know what it's like to live in a small town and be the subject of gossip," Shannon wailed as she backed out with the shoe in her hand.

"Maybe I do." He sat up. "Or not. I do remember enough to know that it doesn't matter what other people think. All that matters is how we feel about each other."

Shannon wrestled the shoe on and then started twisting her hair, holding the pins in her mouth in readiness as her hands quickly smoothed the flaming mass into a semblance of order. Her tirade continued while she worked at her hair.

"Shannon, did you hear what I said?" Jake found his pants on the floor where he had left them the night before and quickly slid into them; Shannon's nervous tirade against the small town gossips had galvinized him into action. He grabbed her hands in both of his. "Shannon?"

"What?" she asked impatiently, breathlessly.

"Did you hear what I said?"

Her deep green eyes were wide with fear, reminding him of a doe right before a wolf takes her down by the throat. She was terrified.

Jake took her face in his hands, easing her fear, calming her agitation. "I love you."

"I love you too."

"Everything will be all right." He looked into the green depths of her eyes. She didn't believe it any more than he did.

Her lower lip trembled as she nodded. "I need to go."

"I'll be over in a while."

Shannon flew out the door, throwing her shawl over her shoulders as she went. Jake looked around the cabin, running his hands though his hair as his eyes, mind and heart searched for an answer to the ever-deepening dilemma he found himself in.

"You forgot your coat," he said to the closed door.

Chapter Seventeen

"So how long do you think it will take?" Cole walked over to the window of Jason's study to check on the progress being made on the bunkhouse in the valley below. Luckily the weather had been mild enough that the men were able to work in their shirtsleeves. They were certain they would have the bunkhouse habitable again by Christmas.

What a shock it had been for Cole and Grace to come home from their interrupted honeymoon and find the devastation that had been done to the ranch. Their chance meeting with Constance had almost been too much for Grace, who was tormented by the knowledge that their marriage was illegal. At least her cabin had escaped with just minor damage, which had quickly been fixed. And Justice had recovered completely from his wound and was now bouncing around in the yard with the boys, playing a game of fetch. Cole never would have forgiven himself if his dog had died while he was gone.

Cole was worried about his wife. About Grace. He refused even to consider Constance in that role. She had given up her right to that title more than fifteen years ago. The woman was without a conscience. How could he have been so blind as to have missed that when he married her? *Because you weren't looking at her with your brain, you fool.*

How many times had he chastised himself in the past few weeks? How many times had he looked at Grace's sad brown eyes and hated himself for the pain this was causing her.

Grace didn't blame him. How could she when he'd had no idea Constance was still alive? He had honestly considered himself a widower all these years and hadn't thought any more about it. He had seen Constance's grave. He had mourned the waste of life and years. He was sorry it had turned out that way. But he hadn't been sorry to be free of her. They were two totally different people who wanted totally opposite things out of life. Apparently Constance had found what she wanted and so had he, after all these years. . . .

Cole's hand ached to close around Constance's elegant throat. He could not believe that she'd had the gall to call the child that he and Grace were expecting a bastard. And if the child was born without the benefit of carrying his name, it would be her fault. The eventuality was something she would enjoy. Sabotaging his happiness and the future of a child, just for the fun of it. Just so she could have the last word.

"She abandoned you, Cole." Jason looked up from the book of law that was open on his desk. "All you have to do is provide witnesses who can corroborate the date she left and that you have not lived as man and wife since. It's just a matter of filing the papers."

"Paperwork," Cole said skeptically.

"Yes, a lot of it."

"The baby is due in three months." Cole turned back to Jason.

"It could happen a lot faster if you could get Constance to cooperate."

Cole let out a hollow laugh. "There is no way that is going to happen."

"Have you tried asking her?" Jason walked over to stand next to his friend. "You said she's in town. Why don't you give it a try? Explain the inevitability of it all. Surely she must have some feelings for you. After all, she did marry you."

"I was a fool."

"It happens to the best of us sometimes," Jason said quietly. Cole knew he was remembering his own life, the mistakes he had made with Jenny's grandmother so many years ago. He had lost her. Cole was determined that he would not lose Grace. Not when it had taken him so long to find her.

"Surely she can't be that unreasonable," Zane asked later as he rode to town with Cole on the wagon. Jenny had given them a shopping list that was a mile long. She was determined that they were going to have a nice Christmas in spite of the damage to the house. Zane had decided that shopping was much better than the frantic construction going on down at the bunkhouse. Besides that, with all the commotion at the ranch, it had been a while since he had paid a visit to the ladies

GET THREE FREE* BOOKS!

SIGN UP TODAY TO LOCK IN OUR LOWEST PRICES EVER!

Every month, you will receive three of the newest historical romance titles for the low price of $13.50,* up to **$6.50 in savings!**

A **$19.97** value!

As a book club member, not only do you save **32% off the retail price**, you will receive the following special benefits:

- **30% off** all orders through our website and telecenter (plus, you still get 1 book FREE for every 5 books you buy!)

- Exclusive access to dollar sales, special discounts, and offers you won't be able to find anywhere else.

- Information about contests, author signings, and more!

- Convenient home delivery of your favorite books every month.

- A 10-day examination period. If you aren't satisfied, just return any books you don't want to keep.

There is no minimum number of books to buy, and you may cancel membership at any time.

* Please include $2.00 for shipping and handling.

NAME:_____

ADDRESS:_____

_____

_____

TELEPHONE:_____

E-MAIL:_____

_____ I want to pay by credit card.

__ Visa   __ MasterCard   __ Discover

Account Number:_____

Expiration date:_____

SIGNATURE:_____

*Send this form, along with $2.00 shipping
and handling for your FREE books, to:*

Historical Romance Book Club
20 Academy Street
Norwalk, CT 06850-4032

*Or fax (must include credit card
information!) to: 610.995.9274.
You can also sign up on the Web
at www.dorchesterpub.com.*

Offer open to residents of the U.S. and
Canada only. Canadian residents, please
call 1.800.481.9191 for pricing information.

in town. He was sure they were all dying to see him. And Chase had given him the perfect excuse to go.

"She's a spoiled brat, or at least she was when I was married to her," Cole said as he guided the team down the familiar trail.

"If she was such a spoiled brat, why did you marry her?"

"Why do you think?"

Zane thought about it for a second. "That good, huh? Can't wait to meet her."

"Zane, my boy, she would chew you up before breakfast."

"Sounds like the answer to all my prayers," Zane said with a wide grin.

"You'd best pray that you never wind up with a woman like Constance. It's more like a curse than anything else."

"Grace still making you wait?"

"How is it you have survived all these years without getting shot?" Cole asked in exasperation.

"Just lucky, I guess."

"If you keep on putting your nose where it don't belong, your luck is going to run out," Cole growled. Justice stuck his head between the two men from his place behind the bench on the wagon. His dark eyes showed his concern at the tone he heard in his master's voice. Cole rubbed the wolflike ears of the big, dark mixed breed and Justice panted in contentment as they rolled into town.

"Until that day comes," Zane said, hopping off the still-moving wagon as they passed by Maybelle's, "I'll keep doing what I do best." He dusted off the back of his pants and adjusted his hat.

"What are you up to?" Cole asked as he pulled the wagon to a halt.

"Secret mission." Zane grinned. "Don't worry; I'll catch up with you at the store." He waved Cole away.

Cole popped the reins. "One of these days . . . ," he grumbled at Justice, who had jumped into Zane's place on the bench.

The last thing he wanted to do was talk to Constance. He had liked it better when he thought she was dead. Instead she had been living the high life all these years while he had risked his life every day fighting against the lawless. He couldn't blame her for going after what she wanted. But he did hate the careless way she treated people. The way she had treated him.

He had tried to make their marriage work. He had done everything he could within his means to satisfy her, but she always wanted more. She had known he wasn't rich when she married him. But she had insisted then that what he had was enough. He had been too much in love to realize that she was just using him as a way to escape her overprotective father. She had used him because he was strong enough to stand up to her father.

She had played both of them for fools. The realization of how well she had played him didn't make Cole feel any better about talking with her as he tied the horses in front of the store and made his way over to what passed for a fancy hotel in town. Constance had probably had a fit when she and her so-called companion had checked in.

"Have you got a Constance Larrimore registered here?" Cole grimaced at how threatening he sounded. It was almost as if he were hunting down criminals again.

The clerk checked the register and reported that there was no such name listed.

"Tall woman, dark hair and eyes, well dressed, probably traveling with a gentleman of means," Cole described her.

"Mr. Petty's companion," the clerk responded. "They checked in two days ago." He checked the register for the room number.

"Did he mention what sort of business he was in?" Cole asked. For some strange reason, the name struck a chord in his brain.

"No, but he's been riding out to look at the land. Maybe he's thinking about settling down in the area."

Of all the dumb luck, Cole thought as he climbed the stairs to the room. There would be hell to pay for sure if Constance wound up settling down in Laramie. Cole rapped on the door as he dismissed the thought. Laramie was way too much of a backwoods town for someone of Constance's sophisticated tastes. She'd rather be someplace like New York City, or Chicago, or San Francisco. Or maybe not San Francisco. After all, that's where her grave was. He gave the door another rap, this time with a bit more force behind it.

"Why, Cole, what a surprise," Constance said when she opened the door.

Yes, she's surprised all right. She probably saw me coming from a mile away, Cole thought as his eyes wandered over the lacy robe that fluttered over the expensive undergarments she wore. Or almost wore. Her breasts threatened to spill out of the tightly laced corset that emphasized her impossibly narrow waist. Her satin drawers, cut unusually short, shimmered in the light over silk stockings and lace garters. Her hair was down, the way he had always liked it, artfully arranged so that it spilled over one shoulder in a lush, shiny mass.

He hated to admit it, but she was a strikingly beautiful woman.

"I want a divorce." Cole stepped past her display and into the room. The last thing he needed was for someone to come by and see her standing there, almost dressed. Or maybe almost undressed. Thank God Zane had jumped off at Maybelle's.

"I'm a Catholic, Cole. You know we don't believe in divorce."

"Don't give me that line of . . ."

"Why, Cole Larrimore," she interrupted, "have you lost all your gentlemanly ways since the last time I saw you?" She looked up and down his long frame. "You still have your hat on. Things must be more primitive in Wyoming than I thought."

Cole snatched his hat off and then felt like a foolish little boy for letting her goad him into doing so. He placed it firmly back on his head and pulled a paper from his coat pocket.

"You abandoned me, Constance. I can get a divorce on those grounds. It would just make it easier and quicker if you sign this paper. We can be divorced before the week is out."

"And you can marry your little whore and make it legal?" Constance jumped on his words with sadistic glee as she walked across the room toward a small table and chair, her hips swaying gracefully.

"Don't do this." His reply was curt. It took every bit of his resolve not to wrap his hands around her long, graceful neck and squeeze the life from her.

Constance arranged herself in a delicate chair that

was covered with an exquisite needlework pattern and picked up a fine china cup and saucer. "I love being surrounded by beautiful things, Cole. I carry some things with me wherever I go, just so I feel comfortable, and at home. I've amassed quite a collection of pretty things." She pointed to a small oil painting that sat on an easel next to the door: "Art." Her hand touched the heavily jeweled necklace she wore: "Jewelry." She took a sip of her tea and her dark eyes looked intently into his: "Men.

"What have you been up to for the past few years?"

"That became none of your business the day you left."

"Don't think that I haven't been paying attention, Cole." She crossed her legs as she talked, exposing herself, deliberately taking her time, trying to tempt him, seduce him. Cole fought the urge to throw up.

Had she always been such a whore?

"I read some of the stories about you." She took another sip of tea and then set down her cup. "Seems like you had quite a few adventures with . . . your dog?" She made the hesitation deliberate, baiting him. Suddenly she saw a garter that needed adjusting and bent to fix it, displaying her breasts in all their abundance as they threatened to spill over the corset.

"What do you want, Constance?"

"Nothing," she said simply. "I don't lack for a thing. As a matter of fact, my life is perfect and I want to keep it that way."

"What do you mean?"

"As long as I'm married to you, I don't have to marry anyone else. It's my excuse." She went into a parody of her response to her many suitors. "I'm sorry, darling; you see, I can't marry you. I'm already married. To a lawman, no less. He's down in Texas fighting horrible bandits. And I'm here, having the time of my life." She waved her hand in the air. "You see, Cole; I need a husband to keep from making any ghastly mistakes."

"I can get this divorce without you."

"I'll fight it."

"Why?"

"Why not?" She smiled over the teacup. "I don't have anything else to do right now. Jefferson is off looking at land all the time. I'm quite bored. Fighting a divorce sounds like fun."

"You are insane."

"Oh, come on, Cole, doesn't it sound like fun?" She pouted prettily. "After all, you'd get to drag my name through the mud. Maybe your little homesteader could watch. Imagine what it would be like. She could sit there with her scarred face and swollen belly while you tell the judge what a bad wife I am."

I am going to kill her. He was actually surprised that he hadn't already.

Constance yawned delicately as if she were suddenly bored with the conversation. "You will have to excuse me. I find that I simply must have a nap before lunch."

Cole looked at the paper he still held in his hand. "Please sign this, Constance."

"Don't be ridiculous, Cole." She rose and showed him the door.

What am I going to say to Grace? Cole thought as the door closed firmly behind him. He wondered if a judge would convict him of murder if he walked back in and acted on his impulse.

"I need a drink," he said as he walked down the stairs.

* * *

Zane stretched and growled under the tumbled sheets. "Dang that felt good," he said as the whore snuggled up to him. "I swear, Missy, you are the best gal here."

Missy giggled in delight. She was sweet, gullible and loved to talk. She would talk nonstop about nonsense, even while doing the deed. Most of the time she didn't even know what she was talking about. Mostly she would just repeat what she had heard.

That was why Zane had come looking for her today. Chase wanted information on the men who had attacked the ranch. The sheriff had come and collected the bodies with an unconcerned air. No one had claimed them. No one came forth to identify them. It was just a random attack out of the blue, as far as the sheriff was concerned. No need for them to worry. Probably wouldn't happen again.

It wouldn't, as long as Chase had a say in the matter.

Zane had to laugh when he recalled the orders Chase had given him.

"Go to Maybelle's and find out if there are any new men in town. See if anyone is just hanging out. Go to the saloon and see who's there. They should be easy to find. They'll just be waiting." Chase's eyes had had that dark look they got when there was a threat to those he loved. Zane was glad he would be the one standing beside Chase instead of against him. Chase was deadly in a fight. And for some reason, he believed the fight hadn't really started yet, even after the attack on the house. Someone was after the ranch. Chase wanted to know who and he wanted to know now. Maybelle's was the best source of information in these parts.

And I am the man for the job, Zane thought to himself

as Missy rattled on about the rich man who had just come to town with his lady friend. The man had come to the brothel and had a private meeting with Maybelle. Maybelle had said that if any men came into town looking for work, the girls should let her know. But only if they were mean and stupid. Missy quickly covered her mouth and giggled.

"I shouldn't have said that," she said airily. "Maybelle thinks all men are stupid."

"We are, honey," Zane said as he curled an arm around her waist. "We're dumber than a box of rocks when we get around somebody as pretty as you."

"Zane, we can't do it again. You know you only paid for one time." Missy pouted.

"But darling, you know I'm one of Maybelle's oldest and best customers." He worked his charms with his hands and his mouth. "Besides, it's not like somebody's waiting downstairs for a turn. Not so early in the day. You're the only one working right this minute. You're the only one having any fun."

Missy melted against him and opened her legs wide to receive him as Zane entered her and congratulated himself on having a very good day. He had gotten laid, not once but twice, he had managed to get out of the heavy construction on the bunkhouse and he had gotten information for Chase. Maybe later he could talk Cole into buying him a drink at the saloon. Life was good.

So why did he feel something was missing? Why did he have to keep convincing himself of his good fortune? And why was he thinking about concerns like this when Missy was doing that thing she did with her hands and . . . and . . . intelligent thought left him as physical need took over and he collapsed against her, too spent to think.

Life was good.

Chapter Eighteen

The answers to his many questions about the past still had not come, but that didn't keep Jake from whistling a merry tune as he hiked through the fresh snow toward the barn. The late morning air was crisp and clear and even the squirrels seemed to be in a festive mood as they scampered up and down the wide trunks of the oaks. Jake smiled as he realized that the tune he was whistling was a Christmas carol, something along the lines of "Deck the Halls" if his memory served him, which it didn't.

He even smiled at his joke, silly as it was. Then he had to laugh when he realized that, like Shannon, he had also gone out without his coat. It didn't matter at all. The day was beautiful and Christmas was coming. He imagined the look on Shannon's face when he gave her the shawl. Then he smiled voraciously as he imagined

Shannon wearing nothing but the shawl. He pictured the shawl slowly being lowered and more and more of her satin smooth skin being exposed to his gaze, his hands, his mouth.

As he approached the barn, he heard the low growl of the orange cat. It rumbled out into the frigid air and then climbed into a yowl. The cat flew out of the door, taking a moment to arch its back and hiss at whatever it was that had disturbed it. The animal flew by Jake with its ears flattened and retreated to the darkness beneath the stoop at the back door of the great white house. Jake shook his head at the cat's antics and stepped inside the barn, wondering what kind of creature he would have to battle inside.

The milk cow mooed frantically when he came in. She needed milking. Jake rubbed the spotted forehead and wondered where Mose was and why he had ignored the animal. Surely Cook would have wanted milk for breakfast. He had even seen her do the milking on occasion, although the cow usually suffered in that case because the woman took her frustration with Mose out on the poor animal.

The dun had his head out and his ears pricked as he looked over the door of his stall. Jake ran his hand down the horse's neck and checked the feed and water. At least his horse was fine; he had made sure of that before he went to Shannon's the night before.

He looked around for the bucket and found one sitting by the door. The cow stomped her foot and mooed again as he came toward her stall.

"I'm going to take care of you. Quit your whining." Jake had to smile. "You sound just like Shannon, boss-ing me around. You even look like her with your red-and-white hide." Jake opened the door to the stall. "Don't tell her I said that, or she'll kill me."

The words had just left his mouth when something came crashing down against the back of his head, dropping him to his knees. A broken leg off the milk stool landed in the straw before him as his ears rang and stars exploded in his mind. Without thought, Jake raised his arm to stop the next blow and rolled toward his attacker, taking the man's feet out from under him.

The man landed in the stall and Jake backed away, willing his brain to function as he fought the ringing and the pain that was still shooting from the back of his head. He needed time; time to get his bearings, time to think, time to figure out what was going on. What was happening? Where did this . . . why . . . Shannon . . . Shannon was in danger.

The attacker quickly gained his feet and Jake continued to back away. Jake came up against a post and used it to pull himself up. The man caught him in the stomach and Jake's air left his body in a whoosh as the impact knocked him to the floor again.

This guy is going to kill you. The thought flashed through his brain. He couldn't concentrate. It had all happened too fast and now he couldn't breathe. Jake felt himself being raised by his lapels and saw the fist coming toward his face. His arms flailed about for something, anything that would save him. He found a horseshoe, forgotten in the straw, and swung it around, knocking his attacker in the side of the head. As the man fell away, Jake scrambled to his hands and knees and desperately sucked in air.

Get up, get up now. . . . His mind was working at least.

Jake staggered to his feet. He heard a noise behind him, a whistling, a whine, air being sliced by a length of rawhide.

The whip hit his back, shredding the thin fabric of his battle jacket, ripping the shirt, tearing across the mass of scars, bringing blood and long-damaged flesh away with it as it was raised to do further damage.

A dam burst inside his head. A vortex of images swirled into place. Once again he was a boy of fifteen, spread facedown over a scarred table with hands tied to the legs and his back bared for the whip. A woman and two girls were sobbing in the yard behind a small cabin that stood next to a church in the lake country of Minnesota.

"Ye've got the devil in ye boy and we must cast it out." He heard the words as clearly as the day they were spoken. And felt the sting of the lash once again on his raw back. A back that had hardly had time to heal from the last lashing. His father was obsessed with vanquishing the devil that caused him to do the things he did.

It had been years later, when Jake met Jason Lynch, that he had discovered he had not done anything more than any other normal boy of his age. The realization had come almost too late to undo the damage done in his formative years.

Slowly, slowly, he had allowed them in. He hadn't wanted to, but the walls he'd built to protect himself had gradually weakened. First there was Caleb, whose eyes saw all that was hidden. Then there were Ty and Zane and finally Jamie and Chase. He had discovered through their friendship that he was not evil. But even friendship was not enough to keep him from fighting the demons that had been planted inside by the endless beatings and belaboring. It could not keep him from feeling guilt that he was not good enough or pure enough to please his father. He had used his past as an excuse all these years to distance himself from others because it was easier to pretend that he didn't care than to care.

He had also found that it was easier not to deserve love than to love. He had tried to love his father and all his father had ever done was hurt him. He had loved his mother and she had stood by and watched his father beat him bloody. It was easier for her to feel sorry for him than to put up a fight for him. It had become easy for them all to make excuses.

It had become easy for him to kill. Easier each time. This time he was going to enjoy it. Because he had vowed to himself and to God that no one would ever take a lash to him again.

The devil that his father had been so sure of came boiling up from deep inside Jake. The demon erupted to the surface with a snarl and before the lash could land again, the whip was ripped away and flung against the wall. The dun reared in his stall as the two men crashed against the wooden panels. Jake slammed the man's head against the wood and wrenched him away, spinning him up against a post and ramming his head against it. He grabbed the man's jacket in one hand and backhanded him with the other. He released his hold and drew back to punch him in the jaw. The man managed to block the blow and Jake came around with a left. His opponent staggered and Jake relentlessly attacked him again. The man blocked with his shoulder and struck Jake in the neck, gagging him. Jake staggered back and then put his head down, driving himself and his attacker up against the wall.

The man's eyes widened as he landed against a pitchfork that had been casually left leaning against the wall. The impact of the two bodies in motion buried the tines into the base of his neck. It wasn't the stabbing that killed him. It was the slow shutdown of his nervous system as his body was disconnected from his brain. He knew he was dying. He could feel it. Jake's pale blue eyes watched intently as the life left his attacker's body. The man saw the gates of hell. Jake knew exactly what they looked like. He had been there.

Jake took a moment to look at his attacker. He wore a uniform. The man was one of the Union deserters. One of five. One dead, one injured by Shamus and probably in the hospital now. With Shannon.

His ice-blue eyes narrowed as Jake pulled the sack that contained his guns out from under his cot. They fell into place on his hips, once again where they belonged. Without consciously thinking about what his hands were doing, he went through the routine of checking the guns and spinning them back into place where the leather of the holsters was slick from years of use. Jake's mind was on other things. Like what he would do to the deserters if Shannon were hurt. The Henry stood in the corner, but he ignored it. He wouldn't need it today. He planned on doing his killing up close and personal. The pair of guns filled his hands comfortably. They were cocked and ready.

Jake checked the passage from the barn to the house. Only one set of tracks showed in the snow that had fallen at daybreak. The men must have arrived sometime during the night and kept the doctor along with Mose and Cook hostage inside. The one Jake had killed had come out sometime after the snow had stopped to snoop around in the barn, probably hoping to find a better horse than the one they had stolen from Shamus.

Jake decided to exit from the back of the barn and circle the house one time, just to make sure he had the numbers right. With luck, the remaining four would all be inside, close and convenient for killing.

Virgin snow surrounded the huge expanse of lawn that fronted the house. The creak of leather and the rattle of bits gave evidence of a group of horses left in a dense stand of hemlock. Jake made his way from tree to tree, cautiously circling and checking to make sure there would be no attack from an unknown source. He had let his guard down. He had become lazy in the past months. He should have remembered that he was a soldier still and there was a war going on.

The attack! He remembered the attack! Jake straightened behind a tree with the guns in his hands as the sounds and sights of that day filled his mind.

Caleb. Caleb had gone down. He saw it as clearly as he saw the mountains springing up around him. But Caleb had survived. He must have; how else would his drawings have wound up in the cave? *Please God, let Caleb be alive.*

Ty and Cat. He remembered seeing Ty on the trail and Cat behind him. Had they survived? Ty would die trying to save all of them. *Ty would die to keep Cat alive.*

Willie. Willie had died. That was the last thing he had seen as he flew off the horse and began the deadly descent down the hill, the horse rolling over him, crushing him, breaking him several times over before he landed, unconscious at last, in the cool water of the stream.

Were his friends still alive? Jake noticed that his hands were trembling. Was it from cold or fear?

Shannon. Please God, let Shannon be safe. He didn't want to think of what would happen to his fragile soul if she wasn't. The demons were too close as it was. All of the pain, all of the loss of his childhood, was like a fresh wound after years of being buried deep. He needed Shannon.

Those bastards had Shannon.

Jake completed his circle, confident that all enemies to his future were inside the building. He crept up to a window on the ward where he had been a patient. That was where they had left Shamus the night before.

The end where he had lain was empty, but then he saw a flash of bright color close to the door. Jake ducked beneath the long bank of windows and made his way stealthily toward the other end of the row. Quietly and cautiously he raised himself up far enough to peer over the sill.

Shamus lay in a bed with his head bandaged and a pale and suffering expression on his face. The man was probably in sore need of a drink. Jake couldn't say as he blamed him. Doc Blankenship was leaning over another bed, where a patient lay. Most likely the man Shamus had shot. A man holding a gun stood on the other side and behind him was Mose in the corner. Where was Shannon? There had to be two more men. Cook was missing too.

Most likely after medical attention, they wanted food.

They probably had Cook in the kitchen fixing food. But that didn't account for Shannon. Where was she?

He'd kill them all. And if they had hurt her, he'd kill them slow.

A crash from deep inside the house alerted him to the fact that someone was moving around. Dr. Blankenship cursed and looked at the man holding the gun in exasperation. Jake watched as the man gave Doc a threatening look before he stepped into the hall.

Jake tapped on the window with the tip of his finger. Dr. Blankenship was engrossed with his patient but Mose glanced his way.

The wizened old man smiled widely. Mose held up his hand with the five fingers spread apart and pointed at it with the other.

Jake held up four fingers and Mose nodded excitedly.

"Shannon?" he mouthed.

Mose held up his hands so they resembled claws and jerked his head toward the hallway.

She was fighting them.

Mose started shaking his head and Jake ducked down below the sill just as the man holding the gun came back into the ward.

Two men accounted for, one of them wounded and under the treatment of Dr. Blankenship. That left two men somewhere else in the building, most likely with Shannon and possibly Cook.

Surprise was on his side. Jake liked the odds. He stealthily crept toward the back door.

Cook was in the kitchen, cursing and cooking. That woman would give a hardened soldier pause, the way she carried on. She was alone. They must have forced her good behavior by threatening the others. Jake moved past the kitchen, glad that her tirade was loud enough to cover the sounds of the creaking floorboards.

He came upon the office where Shannon had treated his hand. The rumbling of deep voices led him to the conclusion that the other two were within, possibly with Shannon. The door was tightly shut and there was no way for him to look in without giving himself away.

Jake leaned against the wall and considered his dilemma. Two were within, another two were in the ward. He could break down the door, at least he hoped he could, and take out the two easily with his guns, but that all depended on where Shannon was. He would not risk her life under any circumstances. And then there was the problem of the man in the ward who was holding a gun on Doc Blankenship and Mose. Could he sacrifice their lives to save Shannon? What about her father?

Jake suddenly realized just how alone he was. He desperately missed his friends. How many times during the years had he shut them out? How many times had he gone off on his own without a word or a reason because it was easier that way? He had even done his mourning in private when Jamie died, determinedly acting as if it didn't affect him as deeply as it did the others.

He had been a fool. What he wouldn't give to have his friends at his side now. They would know what to do. They would take care of Shannon, just because they knew that he loved her. All he was good for was busting in with guns blazing.

Jake suddenly realized how lucky he was just to be alive after all his years of recklessness.

How much longer could his luck last?

He sidled up to the door, leaning an ear against it, hoping to hear something that would give him a clue as to Shannon's whereabouts. He was surprised that she hadn't screamed the house down. Knowing her, she had probably given all of them a severe tongue-lashing.

She was probably gagged. He was going to kill them.

The rumbling continued behind the closed door. They were arguing about something. He had to be sure of Shannon's location. He needed help.

Jake's gut twisted as his mind made the logical decision. He'd take out the two in the ward first and then he'd have Doc Blankenship and Mose on his side. He wasn't sure how much help they would be, but at least they could watch his back. He quietly made his way to the ward.

It was easier than he expected. Jake merely stepped through the door and placed a pistol at the back of the deserter's head.

"Drop your gun." He fought back the urge to blow the man's brains out.

"Mister Jake! Praise the Lord!" Mose cried.

The man cursed as he dropped his gun and raised his arms in the air.

"Where's Shannon?"

"Those other two took her off." Mose picked up the gun. "She was fightin' like a wildcat."

Jake shoved the deserter into the corner that Mose had occupied. "What's the story with this one?" he asked Dr. Blankenship.

"He took a bullet in the lungs." Doc kept his attention on his patient. "He's bleeding in there somewhere but I can't find it."

"If my brother dies, I'll kill all of you," the first man snarled from his place. Jake took a moment to look at him.

Lean and hard best described him. Jake wondered if he had always been bad or if the war had made him that way. It changed people, bringing out the best in some and the worst in others. It looked like it had done a number on this one.

"Are they still shooting deserters?" Jake asked.

"You tell me," the man snarled back. "Looks like you're taking a break from the lines yourself, Reb."

Jake couldn't argue with that. "Where I come from, they hang horse thieves."

"I wouldn't call what we stole a horse." The man was sizing him up, looking for an opportunity. Jake couldn't argue with his statement about Shamus's horse either.

"Where is Shannon?"

"My other brother is getting to know her better." The man smiled. "He has quite a way with the ladies. He's the lover in the family."

"And which one are you?"

"The mean one."

Jake knew the man was trying to make him mad. Trying desperately to goad him into making a mistake so he could get the upper hand again.

"Mose. You keep this gun on him. If he moves, shoot him."

"Yessur, Mister Jake, I'll do it."

"Doc?"

"Go take care of Shannon. Do what you have to do to get these bastards out of my hospital."

"Mister Jake?" Mose called as he stepped back into

the hall. Jake turned to look. "Does you remember now where you come from?"

"Yes, I do, Mose. I come from Wyoming."

"Wyoming, how 'bout that . . ." Mose was actually chuckling as Jake moved back into the hall.

Chapter Nineteen

Shannon did her best to ram her heel into the man's instep but her shoes were worn and she couldn't get much force behind the motion as she was sitting in a chair. She still felt some satisfaction, however, as the man danced away. Too bad she couldn't have given him a quick knee in his privates like she had the one who had been sent out to the barn.

The last thing she had expected to find when she came into the hospital earlier was five deserters from the Union Army. She had been preparing herself for a moral tongue-lashing from Mrs. Farley and the Reverend Mullens.

When she came into the ward and saw the men standing around with guns drawn on Dr. Blankenship and Mose while her poor Da lay helpless in his bed, she had been utterly shocked. She should have run. She should have warned Jake. How long would it be before he showed up, only to get himself killed?

Still, they didn't know about him. Unless the one who had disappeared toward the barn had figured out that it wasn't Mose who slept out there in the tack room but someone else. She fervently hoped Jake was still in the cabin where she had left him.

She felt her cheeks flaming above the rotten handkerchief that they had used as a gag. How could she be thinking about the night of passion she and Jake had just shared instead of figuring out a way to escape the predicament she was in? Her mortal life was in danger. But at least she would die knowing that bit of heaven she had experienced with Jake. Shannon wondered briefly if she would go to hell. She had always tried to do what was right and she knew that making love to a man without the blessing of marriage was a sin, but surely under the circumstances, the Lord would understand. Surely.

The one called Frank was looking at her again. She had figured out that three of them were brothers. The one shot, the one in the ward and this one. They all had the same look about them: mean. Although the one called Frank would be considered good-looking by some. The wounded one was younger and didn't look as jaded as the older ones, but maybe it was because he was hurt. Pete, they had called him, and the third one was Mitchell.

The other two seemed to do whatever the three brothers said. Frank and Mitchell bossed them around, sending the one off to search the barn, telling the other to tie her hands and gag her, and barking orders at Dr.

Blankenship like he could just snap his fingers and make his brother better.

Maybe she shouldn't have jumped on Mitchell's back when he leaned over Da's bed and threatened to gut him if Pete died. The side of her head was still ringing from the blow he had given her, making her realize that the few times Da had struck her were nothing compared to this violence. She would bruise up for sure. And wouldn't that look nice when she sang at the Christmas service.

You'll most likely be dead and buried by Christmas, Shannon. She watched the two men as they put their heads together. They were talking about her. The unrelated one was all for having his way with her. Shannon squeezed her legs together tightly as she caught bits and pieces of the conversation. *Please, God, no. Not after Jake.*

Frank wanted to wait for Mitchell. But that didn't keep them both from teasing and tormenting her. They kept looking at her as if they wanted to strip her clothes off. And the unrelated one kept playing with her hair, which had lost all its pins when she jumped on Mitchell's back.

It was a game. They were bored and they were mean. They were tired of waiting around. How long would it be before they got tired of waiting for Mitchell to come and give them permission to rape her?

Four of them. There were four of them, possibly five. Would she have the strength to fight them off? Would she survive it? Would Jake still want her after they had used her?

Jake. Please, God, keep him safe and away from this

madness. Let them just leave and leave us all in peace.

He would come for her. If there was any way possible, if the one in the barn didn't find him and kill him, he would come. But how could he possibly fight all of them? He would die trying. That's the way he was. He was protective. He had even bought her a coat because he was worried about her not having one. He would come if he could.

How long had it been? It seemed like ages since she had been shoved into the office and tied to the chair. Surely the man who had gone out had had plenty of time to search the grounds by now. He could be in her cabin right now, standing over Jake's dead body.

But they hadn't heard a thing. Surely there hadn't been a gunshot; one of them would have checked if there had been. But that didn't mean it couldn't have happened. Jake hadn't worn a weapon in all the time she'd known him, except for yesterday when he'd carried his rifle. But he hadn't brought that to the cabin.

Shannon fought back the impulse to gag as the stench from the cloth that had been stuffed in her mouth overwhelmed her. Frank was looking at her again.

The door flew open and crashed against the wall beside the jamb as it made the full rotation of its hinges. Two shots were fired before Shannon had time to complete a blink of her eyes. The two men fell to the floor, their mouths hanging open in shock and surprise as their lives left their bodies. Shannon looked on in amazement at Jake as the twin guns twirled their way back into their holsters.

He pulled the putrid gag away. "Are you hurt?" He grabbed her shoulders and lowered himself to eye level. "Did they hurt you?"

All she could do was shake her head. She still could not believe what she had just seen.

Jake went to work on the knots that tied her in the chair. As soon as he had one arm free, Shannon threw it around him. She was trembling. How had he killed both men so quickly?

Jake worked at the knot that held her other arm to the side of the chair. Shannon looked over the wild tufts of his pale blond hair and saw Mitchell standing in the door with a gun in his hand.

"*Jake!*" she screamed and shoved herself up with her legs, moving him away from the bullet that was speeding toward his back. Jake tumbled off to the side, snarling, rolling and drawing his pistol in one quick motion and firing toward the door.

"No!" he yelled as the bullet hit Shannon in the gut, slamming her back. Her bright red hair flew up, as the blood spewed forth with a gush from the wound.

Jake's bullet grazed across Mitchell's cheek and he ran from the room with his hand pressed over it to staunch the flow of blood. Jake wanted desperately to go after him and finish the job, but Shannon was hurt. She was bleeding. She had taken the bullet that was meant for him.

"Shannon!" Jake fell to his knees in front of the chair. The knot would not come undone. Her head lolled forward and her hair fell back around her face and into her lap. The blood was soaking it, turning the bright red into a dark burgundy as it flowed forth onto her skirt. "Oh God, please no. . . ." Jake fought the knot and finally freed her arm.

He pushed her hair back, looking into her face, searching desperately for a sign of life. He pressed his hand against the wound and she moaned.

"Doc!" Jake yelled as he gathered Shannon into his arms. "Mose!"

Cook came running down the hall from the kitchen with a large knife in her hand. Dr. Blankenship and Mose came staggering after her.

"He had a knife in his boot, Mister Jake," Mose was explaining. He stopped cold when he saw Shannon's lifeless form in Jake's arms and the stricken look on his face.

"He's gone," Doc said as he looked at Shannon's wound. "He dragged his brother off with him. They won't get far in the shape the younger one's in."

The sound of horses running confirmed Mitchell's escape.

"Doc?" Jake's voice broke.

"We got to get that bullet out, son." Doc led the way toward the surgery.

Dr. Blankenship cut Shannon's clothes away, revealing the pale porcelain-white of her skin. The wound was an angry hole in her stomach. Jake wiped at the blood while Doc searched for instruments. Cook produced a pot of hot water and then left as quietly as she had come.

"Is she going to die?" Jake asked. The blood kept on coming.

"I've seen worse." Doc placed some instruments in the water and then pulled one of them out with a pair of tongs. "Let's hope she doesn't feel this," he said as he inserted the probe into the wound.

Shannon jerked against the table.

"Hold her down, son," the doctor instructed Jake as he moved the instrument around.

Jake held her shoulders against the table and watched in desperate fascination as Dr. Blankenship searched for the bullet. *Please, God. Please, don't take her away from me. Not now, not when I've finally got a chance to do it right. . . .*

"Got it!" he announced. He reached for a large set of bullet forceps that were still soaking in the water while he held the probe inside her. Jake's stomach turned as he saw the forceps go in, widening the hole that marred the perfection of her pearly skin.

"Hold on, Shannon, we've almost got it . . . ," Jake whispered.

The bullet landed in a pewter bowl with a clang and Jake let out the breath that he hadn't even realized he'd been holding.

"Now we just need to get this bleeding stopped," Doc said, more to himself than to Jake.

Jake smoothed the bright hair back from her pale face. "Shannon, Doc did it, he got the bullet out . . ." He realized he was rambling but he didn't care. He needed desperately to know she was all right. If only she would open her bright green eyes. If only she would say something . . .

"I dragged them bodies out and put 'em with the other one," Mose reported from the door. "Is Miss Shannon gonna be all right? Her daddy's wantin' to know what's going on."

"Tell him when we know something, he'll know something," Doc barked over his shoulder. "Best send somebody for the magistrate too."

"Is that fine with you, Mister Jake?" Mose asked.

It took Jake a moment to understand what Mose was

asking. "It's fine, Mose, I don't have a problem with the law being around." Jake had to give Mose credit for figuring out a lot of things on his own. Jake hadn't been sure of whether or not he was a wanted man. He wasn't. He could be proud of that much in his past.

Cook reappeared carrying Shannon's gown. She cast a sardonic look at Jake as she laid it at the foot of the table. Jake had the decency to look away. He knew the tumbled state of the sheets in Shannon's cabin told the story clearly enough for anyone who entered.

"Think you can carry her into the ward?" Doc asked as he wiped his hands. The wound was heavily padded and wrapped with as much bandage as the doctor could find. "Without disturbing the wound?"

Jake nodded in affirmation. With extreme care, he slid his arms under Shannon's limp form and lifted her tenderly to his chest. Her head lolled against his shoulder and a small whimper escaped from between her parted lips.

Doc led the way to the ward. "We'll put her next to her father. You know she'll be worried about him when she wakes up."

When she wakes up. Jake caught the words and held them close. When, *not* if. *She's going to wake up. . . . she has to.*

Gently he lowered her to the bed. She was fragile. She was precious. The bright red of her hair stood out starkly against the sheets and against her face, which was so pale that her lips had taken on a bluish cast. Jake smoothed back her hair and looked at her closely. The few freckles scattered across her nose seemed darker against the translucent frailty of her skin. The veins beneath her skin were much more prominent than usual. How could anyone be so pale? How could anyone so full of life be this lifeless? He sank into the chair that had mysteriously appeared beside him.

Jake gathered her hand in his. He held her fingers together in one hand while the other caressed her cheek.

"Shannon. . . ." Jake put his head down on the mattress and wept. As he cried, he remembered the last time he had done so. It had been twenty-odd years ago and he had been just a boy barely old enough to go to school. He had promised himself then that no matter what happened, no matter how hard his father beat him, he would not see him cry again. Luckily for Jake, his father was far, far away.

Chapter Twenty

"You gwanna eat sumthin', Mister Jake?" How many times had Mose asked him that in the past few days? "You has to eat."

Jake looked at the tray of food that Mose held out for him. Why bother? He knew it would be tasteless and flat, just as his life was at the moment.

"Best ye eat somethin', boy," Shamus added from his bed. "She's not going anywhere anytime soon."

Jake wondered once again how the man could be so cavalier about his daughter's health. Yes, she was still alive. Yes, she was still breathing, but that was all she was doing. She hadn't moved since he had placed her in the bed—how many days ago was it? Jake realized he had lost count of the days.

"What day is it, Mose?" Mose had announced the days when he had been a patient. Why had he stopped now?

"It's Friday, December the twenty-third, Mister Jake."

Two days until Christmas. Shannon was supposed to sing on Christmas Day for the church service.

"Shannon, wake up. It's almost Christmas." How many times had he begged her to wake up since she'd been shot? How many times had he wiped her brow and squeezed her hand? How many times had he told her he loved her?

More than he could count.

Half of the town had come by. He had not realized how much the small town cared for one of its own, even one who was a bit of an oddity. Ingrid had come, Mrs. Farley, Reverend Mullens and assorted members of the choir . . . a steady parade of people had come by and looked at her still form and declared it a shame that something so bad had happened to such a sweet, hard-working girl. The Christmas service would not be as grand without her wonderful voice. The choir would miss her. Her solo would have been beautiful. On and on they went with their platitudes and their sympathy. Jake willed them on their way so he could have her to himself again. So he could beg her to wake up and look at him with those vivid green eyes. He had so much to tell her. He wanted to tell her everything. He had waited his entire life for someone to talk to and now that he'd found her, she couldn't listen.

"You sure you don't want none, Mister Jake?" Mose asked again. "Cook will bite my head off if I go back in there with this tray full o' food."

"Eat, boy, she'll wake up when she's good and ready," Shamus assured him. "She's a stubborn one, she is. Like her mother, God rest her soul. Got her green eyes straight from her."

Jake wished he could kill him. Or least hit him. He

couldn't for the life of him understand why Cook had suddenly taken a liking to the man. She had personally taken over his care and fussed over him like he was an invalid. Jake was sure Shamus was still lying about just for the attention he was getting from the woman. He sure hadn't given up on getting Mose to sneak him in a bottle of whiskey. Jake figured that Shamus's craving for a drink would win out over all the babying and he would soon slip out the door and visit the tavern.

"Leave the tray, Mose," Jake said.

"Yassur." Mose grinned widely. "I done took care of yo' horse today too. And all the rest of 'em that got left behind. That stable is purt near overflowin' with horseflesh now. And that orange cat sho' do miss you. He was all over my shoes today a yowlin' and a hollerin', 'where is Mister Jake?'" Mose took his time leaving, mixing meows into his language in imitation of a cat pretending to speak. Jake shook his head at the man's antics and stirred the eggs around on his plate.

Had she moved her hand? The tray had quivered just a bit where Mose had laid it on the bed next to Shannon's arm. Jake moved it to the bed behind him and picked up her hand.

"Shannon?" He squeezed her fingers. "Can you hear me?"

An eyelid fluttered.

Jake leaned closer and looked into her face. "Shannon, open your eyes."

Her forehead wrinkled and her mouth twitched.

"Shannon?"

A green eye appeared only to hide again behind a pale lid.

"Shannon, wake up, please wake up."

Both eyes blinked against the light of late morning. They concentrated on the ceiling for a moment before they turned and focused on his face.

"What happened?" she whispered from lips that felt parched and dry.

"You were shot." Jake gathered both her hands in his. "You saved my life."

"Again?" Her smile danced weakly at the corners of her mouth.

"Several times over," Jake laughed as he planted a kiss on her forehead. "And that's not the half of it." He smoothed back a lock of her bright red hair. "We've got a lot to talk about."

"We do?" Her hand drifted down to the padding on her stomach. "I remember, you shot them. How did you do that?"

"It's just something I can do."

"Looks like ye got yerself a gunfighter there, daughter," Shamus chimed in from his bed.

"Da? Are you fine?" Shannon turned her head to look at him.

"Aye, that is, I will be as soon as the doctor turns loose of some of his whiskey."

"Da!"

Jake laughed and she turned back to look at him.

"You got it back," she stated simply.

"I did."

"How?"

"It just happened." He snapped his fingers. "Just like that." He didn't add what had triggered it. That was still something he did not want to think about.

"So you'll be leaving soon?" The fear showed in her deep green eyes and pale face.

"As soon as you're able to travel," he said as he leaned in to kiss her.

"No wife?" she whispered, as his lips lingered. She was still afraid of what her father would hear.

"Only a few close friends," Jake whispered back. "I can't wait for you to meet them. All of them."

Her answering smile was glorious.

"So our patient has awakened!" Dr. Blankenship said as he came into the room. "We were beginning to think you were going to stay abed longer than Jake did."

"There are some who would be calling me lazy if I lay about that long," Shannon retorted saucily.

Dr. Blankenship took a moment to examine her wound. "You gave us quite a scare, young lady." He looked over his glasses at Jake. "Quite a scare." He moved the wrappings back into place. "Plenty of rest and you'll be fine," he said as he patted her hand. "And for you, I recommend some exercise," he said as he moved to Shamus's bed.

"Exercise!" Shamus exclaimed. "All I need is a drink of fine whiskey and I'll be fit as a fiddle."

Dr. Blankenship flipped back the blankets. "Exercise. You've lain about so long that you're about to blend into the woodwork. Now get up. We're going for a walk."

"And leave me only daughter here unchaperoned with this gunslinger?" Shamus protested. "Why, her mother and her Gran would be spinning in their graves."

"Then both of them would be getting more exercise than you." The doctor pulled at Shamus until he rose from the bed, protesting the awful treatment he was receiving.

"Come on, Shamus. We'll go see Cook and you can tell her all about how evil I am. As a matter of fact, you two can compare notes. I'm sure she has plenty of tales to tell on me."

Jake and Shannon watched them leave with their heads together, chuckling as the two men argued their way down the hall.

"What do you think of Wyoming?" Jake asked when they were gone. He leaned in close, enjoying the feel of her hands in his, knowing that now when he squeezed them, they would respond.

"Can't say that I have ever thought of it," Shannon replied. Why did she feel so giddy inside? Was she weak because of the wound, or was it because Jake was sitting here holding her hand and grinning like an idiot? She wanted to laugh out loud just for the joy of it but was afraid to do so, because of her injury.

"Well, maybe you'd better start."

"Is that where we're going?" Why did it give her such joy to ask that question?

"After we go to North Carolina."

"What's in North Carolina?"

"The woman who wrote the letter."

"And she is?" Shannon dreaded the answer despite his previous assurance that he had no wife.

"A friend. I worked for her father. Before the war. And her husband was not only my friend but my commanding officer. I have to find out what happened to them all." The foolish grin of joy at having Shannon awake faded as his concern for his friends took its place.

"They were with you when you were attacked?"

"Yes," Jake said, wrestling with his fear and worry over Cat, Ty and Caleb. "They must have thought I'd died."

"They wouldn't have seen you; I didn't until I was right on top of you."

"Caleb must have survived. He was the one who drew the picture that you found in the cave." "And you remember that too?"

"Yes, he drew it after one of our battles." Jake leaned back in his chair as he kept his hold on her hand. "The boy, the one you saw, his name was Willie."

"You were close to him," she said as the pain filled his pale blue eyes.

"As close as I'd let him be. He followed me around like a puppy. I was always pushing him away."

"It wasn't your fault that he died. It was the war."

"I know." It was good to have his memory back, but the sight of Willie dying was one he wished he could forget again. "I had even promised to take him back to Wyoming when the war was over." He would never forget the joy on Willie's face when he had told him that. He still didn't know why he had offered, but at the time it had seemed like the thing to do. The right thing to do.

"You have a good heart, Jacob Anderson. I knew it from the start."

"I haven't, not always."

"When you didn't remember, your true self came through. You couldn't hide that part of you."

"I've done a lot of things that I'm not proud of, Shannon."

"You've done good things too."

"How do you know?"

"I just do. Why else would a boy named Willie follow you around?"

"He had scars on his back just like mine." Jake

dropped her hand, suddenly frightened. The conversation was getting too personal.

"How did you get them?"

"From my father." His voice was that of a grown man, but he felt like a frightened boy when he said it.

Slowly, carefully, Shannon rose from her bed, ignoring the flash of heat that radiated from her wound. Her head swam and the room spun, but she willed herself to get up. To go to him before he closed her off. She saw the fear in his eyes and knew that he was remembering something. A horrible memory.

"What are you doing?" His eyes narrowed as he fell into his old habit of self-preservation.

"Shhh, it's all right now," she said as she gently wrapped her arms around his shoulders.

Jake blinked against the sudden warmth that enfolded him. His arms slowly twined around her waist, taking special care not to touch the wound, and his head rested against her breast.

"You didn't do anything wrong," she whispered against the pale blond tips of his hair.

I didn't do anything wrong. . . . He held her close as her warmth and her love enfolded him. He felt the guilt fall away. It wasn't his fault his father was crazy. He hadn't done anything wrong. Relief flooded through him. Tears filled his eyes as the burden he had been carrying fell away. He had cried twice in the last week. That was more than he had cried in the last twenty years. The wall he had built around himself came tumbling down and he found that he liked what he saw behind it. There was hope and there was a future. There was Shannon.

Chapter Twenty-one

Jenny looked once again at the dining room table. It still looked like a puzzle with a couple of pieces missing. With half of the china broken in the attack she'd had to fill in with some of the everyday dishes. The montage of mismatched plates and glasses aggravated her sense of order and well-being. She wanted this Christmas to be perfect after all they had been through in the past few weeks.

"Momma?"

"In here," she called out to her son. Chance came into the dining room, tracking mud behind him.

"Chance!" Jenny yelled. "I just cleaned the floors!"

Chance looked down at the clumps of mud that clung to his boots. "Sorry, I forgot."

"What have you been into?"

"I've been helping Zeb. Can I have a cookie?"

"Where is Fox?"

"He's still helping. Can I, Momma?"

Jenny felt her stomach tighten as she realized that the boys would need another bath before dinner. She had a million things to do before the house would be ready for the Christmas Eve festivities, and she had nowhere to turn for help. The men were still out searching for the perfect Christmas tree and Agnes was frantic in the kitchen, trying to get all her baking done so she could get to town and spend Christmas with her brand-new granddaughter. Amanda had literally stayed in her room since the attack, not even coming down for meals. The few times anyone caught sight of her, she looked lifeless and soulless, as if she were doing her best to remain unnoticed. Jenny knew she was still shaken by the attack and terrified of seeing the ghost that had warned them out of the house. Jenny wished she had time to sit down and talk to her, but the few attempts she had made to enter into conversation with Amanda had been unsuccessful. Chances were Amanda wouldn't believe her explanation that the ghost was her dead brother Jamie anyway. And with all the repairs that needed to be made to the house, along with the clean up and getting ready for Christmas, Jenny just didn't have time to deal with any more problems at the moment.

She hated to put any additional stress on Grace. She had been sad and discouraged since she had returned from her aborted honeymoon. Jenny couldn't say that she blamed her either. Jason kept telling Grace not to worry, that it was just a matter of time before the papers could be filed, the divorce granted and the two of them legally married. But it was winter and Cole's marriage to Constance had taken place in Texas. It could be months before they heard anything. More months than Grace had left in her pregnancy.

"Please, Momma?"

Jenny knelt down and wiped at the mud on Chance's face with the corner of her apron. His brilliant blue eyes, so striking in his dark face, watched her earnestly as she cleaned off most of the dirt. Jenny leaned back and assessed her efforts with a sigh. On top of everything else, she had been experiencing morning sickness that lasted way into the afternoon. She and Chase had wanted to announce her pregnancy on Christmas Day, but with the way she had been running to the privy, everyone probably had it all figured out by now.

"Have you had your lunch yet?"

"Yes, Grace fixed me and Fox and Zeb some lunch and we ate it all gone."

"Then go ask Agnes if she has any broken cookies and you may share one with Fox." His quick smile lit his face. "Wait, take your boots off and put them on the porch."

Chance dropped where he stood in the long hall and kicked his boots off, using his feet. The mud that was caked to them flew in every direction as he pushed them off and then proudly carried them to the back door. Jenny shook her head. She couldn't be mad at him when she had done the same thing in her childhood. And just like her mother, she was going to have to mop again. At least she had saved Agnes from another disaster in her kitchen. She also knew that the generous woman would fix her son a plate full of cookies, along with a large glass of milk. But it was Christmas, so let her spoil him. Why should Agnes be different from everyone else who lived on the ranch?

Jenny decided there wasn't anything more she could do for the dining room. The parlor was still waiting for the tree. Jason's study had been cleaned and the treats set out for the men to enjoy. The presents were all wrapped and stacked so he could pass them out to each and every one. Jenny hoped that the trunk full of gifts and necessities that had been sent to Cat and Ty in North Carolina had arrived safely. Cat's last letter had said that even though she had money, she could not find a thing to spend it on. The war and Yankee blockades had wrung everything out of the South.

Three faces would be missing from the group as they gathered around the table this year. During the war they had prayed for the safety of Ty, Cat, Caleb and Jake. They had prayed for their safe and quick return. Jenny hoped Cat and Ty would be back by next year. Surely the war could not last that much longer. Caleb was already back, but still not himself. War had taken a heavy toll on him, depriving him of far more than his leg. Jenny guessed that he missed Jake worse than he let on. They all did. She wished again that she had known him better. He had always been there for her but had never said much. At other times, his dry humor had put them all in stitches. He had shared their tragedies and triumphs. He had been a part of their lives. Now he was gone, never to return. Jason had plans to put a marker for him up on the hill next to Jamie's. He was just waiting for Ty and Cat to come home to do it. And they had their own plans to memorialize him, she and Chase. The babe, if it was a boy, would be named after him.

Jenny ran a hand over her still-flat stomach and wandered into Jason's study to look out the window toward the ridge where her twin brother's earthly remains lay. The pain always seemed so close at Christmastime.

Was it because of all the happy Christmases they had shared as children? Her mind was filled with an image of Ian, her tall and handsome father, laughing with joy as she and Jamie squealed in delight over the presents hiding beneath the tree. Then there was her mother, Faith, graceful and shining with love as she joined him. Had there been any two children who had been more blessed? Jenny didn't think so as the memories of her childhood flitted through her mind.

Even when the two of them had been sent to the orphanage after the murder of their parents, they had had each other until fate had separated them for so many long years. Jenny smiled wistfully as she recalled the days after she had finally found Jamie. The last Christmas they'd spent together was a bittersweet memory. They had talked late into the night. Jenny was newly pregnant and keeping it a secret. Jamie was desperately in love and ready to marry the girl of his dreams. A week later he was dead, murdered in the street on his wedding day.

A tear trickled slowly down her cheek as Jenny looked out the window toward the grave of her brother. "It's not fair," she said with a fist clenched at her side. Would she ever stop feeling the pain of his loss? She knew the answer. She would be old and gray and on her deathbed and still miss Jamie. He was a part of her. They had shared a bond that few would know. Not even Chance and Fox, as close as they were in age, shared the kind of closeness she'd had with her twin.

Jenny wiped her eyes with the back of her hand. She didn't have time for this. The mud was quickly drying on the floor. The decorations for the tree were still in the attic. The boys needed a bath. Her list was long and still she stood in the study, looking out over the ridge, missing a brother who had been gone for almost four years.

The pain was still as fresh as if it had happened today.

The sounds of footsteps in the foyer bought her back to the present. Jenny made sure her tears were hidden as she turned to see who it was.

"Momma, I brought you a present!" Fox said as he ran into the study. Zeb stood in the doorway, grinning broadly. Her musings must have been deep. She hadn't even noticed the two of them coming up the hill.

Jenny knelt to her nephew's level as he came to her with grubby hands cradling a tiny bird's nest. "We found it in the barn. Zeb said it fell down from the rafters." Fox relayed his knowledge with a serious expression on his winsome face.

Just like his father, Jenny thought as she examined the perfect little nest. "It's beautiful," she said as she saw how proud he was of his find.

"Can we put it in the Christmas tree?"

"Yes, you may."

Fox grinned up at Zeb as if they had a conspiracy going on.

"Fox?" Jenny asked as he turned toward his large companion. "Can I have a hug?" Jenny spread her arms wide as she knelt on the floor. Fox turned back and ran into her arms, carefully cradling the nest. Jenny hugged him tight, trying her best not to crush him as her longing for Jamie coursed through her body. *Thank you, God, for this child. Thank you so much.*

"Why are you crying?" Fox asked. His wide blue eyes were full of concern.

Just like Jamie. "Because I'm happy." Jenny sniffed as she checked the buttons on his coat. "Agnes has cookies in the kitchen if Chance hasn't eaten all of them. Why don't you go see what's left."

Fox deposited the nest in her hands and took off at a run toward the kitchen.

"That boy sure do notice the little things," Zeb said as he watched Fox run down the hall.

"His father was the same way," Jenny said as she dried her eyes again. "He could sit for hours and watch a gopher hole."

"I hear tell he was a fine man, Miz Jenny," Zeb said. "I sure do appreciate you givin' me some of his clothes and such."

"I'm glad to see that somebody can use them." She didn't add that it pained her to see Jamie's things on his body, not because she resented Zeb's wearing them, but just because she still missed him.

"Y'all done been real good to me, Miz Jenny, and I surely am grateful."

"Thank you, Zeb." Jenny stood and placed the nest on Jason's desk. "You will be joining us tonight, won't you?"

Zeb looked shyly at his feet. "Are you sure you want me at the table, Miz Jenny?"

Jenny walked over and placed her hand on his arm. "Zeb, we all want you at the table. You are an important part of this ranch, and besides that, my boys adore you. Can I count on you to be here?"

"Yes, ma'am, I'll come." His smile stretched from ear to ear.

Squeals came from the front of the house, followed by the sounds of pounding feet. "Momma, look at the tree!"

Jenny and Zeb went into the hall. Chase had a boy on each hip as he turned to look at his wife with glowing eyes and a soft smile. "We brought it around to the front," he explained. "It was too big to drag up the hill."

"What?" Jenny said as she walked toward them, suddenly glad she hadn't mopped the floor for the second time.

"It's huge!" Chance announced. Fox nodded in agreement, blue eyes as wide as saucers.

Jenny walked out onto the porch. A tree, twice as long as the wagon it lay on, greeted her, along with the smiling faces of Zane, Caleb, Cole and Jason. Justice wagged his tail from his perch on the bench.

"It's a doozy," Zane said, obviously pleased with himself.

Jenny looked at it in amazement. "Are you sure it will fit through the door?"

"We'll make it fit," Chase said assuredly.

"It better fit, or I'll be shooting someone," Cole said as he looked at Zane.

"Dang," Jenny said. All other words had failed her.

Chapter Twenty-two

Jake had told her everything. Shamus had been moved to another room since he refused to leave the comfort of the hospital, using his daughter's injury as an excuse. They all knew the truth, especially Cook, who volunteered to take care of him. What she really meant was spoil him, but no one minded. They all figured he needed some spoiling.

So when Jake and Shannon were finally left alone in the ward on the morning of Christmas Eve, Jake explained about growing up in Minnesota, the only son of a preacher who saw the devil in everything around him. He told her about the meals that grew cold and stale while his father's blessings ran on and on and how if any of them dared to move an inch during the ramblings, they would go hungry. He told her about the fire-and-brimstone sermons that would last all day with some of the parishioners passing out from hunger. He told her about the constant beatings that he received as a boy for the slightest infraction of his father's stark and sadistic rules, and then the whippings that came when he reached his teens and started to grow and change.

Jake told Shannon of his decision to run away when he was fifteen years old. He told her of how he stole food just to survive. He told her of how an outlaw gang took him in instead of killing him for stealing from them. He had expected to die that day. He had wanted to, but instead they took a liking to him, felt a kinship with him. They taught him how to handle a gun until he was the best one of the bunch and they grew fearful of him. He was nothing more than a boy of seventeen and they were all afraid of him. He told Shannon of the day when they were robbing a bank where a trap had been set for them. He was the only one who got away. The only one who survived. He had realized then that by living as an outlaw, he was proving his father was right. But more than anything, he wanted to prove that the preacher was wrong. He had drifted then, making a living by hiring himself out as a gunman. He managed to survive those years without getting into trouble with the law although he had done his share of killing. He had finally met a man named Jason Lynch who saw something promising behind the deadly façade he maintained. Jason had taken him on as a cowhand on his ranch. At first he had been bored with the day-to-day routine, but there was something about hanging out with the other hands, something about the camaraderie that made him stay. He felt like he was part of a family. He felt as if someone cared whether he lived or died. He had found a home.

Jake told her of his life there. He told her of his

friends. He told her of how Jamie and Chase had come to work with them, and about Jamie's sister, Jenny, turning up after Jamie had searched for her for years. He told Shannon about the fun they had, about the day he threw Jenny and Cat into the puddle and the ensuing mud fight. He told Shannon about the cattle drive and how Jenny and Jamie had decided to pay a visit to their old home in Iowa and about the man who took Jenny.

As he told the tale of Jenny's rescue, Jake realized that he knew exactly how Chase had felt that day. He had lived it himself when he realized that Shannon was in danger. Jake held on to Shannon's hand as he told her the story. He never wanted to feel that desperate, hollow anger again.

He told her about Jenny's recovery after the horrible things that had happened to her. He told her about the wedding with all the frills and lace that Cat could come up with in the wilds of Wyoming.

He told her about the dance and the fight and how they had all spent the night in jail and how they were all more afraid of Jenny than of the law, and Shannon laughed at the telling.

He told her about Jamie and about his dying, and she told him about Will and his dying. And he knew that her loss had been greater. He knew something then of what Jenny had felt. And Chase, who had loved Jamie as a brother.

Then Jake told her of his time at war, how he was seeking his own death fighting for a cause that his father was against. He told her of Willie and of the battles. He told her how he would charge into the midst of the fighting with no thought for anyone or anything but killing and dying.

And once again she told him it was not his fault. Not any of it. He believed it now.

They spent all of Christmas Eve day talking, except for the times when Shannon napped, dozing off in the middle of a conversation because she was still weak from her wound. Jake stayed by her side the entire day. He was there when she fell asleep, there when she awoke.

Finally, when night had come and the talking was over, he crawled into the bed next to hers and sought his rest, weary and relieved after all the worry of the past few days. Jake wondered as he lay there listening to the peaceful breathing of Shannon in the other bed what his friends were doing back in Wyoming. He recalled the joyous Christmases they had shared through the years and he fondly remembered the last Christmas he had spent there. Jamie had been alive and Jason had gifted them all with the Henry rifles. Since then he had been at war and the men had passed the holidays as most soldiers do, remembering the good times that had passed. All of Jake's good memories settled around the ranch and his friends. He said a prayer for Caleb, Ty and Cat, hopeful that they had survived the attack, and hopeful that they had escaped and made their way back home instead of being imprisoned in the North. It was all he could do for them at the present. He finally fell into an exhausted sleep, content with the world around him.

Jake blinked his eyes and wondered where he was for a moment. The way the sunlight danced through the window and illuminated the floating dust motes told him it was late morning. Late Christmas morning. He stretched lazily and turned to greet the love of his life, only to find that she wasn't there. Her bed was not only empty, it was neatly made up.

"Shannon?" he called as he threw back his blanket and began the search for his boots.

Mose stuck his head through the doorway. "'Bout time you got up, Mister Jake. It's purt near onto lunchtime."

"Where's Shannon?" Jake jerked on his boots.

"She done gone up to her cabin to take a bath. And she said fer you to take one too, soon as she's done with the tub. She's gwanna sing fer the Christmas service and the entire town is coming to hear it."

"She's what?"

"She done rolled out of bed this mawnin' and said she's gwanna sing."

"What did Doc say?" Jake asked as he stepped into the hall.

"He said if she feels like singin', then to go on and do it." Mose goosed Jake in the side with his elbow and gave him a laugh and a wink. "Doc done said she can do whatever she feels like doin'."

Jake went on down the hall, ignoring the innuendo.

"Cook left you some breakfast in the kitchen," Mose called after him. "Mister Jake?"

"What?"

"Merry Christmas!"

Jake turned and looked at the wizened figure grinning broadly in the hall. "Merry Christmas, Mose."

It was a beautiful day. Jake stepped out onto the back porch munching on a biscuit-and-egg sandwich, and greeted it joyously, greedily sucking in the crisp, clear air. It had snowed again during the night, just enough to blanket the earth with a clean covering and swell the naked branches of the big oak trees. In the distance the sound of sleigh bells could be heard as a family passed by the road out front, on their way to enjoy Christmas festivities.

Had there ever been such a glorious morning? He could not recall. But then again, he had never been in love before. He had also never been free of the guilt he had carried since he was a small child. Shannon had absolved him of all his sins with her love. Wasn't it amazing how being in love could change one's outlook? But what was that smell? It wasn't the usual rotten-egg smell coming from the hot springs. Jake lifted an arm and realized that the smell came from his body. He was still wearing the shirt he'd had on when he was attacked in the barn. The front of it was crusted with Shannon's blood, and he felt a draft along the back where it had been torn by the whip. Luckily he had another shirt. As a matter of fact, it was a shirt that Jenny had made and given him before they had left for the war. But that was the extent of his wardrobe. His boots were in good shape—they were still practically brand-new—but his pants were worn and his shell jacket was frayed.

He needed something decent to wear. After all, he was going to church to hear Shannon sing.

"Mose?" Jake yelled as he stepped back inside the house. "Mose, where do you keep the clothes?"

"What clothes?" Mose asked as he came down the hall.

"The clothes from the soldiers, the ones who don't make it." His words sank in. *Some of them don't make it. Some of them do.* He was a lucky man. A very lucky man.

Mose smiled his broad smile. "I think I knows what you're looking for," he said and he encouraged Jake to follow him up the stairs. They both came down a few minutes later, pleased with what they had found in the stores Doc kept for the soldiers who passed through the hospital.

"I'll fetch you the tub just as soon as Miz Shannon gets done with it."

"Thanks, Mose," Jake said. "I'll be back as soon as I talk to Reverend Mullens."

"I'll make sure Cook takes care of the rest of it, Mister Jake."

"And make sure that she doesn't tell Shamus," Jake added. "That old fool would give it away for sure."

Mose went on his way, cackling over the secret Jake had shared with him upstairs. "Miz Shannon sho' is in fo' a surprise. Them's lots in this town that's in fo' a surprise. Miz Shannon's about to get the bestest Christmas present ever. Won't Doc be proud when he hears about it? Yesum, it's gwanna be a Merry Christmas fo' sho'."

Shannon looked at the group gathered around the table for the afternoon meal. Doc, Cook and Mose all looked as if they were about to bust wide open. They kept goosing each other and smiling as if they were sharing some sort of joke. Her father had his head buried in his plate, shoveling in the wild turkey, dressing and sweet potatoes as if he hadn't had a decent meal in a year, which was more than likely the case, at least since she had moved out. Jake was nowhere to be seen although Mose assured her that he would join them as soon as he was done gettin' fixed up. They had said the blessing and gone on without him as if they couldn't wait to get the meal over with.

Shannon was bewildered, to say the least. She had risen early that morning, feeling fine, although her wound still pained her a bit. It had thrilled her to see Jake still sleeping in the bed next to her, although she would have liked it more if he had slept with her. She still got all trembly inside when she recalled the night they had spent together. And now he had his memory back and had assured her that nothing stood in their way. He wanted to take her to Wyoming. She planted a kiss on the stubble of his cheek and went to her cabin. She was going to take a long, hot bath and wash her hair. She was going to put on her nice dress and she was going to sing in the Christmas service. It was a glorious day. Never mind that she didn't have a present under the tree, or even a Christmas tree for that matter. She had received the best gift ever. She had received love.

The snow hanging on the branches of the hemlocks and pines was more beautiful than the tree Mrs. Farley had every year, which was hung with fine glass ornaments and lit with candles. The crisp, clean feel of the air was more wonderful than any room full of festive people celebrating the season with fancy punch and tables laden with pretty dishes. The sounds of the birds chirping and the squirrels scampering from branch to snow-covered branch was more glorious than any carol that had ever been sung, although she hoped to give them some competition later when she did her part in the Christmas service.

Shannon did a pirouette in the snow and kicked at a

drift, heedless of both the flakes that slipped into her shoe and the wound in her gut, although it did hurt sometimes. She didn't care. Nothing mattered except for the man who lay sleeping in the ward. Jacob Anderson. She loved Jacob Anderson and he loved her. It was the best present she had ever received. She would treasure it forever.

Shannon took special care to make sure she looked her best before the afternoon meal. She put on her fine green dress with the lace collar and tried her best to pin her hair up into a tidy bun, only to have a few tendrils escape and hang down her back. She finally decided she had done all she could with it and added the green ribbon. She left her shawl hanging on the chair. She would brave the cold rather than detract from her outfit. If it got cold enough, she'd come back for the coat that still lay where it had been dropped before Jake . . .

Shannon's cheeks turned a fiery red that had nothing to do with the cold air as she recalled once again the night they had spent together. And wondered when they would come together once again.

"You're a wanton for sure, Shannon Mahoney, thinking of sinning like that on the birthday of our Lord," she said as she looked in the mirror that hung on the wall. "And after He answered all your prayers too."

She had gone back to the big house, expecting to find Jake, but instead she had found the mysterious actions of Doc, Cook and Mose as they all gathered around the table for the feast Cook had prepared. And bless her heart, the woman was practically doting on her father, making sure he had a tender cut of meat and that his rolls were warm enough to melt the butter. And Da was doting back, touching her hand and smiling sweetly. Their obvious fondness for each other would almost be embarrassing if it hadn't been such a relief to her.

Because she was leaving. She was going away with Jake. Never mind that he hadn't said another word about it since she'd woken up. Never mind that he hadn't said anything else about their relationship beyond declaring his love. She was going with him.

Jake slid into the seat beside her and dropped a quick kiss on her cheek. Shannon turned to him and then had to look again. He was wearing a coat made of a warm gray wool and his shirt was neatly buttoned to the neck. A look down showed a pair of black pants tucked into freshly polished boots. The only thing familiar was his shirt; she knew it to be the one from his saddlebags.

"What are you . . . where did you . . . Why?" she started.

"Dang if this don't look delicious," he interrupted her as Doc and Mose began the process of passing platters.

"Hmm, try those sweet potatoes there, Jake. They are wonderful," Doc said.

"And the rolls will purt near melt in your mouth," Mose declared.

"Smells great," Jake said as he slapped a heaping mound of dressing onto his plate and then covered it with gravy.

Shannon looked around the table with her mouth hanging open. Jake reached over and touched her beneath her chin, settling her mouth back into a closed position. "Haven't you heard? It's not polite to eat with your mouth open," he whispered in her ear and then proceeded to take a huge bite of turkey.

She wondered briefly if the world had gone daft.

Then wondered again if perhaps she was the one who had gone off the deep end.

"You gonna eat that?" Shamus asked, pointing to the freshly buttered roll on her plate.

"Yes, Da, I am," Shannon said and joined the meal. Soon they were all feasting on a pumpkin pie and giving voice to what a wonderful meal it had been.

"Hope you don't mind excusing us for a minute," Jake said as he rose and took Shannon's hand.

Everyone agreed that they wouldn't mind, except for Shamus.

"Where are ye off to in such a rush?" he asked, only to have Cook throw an elbow into his stomach.

"Mind yer manners there, Shamus," she exclaimed. "And help me stack the plates."

"Stack the plates!" Shamus exclaimed. "After I've been wounded?"

"If you're fit enough to eat like a horse, then you're fit enough to work like one," Cook said with her hands on her wide hips. "Now get off your duff and help me with the dishes."

Shamus shook his head and went to the appointed task, wondering briefly how his world had gotten so turned around.

Jake winked at Cook and led a still bewildered Shannon by the hand to the front porch.

"Don't you think it's a bit cold out here for conversation?" she asked as she shivered in the chilly air.

"Have I told you today how beautiful you are?" Jake asked with a smile. He picked up a package wrapped in brown paper and tied with green ribbon. "Merry Christmas."

"It's a present?" she asked, still a bit confused by all the mystery that had surrounded their meal.

"Yes, it is," he replied. *The joy is in the giving. . . .*

"For me?"

"Yes." He could not recall a time when he had received a present that had made him feel more excited than this.

"But I didn't get you anything."

"Yes, you did," he said as he gently kissed her protesting lips. He was enjoying this. He wished he could give her presents every day.

Shannon held the parcel in her hands as if it were made of the finest crystal. "I did?" The day was getting stranger by the minute.

"Why don't you open it?" Jake led her over to a set of chairs and took the one opposite her. As soon as he was settled, he felt like jumping up again. He could not recall a time when he'd ever felt so lighthearted. He almost felt like a kid, but not the one he had been. That child had not known joy, only drudgery and pain.

Shannon looked at the package and wondered what mischief was afoot. "I can't recall the last time I got a present. And I've never had one that was wrapped." She timidly pulled at the green ribbon.

"It won't be the last, I promise you."

Shannon looked at him, her green eyes brimming with happy tears.

"Open it," Jake said, his pale blue eyes dancing as he watched her. He was so excited that he wanted to jump and yell, just for the fun of it.

She finally caught the excitement he felt and pulled the ribbon away. "What should I do with it?" she asked as she held up the ribbon, letting it stretch to the floor.

Jake grabbed it from her hands and quickly tied it around his neck like a string tie with the ends dangling over his coat.

"Have you gone daft?" Shannon asked as she stifled the laugh that threatened to erupt behind her hand.

"Just consider me a present that you can open later," Jake said and enjoyed the fact that she blushed a deep red all the way up to the roots of her hair. "Hurry up and open it."

Shannon rapidly tore at the paper and then her jaw dropped when she saw the exquisite weave of the fabric inside. She held the shawl up before her and saw the wonderful detail of the embroidery.

"It's lovely," she exclaimed. "I couldn't wear it. It's too beautiful."

"I meant for you to wear it and enjoy it." Jake stood up and took the shawl from her hands. "Stand up."

Shannon stood and he draped the shawl over her shoulders. He crossed it over in front, wrapping his arms around her gently, remembering to be careful of her wound. Shannon reached up to caress his arms as he held her to the solid strength of his chest. She could feel his heart beating against her back, and the heat from his body filled her with warmth.

"I love you, Shannon Mahoney," Jake whispered in her ear and then kissed her cheek.

"And I love you, Jacob Anderson." She leaned her head back on his shoulder so their lips could touch. "It's the loveliest present anyone ever received."

"It gets cold in Wyoming. I expect to see you wear it often."

"The shawl is too pretty to wear every day. I would wear it out in no time."

"When you do, I'll buy you another."

"You will quickly run out of money if you spend it all on me."

"Are you planning on arguing with me about everything?" he asked as he laughed at her protests.

"Dolt. Am I foolish to want food in my belly instead of pretty things?"

"Well, you did say you were practical." A sudden burst of memory came and caused him to laugh harder. She turned around to look at him.

"Shannon, I'm not a rich man by any account, but I have plenty of money," he said when he could talk again. "I just remembered I have quite a bit of money in a bank in Wyoming. I put everything I've ever earned into that bank. I never had anything to spend it on except for a few necessities." He didn't add that those necessities consisted of a couple of trips a month to Maybelle's. He also reminded himself to have a serious talk with Zane when he got back to Wyoming.

The sound of bells filled the air and they looked up to see a family going by in a gaily decorated sleigh drawn by a high-stepping bay.

"Merry Christmas," they called from the road, waving as they went over the bridge into town.

"Merry Christmas," Shannon and Jake called back.

"I must get to the church in time for practice," she said as she looked up. The sun was beginning its descent in the sky. "I haven't told the reverend yet that I can sing today."

Oh, but he already knows, Jake thought as Shannon hastily picked up the paper from the porch floor.

"I'll walk you over there," he volunteered.

"You will?"

Jake held out his arm for her to take. Shannon grasped it and they stepped off the porch together, only to slip and slide in the snow. Jake caught himself and then managed to keep Shannon from taking a tumble. They both laughed gaily as her hair tumbled from its pins and the green ribbon wrapped around it fluttered to the ground.

"Are you sure you're ready for this?" Jake asked as he rescued the ribbon and Shannon quickly tied her hair back.

"I am," she answered, taking his arm again as he gave his smiling approval to her hair. She gave the green ribbon around his neck a tug and he quickly smoothed it down, enjoying the whimsy of wearing it.

"And so am I," he said as they took off down the path toward the road and the church.

Chapter Twenty-three

The church filled up quickly as the late afternoon sun dipped behind the mountains and dusk descended. Candles were lit in the windows and the organ played hymns as the people of the town and surrounding farms made their way down the aisle and filled the pews. Jake took his place in the back row and later made room for Mose as he shuffled in. Mr. and Mrs. Farley paraded in, the Mrs. wearing a new bonnet embellished with flowers and ribbons and topped with a nest and a bird. Jake wondered if the cardinal perched atop the creation was a real one that had been stuffed or merely a replica.

Doc walked by and gave Jake a squeeze on his shoulder before he moved on toward the front. Cook arrived, poking at Shamus as he muttered about something that was obviously bothering him. When he saw the state of the older man's clothing, Jake realized that Shamus had also raided the coffers on the second floor. Shamus crossed himself and dipped before he entered the pew beside Cook, shaking his head as he took his seat. Jake recalled Shannon saying something about her father's being Catholic. Maybe he had problems worshipping in another denomination's church. He also recalled his father mentioning at one time or another that Catholics were the devil's work. Jake wondered if it mattered to God what name was on the sign over the church doors. He couldn't even recall what name labeled the church he was sitting in.

The building was soon overflowing with people, lit by the soft glow of the candles and filled with the rising swell of the organ. The Reverend Mullens took his place and welcomed his parishioners. He opened his Bible and read aloud a passage from Luke, chapter two, verse one.

And it came to pass in those days that there went out a decree from Caesar that all the world should be taxed. . . .

Jake listened to the telling of the Christmas story and as he listened, he recalled a Christmas in Wyoming four years ago when they had all gathered in the parlor of the big house and Jamie had read the passage to them. It had become real for him that night. It was as if it were the first time he had heard the story told, and it finally made sense to him. God had made the sacrifice of His son to save the world. Jamie sacrificed himself to save his sister and his friend. What greater sacrifice could there be than to lay down one's own life for another?

What a fool he had been seeking his death just to get back at a father who didn't care one way or the other. How many times had he charged heedlessly into battle and put Caleb and Ty at risk? Life was precious. He was so lucky to be alive. Never again would he take it for granted. God had granted him a precious gift. He had spared his life and then given him a reason for living.

The reading of the Scripture was over and the choir gathered to sing.

Jake bent his head and placed a hand over his face, squeezing hard at the bridge of his nose to keep from laughing out loud. Mrs. Farley and her hat were monopolizing more than their fair share of the platform. And besides that, the bird threatened to fall off and land on Shannon at the end of each line of song as the woman moved her head to emphasize the screech of her voice. Shannon and the rest of the choir bore it all with patience and fortitude, although Shannon did occasionally bite her lip to keep from laughing. The congregation winced occasionally as the buxom storekeeper hit the high notes but on the whole, people were full of Christmas spirit and smiled their appreciation of the choir's efforts. Finally the concert was over and the reverend once again took the podium.

His message was one of peace. It was a simple plea for neighbor to forgive neighbor. Jake wondered if all the churches across the land had the same message given to them on this day. He wondered if the generals and admirals and presidents of a nation split in two were listening. It all sounded so simple while sitting in the back row of a tiny church in the wild mountains of West Virginia. All they had to do was forgive and forget.

The amen was said and Shannon stepped up on the platform. The organist played a note and she began.

Hark the herald angels sing . . .

Jake had heard her sing it before, but not like this. The church was too small to hold the glorious sound. Her voice sailed up to the rafters and beyond. It filled the church and filled the people who sat awestruck with the beauty of it. It spilled forth from her body. She overflowed with love and compassion for all who listened. She glowed.

They wanted to hear more and yet were afraid to; the beauty of her voice was without measure.

Jake sat mesmerized as she sang the words, proclaiming the heavenly message. He wondered if perhaps Shannon could have been one of the angels who announced the Lord's birth on that night so long ago. Perhaps she was. Perhaps she had sung in the heavens and had then been sent down to Earth. To save him.

He didn't deserve it but he did appreciate it. He would spend the rest of his life showing her how thankful he was.

Shannon stepped off to the side of the platform and remained where she was after Reverend Mullens whispered in her ear.

"Praise the Lord," Reverend Mullens said when he turned to face the congregation.

"The Lord be praised," the congregation answered, knowing that he had been praised greatly.

"Before I give the benediction, there is a young man here who would like to invite all of you to be a part of something special."

"Go get her, Mister Jake," Mose hissed as Jake stood and made his way to the front of the church.

Shannon cast him a sideways look as he walked down the aisle. She shifted nervously when he came up on the platform and knelt before her, taking her hand in his.

"Shannon Mahoney, will you marry me?"

"Are you daft?" she whispered as she anxiously looked around to find that everyone was watching the proceedings.

"No, I am not daft, in spite of what you think. Will you marry me?"

"You mean now?" She was certain the entire world had gone off-kilter despite what he said. Or perhaps worse, she was dreaming, a victim of a fever and a fatal wound.

"Yes, right now, this minute in front of all these witnesses." The congregation laughed as Shannon gazed down at him with green eyes full of surprise.

Shannon looked up and around at the glowing faces. They were all smiling encouragement in her direction, except for Cook, who had slapped a hand over Shamus's mouth. In the back she could see Mose's wide grin as he stood to watch the proceedings. Her eyes caught Dr. Blankenship nodding his head up and down. "Say yes," he mouthed in her direction.

"Shannon?" Jake asked. Still kneeling, he suddenly felt extremely vulnerable.

She shook her head as if to clear away cobwebs. The entire world had gone crazy, leaving her the only sane one.

"Marry me?" He said it quietly this time, as if he was afraid of her answer. His pale blue eyes looked up at her earnestly and she saw the vulnerability behind them. He had given her his heart and she held it in her hand. She could choose to cherish it, or she could choose to throw it away. His entire future and hers depended on the answer she gave him.

"Of course, I will, you dolt." Her green eyes danced with merriment. "Now get up before you make a greater fool of yourself."

The congregation laughed again as Jake came to his feet and grabbed her shoulders, planting a kiss on her mouth.

"You're not supposed to do that until after the ceremony!" someone called from the back.

"He's also supposed to ask her father for her hand, but he's yet to do that," Shamus groused. Cook jabbed him again with her elbow. "Enough, woman, I'm growing a hole in my side from your constant poking!"

"Da, he saved your life. The least you can do is give us your blessing."

Cook jabbed Shamus again. "Consider yourself blessed," he said as he rubbed his much-abused side.

Reverend Mullens opened his prayer book as Jake and Shannon took a place before him. "Dearly beloved . . . ," he began.

They held hands and looked into each other's eyes and recited the vows as the reverend instructed them. Jake squeezed her hand when she promised to obey and her smile danced at the corners of her mouth as the words came tumbling out in a rush. Jake blinked as if waking from a dream when the reverend asked for a ring.

He had forgotten about the ring.

Jake looked around as if in a daze. He didn't have a

ring. Would the marriage be binding without it? The green ribbon he had tied around his neck in a moment of whimsy suddenly felt as if it were choking him.

Shannon chewed on her lip as he hesitated, suddenly fearful that he had changed his mind about marrying her.

"I don't have a ring," he whispered loudly enough for Shannon and the reverend to hear. Fortunately his voice carried to the first few rows of pews.

Mrs. Farley, who had started sobbing loudly into her hankie at the onset of the ceremony, raised her wide girth from the front pew.

"You can have mine," she sobbed as she wrenched at the gold band she wore on her pinkie. "Bless your hearts, I'm so happy for both of you," she continued amid sobs as she worked at the ring. "It's stuck," she hissed at Mr. Farley. The red bird bobbed on top of her bonnet as if it were jumping up and down, trying to watch the ceremony over the tips of the flowers.

A draft was felt as the door at the back of the church opened and closed and Mose came running down the aisle with snow in his hands. He slapped his hands around Mrs. Farley's hand and the old woman's eyes widened in shock as if she were under attack. She jerked her hand away and the ring was left behind. Mose wiped it on his sleeve, blew on it, shined it on his shirt and then dropped it onto the open pages of the prayer book.

Mr. Farley rolled his eyes as his wife settled back next to him and loudly blew her nose. Mose settled in on the other side of the man as if he'd been sitting in the front pew of the church his entire life.

"Thanks a lot," Mr. Farley scolded Mose. "Now I'm going to have to buy her that diamond ring she's been after." Mose just smiled at him and nodded.

"With this ring, I thee wed. . . ." Jake slid the band onto Shannon's finger and was not surprised to find that it fit her perfectly. As she fit him.

And in the soft glow of candlelight in the early evening of Christmas Day, they became husband and wife as the entire town looked on. The congregation erupted into a cheer when they kissed.

"Oh, this is so wonderful," Mrs. Farley exclaimed as she jumped to her feet. "Everyone's invited to our house for cake and punch!"

Mr. Farley rolled his eyes at his wife's generosity. It was going to be a very expensive Christmas for him.

"I hope they'll break out the whiskey too," Shamus added as Cook kissed him on the cheek.

"You need to sign the certificate before you go," Reverend Mullens said to Jake as people began to mill about the happy couple. He pulled out the parchment that he had prepared after Jake's visit earlier in the day.

Jake kept a tight hold on Shannon's hand as several from the congregation came up to offer their congratulations. He didn't know any of them except for Ingrid, who wrapped her arms around Shannon's neck and sobbed with joy.

"I'm so happy for you, dear one," she exclaimed as she dabbed at her eyes.

"Thank you," Shannon replied breathlessly, still not sure of what had happened.

Reverend Mullens tugged on Jake's sleeve. "You need to sign this to make it all legal," he explained.

Jake pulled Shannon away with him to the pulpit where the parchment lay. Reverend Mullens handed Jake a pen and he signed his name with a steady hand

and then held out the pen for Shannon to take.

She looked up, panic-stricken. He didn't know that she couldn't read or write. She hadn't had a chance to tell him. Would he still want her if he knew how ignorant she was? She had to tell him. . . .

"I can't," she said with a trembling lip.

"Can't what?"

"Can't read or write." Shannon looked at the toe of the worn shoe that poked out beneath the hem of her dress. "I don't know how. I never learned."

Jake dipped his head to look into her fearful green eyes. "How old are you, Shannon?"

"Twenty-two." Had he thought her younger? Was she not only ignorant but also too old?

"That's how old I was when I learned how."

"To read and write?"

"Yes." He smiled encouragingly. "Remember me telling you about my friend Jamie? He's the one who taught me how." Jake placed the pen in her hand and then put his hand over hers and guided it to the page. He took her hand through the motions of spelling out her name on the line. "We'll do it together," he said into her ear as the letters spilled forth from the pen. "As husband and wife."

Mrs. Farley put out quite a spread. Jake wondered who all the fancy treats were originally for as she brought out cakes and cookies for the celebrants who showed up at the impromptu wedding reception. He shook hands with people he had never seen before and watched Shannon be hugged and kissed by people she had known her entire life. Shannon glowed as she was congratulated and Jake heard the whispers of the townspeople as they remarked on how beautiful she was. And they had never noticed. Jake was proud to know that he had seen her beauty from the beginning. He was proud to have her stand tall beside him. He was also happy that he had a few inches on her, although if she ever took to wearing heels he was in trouble.

Shamus held court in one of the corners and told a rather embellished tale of how he had rescued his daughter and her fiancé from the clutches of the Union deserters. Of course, poor Shannon had been accidentally shot during the incident, but she was much better now. Jake and Shannon ignored him and let him have his day. They had more important things on their minds. When Shamus broke into song, they slipped away, unnoticed by all except for Dr. Blankenship, who saluted Jake with a tip of his cup as they passed through the room. Doc was satisfied that his job was done. He had seen to Shannon's cabin earlier in the day.

He suddenly realized that he was going to miss her.

The stars in the night sky were as bright as the candles that gleamed on Mrs. Farley's tree. Jake held on to Shannon's hand as they stood on the Farleys' porch and looked up at the night sky. He said a prayer for the safety of those who were still fighting the war. He hoped that Caleb and Ty were safe somewhere. He hoped they were still alive.

"What are you thinking?" Shannon asked as she stood next to him with her precious shawl wrapped tightly around her shoulders.

"I'm thinking about how lucky I am." He brought her hand up and kissed it. "I'm also thinking about my friends and wondering what they're doing right now."

He turned and touched the side of her face. "But mostly I'm thinking about how much I love you."

Shannon let out a sigh and the air between them fogged as he kissed her. "It's been a long and exciting day," Jake said as his lips lingered on hers.

"It has," Shannon answered with her lips barely touching his. "Perhaps we should seek our rest."

"You are very practical, wife."

"It's one of my best qualities, husband."

There were just a few inches between them, and their eyes sparkled and danced at the easy banter.

"I can think of other qualities of yours that I like better," Jake teased.

"Would you care to list them for me?" Shannon teased back. The creak of the door behind them, followed by a loud clearing of a masculine throat, brought their heads apart abruptly.

Doc made a show of stretching and yawning, then pulled out his watch.

"Isn't that funny, I was just thinking the same thing," Jake said as he took Shannon's hand again and led her off the porch.

"Better hurry up, son," Doc said. "Before you come under the influence of a very powerful woman."

"Oh, she's making plans, is she?" Shannon asked.

"I'd run if I were you."

Shannon gathered her skirts and they took off down the road, slipping and sliding when they hit an icy spot. Doc leaned on the banister and enjoyed the sound of their laughter as it faded over the bridge.

A fire had been laid in the stove and the bed made up with clean sheets and an extra quilt. On the table was a vase with pine boughs and holly, which filled the room with a wonderful scent. There was also a plate covered with a cloth that held enough food so they wouldn't have to worry about breakfast.

Shannon looked about in awe, still thinking that somehow she was dreaming. She touched the gold band that shone brightly on her finger. It seemed real enough. She turned to see Jake lighting the fire. He seemed real. She could reach out and touch him if she wanted, and she wanted to very much.

Jake looked up from the stove and smiled. She was just standing there, looking at him as if she were afraid he was going to disappear into a puff of smoke and drift up through the stovepipe and into the night sky. He couldn't blame her for thinking that way. He still found their wedding a little hard to believe himself. But yet here he was, newly married and about to experience the joys of the marriage bed. He was blessed.

Shannon carefully folded her shawl and placed it on top of the small cherry bureau that held her few precious belongings. She suddenly wished that she had a pretty, lacy nightgown to put on. But this night was completely unanticipated.

Jake took off his coat and laid it on a chair before he came up behind her and wrapped his arms around her. "Was it right that I did it this way?" he asked. Shannon looked into the mirror on the wall and found him looking back at her with hopeful pale blue eyes.

"It was the most wonderful wedding I could have wished for," she said breathlessly as the realization that she was truly married to Jake sank into her still-muddled brain.

"I could have waited and given you time to plan and do all the—"

"No," she interrupted. "It was perfect." She turned in his arms to face him. "It was more than I ever hoped for."

"As you are to me," he said tenderly, touching her lips with his. "You saved me, Shannon. In more ways than you'll ever know."

The kiss deepened as their arms went around each other and they held each other close. They couldn't get close enough and realized there were too many layers of clothing between them. Shannon reached up and pulled away the silly green ribbon from Jake's neck. He laughed joyfully and pulled the ribbon from her hair. Shannon unbuttoned the top button of his shirt and worked her way down, trailing her lips behind her fingers. Jake responded by pulling the pins from her bright red hair so that it fell shining down her back.

She pulled the shirt down his arms and ran her hands over the breadth of his chest, her hands tracing over the pattern that had become so familiar during the time he had been unconscious and under her care. They traced over the ridges in his stomach where the muscles jumped and twitched at the mere touch of her fingertips.

Jake sucked in his breath and caught her hands as they teased at the waist of his pants. He suddenly realized that he had never undressed a woman before. The scantily clad whores at Maybelle's shimmied out of their costumes in the blink of an eye. He didn't know where to begin, but he knew for certain where he wanted to end. Shannon turned her back to him as if she were reading his mind and gathered her hair into her hands to expose a row of buttons down her back.

His fingers had no trouble finding their way. Moments later, the dress that matched her eyes was spread wide enough for him to slip it over her shoulders, exposing the soft pearly white of her skin to his lips as he dropped gentle, teasing kisses on her shoulders and neck. Shannon pulled the dress down and leaned back against his frame as his hands came around her trim waist and up to caress her breasts.

"Shannon," he groaned and she felt his wanting against her back.

The need suddenly became urgent and the rest of their clothing seemed to disappear as hands roved and lips followed. Hand in hand they walked to the bed, pulled back the quilts and tumbled into the soft layers of warmth.

Jake pushed back her hair and looked down into the deep green of her eyes. "I love you, Shannon Anderson."

"As I love you, Jacob," she said, looking up into the pale blue of his eyes. And she noticed then that they no longer held the look of ice. Now they were warm and smiling like the sky in early summer. And as he came to her, the warmth of his eyes spread through her body and she realized she would never be cold or lonely again. Not as long as she had Jake.

Chapter Twenty-four

Cat looked up from the laundry tub as the children ran circles around her, chasing a gaily painted hoop. It hadn't been much of a Christmas for the slaves who remained on what was left of her husband's family plantation, but she had done the best she could with what had been available. At least they were now free. Cat figured that their freedom was more than they had ever hoped to have.

"Why don't you let me finish that for you, Miz Cat?" Ruth said as Cat curled her spine and pressed her fists against the small of her back. A bead of sweat trickled between her breasts. It was a warm day for the end of December; a lot warmer that what she was used to in Wyoming. But then again, it had been a few years since she had spent a winter in Wyoming.

"Don't worry, Ruth," Cat said to the former slave. "I got my monthly. There's no baby inside of me."

"Don't you worry none, Miz Cat. It will come in the Lord's own time."

How many times had she heard that in that past few months? Since she had returned to the plantation with Ty after participating in his escape from prison camp, Ruth and Portia, who had practically raised Ty along with her own son Zeb, had watched over her like a pair of hawks. They hoped, as she did, that she would become pregnant again; the loss of her baby the previous summer had nearly killed her.

The Lord's own time . . . Cat wondered when her time and the Lord's time would come together. It wasn't for lack of trying on her part and Ty's. They definitely had that aspect under control. She looked up to see her husband, who was supposed to be recovering from a broken arm, scrambling over the roof of the house that was being built on the foundation of the one that had burned. Ty's older brother Parker handed up a tool as Ty leaned dangerously over the edge of the framing. Cat almost wished that he would fall off the roof again so he wouldn't have to go back to the front. Not that she really wanted him to be hurt, but then again maybe she did. It would be worth it if the injury saved his life.

Cat watched as the brothers laughed together over a comment that Parker had made while handing up the hammer. Parker had changed greatly from the stern, humorless man he had been when she had met him at the onset of the war. He was now more compassionate and caring. Cat considered this to be a blessing, considering what Parker had experienced. After all, he could have easily gone the other way. He had been through his own type of hell while Ty had been in prison camp. A roving band of Union soldiers had attacked the plantation. Parker had been grazed in the head by a bullet and the Yankees had thought him dead. Lucy Ann had taken advantage of his injury and run off with the soldiers who fired the house. Cat personally hoped that her sister-in-law had been dealt her own brand of justice after the evil things she had done to Zeb before he left the plantation. Portia and Silas had cared for Parker until he recovered from his injuries and grief. He owed his life to them.

Cat mused that despite everything that had happened since she'd first come to North Carolina, one thing hadn't changed: she was still waiting for the war to end. But at least now she and Ty would not be apart. They had managed to sneak between the lines after his escape from the prison in New York. Ty's commanding officer in Richmond had given him a month's leave to recover his health. They had come back to the plantation to find it in near ruin. The house was gone, half the slaves had run off and there was no money left. They had thrown themselves into the rebuilding of the house, a task that Ty wasn't physically ready for after his months of imprisonment. He had fallen off a ladder on the last day of his leave and broken his arm, which had delighted Cat. It kept him safe with her instead of in the middle of the war.

Instead of the luxury she had enjoyed before when she had stayed in the huge manor house, the two of them were now living in one of the slave cabins. Cat found that she didn't mind the primitive conditions at all, for now she had her husband with her. She would live in a cave and not mind, as long as Ty was with her. Cat realized that it might come down to that before too long. It was difficult to tell what their living conditions would be like when they went back to the front.

"Somebody's coming, Miz Cat," Ruth said as she wrung out the clothes. Cat looked up the the long, oak-lined drive. Two riders were slowly coming toward the remains of the house. She waved at Ty, who looked at her, and then in the direction she was pointing.

Cat considered the food available for dinner. Two more mouths shouldn't be much of a burden. She only hoped that they were bringing good news with them instead of the usual bad. If only the newcomers would say the war was over and Ty didn't have to go back.

She was surprised to see Ty suddenly scramble down the ladder and start running down the drive. One of the riders jumped off his horse and took off his hat to reveal pale blond hair.

"Oh, my God," Cat said.

"What is it?" Ruth asked.

Cat let out a whoop and took off at a run, sparing no thought for the stack of clean clothes that landed on the ground, knocked off the table in her haste.

Ty and Jake were wrapped up in each other's arms. Tears ran down Ty's face as they both laughed and talked at the same time.

"I thought you were dead," Ty said.

"I almost was," Jake replied as they pounded each other on the back and laughed for the sheer joy of it.

"How in the world?" Ty asked

"It's a long story," Jake answered. "I'm just glad to see you survived, too."

"You'll never believe everything that has happened since then," Ty said.

"Where's Caleb?" Jake asked.

Ty stepped back and put his hand on Jake's shoulder.

The pale blue eyes looked at the darker blue of Ty's with dread.

"He survived," Ty said. "But he lost his leg."

Jake bent his head as relief washed over his body. Caleb had survived. The next second he landed on his backside in the dirt as a petite wildcat hit his chest.

"You're alive!" Cat cried as Jake hugged her tight.

"I survived the attack, but the reunion's about to kill me." Jake looked up and smiled at Shannon, who had been watching the proceedings quietly from the back of her horse.

Ty laughingly pulled Cat up with one hand and Jake with the other. Cat wrapped her arms around Jake's waist and held on. She felt as if she were dreaming; she had the sense that if she let go, he would disappear.

"So who's your friend?" Ty asked as Cat finally released Jake and stepped into her husband's embrace.

Jake helped Shannon down from her saddle and placed her arm through his to better present her to his friends. "This is my wife, Shannon. Shannon, these are my friends, Tyler and Catherine Kincaid."

"You've got a wife?" Cat asked incredulously as she looked up at Shannon's glowing face with tilted green-gold eyes.

"Yep, sure do," Jake replied.

Ty and Cat laughed with sheer relief. Ty pulled Jake and Shannon toward him and Cat and the men wrapped their arms around the circle the four of them made, pulling each other close until the tops of their heads were touching.

Cat looked up to see Jake's eyes shining with happiness. "Just wait until everyone back home hears the news," she said as tears of joy ran down her face.

Jake, Shannon, Cat and Ty sat around the table in the small slave cabin and talked late into the night after enjoying a meal together. Portia, who had once been the housekeeper for Parker, fussed over Jake as if he were her own son come back from the dead. The former butler, Silas, who had had nothing to do since the house had burned, smiled widely as he welcomed Mr. Jake back to the fold.

"I just can't believe what happened," Ty exclaimed after dinner as Shannon told her tale of finding Jake in the stream. "All I could see from the trail was your horse. When I went down to look for your body, you were gone. I just figured you'd been blown to bits."

"We heard someone on the trail when Caleb and I hid in the cave," Cat added. "It must have been Shannon going by with Jake."

"We hid in the same cave not too long ago," Shannon said.

"And we found one of Caleb's drawings in there too," Jake added. "How . . . what happened when he lost his leg?"

"He lost it when they first ambushed us," Ty said. "I made him hide with Cat."

"I bet he loved that," Jake commented. "One thing I haven't been able to figure out is how the Yankees knew we were coming down the trail that day."

"They knew because Wade Bishop told them," Ty said.

Jake slapped the table with his hand. "I knew there was something wrong with that bastard."

"Oh, that's not the half of it," Ty said and told Jake the story of Wade Bishop and his own escape from the prison camp and the near disaster with Jenny being taken by the man.

Jake shook his head at how close they had all come to tragedy. "So tell me what happened with Caleb."

"When I saw his wound, I knew it was bad, but I never realized just how bad. I only knew he wouldn't survive in a prison camp."

"So you two hid in the cave until the Yankees were gone?"

Cat nodded her head. "We knew there wasn't anything we could do to help. Caleb never said a word about his leg. I waited until he passed out to cut his boot off and bandage it." Her face blanched. "His foot almost came off in my hand. I knew there wasn't any way to save it."

"She chopped it off with my sword," Ty said.

Cat gave Ty an elbow in the stomach. "I wish you two would quit saying that. When Caleb went home, the first thing he said to Chance and Fox was that Auntie Cat chopped off his leg with a sword."

"You've been home?" Jake asked, his eyes lighting up at the prospect.

Cat brought him up to date with the happenings in Wyoming, including the problems of Cole and Grace. Jake listened in amazement to the goings-on while Shannon tried hard to keep track of all the names he had shared with her.

"So now you have to tell us your story," Cat said when she was done with the news from home. "It's been close to six months since you supposedly died. What have you been up to?"

"Mostly sleeping," Jake said with a grin.

"Dolt," Shannon said and told of his recovery.

"And you really had no memory of anything when you woke up?" Ty asked incredulously.

"I could remember the simple things like talking and reading and riding a horse. I even remembered how to use my guns, but everything else had disappeared."

"He was even worried he might be married and couldn't remember his wife," Shannon added.

"What made you think that you had one?" Cat asked.

"They found a letter in my pocket from a woman. Half of it was washed away."

"The letter I wrote you?" Cat asked in disbelief.

"That's the one," Jake said as Cat burst into laughter.

"He was probably just using that as an excuse," she said to Shannon.

"He had a ton of them," Shannon replied. "I've never seen anyone work so hard at not having a relationship." Jake took her hand, pleased that she felt comfortable with his friends, thrilled that she could say such a thing and not worry about the repercussions.

"Obviously you haven't met Zane," Ty said and the three who knew him laughed together.

"I've heard a bit about him," Shannon said with a smile. She loved the warm feeling that enclosed the group around the table. It was nice to have a conversation with people close to her age. She was also happy that Jake had such wonderful, caring friends who seemed so willing to be her friend too.

"So you woke up after being in a coma for three months without any memories," Ty stated. "How did you two go from that to being married?"

Jake raised Shannon's hand to his lips and deposited

a kiss on her knuckles. "She saved me," he said as he found her eyes with his.

Cat squeezed Ty's knee under the table. Their eyes met and both brimmed with happiness. Not only was Jake alive, but he was undeniably happy. He had come back to them whole and changed for the better.

"Tell us about the wedding," Cat said to Shannon. "I'd ask Jake, but he'd just say 'we got married' and that would be the end of it."

"Oh no, it was very romantic," Shannon began.

"Wait a minute, are you sure you're talking about Jake?" Cat laughed.

Shannon went on in detail about Jake proposing on his knees in front of the entire town. Ty inclined his head toward the door and Jake went out with him.

"So what are we supposed to do now, Major Kincaid?" Jake asked when they had settled into a pair of straight-back chairs.

"If you're asking me for orders, then I'd say go home." Ty tipped the chair back and placed his booted feet on the railing of the porch.

"And what about you and Cat?" Jake asked.

"You know the answer to that, Jake. I've got to go back. It's my duty."

"Just make sure that doing your duty doesn't get you killed."

"Now you sound like Cat."

"I've seen you in battle, Ty. And now you won't have me and Caleb to watch your back."

"You saved my life at the Wilderness Campaign."

"And you probably saved mine more times than I can count. I guess I can stick around and try to even things out."

"No, Jake. Take your wife and go home. Consider that an order," Ty said firmly. "I promise I won't do anything stupid. Chances are we won't see much fighting anyway. For the South, the war is pretty much over."

"I guess we were on the losing side," Jake said as his feet also found the rail.

"Only in the war," Ty said, feeling philosophical. "I'd say that you won."

"I wasn't kidding when I said she saved me, Ty."

"I know. You've changed."

"All that stuff that happened to me when I was a boy, all that anger I carried; it's gone now." It was. Jake felt as if the weight of the world had been lifted from his shoulders.

"You never really talked about it, Jake, and we never felt like we could ask."

"I know." Jake laughed. "I was a real bastard at times, wasn't I?"

"Let's just say we tried really hard to stay on your good side."

"I'm surprised that you could even find a good side of me," Jake said as he reflected on his past. "If Jason hadn't have taken me in, I don't know what would have happened to me. I'd probably be dead now, either shot or hanged, or worse, in prison. Being around all of you always gave me hope and made me think that I could have something better in life."

"Looks like you found it."

"I did. I can't explain how, or why, I just know that Shannon made all the hurt and anger go away."

"A good woman can make a world of difference."

They sat in silent companionship for a moment until Jake broke the silence.

"I'm sorry about Willie," he said.

"So am I. We lost a lot of good friends that day." Ty told Jake who had died and who had lived, only to be sent off to a prison camp in the North. "I've tried to find all their families and tell them what happened."

"Willie didn't have a family."

"He had you, Jake. He worshipped you."

"And see what it got him," Jake said in disgust.

"It's not your fault. Willie made the choice to go to war. He even lied about his age to do it."

"But he might not have gotten killed if he hadn't been following me."

"Or maybe he would have. Maybe he would have been maimed for life. Maybe he would have been wounded and died in a prison camp. The list of possibilities could go on forever, Jake. Believe me, I've been over it a thousand times in my mind. What if I'd been paying closer attention? What if I'd sent Cat home before we got to the caves? What if I'd listened to you and not trusted Wade Bishop?"

"It never ends, does it?"

"No, and you could go crazy trying to figure it out. It's just like Jamie always said. Sometimes bad things happen to good people. Or maybe it was Jenny who said it."

"I guess they would know better than anyone."

"Yes, they would."

"I want to go home, Ty. And when I say 'home,' I mean Wyoming. The ranch. I want Shannon to love it there as much as I do." The words tumbled out in haste as if they were keeping him from achieving his goal.

"She will."

"What makes you so sure?"

"You'll be there, won't you?" Ty said with the wisdom that came from being married longer than Jake.

"I miss Caleb," Jake said. He realized that being with Ty made him miss Caleb all the more.

"Jenny's worried about him. She says in her letters that he hasn't picked up his sketchbook since he got back."

"He hasn't?" Jake found that it bothered him to hear that. Caleb without his sketchbook was as heartbreaking as Caleb without a leg. "Maybe things will be different once we all go back."

"I hope so. Cat doesn't say it, because she knows I'm needed here, but she's worried about things back home. A lot of stuff has happened that adds up to bad news."

"Chase and Cole can handle it."

"I hope so." Ty looked over at Jake. "But I also know that they'll be happy to have you there to lend a hand."

"I'll be there," Jake declared. "Just as soon as we can manage."

"So will I," Ty said. "It just might take me a bit longer to make it."

"Ty, the last time I saw Cat, she was pregnant." Jake felt bad for asking, but he had to know. "What happened?"

"She lost the baby. Right after she got Caleb home."

"I'm sorry."

"Just consider our child another casualty of the war," Ty said bitterly. He had thought he was over the loss by now and was surprised to find he wasn't.

"Can you still have another?"

"We're trying," Ty said. "It hasn't happened yet." His feet hit the floor. "I think the worst part is the disappointment she feels as the months go by and it doesn't happen."

"Shannon's disappointment was hard for me to take too. I didn't want to hurt her, but no matter what decision I made, it was going to cause her pain."

"But it all came out all right in the end."

"Yes, it did. In spite of me." Jake smiled at his joke. "And it will for you too."

"I hope so. I'd rather take a bullet in the gut than see Cat hurt."

"Being in love is a painful experience," Jake decided.

"Yes, it is, but it's worth it," Ty declared.

"Yes, it is," Jake said in wholehearted agreement. He rose from his chair to seek the comforting presence of his wife and Ty followed him to find his own happiness. It did not surprise them to find Cat and Shannon with their heads together, exchanging their own observations on love and men. After all, they had both married extremely wise women.

Chapter Twenty-five

Zane figured he must be getting old. Why else would he think a trip to Maybelle's was going to be boring? Sure it would be nice to have a few drinks, cut loose, and enjoy the company of a sweet gal, but it was getting to be a bit monotonous, having to do it two or three times a week. Still, he was not one to shirk his duty, and Chase figured that Maybelle's was the best place to get information in town. Every cowhand and soldier that came close to Laramie made a trip through her ruby-red doors at one time or another.

At least the weather was good. He'd be danged if he was going to ride through snow or freezing rain just to find out a piece of information. It didn't take a genius to know that somebody was behind all the problems that had been occurring lately. It couldn't be a coincidence that water holes were being fouled, stock slaughtered and homesteads burned.

Whoever was behind it had to be a pretty shady character, that was for sure. Jason, Cole and Chase were convinced it was the man who had shown up in town right before Christmas. A real fancy dresser who looked as if he'd never gotten his hands dirty with work a single day of his life, he'd been seen waltzing about town several times with Cole's first wife on his arm, both of them dressed as if they were sashaying the paved streets of Paris instead of walking the muddy pathways of Laramie, Wyoming. The problem was finding proof that Petty was involved.

Sweet little Missy had confided on one of his previous visits that Petty came to Maybelle to help him find men who were looking for jobs. Zane wondered what kind of skills you needed to work for the man. Did Petty ask his hopefuls if they were proficient at house burning and cattle butchering? Would someone be turned down if he was deemed not angry enough or ugly enough for the job?

What drove men to seek their riches by taking away what others had honestly worked for? Jason Lynch had come to the territory thirty years ago and worked hard to make his ranch one of the most successful in the state. He had done it the hard way too, owning the land that he used instead of taking advantage of the free range. He was always willing to lend a hand to his neighbors and had no problem with letting the homesteaders graze their cattle alongside his. He was even taking on the challenge of building a school at the crossroads, so the children of the local ranchers and homesteaders wouldn't have to come all the way to town. And this Petty character thought he could just waltz in at the last minute, steal away the land and then turn around and sell it to the railroad. He probably planned on doing the same thing all the way to California. Zane shook his head at the audacity of the man.

Zane tied his horse at the post outside of Maybelle's and took a moment to look around the bustling streets of Laramie. It would be good for the town to have the railroad come through. The town would grow and the people who lived in it and worked in it would prosper. But at what cost? Zane had always thought that it would be exciting to live in a big city and experience all the sights and sounds of modern civilization, but then again, he liked things the way they were. Or the way they used to be before Jamie was murdered and the war began. Life would never be that happy or carefree again.

"Dang it, Zane, you're starting to sound like an old woman, whining and crying over a dead cat," he chastised himself as he stepped onto the broad porch in front of Maybelle's.

Behind the red doors was paradise. How many times had he told himself that in the past few years? All the loving a man could handle, for a price. Luckily for him, Jason was giving him extra money to make this visit.

Zane's hand froze on the knob as he considered the implications of that. Jason was paying him to sleep with women. Did that make him some kind of whore? Was it even possible that a man could be a whore? Was there a name for that kind of man? *What the hell?*

Zane stepped back from the door and turned to look around the town again. Nothing had changed in the past few minutes since he'd stepped onto the porch. So why was it he felt so . . . cheap?

"Dang!" he said out loud. His horse looked up at him

and then lowered his head again, falling back into his rest without a worry in the world.

Zane could not for the life of him believe that he was standing on the porch of Maybelle's with gold in his pocket, feeling reluctant to go in. He quickly changed his mind, however, when he heard a crash, followed by a squeal.

Several of the scantily dressed whores were standing at the base of the steps, looking up toward the second floor, where the majority of Maybelle's business was done.

"What was that?" Zane asked the group, who nervously began to scatter when Maybelle appeared at the top of the steps.

"None of your business, honey," Maybelle said as she came swaying down the staircase.

Zane looked around the main room, where two men were enjoying the bonus benefits of having a drink at Maybelle's bar. Women posed and pranced in their undergarments, hoping to entice them to go upstairs and part with more of their coin. Missy wasn't among them.

"Where's Missy?" Zane asked Maybelle as she came to the bottom of the steps. Zane hated standing so close to the woman. Her heavy makeup only served to show her age instead of hiding it. The paint on her lips was too bright and her perfume heavy and sour smelling.

"She's busy right now, darling. Do you want to wait?"

All eyes looked upward as a scream sounded over the forced laughter coming from the main salon.

Zane grabbed the banister.

"Don't you go up there," Maybelle threatened. "I'll cut you off, and then where will you be?"

Zane pushed his way past her as another scream was heard. Maybelle yelled for her bouncer but Zane wasn't worried. He knew Bill had probably passed out by now, as usual. Besides, Bill was his friend.

Just as he thought. The screams were coming from Missy's room. And the door was locked, which was against the rules.

"Missy?" Zane called through the door.

Zane's ears burned as a burst of profanity questioned his parentage and gave him explicit directions on what he should do to himself. The sound of muffled sobs overcame any trepidation Zane felt about entering the room. He threw his shoulder against the door. It held as solidly as a jail cell's.

"Missy!" Zane shouted. He heard the sounds of heavy footsteps on the stairs.

He wasn't leaving until he was sure Missy was all right.

Zane pulled out his gun.

"Put that away!" Maybelle screeched. "You know I don't allow guns upstairs!"

Zane shot at the knob while Maybelle yelled, "What has gotten into you?"

Zane kicked the door open. Missy sat in the bed with a sheet pulled up under her chin. Her lip was bleeding and her eyes were moist with tears. The next thing he knew he was flying across the room. His gun left his hand and went skidding under the bed. Zane felt himself being picked up by the scruff of his neck and tossed into a bureau. Dazed, he tried to roll over but his head plowed into the heavy piece of furniture again.

He managed to twist himself around before the next volley came and found himself facing a man with a fresh scar across his cheek. The man tried to wrap his hands around Zane's neck as Zane used his strength to push his arms away. They pushed back and forth, each one struggling to get the upper hand. Zane felt the hot breath of his opponent on his face. He threw his head forward and struck the man square in the nose with his forehead. Blood spurted and the man fell back, grabbing at his nose as Zane scrambled to his feet.

Zane stood with head pounding and stars still exploding in his head, wondering what had just happened. The heavy smell of Maybelle's perfume added to the assault on his senses and turned his stomach. The man with the fresh scar cursed as he looked at his blood-filled hand.

Zane blinked in shock as the man pulled a knife from his boot. Zane put his hands out. This had gone far enough.

"Why don't we go downstairs and have a drink?" he said as the man with the scar waved the knife in front of him.

"We don't want any trouble here," Maybelle added.

Zane looked toward the doorway, which was quickly filling up with scantily dressed women. He needed to end this altercation before somebody got hurt.

"What's your name, friend?" he asked with his most charming smile.

"Go to hell," the man retorted.

"He said it was Mitchell," Missy said just to spite the man. She stood on the bed with a sheet wrapped around her body, smiling triumphantly.

"So, Mitchell, I'm guessing you're new in town?" Zane warily watched the knife as the reflection from the lamp bounced off its shiny surface.

"You broke my nose," Mitchell replied.

"You nearly broke my skull," Zane retorted as he real-ized that the man was not in a mood to be reasonable or friendly.

Mitchell raised the knife and came toward Zane, who stopped the downward thrust by bracing his hands under the man's arm. At the same time, Missy let out a yelp and jumped on the man's back. The sheet fluttered behind her and then swirled around the three of them as Mitchell tried to shake her off while at the same time attempting to stab Zane.

Zane wrestled with Mitchell and the sheet. Mitchell let out a howl as Missy bit his ear. The three of them fell to the floor with Zane landing on the bottom, Missy in the middle and the sheet twisted around a tangle of legs that kept them all from moving. Zane kept a hold on Mitchell's wrist as Missy's hands found a soft target and squeezed. Mitchell let out a yelp, fol-lowed by another round of cursing. Suddenly a bar-rage of fists and kicks hit the man's back as the other whores decided that they had remained silent long enough.

Zane was at a loss as to figure out what happened next. One minute he was under a sheet wrestling with a man determined to slice him open. The next thing he knew, he was standing against the wall, placed there by Bill, who had awakened from his nap and intervened. Maybelle was hustling Mitchell out the door while the whores were making a fuss over Missy, who sported a split lip and a swelling eye.

"Are you all right?" Bill asked him.

Zane took a quick inventory of his body. Except for a

lump on the back of his head, he seemed to have come through the incident unscathed. "I believe I am," he said. "What was with that guy?" he asked Missy.

"He said he liked it when the woman screamed," she explained. "Then he said I didn't scream loud enough, so he hit me."

"I hate that kind," one of the whores said while the others murmured their agreement.

"He was bragging, too, said he had just walked away from the Union army in Virginia back before Christmas," Missy added.

"He must have skedaddled pretty quick to make it all the way out here," Zane observed. "Maybe he was afraid they were chasing him?"

Missy shrugged. She had said all she knew and didn't feel like thinking about it anymore. She was more excited over the fact that Zane had come to her rescue than she was over the beating Mitchell had given her. The occasional beatings were just a hazard of the job. She usually got a bit of extra money to make up for it; although she was doubtful any would come across after all the hullabaloo today.

"Did you come here to see me?" Missy asked Zane while the others filed from the room.

"Uh-uh," Bill said. "Maybelle said for me to send you on your way as soon as she got the other one out of the house."

Zane swallowed in relief. He didn't like the way Missy was looking at him. It was almost as if she thought he actually cared or something. Sure, she was a sweet girl and he didn't want her to get hurt, but it wasn't as if she was his girl. She was a whore! It wasn't as if he wanted to take her out to dinner or home to meet his family. Maybe it was time he gave another one of the girls a turn.

Zane adjusted his clothes and dusted off his hat, which had miraculously survived the tussle without getting squashed flatter than a pancake. Then he remembered that his gun had slid under the bed. He crawled in after it while Missy hung upside down, smiling sweetly and giving him directions. It wasn't as if he couldn't see it himself, dang it all.

He hit the street with a great feeling of relief washing over his body, which was starting to feel like one huge bruise. He swung up on his horse and bypassed the saloon without even thinking about going in for a drink.

If he had gone in he might have noticed a meeting going on at a corner table. Zane's original quarry, Petty, was surrounded by a group that now included the man with the fresh scar and broken nose. He was nursing a drink given to him by the sheriff.

Zane had other things on his mind as he rode away. He was thinking about the money Jason had given him. Should he give it back or save it for another trip? He mulled the question over the entire way home.

Chapter Twenty-six

Jenny had never thought she'd wish for more snow but right now she was desperate for it. She watched from the door of her cabin as Chase and the rest of the men mounted their horses and rode out toward the south.

"Another day and more prayers," she said to herself as they disappeared over the ridge. She wrapped the quilt tighter around her shoulders. It was certainly cold enough for snow. The wind whipping around the tail of her gown was frigid, but there were no clouds to be seen and the dim winter sun held a promise of warmth to be felt when it reached midday.

If only they could catch the saboteurs in action. Chase and Jason had set up watches at night, split the men into patrols, talked to the sheriff, talked to the army and still had nothing but problems. Water holes were being poisoned, stock were being killed and one home-steader had been burned out. Jason's friend had told him a man named Petty had run him off his ranch several months earlier and now a man named Jefferson Petty had shown up in Laramie with plenty of cash and low bids to buy out anyone who wanted to go. It didn't take a genius to figure out what was going on. So why wasn't the sheriff more concerned about it all?

To make matters worse, Zane had reported seeing a lot of shady characters hanging around Maybelle's. He had even gotten into a fight with one of them, a man named Mitchell with a scar on his face. Chase was sure that they were all hired guns for Petty. But so far no one had been able to put together any hard evidence.

"Can we ride our ponies today?" Chance asked as he wrapped an arm around her leg. Jenny ran a hand through his dark hair, still tousled from sleep. Both boys were obsessed with the ponies Jason had given them at Christmas. Jenny and Zeb had been teaching them to care for them and rewarding that care with rides.

Jenny lifted her son to her hip. "My, you're getting to be big," she exclaimed as he settled against her. "Before too long I won't be able to lift you at all."

"Daddy says that your belly's going to get fat, and me and Fox will have to help with the chores," Chance said as he laid his head on her shoulder.

"Daddy said Momma's going to get fat?" Jenny said with blue eyes dancing. "Well, Daddy is going to have to pay for that remark."

"What's a remark?"

Jenny laughed and kissed her son's cheek. "Go wake up Fox and get your clothes on. I'm ready for breakfast."

Chance ran into the room that had been added on to the cabin and jumped onto the bed he shared with Fox. Jenny listened to their squeals as they fell into their morning ritual of wrestling each other out of bed. The tussling would last until the call of nature intervened and they went to seek the outhouse.

Jenny opened the door of the giant wardrobe, which would afford her some privacy as she dressed. She pulled off her gown and hung it on one of the hooks, then took the time to peruse her figure in the mirror. *Looking pretty good for four months along,* she thought as she ran her hands over the still flat plane of her stomach. *And I haven't heard any complaints about these either,* she thought with a smile as she noticed the heavy swelling of her breasts. She touched the scar over her left breast and noticed that it was beginning to fade somewhat. It didn't seem so long ago that she had used a hot blade to remove the brand of Randolph Mason from her breast, but it would be five years this coming fall. The boys would be four come summer when another little Duncan would make its presence known. So much had happened and yet it seemed like just yesterday that she had come to live at the ranch.

Jenny dressed in her usual uniform of shirt, pants, and boots and then took a minute to make up the big bed that she shared with Chase. The boys were dressed and racing each other out the door, so she took a moment to clean up their room.

"And where are we going to put you, my little one?" Jenny asked the still silent babe in her womb as she looked around the room that seemed to grow smaller with each passing Christmas.

Satisfied that her cabin was as neat as possible considering the residence of two three-year-olds, she made her way toward Grace's cabin, where she knew that breakfast would be waiting in spite of her continued insistence that Grace leave it for her to prepare.

Jenny was at her wits' end as to what to do for Grace. Her friend was only a month away from her delivery and worried that Cole's divorce would not come through in time for them to marry before the baby came. If only Constance would be reasonable and sign the papers, but Cole's second visit had been as unproductive as the first. Constance seemed to be taking joy in the fact that she was causing Cole pain. Jenny had yet to meet her, although she had caught sight of her on one of her trips to town. She had resisted the urge to rip her heart out because she had the boys with her. She had also imagined what would have happened if Cat had been around to see the woman mincing about the streets of Laramie in her fashionable clothes. There was no doubt in Jenny's mind that a significant amount of mud would be involved in any meeting between Cole's wife and the feisty Cat.

Amanda was another dilemma that needed solving. It was as if she had turned into a ghost and haunted the upstairs of the big house. She had made a brief appearance during the Christmas festivities, but had then faded back into her room without even taking time to open her gifts. Cole was torn between the two women in his life and frustrated because he didn't have the answers for either of their problems.

Jason and Chase were worried about the goings-on around the ranch and in the outlying areas. Caleb had become even quieter than he'd been before the war. His sketchbook still sat untouched in Grace's cabin, where he had left it the day Jenny had returned it to him. At least its location was a blessing. It could have been burned up in the fire at the bunkhouse.

Even Zane seemed to be in low spirits. He had not been his usual silly self since the turning of the New Year. Jenny wasn't sure if she should be grateful for that or not. He was definitely different. Maybe it had to do with the fact that Maybelle's whores had had to rescue him from a sure beating.

The only one who seemed to be thriving was Zeb. The former slave had settled into his life in Wyoming as if he were born to it. Jenny wondered sometimes if he ever got lonely for his family. If he did, he never showed it. She smiled as she watched him come off the porch of Grace's cabin with a boy on each shoulder and Justice following at his heels. The boys seemed to be eating something, so Jenny accepted the fact that they had been fed and left it at that.

She knew she had overslept. It was the babe causing her tiredness. She needed to stop being so lazy, because who knew how much longer Grace would be able to keep up with her chores. Jenny would have to take over the cooking and the washing for all the men who lived on the ranch. She really wasn't looking forward to that responsibility. Never mind the hard work; it was the time away from the boys and her horses that she resented having to give up.

Maybe Amanda could help. Jenny gave up on that thought as soon as it crossed her mind. Amanda was terrified to be in the presence of the men. Only Jason and Cole could talk to her without making her tremble in fear. Jenny wondered again what kind of abuse she had suffered during those long years when Wade Bishop held her captive.

Caleb could take over some of the indoor chores, but Jenny hated to ask him. It would be a blow to his pride that he would never recover from. Chase had told her that he was as good as ever on horseback, but was still rather awkward on the ground.

Maybe she should ask Jason to hire someone to help out. It smarted her pride to have to admit that she just didn't feel up to all the work that was waiting. There were women she knew who worked from sunup to sundown and took care of a house and family on the side. And one of them had just been burned out by someone who was trying to steal her family's land. Who knew how many others would suffer the same consequences before the troublemakers were stopped?

With those worries on her mind, Jenny walked into Grace's cabin and found the older woman bent double over the table.

"Grace!" Jenny ran to her friend and helped her into a chair. "Are you all right?"

"I don't know," Grace panted. "My back is killing me!"

"Where does it hurt?" Jenny was afraid her labor had started. It was too early yet for the baby to come.

"Across my shoulders," Grace replied.

Jenny heaved a sigh of relief and massaged Grace's shoulders, bringing sighs of relief.

"I was afraid you had gone into labor," Jenny said as she rubbed out the knots across Grace's neck.

"No, I was wiping the table and just had to rest a minute. My back was tied up in knots."

"You're worrying too much, Grace," Jenny commented.

"Isn't this a case of the pot calling the kettle black?" Grace asked with unusual good humor.

Jenny responded by giving Grace's arm a playful pinch and picked up half a biscuit left behind on one of the boys' plates.

"I guess this means that you didn't get sick this morning," Grace said as Jenny wolfed down the biscuit.

"No, the morning sickness has been over for a few weeks. Now I just feel like sleeping all the time."

"Maybe you're just remembering the last time," Grace commented as she studied Jenny.

"I did manage to sleep away the first few months of Chance's pregnancy," Jenny said as she scooped the remaining scrambled eggs from the skillet.

"And who could blame you?" Grace answered as she remembered the horror of those months after Jamie's murder.

They fell into the easy companionship of shared work. They cleaned up the breakfast dishes and then Grace began the preparations for lunch while Jenny tackled the never-ending chore of mending.

"Maybe we could talk Amanda into doing the mending," Grace said, taking a break from her work to sit down in a chair.

"It would be a big help if she would," Jenny said as she sewed a pocket that had been ripped away from Caleb's shirt.

"I feel like we're not really doing much for her," Grace confided.

"There's just so much going on," Jenny agreed. "And I'm sure that what happened at the house just added to her fears."

"Cole is worried about her, but he just doesn't know what else he can do."

"It's just like everything else, Grace. It's going to take time."

"Maybe you could talk to her?" Grace suggested.

"Do you mean tell her about what happened to me?"

"It might give you some common ground. Maybe give her something to relate to?"

Jenny snapped a thread with her teeth as she mused on Grace's suggestion. "I don't know, Grace. My experience might sound rather trivial after what Amanda's been through. We don't know how many men were forced on her."

"That's true," Grace said.

"I have tried to talk to her, but it's so hard. It's as if she's afraid to open herself up and let anyone know what's going on inside."

"All I know is she can't go on like this. It's almost as if she doesn't want to be alive."

"Are you and Cole afraid that she might try to hurt herself?"

"I don't know. Possibly. We talk about it a lot, but we never come up with any answers."

"Sounds a lot like everything else that's going on around here," Jenny said with a wry smile.

Grace flipped her dish towel toward Jenny as she awkwardly rose from her chair. "At least somebody's in a good mood this morning."

"I didn't start out that way. I woke up just as worried as I went to bed. But then Chance said something that got me out of it."

"So what were the little man's words of wisdom?"

"He told me that Chase said I was going to get fat."

"I'd kill him."

"I plan on it." The two women shared laughter as they went back to their tasks. The sounds of Justice's barking overrode their joyful noise and Grace went to the door to see what the fuss was about.

"Oh, my God," she exclaimed and turned to look at Jenny with her mouth hanging open.

"What is it?" Jenny asked as she came to the door to look over Grace's shoulder. A tall woman with long red hair stood at the bottom of the step while her companion tied their horses to the rail. Justice stood guard on the porch, alternating between barking and looking to Grace for instruction. The man walked from between the horses and took his hat off as he looked up at the two women in the door of the cabin.

"Grace, you've put on a bit of weight since the last time I saw you," Jake said as he smiled up at them.

"Jake, if I wasn't so thrilled to see you right now, I'd wring your neck," Grace cried. "I might just wring it anyway." They met halfway, with Grace doing her best to hug the life out of him despite the difficulty posed by her protruding belly. Jenny waited impatiently to take her turn.

"How in the world?" she managed to get out between the tears.

"It's all a long story and I want to tell it only once," Jake said. He held out his hand to the woman at the bottom of the steps. "I will share the best part," he said as Shannon came up beside him. "This is my wife, Shannon."

"Your wife?" Grace asked incredulously.

"My wife," Jake assured her.

Jenny stepped up to Shannon and took her hands in her own. It amused both of the women to see that they were of the same height.

"Welcome to the family, Shannon," Jenny said as she hugged her.

"Thank you," Shannon replied in her delightful brogue. "I like it very much, so far."

Jenny looked at Jake, who was beaming with pride. "I see you've done a good job of taming this wild beast," she said teasingly.

"It took a bit of work, but once I got his attention, it was easy," Shannon replied in the same teasing tone.

Jake rolled his eyes at the banter. "I can see that I'm going to have problems with both of you."

"Speak for yourself there, cowboy. From what I can see, Shannon is an answer to prayer," Jenny said. "Now come inside and tell us why you're not dead."

"Do you mind if Shannon tells the story? I need to find Caleb."

Jenny looked into the pale blue eyes that were full of concern for his friend. "They went toward the south pasture." Jake untied his horse. "Jake," Jenny said as he swung up. "We've got trouble, so don't try to surprise them. You might wind up really dead this time."

Jake's pale blue eyes narrowed as he looked into the deep blue of Jenny's. It was a look she knew well, but this time it was steady and sure instead of edged with anger. It gave her a strange sense of comfort. Jenny placed an arm around Shannon's shoulders as Jake took off at a full gallop over the ridge.

"Come inside, Shannon, and tell us everything," Jenny said as she led Jake's wife into the cabin. "And take it easy on both of us, because we're expecting. . . ."

"Rider coming," Chase said. They didn't doubt him. He had proved through the years that his dark eyes and sharp ears gave him an edge the others did not possess.

Chase, Cole, Jason, Caleb and Zane turned their

horses and lined them up side by side toward the direction where a dim figure could be seen approaching.

"It's not Dan or Randy," Chase informed them as he surveyed the rolling plains covered in winter's drab colors. Dan and Randy were riding the northern borders of the ranch, where things had remained peaceful. Chase hated the thought of going off and leaving his family alone with so much trouble surrounding them, but the work needed to be done and the ranch needed to be protected. He would have felt better if someone could have stayed behind, since Zeb still wasn't good with a gun. But Jenny was better with a weapon than most men and Grace had proved herself quite capable with a rifle. It was just another dilemma added to the never-ending list that became more overwhelming each day as the trouble mounted.

"Don't recognize the horse either," Cole said as he made sure his rifle would slide easily from the stock, just in case.

"Don't be in such a hurry," Jason warned him. "It might be one of the locals needing help."

The men had been on their way to look at the homestead that had been burned out the previous day. Their journey had been interrupted by the discovery of another dead steer. They had found the body in a ravine, the blood from the slice in its throat freezing the carcass to the ground.

"Dang," Caleb said as he watched the approaching rider.

"What is it?" Chase asked.

Caleb shook his head. "Nothing. I just thought I recognized . . ."

"Dang," Zane said and then let out a whoop.

Chase looked closely at the approaching rider. He dug his heels into the buckskin and the horse took off with a leap; Zane and Caleb were right behind him.

The three men galloped toward the rider, who had pulled his dun-colored horse up abruptly before sliding to the ground to wait for the group that was quickly approaching.

"Yeehaw!" Zane yelled as he flew off his horse and rolled Jake onto the ground with him. Jake landed flat on his back with Zane sitting on his stomach screaming his lungs out. Chase jumped down and pulled Zane off so Jake could breathe. The two men hauled Jake to his feet and alternated between pounding on his back and hugging his neck.

"Dang," they all said at once as Caleb watched from horseback.

"Why aren't you dead?" Zane hollered.

"You nearly killed me, you dang fool," Jake hollered back. "All these dang reunions are going to be the death of me."

Chase quietly grasped the bridle of Caleb's horse as he danced around, agitated by the commotion under his feet. Caleb balanced himself against the horse as he dismounted and found the ground with his feet.

Jake looked at his friend as he began to move forward awkwardly. "Dang, Caleb," Jake said, swallowing hard as he realized how lucky they were to be alive. Both Ty and Caleb had lost something precious to the war. He, on the other hand, had come out a winner. He should have been dead, but he was alive and he was whole. He had found a woman to share his life with and he had put his demons to rest. He was a lucky man. Life had brought him a windfall of blessings.

"Dang but if it ain't good to see you, Jake," Caleb said with a glow in his warm brown eyes. The two men embraced, friends from the beginning, now as brothers after sharing the horrors of war.

Zane dashed at his eyes and cleared his throat. Chase grinned as Jason and Cole joined the group.

"Well, it's about time we had some good news around these parts," Cole said.

Jason dismounted and gave Jake a fatherly hug while the other man ignored the sudden barrage of questions that were being thrown at him.

"Can't it wait until we get back?" Jake asked.

"Nope," Zane said. "You're going to tell us about it on the way back."

"If I tell you about it now, it will spoil the surprise," Jake said with a sly smile.

"Surprise?" they all asked at once.

"Does Ty know that you're alive?" Caleb asked as they all turned to remount their horses.

"I saw him," Jake said. "Cat too. They're doing fine and itching for this war to be over with." He studied Caleb's stance as they stood next to his horse. "Do you need a hand up?"

Caleb swung up into his saddle. "I can manage," he said, secretly grateful that he had made it without much trouble.

Jake smoothed out a rein that had become twisted against the neck of Caleb's horse. "Sometimes you've got to be dead before you learn how to appreciate the best things in your life," he said as he looked up at Caleb. "I sure did miss you."

Caleb smiled down at Jake. "If I had to choose between this and you, I'd choose you a hundred times over," he said as he moved his hand over his missing leg.

"Dang if you all don't sound like a bunch of women," Zane said. "Now let's get a move on. I want to see the surprise."

"One thing, Zane," Jake said as he moved the dun in beside him. "If you so much as touch this surprise, I'll kill you." Jake took off on the dun, falling in beside Caleb.

"Dang," Zane said, grinning. "Can't wait to see what it is."

"You say Mister Jake's alive?" Zeb asked as he sat down at the table.

"Who is Jake?" Fox asked.

"Jake is one of your friends, just like Caleb and Zane," Jenny explained to the boys as she set their plates down before them.

"Why was he dead?" Chance asked.

"He wasn't, darling, we just thought he was." Jenny looked to the other adults in the room for help. It was still hard for her to comprehend what had happened, much less have to explain it so a child could understand.

"He was lost," Shannon explained, easing into a chair between the two boys. She had pitched in to help prepare the lunch while she answered all the questions that Jenny and Grace had thrown her way. "And nobody knew where to find him. And he couldn't remember where he lived."

"Why couldn't he remember?" Fox asked.

"He had a bump on his head," Shannon explained.

"Oh," Fox said and took a big gulp of milk. Both boys seemed satisfied with the answer, and Jenny gave a sigh of relief. Sometimes their constant questions were beyond her patience. She gave Shannon one of her wide grins and was pleased to get one in return. Jenny could not remember ever warming up to someone so quickly. She was usually more guarded around new people, a hard lesson she had learned after spending several years on her own. Shannon seemed to fit right in. She had helped out with the chores as naturally as if she had been working with Grace and Jenny all her life. Jenny soon realized that Jake's wife was an answer to prayer in more ways than one.

"I bet they've been whooping it up all over the countryside," Zeb said, laughing at the thought of it.

"I'm sure it was quite a reunion," Grace added.

"It sure is nice to have some good news for a change," Jenny commented. "Most of our days have been full of trouble," she explained to Shannon.

"We noticed quite a bit of it on our way out here," Shannon replied. "It's as if the war has torn the entire country apart."

"So how are things back East?" Grace asked. "Was there any fighting going on around you?"

"We missed most of the fighting in my town, but we saw quite a few of the wounded. We never knew from one day to the next who would be brought in. We just treated the wounded, no matter what uniform they wore," Shannon said.

"Thank goodness for that," Grace exclaimed. "I'd hate to think of Jake not getting help because he wore a Confederate uniform."

"I didn't even think about it when I found him," Shannon replied. "I just knew he was hurt."

"Thank you for saving him," Jenny said as she slid into the chair next to Shannon.

"It was my pleasure, believe me," Shannon replied with a twinkle in her deep green eyes.

Jenny flashed her grin. The day just kept getting better and better as far as she was concerned.

"I've got something for you," Shannon said to Zeb.

"For me?" Zeb asked in surprise. He was still reeling from the generous gifts he had received at Christmastime.

"It's from your mother." Shannon pulled a folded piece of paper from her pocket. "She figured we'd make it here quicker than the mail."

Zeb held on to the paper as if it were made of fine crystal. "You saw my momma?"

"Yes. She said to tell you she's doing well and taking good care of Mister Parker."

Zeb smiled widely, something he had been doing lately with amazing regularity. "Dang," he said. "My momma wrote me a letter."

"Cat's been teaching her, Zeb. You knew she would," Jenny said.

"Yep, I guess I did." Zeb excused himself from the table. "I 'spect I'll go read it now," he announced proudly and left for the bunkhouse with his prize in hand.

"Well, I don't know about everyone else, but I think we should have a party," Grace said as they watched him leave.

"A party!" the boys squealed joyfully.

"Sure, why not?" Grace said, tousling both of their heads. "I can't think of a better reason to celebrate. After all, we've had a miracle and a marriage show up on our doorstep in the same moment. Sounds like a good enough reason to me."

"A party?" Shannon asked in awe. Just like that at the drop of a hat. They were going to have a party.

"I'd better go talk to Agnes and see what she has

stashed away in the cupboard," Jenny said. "Maybe we could get Amanda to pitch in too."

"Oh, I hope so," Grace said. Her face was shining with excitement. A party would be a nice change of pace, especially with all the doom and dread that had been surrounding them since before Christmas. A party would make them forget their troubles for a while. Grace pulled out her recipe box as Jenny left to go up to the big house with her boys trailing after her. "Let's see what we can whip up in a hurry for our party," she said to Shannon as she put the box down before her.

"I'll do what I can," Shannon said. "Just so you know, I don't read very well yet, but I'm great at following directions." She leaned toward Grace with a confiding tone and a wry smile. "Please don't tell Jake I said that."

Grace laughed out loud and once she started, found it hard to stop. "Oh my, Shannon," she said with tears of joy in her eyes. "You *are* the answer to our prayers."

Chapter Twenty-seven

Parties were good for the soul. So was moderation. Jenny looked around in disgust at the snoring bodies that lay about the parlor in the big house. Even Jason was slumped in an undignified position with his head tilted back and his mouth wide open as he slept in his chair. The party had started out well enough. They had eaten some special treats and talked and joked. Jake had bragged about Shannon's voice and after a little begging she had brought out her guitar and entertained them with some songs. Her voice was beautiful and had held them all transfixed. Jason had been so inspired that he'd brought out his private stock of brandy to drink a toast to Jake's homecoming. Which led to a toast to Jake's wedding. Which led to a toast to Cole and Grace's hopefully soon wedding. Which led to a toast to their baby and a toast to Jenny and Chase's baby and so on and so forth. When Randy left and then returned with a mysterious-smelling jug of moonshine, the whole group went to hell in a handbag as Zane had remarked over and over and over again.

"Men," Jenny snorted in disgust. The odor emanating from the room was enough to choke a horse. Even Zeb had joined in the fun, shyly hanging back in the corner until Zane had dragged him into the middle of things and made sure that his cup was filled. Unfortunately the big man had passed out right in front of the doorway, which made it a little difficult to get in and out of the room. Jenny stepped over his snoring form and made a face at the racket that greeted her.

The women and children had retreated upstairs to find soft beds when the rowdiness started. Grace and Jenny had abstained due to their condition and Shannon had declared she had no use for liquor but if Jake wanted to make a bigger fool of himself than he already was, then he should go on and drink. The sass that had passed between the two of them had been surprising to the others at first, but they soon understood. Shannon gave as good as she got. She was the first person who had not tiptoed around Jake and his short fuse. Unfortunately for Jake, Zane relished the thought that he could now antagonize Jake and not get shot for doing it.

Jenny wondered what Amanda had thought of all the whooping and hollering that had gone on downstairs. She had declined to join the party. To her Jake was just another unknown man she needed to avoid.

Fat chance of any work getting done today, Jenny thought as she surveyed the sleeping men. Jason and Caleb had snagged the wingback chairs that flanked the fireplace. Cole had gotten lucky and landed the couch, which was a bit short for his long, rangy frame. Jake had landed in a chair with an ottoman and didn't seem to be suffering too much. Zane, Randy and Dan made a circle in the middle of the floor with heads propped up on the backs and legs of one another. Chase was in the window seat, still propped up as if he were looking out the window. Jenny spared her husband a minute of mercy and ran her fingers through the feathers of his dark hair.

He stirred without opening his eyes and snared her about the waist with his arm.

"Are we dead?" he asked as he leaned his head against her breast.

"It smells like it," Jenny said as she dropped a kiss on top of his head.

"Where are the boys?"

"Still asleep upstairs. Agnes is fixing breakfast for everyone up here."

"I think I'll pass," he said blearily.

"I guess this is one of those times where you reap what you sow."

"Jenny," he said slowly as if his head were about to fall off his neck and roll around on the floor. "If you give me one more word of wisdom, I will throw up."

Jenny moved away and his head clunked against the frame of the window.

"Ow! What was that for?"

"That was for telling the boys I was going to get fat!" Jenny chuckled evilly.

Chase tried to grab her and missed, even though his eyes were wide open. She saucily stuck out her tongue and flung a pillow at him.

"Sleep it off," she commanded as she picked her way

through the room toward the door. Chase took the pillow and rolled onto his side, trying his best to fit his long frame onto a cushion half his length. Jenny caught her foot on someone and barely kept herself from falling on her face.

"Oh, Missy, that feels so good," Zane said as Dan shifted his legs beneath Zane's head.

Jenny rolled her eyes and made her way to the kitchen. Shannon and the boys were sitting at the table talking to Agnes.

"I found these two sleepy heads in the hall," Shannon explained.

"I think they'll be the only ones of the male persuasion awake today," Jenny declared as she gave the boys each a quick kiss.

"Is it that bad?" Shannon asked. She had memories of her father's drunken spells and resulting hangovers.

Jenny saw her fear. Obviously, she had some painful times behind her.

"No, they just needed to blow off some steam. They'll be fine as soon as they all throw up and have a shower."

"Sounds lovely," Shannon said, wrinkling her nose in disgust.

"Is Grace up?" Jenny asked.

"She's down at her cabin," Agnes chimed in. "She's got a list of things she wants to do today and was anxious to get started."

"We're going to town," Shannon explained. "I told her I'd take over the cooking. I want to earn my keep."

"I've no doubt that you will," Jenny said. "I'm just happy that you're going to stay."

"Where else would we go?" Shannon said. "This is Jake's home."

"And it's yours now too."

"Thank you. Although it might take a bit of getting used to. Everything here is so big and spread out. I didn't know you could see so far. At home you stepped out your door and onto the next mountain. They were that close."

The boys looked up with wide blue eyes at Shannon's description of her home. "Could you really?" Fox asked.

Shannon bussed the swirls of his bright copper hair. "Not really, it's just a way of saying things."

"I like the way you say things," Chance declared. "And your songs."

"Thank you. Maybe I could teach both of you how to play the guitar."

Their eyes grew as wide as they had been on Christmas morning and they nodded silently, afraid that if they spoke, the wonderful opportunity would be denied them.

Grace blew into the kitchen with her cheeks rosy and her brown eyes twinkling. Jenny could not remember the last time she had seen her in such a good mood.

"It's the babe making her that way," Agnes confided. "She's feathering her nest."

Jenny agreed with the housekeeper. She remembered feeling that way herself; she had made use of the energy to sew tiny garments for Chance.

"Do you think we could rouse up one of the men to hitch the buggy for us?" Grace asked.

"Don't bother," Jenny sighed. "I'll do it."

"That bad?" Grace asked.

Jenny just smiled and nodded as she left the kitchen for the barn.

"I'd love to come along," she said later when she

brought the buggy around. "But I wouldn't dare leave the boys in the middle of all this."

"We'll be fine," Grace declared as she took up the reins. "It's a beautiful warm day and Shannon can learn her way around town."

"Just keep an eye out," Jenny warned the two women.

"We'll be fine," Grace said as she popped the reins and the horse took off down the drive.

Jenny watched as the buggy disappeared over the ridge. She wondered if the strange feeling nibbling at her was because Grace didn't go to town much and hardly ever on her own. But then again, the baby was announcing that its time was near by giving Grace the urge to get everything ready for its coming. Besides, Shannon looked quite capable of handling anything that came along. She seemed to be as strong as an ox and had seen a lot of the world by nursing the wounded of the war. The two women should be fine.

Jenny wondered if she should have taken the time to put a rifle in the buggy.

"Who's that?" Shannon asked Grace as her companion stopped tying the buggy to look at a couple dressed in expensive clothes standing on the porch of a hotel.

"Cole's soon-to-be ex-wife," Grace spat out in disgust. She bent her head self-consciously as she spoke, as if to hide her scars.

Shannon couldn't help noticing that the couple was observing them also. "I'm glad to see his taste has gotten better," Shannon said, giving the over-dressed woman a returning stare. She knew Grace was self-conscious about her face. Jake had told her about the scars, but after her first meeting with Grace, Shannon had hardly given them a thought. There was so much more to the woman that the scars faded into the background. *As it should be,* Shannon thought. *Grace will be beautiful long after that one's looks have faded.*

Grace gave Shannon a smile of gratitude as Constance whispered in her companion's ear. The man took out his watch and checked it and then nodded in agreement as Grace and Shannon went into the general store. Grace went about the business of introducing Shannon to the storekeeper and put her name on the list of those approved to sign for Jason's account.

Shannon was nervous as she signed her name to the ledger. It was the first time she had done it on her own without Jake there to guide her. He had been teaching her to read and write since they left North Carolina and she had made great progress in her learning. She checked the signature and was proud to see that it didn't look a bit shaky, in spite of the way her hand had felt while holding the pen.

The two women finished their business and were on their way back to the ranch just as the winter sun hit its zenith.

"Sometimes the snow gets so deep that you can't even get to town," Grace said as the horse moved over the trail at a smart pace. The ground was firm beneath the hooves and wheels and the ride remained relatively smooth. Both women were taken with the beauty of the warm winter day. Grace seemed to be determined to enjoy it since she knew it would be a long while before she would get out again.

"Sometimes at home you could take a step and disappear in a drift as high as your head," Shannon said.

"Which was dangerous since you never knew when you might be stepping off the side of a mountain."

"I would imagine so," Grace said. "It sounds beautiful though."

"It was. And it's beautiful here in a different way." Shannon looked around at the wide expanse of rolling prairie. "It doesn't seem to be as wild as the woods back home, but then again it is. We saw buffalo on our way out. It was a bit scary to hear all the noise of their running but exciting too."

"That is the way life is out here. One minute it's so quiet and peaceful and it seems like you can see into forever. The next it's a battle for life and death. And that's just the challenges nature throws at us."

"Of course, when man gets involved, it makes things worse," Shannon commented.

"That has been the case lately," Grace agreed.

"I couldn't turn around back home without a busy-body meddling in my affairs," Shannon laughed. "One even took full credit for Jake's marrying me, which was fine. We got a party out of her at least."

"I see that Jake survived it. From what I saw this morning, it might be a while before he recovers from this latest party."

"It will be funny to see the men walking about on their knees."

Grace laughed at Shannon's dry wit and quickly dismissed the twinge in her back. They would be home soon enough. She'd worry about it then.

Before their laughter died, the buggy was surrounded by a group of riders. Grace snapped the reins to drive the horse through, but one of the riders caught the reins and the poor animal could only rear within the traces. Shannon placed a protective arm around Grace's shoulders as the reins were torn from her grasp. Both women were shocked to see a familiar face in the group that held them captive.

"Well, I'll be damned," swore a man with a scar on his face and a crook in his nose. "I lost both of my brothers because of you." He spat the words at Shannon, who sat tall and straight on the seat beside Grace.

"Well, isn't this sweet?" Constance was obviously enjoying herself. "Here I was thinking I was lucky to run into someone I know and my friend Mitchell has done the same. It's a small world, isn't it, ladies?"

"You and me are going to have one hell of a reunion," Mitchell promised loudly. "I hope your man is around so he can watch it."

Shannon's green eyes shot daggers. "I've known a lot of men in my time that talked big and had nothing to back it up." She cast a look toward Mitchell's crotch. "I'm pretty sure you're one of them."

Mitchell's scar grew vivid as his face flushed with anger and embarrassment. It didn't help the matter at all that the other men were enjoying the put-down as much as Shannon was. He kicked his horse up to Shannon's side of the buggy.

"You'll be screaming by the time I'm done with you," he promised.

"Coward," Shannon retorted and turned her head away to ignore his threats. She noticed that Grace looked pale and wondered perhaps if she should have kept her mouth shut.

"Could we hurry things up a bit?" Constance called out. She wondered why she seemed to be the only one having fun. After all, she was about to make Cole squirm and beg her for mercy. She couldn't wait.

What luck it had been for their plans to have Grace show up in town. Petty had known from the start that Jason Lynch would not sell off any part of his ranch. He was more the type to give it to the government to aid the cause of progress. What a waste! They had quickly decided not to lose any time making offers that would just be refused. What they needed was leverage. They must take something that Jason wanted badly. Just by greasing the right palms and making the right connections, they had found out all they needed to know. Jason Lynch was very attached to his people. He even considered the people who worked for him to be family. The ploy to kidnap the great-grandchildren had failed drastically and had resulted in the loss of all of their men. And after getting a look at the father of the boys and hearing stories about him, Petty had decided that taking that route was just too dangerous. The man was practically insane when it came to his wife and sons. Jason's daughter was back East with her husband. But Grace was here and handy. And even though she was carrying Cole's child, Jason felt a great deal of affection for the woman. There had been those who had thought for years that Jason would someday marry her. Constance wondered for a moment if Jason had bad feelings toward Cole. It was almost funny to think about it. Two of the best-looking mature men in the West and they both were infatuated with a woman with a scarred face. What was it about Grace that was so special?

The group of men kept the buggy surrounded as they led the horse and two women down the trail. Grace's mind scrambled as she tried to guess where their captors were taking them. They took the cut and she quickly realized that they were headed to the cabin where Fox's mother and grandfather had lived. It still stood deserted after all these years as far as she knew. Then Grace recalled looking at the proposed route for the railroad and knew that Constance and her friend had probably bought the place for a song.

"Do you mind telling me what's going on?" Shannon whispered to Grace.

"I think we're being kidnapped," Grace whispered back.

"Well, I can understand why Mitchell wants me, but what has this got to do with you?"

"I really don't know," Grace confided. "But I'm sure whatever it is, it isn't good for either one of us. These are the men responsible for all the bad luck that everyone's been having."

"I think I already had that part figured out," Shannon said as she squeezed Grace's hand in her own.

"Don't worry, Cole and Jake will come," Grace assured her.

"They'll have to wake up first," Shannon said as casually as she would say "pass the milk."

Mitchell was looking at her. Jake would have to kill him.

Chapter Twenty-eight

Jenny wasn't the least bit surprised when the empty buggy showed up at the barn. She had almost been expecting it. Zeb grabbed the reins of the horse as he showed up without his passengers and did a quick examination of the seat. An envelope was pinned to the seat by a knife. Zeb pulled it out and handed the letter to Jenny.

"They want to talk to Jason. They want to make a trade. Grace for the ranch," Jenny quickly summarized. "We're supposed to wait to hear from them again."

"Can they do that, Miss Jenny?"

"Some people think they can do anything they want." Jenny's mind raced as all the possible tricks and complications that could occur circled her brain. Luckily hers was working. She wasn't sure about the men's brains at the present time.

"Run up to the house and kick everyone awake."

Jenny had seen a few bodies wandering by while she worked with one of her colts. She was pretty sure Chase was in the shower and had heard Cole hacking and coughing as he went into Grace's cabin. "And, Zeb, watch out for Jake."

"Yes, ma'am, I knows that much," Zeb said as he took off up the hill.

The top of a dark head over the shower stall confirmed that Chase was inside. Jenny threw the door open and ignored the passion that sprang to life, flashing deep within his dark eyes.

"We got trouble," she announced as she handed him a towel.

"Grace?"

"Yes, Shannon too, as far as I know." It didn't even surprise her anymore when he knew what she was thinking. "I told Zeb to watch out for Jake."

Chase quickly dried off and jerked on his clothes as Jenny read the letter. Both had their ears tuned for any commotion. They weren't sure of how the new Jake was going to react.

"We need to find them before they contact Jason again." Chase had quickly come to the same conclusion as Jenny. "What do I have to do to convince you to stay behind?" Chase asked as they walked between the cabin and the bunkhouse.

"Don't worry, I will," she promised. "After all, it might all be a distraction so they can attack the ranch again."

Jenny's words stopped Chase dead in his tracks. "So who should stay and who should go?"

"There's no way Jake and Cole will stay put. Take Caleb with you, since he's probably the only one Jake will listen to. The rest of us will stay here and wait for the next message. Of course, we'll all be in the house with rifles ready."

Chase dropped a quick kiss on her cheek as he saw the determined faces of his friends coming down the hill.

"I love you," he said.

"I know. I love you too."

They still had to tell Cole.

Shannon was more worried about Grace than she was about herself. She could feel the tensing in the woman's body as they sat side by side against the wall with their hands tied in front. Mitchell had remembered the fight she had given him before and was not about to turn his back on her. She was sorry. She had wanted to remind him.

They were arguing about what to do with her.

Mitchell was certain that she was of no consequence to anyone here since he had just seen her over a month earlier in West Virginia.

Constance declared that she could be Lynch's daughter, who was reported to be back East. She could have come home.

Shannon and Grace were perfectly content to let them think that. All Shannon had to do was keep the Irish lilt out of her voice. She could, as long as they didn't make her angry. It had a tendency to come out more when she was mad. It wouldn't take much to get her that way.

Mitchell was still looking at her. He wanted his revenge and he wanted it now.

It was almost amusing to watch the two of them argue back and forth, except for the fact that if Mitchell won, Shannon was done for. She was confident that she could probably give him something to think about if it was just the two of them, but the way the rest of the men were looking at her . . .

They needed to buy some time. They knew that the horse and buggy had been turned loose and that the animal would go directly home. It was just a matter of praying that the men would be conscious enough to realize what had happened and track the buggy's trail back to where the women were being held. Shannon was confident that Jenny would make sure they got to it, even if she had to personally wring each one of their necks in the process.

Grace let out a small gasp, so quiet that Shannon had to look at her to make sure she had heard it.

"Are you all right?" Shannon whispered.

"I don't know," Grace whispered back. Her face seemed flushed and she was holding her mouth in a tight line.

"Is it the baby?"

"Quiet!" Constance yelled.

She didn't seem as elegant when she screamed in that manner, Shannon observed. It was more like Mrs. Bradshaw back home when she was hollering at her pigs after they went wallowing in the deep wood.

"Yes," Grace managed to answer.

"Count in between," Shannon advised.

"I said quiet." Constance looked down her nose at the women and popped her riding quirt on the side of her skirt.

"Is that supposed to scare me now?" Shannon asked with a bright red eyebrow cocked in question. *You didn't keep it out that time, Shannon*, she thought, but stopped worrying as Constance's face flushed a deep shade of purple. Shannon needed to get her attention away from Grace. Constance was looking at her much too closely.

"How would you like it if I gave you a set of scars to match hers?" Constance's rage was barely contained as she bent over Shannon.

"Better that than looking like you," Shannon fired back. *That ought to get her attention away from Grace.*

"Let me have her," Mitchell said. "I'll give her more scars than you can count."

"My father would love that, for sure," Shannon said, adding to the confusion. "He won't be as generous for damaged goods."

"See, I told you she is Lynch's daughter." Constance smiled in victory.

"She's not his daughter. Just listen to her talk!" Mitchell yelled. "Why would Lynch's daughter be working in an army hospital?" Mitchell refused to believe it.

"My husband was wounded," Shannon replied with a vicious grin. "You remember my husband, don't you?"

Mitchell touched the fresh scar on his face. "I'll remember him the same way you'll always remember me," he said with a sneer. "As a matter of fact, let's have a look at the scar I gave you. We can see who's healed faster." He jerked Shannon to her feet and pulled at the shirt tucked into the waistband of her skirt.

Shannon returned the favor by clubbing him in the jaw with her bound hands. Mitchell struck back, but Shannon stood her ground as the imprint of his fist turned red against the porcelain white of her skin.

"I see someone's given you a present also," Shannon

said victoriously. "I don't recall seeing that the last time we met."

Mitchell's hand moved without thinking to the bruise on the bridge of his nose and then he drew it back as if to strike her again.

"Enough," Constance yelled. This time she followed up her command by laying her quirt across Mitchell's chest.

Shannon licked the blood off her lip and grinned her victory.

"You forget that I'm giving the orders here," Constance reminded the men. "And if you want to earn your pay, you'll do as I say." She kicked at the men who were within striking distance. "The rest of you, get outside and keep watch. They might just figure out where we are and do something foolish." The men begrudgingly left the cabin. They had been enjoying the arguments. Mitchell followed, giving all the women a promising glare.

"You've beat them to it," Shannon said to Constance. She heard the sharp intake of Grace's breath behind her. She prayed that Grace hadn't gone into labor. They needed more time. She wondered how long it would take for Jake to find her.

Constance looked at her in complete shock.

"Do you think they're just going to sit around and wait to hear from you? Ask your friend what my husband did when last we saw him."

"He won't do much when he sees you with a gun at your head." Constance restlessly stalked around the cabin.

"That one and his brothers thought the same," Shannon continued, making sure she kept her body between Grace and Constance. She was fairly certain that Grace was in labor. Her breathing had become louder, almost as if she were panting like a dog. "You'd best let us go before you wind up dead," Shannon said. "Like the brothers."

Constance whirled and slapped her quirt on the table. Grace jumped at the noise.

"Oh my," Constance purred as she walked past Shannon. "The not-quite Mrs. Larrimore doesn't look so good." She walked over to where Grace sat against the wall. "Is it time for your precious little bastard to make its appearance in the world?"

Shannon swung with all her might. Her bound fists came up and hit Constance square in the nose. Blood spurted and she fell back against the table. Shannon hit her again and the woman's dark eyes rolled back into her head as she fell to the floor, unconscious.

"You don't know how many times I wanted to do that," Grace panted.

"How are you?"

"I'm not really sure," Grace's voice was stronger than her answer.

"Can you stand?"

"If you help me." Grace extended her bound hands.

"How close are they?" Shannon asked as she pulled Grace to her feet.

"Very," Grace replied as she bent over double. "How long do you think we have before someone comes?"

"If you mean the fools outside, I'm surprised they haven't come checking already with all the noise Her Majesty made as she crashed to the floor."

"Do you think her nose is broken?" Grace looked down at Constance without pity.

"I dearly hope so," Shannon said. She went to the

cupboard in hopes of finding a knife to cut their bonds. "Do you think the men will be able to find us?"

"Chase can track anything. And besides that, this cabin belonged to Fox's mother."

"I bet they didn't know that," Shannon said with a smile of victory. She had found a knife in a drawer. It looked as if it were too dull to cut butter but she'd give it a try. Grace held out her hands and Shannon went to work, slowly sawing at the strands. It seemed to take forever, especially when Grace was overcome every few minutes with labor pains. The rope eventually frayed apart and Grace was able to untie Shannon.

Shannon used the rope to tie up Constance and added a gag just to see the look on her face when she woke up. Then the two women crept to the window.

They could see the men scattered about, all watching the area around the cabin. Mitchell was nowhere to be seen, but Shannon figured he was out of her sight line, possibly even behind the cabin or in the small barn off to the right.

"So what do we do now?" Grace asked.

"Try to sneak out the back?" Shannon suggested.

"That might be a little difficult for me," Grace said. "I think my water just broke."

Chapter Twenty-nine

"I guess brains aren't a requirement for employment with this guy," Cole said as he handed the spyglass back to Chase.

"They probably think we're just going to sit around the ranch and wait to hear from them," Chase said. "You get six?"

"Yes," Cole said as he backed out from beneath the stand of scrub trees on a small rise close to Sarah's former cabin. Chase had not had any problem following the buggy tracks back to the cut. They had circled around to the rise after that to see what awaited them. They had a clear view of the cabin and barn from their post on the hill. The problem was that the men surrounding the cabin would also have a clear view of them when they rode in. "Of course, we don't know how many are inside or in the barn."

"Let's play it safe and say ten," Chase said. "Maybe it

will make Jake slow down a little." He looked toward the horses, where Jake waited beside Caleb. The look on his face was murderous. Chase remembered the feeling well.

"I know exactly how he feels," Cole said as he looked back. "And I reckon you know more than anyone else."

"I hope I never feel it again. Three times was enough for me."

"Three?" Cole asked. He remembered the last time in New York when Jenny had been captured by Wade Bishop. He had heard of another time involving a man named Randolph Mason.

"The first time was just after I met Jenny at the orphanage. She was sold off to a man named Miller. Jamie and I searched for five years and never found a trace of her. She wound up finding us. You know about the other two times."

"What did you see?" Jake asked as the two men mounted their horses. His eyes had narrowed into slivers of ice.

"Ten or so. All scattered about and hoping for trouble. The women are most likely inside the cabin," Chase informed him.

"So we just ride in from all directions?" Jake asked.

"Attack on all fronts," Caleb added, recalling battle plans from the war.

"They'll see us coming from a mile away," Chase said. "They'll have too much time to do something foolish."

"Like use the women for a shield," Cole spat out in disgust. "We're going to have to take it slow and easy and hope that we can surprise them."

"I think I can circle around and come in through the

barn," Chase said as he knelt on the ground and used some small stones to form a diagram. "If Cole can get up close on foot, coming in from this side, and Caleb can come in from behind on horseback, then they won't know which way to turn."

"So where does that leave me?" Jake asked.

"Coming right down the drive with guns blasting."

Jake nodded with a grim smile on his face.

The men once again checked the loads on their weapons.

"So what's our plan if they do use the women as a shield?" Caleb asked.

"Hope that my aim isn't off," Jake said grimly as he wheeled his horse to make his way toward the front of the house.

"Don't do anything foolish, Jake," Cole called after him. "Remember that they've got my woman too."

Jake kept going.

"Dang it, Jake!" Cole called. Caleb placed a comforting hand on Cole's arm.

"He won't do anything to hurt Grace," Caleb assured him. "It's just his way."

"He'll probably go off half-cocked and get us all killed," Cole griped.

"That might have been true a few years ago, but not anymore," Caleb said. "He's got a reason to live now."

"And I've got two of them," Cole replied.

He had done this before. Jake's gut tightened as he remembered the time several years earlier when Jenny had been held captive by Randolph Mason. They had attacked a similar cabin in a similar way to gain her freedom. He had seen the promise of death in Chase's dark eyes that day. He wondered if his eyes were as easy to read as Chase's had been.

Jake also remembered the condition Jenny had been in. She had been brutally beaten and raped to the point that she wanted to hide herself from Chase. Was Shannon suffering the same fate at the moment?

He would kill all of them. The thought of Shannon being hurt exploded in his brain, creating a red haze that was impossible to see through. It took every bit of his willpower not to send the dun racing down the trail toward the cabin. He needed to wait. He needed to give the others time to get into position. He needed to save Shannon. Jake quieted the dun, who was tossing his head, having sensed the agitation of his rider.

"Easy," he said to the horse as it danced beneath him. Jake realized that the dun was as anxious for the coming battle as he was. Knowing that the horse would not falter beneath him calmed his insides and he fell into a comfortable resolve about what was to come. He had done this before. He had faced death hundreds of times and never worried about the outcome until now. This time it was for everything in his life that was good. This time he had to win.

He despised Petty's making Shannon and Grace weapons in his battle for the land. It wasn't really surprising since he was attempting to steal it away from a man who had worked long and hard to keep it. Jason had earned the land after buying it honestly, adding to it piece by piece until he had built a small empire by the sweat of his brow. Men like Petty thought they could just come in and take whatever they wanted. But this time he had made a mistake. He had taken Jake's wife.

They were all going to die. If one precious hair on her flaming red head was injured in any way, then they would all die.

He couldn't stand to think about it.

He stopped the dun on a curve behind a clump of bushes and waited for Chase's signal. The dun chewed on his bit, his body tense, waiting for the signal to bunch his muscles and leap into battle. Jake looped the reins around the saddle horn and drew an ivory-handled revolver into each hand. He knew without a doubt that the dun would stay true to the course.

A rabbit hopped into the middle of the trail, long ears perked and whiskers twitching at the horse and rider that stood quietly at attention, poised and waiting.

Jake wondered how many men Chase and Cole would silently take out before Chase gave the call.

Jake heard it then, the call to attack, the sound of a bird of prey as it strikes its unsuspecting victim. The dun jumped as Jake squeezed his calves against the animal's sides, and they took off as one down the drive.

It wasn't that far, but the distance to the cabin seemed interminable. He knew Shannon was inside. The men protecting it had scattered for cover as soon as the shots started.

Jake saw it all as they raced toward the cabin. He saw a man fall, struck by a bullet from the gun in his right hand. He saw Cole drop to the ground and roll, shooting from the hip as he came up again. He saw Chase and another man crash through the rotten boards of the forgotten corral and caught the flash of light off a knife blade and knew that Chase had taken his opponent.

Jake heard the sound of gunshots from behind the cabin and knew that Caleb was there as he dropped a man who made the mistake of sticking his head up from behind the well. He was relieved to see Caleb ride around from behind and then angered to see three men crash through the door of the cabin to the inside.

The dun kept going until a bullet landed at his feet, shot through a window of the cabin. Jake grabbed a rein and pulled the animal off before he had a chance to go crashing through the door. There was no doubt in his mind that his horse would have done it, if given the chance.

Caleb wheeled the animal and they both sought cover as bullets rained around them, all coming from the broken windows of the cabin. Jake jumped off the dun and sent him away with a smack to his hindquarters. Caleb grabbed his rifle just as Jake yanked him off his saddle. They both dived behind the well just as Caleb's horse took off, following the dun.

"Thanks," Caleb said as he dragged his leg around.

"Don't mention it," Jake said, looking toward the cabin. "How many do you think are in there?" They both settled with their backs against the well as the shots continued.

"Two or three, maybe more."

"I wonder how much ammo they've got," Jake said.

The shots stopped as the men inside realized they weren't hitting anything.

"I figure they're wondering the same thing right about now," Caleb observed.

Chase signaled from the door of the barn that he was clear and Cole did the same from a position behind a woodpile.

"I reckon they'll be wanting to start the negotiations about now," Jake said in disgust.

"Hey," a voice called from inside. "We've got your women."

Cole stood up slowly with his hands out at his sides. "So what do you want in exchange?"

"We want to talk to Lynch!"

"This doesn't concern him," Cole said, watching from the corner of his eye as Chase pointed to the back of the house. He wanted Cole to keep them talking so he could make his way around.

"He's the one with the money; he's the one we want to talk to."

"First you've got to show us that the women are unhurt. Let us see the women and we'll send for Jason," Cole said.

"We're going to be here all day," Jake griped.

"Let him talk, Jake, he's done this type of thing before."

"How 'bout if we send your wife out?" the voice yelled from the house.

Jake looked over at Cole in disbelief. They were going to send out Grace! What did that mean for Shannon? Was she hurt or were they just being merciful because Grace was pregnant?

"We need to see both of them," Cole yelled back, hoping he hadn't made a mistake. He desperately wanted Grace to come out, but not at the cost of Shannon's life.

"Your wife will tell you all you need to know," the voice yelled back.

Jake and Caleb peered around the sides of the well as they heard the creaking of the cabin door. A figure came hurtling through as if she had been pushed from behind. The men watched dumbfounded as Constance squared her shoulders and gathered as much dignity as she could muster, considering her hands were bound and she was gagged. She was also sporting a set of black eyes and a considerable amount of blood beneath a nose that seemed to be slightly askew on her once-perfect face.

"Here's your wife, Larrimore." The voice was laughing. "No need to thank me."

Constance found Cole with her eyes and marched straight for him.

"Dang," Jake said as they watched her passage.

"This might be funny when we tell it," Caleb said.

"No doubt Zane will enjoy it," Jake said as he leaned back against the well.

Shannon smiled victoriously as she watched Mitchell shove Constance through the door. She had known Jake would come, and the others too. And if it had not been for poor Grace and her water breaking, they would have been out the door with the first shot. She didn't know how Grace had borne it as long as she had. She had barely made a sound even though the pains were getting longer and closer together. Shannon knew when they came because she kept a tight hold on Grace's hand.

"You'd best send for a doctor along with my father," Shannon said tartly as Mitchell and the other two watched from their hiding places beside the windows. "Unless you're experienced at delivering babies."

"That's women's work," one of them said. "You can handle it."

"I've never attended a birth before," Shannon informed him. "And this one has complications."

"What do you mean 'complications'?"

"The babe is coming early," Shannon sneered. "Perhaps it was the excitement of being kidnapped by a pack of fools."

Mitchell turned and looked at her in exasperation. "Somebody shut her up."

"Go ahead," Shannon challenged. "Then you can deliver the babe all by yourself."

"Looks like they're sending someone for Lynch," one of them remarked.

"It's the crippled one," another said.

"What happened to the breed?" Mitchell asked his companions. One of them went to the window that looked out over the back and shrugged his shoulders. "Keep a lookout for him. That one is dangerous."

Caleb was going for help and Chase was nowhere to be seen. She hoped he was working on getting them out. Shannon absorbed the information as Grace squeezed her hand again, this time with a moan.

Shannon wiped the sweat from Grace's forehead with a handkerchief she had found in Grace's pocket. Grace was pale and her dark brown eyes were huge in her face.

"It's getting close," Grace panted.

"Her time is getting near," Shannon announced to her guards.

"And?" Mitchell shot back.

"We need some water, preferably boiled. And she needs to be in a bed, not sitting on the floor." Shannon stood up, hoping her height would intimidate them.

The men shrugged off her orders.

"Jason Lynch will not pay for a dead woman and a dead baby," Shannon informed them, with her hands on her hips.

"No, but he'll pay for his daughter," Mitchell said.

"His daughter is in North Carolina. She's just a little over five feet tall and has curly brown hair. Our eyes are close to the same color, but that is about all we have in common." Shannon let loose with her tirade. She was getting tired of the games the men were playing. Grace needed help and she needed it quick.

"I knew you weren't his daughter," Mitchell said with a smirk.

"Idiot."

Suddenly Grace let loose a wail. It started low and built as if she were riding the crest of her pain. The men all turned to look at her. At the same moment Chase crashed through the window that faced the back.

Shannon tried to cover Grace as gunfire was exchanged but was stopped as Mitchell grabbed her by her scalp and pulled her back. She felt the cold barrel of the gun against her temple. The other two men lay where they had fallen.

"Make a move and she's dead," Mitchell said to Chase. He wrapped an arm around Shannon's neck and kept the gun at her temple. Shannon grabbed on to his arm with her hands. She knew she could use her strength to pull it away. It was just a matter of waiting for the right moment to do it.

Shannon felt a shiver go down her spine as she looked into the dark eyes of the man who had tried to save her.

"You'll never make it past Jake," Chase promised him. He stood poised, like a mountain lion ready to strike its prey.

"He's right, you know," Jake said from the doorway. "Put down the gun and you just might walk away from this." Cole stood behind him, his eyes on Grace, who was panting hard.

Mitchell turned, using Shannon as his shield, and was pleased to hear the sharp intake of Jake's breath as he recognized him. "I lost both of my brothers because of you," he spat out.

"You lost both your brothers because you're a fool," Shannon said. She looked at Jake, her green eyes confident that he would quickly find a way to get her out of this predicament. After all, she had seen his work before. But the last time he'd had the element of surprise. This time Mitchell was holding all the cards.

"Your wife has a big mouth," Mitchell snarled as he edged the two of them toward the door.

"She is a bit sassy," Jake agreed, his eyes never leaving Mitchell's face.

"Back off," Mitchell yelled at Chase, who had moved toward Grace. "I'm riding out of here and I'm taking her with me, just to make sure you don't do anything foolish!"

"Idiot," Shannon sighed.

"Will you shut her up?" Mitchell screamed as he edged toward the door.

Shannon kept her eyes on Jake's face. She wanted to make sure Grace would not be in the line of fire. In the next instant she pulled on his arm and slid to the floor. Before she hit bottom she heard the bullet speed past her and felt her captor fall away, hitting the floor at the same time she did.

"Shannon!" Jake's arms were around her. "Are you all right?"

"I'm fine." She could hardly talk with her face crushed against his chest but she let him squeeze her for a moment before she pushed him away. "Grace is in labor."

Cole had already gathered Grace into his arms and was carrying her into one of the bedrooms, which held a broken-down bed frame and mattress.

"What should we do?" Cole asked Shannon as he held on to Grace's hand. Another pain hit her and she arched her back off the bed.

"I don't know, I've never done it before," Shannon admitted.

"I have," Chase said. "Twice, as a matter of fact."

"Hurry up," Grace cried. "It's coming now." Everyone scrambled as Chase barked out instructions.

"I'm afraid it's too early," she said in between cramps. "It will be too little to survive."

"It might not be," Cole reassured her.

"I need to push!" Grace announced. Chase sprang into action, positioning himself at the end of the bed with Shannon beside him. Jake took one look and decided that he would be of better service elsewhere and left the room. Grace's wail followed him out as he picked up a body to drag outside.

Before he could finish laying the bodies out, a thin wail rang out from the bedroom. Jake ran back into the cabin and toward the bedroom.

"It's a girl," Shannon announced with green eyes glowing.

Cole and Grace both had their heads bent over a tiny bundle wrapped up in Grace's coat.

Jake looked at the miniature face, clenched tight in a cry. A dark brown swirl covered the tiny head and a pair of small fists were flailing against the constraints of her wrappings.

"She's not too little?" he asked in a hushed voice.

"She'll survive," Chase assured them all. "Just listen to her cry."

They all laughed as the baby girl forced the cries out as quickly as she drew in breath.

"She's a fighter," Cole said proudly.

"Jenny Catherine," Grace announced.

"I think it suits her," Chase agreed, proud that they had honored Jenny. He left the room to dispose of the remains of the birth with a wide grin on his face.

Jake took Shannon's hand and they quietly slipped away from the new family. He nudged Mitchell's body with the toe of his boot as they stepped out onto the porch.

"Imagine running into someone you know, all the way out here," he said with a hint of a smile.

"It was a bit of a surprise," Shannon replied, looking down in disgust at the man. "I think he enjoyed the reunion more than I did."

"Only for a while." Jake drew her into his arms and lifted his chin to gently kiss her forehead. "I'm glad I killed him. I should have killed him before."

"I'm glad too," Shannon confided. "Although I hope it doesn't get to be a habit."

"I think the worst is behind me." Jake leaned back to look into her deep green eyes. "How about I promise not to do any more killing if you promise not to get into any more trouble?"

"Me get into trouble? I've been mostly minding my own business," Shannon protested.

"Shannon, you've been in Wyoming only one day and you managed to get yourself kidnapped, be in the middle of a battle and help deliver a baby. I hate to think how much trouble you will get into in a week's time."

"It's a lot more exciting than back home, I have to admit."

"There is a lot to be said for peace and quiet."

"I can live with that." Shannon cast her gaze up to look into his pale blue eyes. They were almost translucent, as if she were looking into a stream that sparkled in the sunlight. They held contentment and they held joy, but most importantly they held peace. "As long as we're together, I can live with anything."

"Good, because we're going to be staying in the bunkhouse for a while," Jake informed her.

"Dolt," she replied. "I married you and you expect me to live in a bunkhouse with a pack of cowboys?"

Jake didn't feel like arguing with her. And he had found a sure way to silence her.

With a kiss.

Chapter Thirty

Caleb returned with Jason and Jenny. They were amazed to find Jake and Shannon sitting on the front porch as if they owned the place. The bodies were laid out in the yard and a bloody Constance was fuming from her place on the ground, where she sat with her hands still tied and a gag still in place. The surprise continued when they saw Jenny Catherine Larrimore greedily nursing at her mother's breast.

"So, Cole, what do you plan on doing about your first wife?" Chase asked as he put his arm around Jenny, who was absolutely enraptured with her tiny namesake.

"I guess shooting her now is out of the question?"

"Sounds good to me," Grace said as she looked down at her daughter.

"I'd love to go along with you, but in the long run I'd think you'd regret it," Jason said, not really sure if Cole was serious or not.

"I've got an idea," Cole said. He cautiously rose off the bed, careful not to disturb the new mother and child. He pulled a piece of paper from his pocket. "I've been carrying this around, just in case," he explained.

Constance turned purple again when Cole hauled her to her feet and led her into the cabin. He was sure the gag was muffling a steady stream of curses.

"I'll take this off if you promise to keep quiet," he told her as he seated her in a chair. The room became crowded as Jason, Jenny, Chase, Jake, Shannon and Caleb all piled in to watch the proceedings.

Her dark eyes bulged in anger but she complied.

"Constance, let's make a deal," Cole said as he removed the gag. He put the paper down in front of her. "Sign this and I'll let you go."

"You son of a—"

Cole stuffed the gag back into her mouth.

"You can be married to me in prison, or divorce me and go free. Which will it be?" He removed the gag again to allow her to answer.

"Give me a pen," she sighed and held out her hands to be freed.

Jason produced one.

Constance signed the paper with a flourish.

"I hope you and your little—"

Cole stuffed the gag back into her mouth. Constance jerked it out and dabbed delicately at the blood that had dried on her face. "I hope you know that my nose is broken," she cried.

"I like it," Shannon declared. "I think it gives your face character."

They all burst out laughing as Constance collected what was left of her dignity and left the cabin.

"I guess the only thing left to do now is go after Petty," Jason said.

"There's something you need to do first," Cole said and led them back into the bedroom. He took Grace's hand in his and sat down on the side of the bed. "Grace, I'm a free man. Will you marry me?" He laid the paper down beside her so Grace could see Constance's signature.

"It's about time," she exclaimed with a smile as she cuddled their baby girl, who had quickly finished her first meal.

Jason married them while the others watched. The end of the quick ceremony was commented on by Jenny Catherine, who let out a huge belch and a quivery sigh.

"That makes it official," Jason said as they all laughed. Cole kissed his wife and then he kissed his daughter.

"Let's go home," he said.

"Go on," Chase said. "I've got some unfinished business in town."

"*We've* got some unfinished business," Jake corrected him as he took out a pistol to reload.

"Count me in," Caleb declared.

"Make it quick," Jenny said. "I'm ready for some peace and quiet."

Petty was nowhere to be found. The desk clerk at the hotel reported the man had checked out earlier and left no forwarding address. The men figured that he had seen that his plan had not worked and his men had been killed so he'd packed up and left. Constance had disappeared also. Chase went to the sheriff and told him what had happened. The man said he would collect the bodies and left it at that.

•

"Do you think Petty will try it again?" Caleb asked as they rode home.

"He'd be a fool if he did," Chase said. "We would all be ready for him. Besides, Jason is organizing the landowners that are in the proposed path of the train line."

"I don't like the way the sheriff is handling all this," Jake said.

"I guess he's just mad because we keep doing his job for him," Chase commented.

"Nope, I think he's in on it," Jake replied. "I don't trust him."

"Best listen to him," Caleb said. "He said the same thing about Wade Bishop."

"You did?" Chase asked.

"I did."

"I'll pass it on to Jason," Chase said. "What are you grinning about?"

"I told Shannon we were going to have to live in the bunkhouse."

"Are you crazy?" Caleb asked. "You're going to bring her in with the rest of us?"

"You guys could build us a place of our own. Maybe as a wedding present?"

"Maybe," Caleb said. "But what are you going to do in the meantime?"

"I'm going to take Shannon to Minnesota to meet my father."

The place was not as he remembered it. It was a lot smaller than what his memory told me. The church still stood on the edge of the woods, but it looked as if it had been a long time since anyone had used it. The little cemetery was still there and the cabin that housed the minister and his family. The cabin had fallen into disrepair. There was smoke coming from the chimney, however, and that meant someone was living there. Jake knocked on the door.

"Who's there?" The voice was strong and booming, just as Jake remembered it. It had struck terror in him and in the members of the congregation. Shannon squeezed his hand as they heard the sound of footsteps coming toward the door.

The man was tall and thin, with piercing blue eyes and snow-white hair that stood out wildly from his head. "What do you want?" the man demanded. Shannon felt a shiver go down her spine. It was as if he could see into her soul. She could only imagine the terror he would strike into a small boy.

"I've come to tell you something, Father."

The man cocked his head as he looked into his son's face. "Jacob?"

"I am." Jake looked past him into the darkness of the cabin. "Where's Mother?"

"Dead. As you should be." The man looked him up and down and snorted in contempt when he saw the guns on his son's hips.

"And my sisters?"

"As good as. They run off and are living in sin. You were all full of sin."

"That's what I've come to tell you, Father," Jake said. "I have come to realize that I wasn't the bad one. It was you."

The man drew back his hand to slap him, but Jake stopped the blow by catching his father's fist in his own. The older man fought against him but soon realized his waning strength was no match for his son's.

"I forgive you, Father," Jake said as he released the hand.

"How dare you speak to me that way! You are as full of sin now as you were when you were a child."

Jake took Shannon's hand in his and turned from the porch as the tirade continued. He ignored it. He had made his peace.

"You're a good man, Jacob Anderson," Shannon said as they mounted their horses and rode away from the falling-down cabin.

"If I am, it's because you bring it out in me."

"No, it's because now you believe it for yourself."

He reached out and took her hand as they rode side by side. She believed in him. It was more than he had ever hoped to have. He had been lost and wound up finding everything.

"I'm ready to go home," he said.

"You'd better hope that we've got a place to live when we get there."

Jake leaned over to kiss her. Shannon smiled as his lips touched hers, a difficult task considering they were both on horseback. She had finally figured out how to make the kissing start.

CHASE THE WIND
CINDY HOLBY

From the moment he sets eyes on Faith, Ian Duncan knows she is the only girl for him. But her unbreakable betrothal to his employer's vicious son forces him to steal his love away on the very eve of her marriage. Faith and Ian are married clandestinely, their only possessions a magnificent horse, a family Bible, a wedding-ring quilt and their unshakable belief in each other. While their homestead waits to be carved out of the Iowa wilderness, Faith presents Ian with the most precious gift of all: a son and a daughter, born of the winter snows into the spring of their lives. The golden years are still ahead, their dream is coming true, but this is just the beginning....

Dorchester Publishing Co., Inc.
P.O. Box 6640   _5114-1
Wayne, PA 19087-8640 $6.99 US/$8.99 CAN

Please add $2.50 for shipping and handling for the first book and $.75 for each additional book. NY and PA residents, add appropriate sales tax. No cash, stamps, or CODs. Canadian orders require $2.00 for shipping and handling and must be paid in U.S. dollars. Prices and availability subject to change. **Payment must accompany all orders.**

Name: _____

Address: _____

City: _____ State: _____ Zip: _____

E-mail: _____

I have enclosed $_____ in payment for the checked book(s).

For more information on these books, check out our website at www.dorchesterpub.com.
_____ *Please send me a free catalog.*

Crosswinds
CINDY HOLBY

Ty – He is honor-bound to defend the land of his fathers, even if battle takes him from the arms of the woman he pledged himself to protect.

Cole – A Texas Ranger, he thinks the conflict will pass him by until he has the chance to capture the fugitive who'd sold so many innocent girls into prostitution.

Jenny – She vows she will no longer run from the demons of the past, and if that means confronting Wade Bishop in a New York prisoner-of-war camp, so be it. No matter how far she must travel from those she holds dear, she will draw courage from the legacy of love her parents had begun so long ago.

The Conqueror

JUDITH E. FRENCH

For two long years her father's tiny mountain kingdom had withstood the conqueror's sweeping forces, but now the barbarians storm the mile-high citadel and the women cower in fear. All but the one called *Little Star*. Famed as the most beautiful woman in all Persia, Roxanne has the courage of a fierce warrior and the training of a prince of her people. When she learns that slavery is not to be her lot, but a brilliant political alliance, she vows to await her bridegroom with her snarling leopard at her side and silken seduction at her fingertips. For she is no plaything, but more than a match for any man, even . . . Alexander the Great.

The Barbarian

JUDITH E. FRENCH

Surrounded by the exotic luxuries of ancient Alexandria, courted by the world's most powerful men, Roxanne is a woman of privilege—and one with no memory of her past. Flashes of recollection bewilder her, images of a tiny baby torn too soon from her loving arms.

Then one starless night a stranger enters her silken chamber, startling her with his dark savagery, seducing her with his sensual mastery. Does he hold the key to the mysteries that plague her? His tales of passion and betrayal seem too fantastic to be true, but her heart tells her one thing is as certain as the rising of the sun: She once gave all her love to this daring warrior, had pledged her hand and her honor to...*The Barbarian.*

BRAZEN
BOBBI SMITH

Casey Turner can rope and ride like any man, but when she strides down the streets of Hard Luck, Texas, nobody takes her for anything but a beautiful woman. Working alongside her Pa to keep the bank from foreclosing on the Bar T, she has no time for romance. But all that is about to change....

Michael Donovan has had a burr under his saddle about Casey for years. The last thing he wants is to be forced into marrying the little hoyden, but it looks like he has no choice if he wants to safeguard the future of the Donovan ranch. He'll do his darndest, but he can never let on that underneath her pretty new dresses Casey is as wild as ever, and in his arms she is positively...*BRAZEN*.
